A Pocketful of Noses

JAMES POWELL

A Pocketful of Noses

of Noses

Stories of
One Ganelon
or Another

by **James Powell**

Crippen & Landru Publishers
Norfolk, Virginia
2009

Cover by Gail Cross

Crippen & Landru logo by Eric D. Greene

ISBN (signed, limited clothbound edition): 978-1-932009-36-1

ISBN (trade softcover edition): 978-1-932009-37-8

FIRST EDITION

Printed in the United States of America on recycled acid-free paper

Crippen & Landru Publishers

P.O. Box 9315

Norfolk, VA 23505

USA

www.crippenlandru.com

info@crippenlandru.com

Contents

The Fiction Behind the Fiction

FRIENDS OF THE Ganelon family might be interested to know that San Sebastiano came before they did. While living in Europe in the mid-fifties I heard that Monaco, the little principality in the south of France, had a special department of police that watched heavy losers at the Casino. Any who appeared suicidal were escorted to the railway station and put on the next train out of town. Monaco didn't want to become the suicide capital of Europe.

It was almost eight years before I got around to writing a story about one of these policemen. By then my memories of one brief visit to Monaco and its gambling tables were dim indeed. Rather than be caught up in some mistake of fact I decided to invent my own principality. I called it San Sebastiano and gave it a history from its founding by the crew of a Tarshishman up to the present day. That story, my first published work, was "The Friends of Hector Jouvet" which appeared in 1966.

It wasn't until 1970 that I returned to San Sebastiano with "Coins in the Frascati Fountain" to introduce Ambrose Ganelon IV, the last of a famous family of private detectives whose forbearers had rid the principality of serious crime. The first Ambrose Ganelon, the founder of the Ganelon Detective Agency, had been an armchair detective. Then, true to the vaudeville maxim, don't follow one banjo act with another banjo act, I gave the second a scientific turn of mind. The third belonged to the two-fisted, hard drinking, womanizing school. Ganelon IV, left with no challenging cases to solve, became a detective of the impoverished sort. Using outfits from the family closet of disguises, he eked out a living as a street vendor, a blind beggar who played the musical saw or a sea dog with a fortune-telling parrot, when he could afford to rent the parrot.

What I expected would be one story has turned into more than thirty. This collection offers a sample of the adventures of all four generations of the Ganelon family.

Inventing San Sebastiano freed me from the tyranny of facts. If you go into a large public library you will see a pale crowd of men and women researching books or articles they plan to publish or preparing for courses they intend to teach. And these are all noble things. But there are other researchers there, an even paler crew who accumulate knowledge so they can write letters to the editors of mystery magazines peppered with words like "egregious" and "invincibly ignorant." "Dear Editor," they write, "in your issue of November last I was astonished to find a character in a James Powell story releasing the safety catch of an 1864 sleeve Derringer, model 302, a.k.a. 'the Elbow Smasher.' I think not. That particular model Derringer did not come with a safety-catch until January of 1865."

So I found it simpler to equip the Ganelons with weapons from my own Hungarian company, Hrosco Armaments, and to fill San Sebastiano's sky with Prentiss-Jenkins Hedgehog airplanes and its narrow streets with Plessy-Voltiger electric landaulets, all of my own invention.

Then, to keep these stories from spinning off into space completely, I loaded them down with a ballast of blunt instruments, ironclad alibis, burdens of proof, red herrings of leviathan proportions and conspiracies of planetary size.

I enjoy returning to San Sebastiano. I find it a good place to work. I hope you'll fine it good vacation country and that you will want to come back.

AMBROSE GANELON I

The Flower Diet

S AN SEBASTIANO'S GREAT giraffe mania of 1842 began with the gift of a pair of those fine animals to the Mediterranean principality by the King of the Belgians. The public flocked to see Anatole and Natalie roaming the St. Felix zoo like lofty citadels, their living quarters decked out with blue bunting cabbages and pink bunting roses, twin symbols of the little nation. (In San Sebastiano's charming folklore its first baby citizen had been found inside a cabbage, its first citizeness inside a rose.)

For the next three years everything was giraffe: Canes and umbrellas sported giraffe-head handles, stuffed giraffes crowded toy shelves, giraffe-patterned cravats and giraffe-horn tiaras became the style. Of the innumerable giraffe songs only "Love in the Clouds" has come down to us with its memorable refrain, "Our romance remains aloof/Though we're dancing hoof to hoof."

Even young Ambrose Ganelon, the stocky little founder of the detective agency which today still bears his name, owned a papier-mâché pocket case for his oboe reeds in the shape of a giraffe.

So when Deodat Cavelli and his cost-cutting followers formed a government pledged to making a little go a long way, was it any wonder they were dubbed Giraffists?

In those days, Ganelon hadn't yet gained the prosperity which would make him the sometime prisoner of his armchair from the gout, dependent on a cadre of agents acting as his legs and eyes. Back then he lived in a small, slant-roofed garret at 18 bis rue Blondin, where the landlord's generous daughter, an excellent cook, had taken a fancy to him.

Ganelon never left home without a thorough reading of the morning newspapers, a habit from his penniless university days when he solved crimes from newspaper accounts, selling his findings to Nathan Medocq, then Assistant Prefect of Police. So it was that in the spring of 1845 in the *Factotum du Matin* he saw a small notice that Luiz Falcoa, a Portuguese merchant, late of Venice, invited those of the public interested in curiosa to visit his establishment, the Shop of Far-Fetched Things, on the rue Vanesse.

At the time, Ganelon merely wondered why anyone would choose such a run-down part of the waterfront to set up shop. But a month later, in the gossipy little *Miroir des Boulevards*, the columnist "Flaneur" described something as so preposterous it reminded him of Monsieur Falcoa, the one-eyed shopkeeper in the rue Vanesse, who claimed he could sell his wares cheaply because he knew the alchemists' secret of living on the odor of flowers. Now why, Ganelon asked himself, would a man claim such an absurdity? Before turning the page, he marked this Falcoa down as someone in need of watching.

Meanwhile, under Cavelli and the Giraffists the economy stagnated. Factory workers were laid off or saw their wages reduced by ten percent. A crop failure drove up the price of bread.

Perhaps the journalists turned to Falcoa as a relief from such dreary news. The shopkeeper told them he had learned his useful secret during a buying trip to Trebizond on the Black Sea. Among the passengers on the voyage out was one whose absence at meals Falcoa attributed to seasickness. Later, when they struck up a friendship, the man sniffed his boutonniere and confessed his membership in the Rosicrucian brotherhood that had rediscovered the ancient diet of flowers.

Their first night in Trebizond, Falcoa's friend fell so violently ill the hotel doctor despaired for his life. Having read somewhere of the upas rhododendron of Trebizond, whose nectar held a strychnine-like poison rendering the honey made from it deadly to man, Falcoa wondered if its perfume might be equally fatal to one who fed on the odor of flowers. He immediately chartered a swift ship to carry them far from the place. But death overtook the craft. Before expiring, Falcoa's grateful friend pressed into his hand a crumbling pamphlet on the Flower Diet saved from his Rosicrucian novitiate days.

Ganelon put down the newspaper, wrote "Trebizondian honey?" on his cuff, and frowned at the words.

In follow-up stories, the celebrated explorer Polydor Briant spoke of an ancient tribe at the source of the Ganges who had no mouths but lived on odors—flowers, mostly, or perhaps an apple before a long voyage—while Baron von Klemm, dean of the diplomatic corps, remembered an immensely fat king of Siam who fed entirely on the vast lies his courtiers told him, and Cardinal Jussot pointed to the holy woman in Germany who took no food but her daily communion wafer.

The ever-curious Prince Conrad was the first to invite Falcoa to dinner. That is to say, while the royal family ate, Falcoa now and then smelled the single red rose on his plate and touched his napkin to his lips. Afterwards, he endeared himself to the royal children with stories of his adventures in far-off Canada, a land doomed many times over because it had been built on a vast snowman graveyard.

Soon Falcoa was taken up by fashionable hostesses and would sit smiling while the table fed and stared. Once he was asked if his odd diet hadn't cost him the sight of an eye. Falcoa blamed his eye patch on an accident, insisting he had never been sick a day since learning to live on flowers.

Later, speaking before the Culture and Agriculture Society, known popularly as the Poet and Peasant Club, Falcoa told his audience, "Feed as animals do and you nourish the body. But the nose is the mouth of the soul." When the painter Marbeuf rose to ask if he could teach others to feed ethereally, too, Falcoa shook his head. "Society is not yet ready for the Flower Diet," he replied.

The next morning, Ganelon looked up from the newspaper account of the speech with a furrowed brow. If Falcoa wasn't setting himself up as a teacher, what *was* the man after? He certainly wasn't in it for the free dinners.

The rue Vanesse was a short, dismal street smelling of bilges, rotting rope, and stale fish. Warehouses shouldered their smaller neighbors aside and shouted down the tiny shop signs with names ten feet tall. Drays filled with bales, hogsheads, sacks, immense baskets and boxes crammed the street. Here and there an alleyway gave Ganelon a glimpse of the ship-filled harbor, a mass of masts, spars, and rigging. Commerce streamed around him on all sides. The noise was deafening, horses' hooves and harness, wagon wheels on cobbles, the draymen's cry.

Falcoa's shop occupied the ground floor of a narrow three-story building, its front door well strapped with iron, the small shop window heavily barred. Ganelon instinctively looked upward and found the bell hanging beneath the pitch of the roof. A few old buildings like this still remained in the principality. In their time they had been banking houses, the external doors and windows wired up to machinery in the garret. Any attempt at forced entry would have set that alarm bell ringing.

Ganelon stepped through the front door and into a small hallway. A narrow staircase curved upwards. Beneath it, a second door led into the Shop of Far-Fetched Things. If Falcoa sought notoriety to promote his business, he had failed. The place was empty, no fanciers of curiosa, no debt-ridden heir come to buy Trebizondian honey for a wealthy aunt with the sweet tooth; indeed, no honey pots.

After the crush of commerce outside, the shop seemed quiet as a chapel. Indeed, one wall of shelves held statues of alien gods and goddesses. But then, as if to cancel them out, another held alien devils and demons. Ganelon looked around. Those carved boxes and urns there offered many hiding places for ship's biscuits and hard sausage. But if they did, they wouldn't be left unattended.

Here Falcoa entered through the shop door, a fragile, bookish-looking man, his pallor enhanced by the black eye patch, carrying an ivory stirrup cup bound around with silver. "Forgive me, sir. I was up in my workshop making a small repair." Shyly he offered the cup for examination.

"Narwhal?" asked Ganelon. "Russian ivory?"

"Unicorn, sir," insisted Falcoa quietly. "Which has the power to purify a poisoned cup." He lay the object across two wall brackets above a table which bore a porcelain goblet on an ormolu base.

"Griffin's egg?" asked Ganelon.

The shopkeeper brightened. "The gentleman is a connoisseur?"

"My name is Ambrose Ganelon. I am a detective of the unofficial sort."

"How may I help you?"

Before answering, Ganelon took up several discreet price tags. "You sell the fabulous for knock-down prices."

"It is the age which holds them cheap, sir. I confess I have little head for business. But I am a patient man. I trust in human nature. Things change." He spoke as if these words gave him no pleasure.

"Then how convenient you don't eat."

"Ah, you've heard of that," smiled Falcoa. "Yes, the very air around us is rich with nourishment if we but know how to harvest it."

He might have continued in this vein but Ganelon interrupted him. "I hope, Monsieur Falcoa, you haven't come among us to fish in troubled waters."

"I admit I sometimes feel like the owl, which, some say, soon turns any place it dwells into a ruin."

"Please remember, I dwell here, too," cautioned Ganelon. "I'll have my eye on you."

"Yet the hand is quicker than the eye," replied Falcoa and, making a magician's pass, he reached behind Ganelon's ear. But instead of a coin, a pure white dove, or the ace of spades, the hand came back empty.

The two men exchanged bows as if they understood each other.

Telling himself that the shop's most far-fetched thing was Falcoa's nose, Ganelon returned to the street. He also noted a man in a doorway across the way dressed in that peculiar shade of black only police agents wear.

Ganelon was at his oboe that evening when he heard a step on the garret staircase, then a knock. He opened the door to find Prefect of Police Nathan Medocq.

A thin, sharp-elbowed, and smiling man, Medocq seemed all spine and teeth, like a sinister pocket comb. He had a large spice of the scoundrel in him. Most recently, when Giraffist economies obliged the secret police cadets to furnish their own disguises, he let it be known that those who wished to graduate must buy their beards from him. Reportedly it was quite a sight when the cadets paraded in for their diplomas wearing identical bright red, waist-length beards.

Invited inside, Medocq surveyed the room with a quick glance and used his walking stick to push aside the curtain which hid Ganelon's bed and washstand and to peek under the cushion on the offered chair. "You paid a visit to Monsieur Luiz Falcoa today. Why?"

"Why not?"

The pocket comb bristled. Then it shrugged and settled back in the chair. "All right, I have his house watched. I have him followed, hoping he'll lead me to some nest of conspirators. I've had the man under surveillance since he stepped ashore carrying Parma violets."

Ganelon understood. Napoleon said he would return from Elba with the spring violets. His people adopted the flower and wore the color as a show of faith in his promise. Medocq and his reactionary friends hated the dead emperor's followers most of all.

"I even ordered his place searched while he was out on one of his evening walks," admitted Medocq. His look turned sheepish. "The front-door lock was one of those damned new unpickable Bramahs. So my men tried to force a second-floor window and set off the old alarm bell. What a row with the uniformed police before they could identify themselves!"

Ganelon expressed amazement the alarm system still worked.

"Two years ago a sea captain named Jacobi bought the building and spent the time between his last few voyages before retirement restoring the wiring and oiling up the gears. Machinery's his hobby. He occupies the third floor."

Medocq laid a finger alongside his nose and renewed his smile. "Scratch a sea captain, find a smuggler, as the saying goes. So I hinted to Jacobi that certain pending charges might be overlooked for his cooperation."

"The next evening my search team was waiting in the next street when Falcoa passed by at the start of his walk. Jacobi had left the front door unlocked for them. They combed the shop and upstairs living quarters and found nothing of an incriminating nature. By then his Flower Diet was all over the newspapers. So I had my men look into that, too. Nothing. No food, not a crumb. Not a fork, not a spoon. Not a pot. The man doesn't eat."

"He eats," insisted Ganelon.

"You think it's some kind of confidence game? I suppose. Hardly a matter for our underfunded secret police, then. Still, I'd like to keep an eye on him."

"Tell me about his nightly walks," asked Ganelon.

"He walks. He stops nowhere and speaks to no one." Medocq thought for a moment and laughed. "Perhaps he's working up an appetite. On his way back he always buys a bouquet from an old flower woman on the Boulevard Tancredi, inhales deeply thereof, and returns it with a polite bow."

"And what does Venice say?"

"According to them, Falcoa had a small antique shop in the Campo San Bartolommeo. But their report left me with a curious impression. Something tells me that if we ever tried to send Falcoa back, Venice would not take him."

As Ganelon lay in bed that night other matters should have occupied his mind. In three days he would leave for London where, under orders from General Lionel Gaston, the head of San Sebastiano's military intelligence, he was to steal the plans for the Perkins Steam Machine-Gun. Yet he found himself staring up into the angle of darkness pent up beneath the eaves, pondering Falcoa's swindle, wondering when the man would drop the other shoe and what shape that shoe would take.

The next evening, with Medocq's permission, Ganelon waited with two secret-police agents across from the dark shop on the rue Vanesse. Light burned in Falcoa's second-floor windows and in Captain Jacobi's above them.

Then Falcoa's light went out and a minute later the shopkeeper appeared at the front door, which he locked behind him before he started down the street.

Ganelon and an agent who wore the faded remains of a black eye from the botched break-in attempt followed after him. This most unprofitable walk went just as Medocq said. In an hour or so, they were back in the rue Vanesse.

Falcoa unlocked the door and disappeared inside the building. Ganelon and his companion rejoined the other agent across the street. The light came on in Falcoa's rooms. After a few minutes a dimmer light replaced it.

"Settling in for the night," said the agent with the black eye. "He reads in bed by candlelight. No leaving a warm bed to turn out the gas. I pull that trick myself. In a half-hour or so he'll blow out the candle and go to sleep."

Ten minutes later, the third-floor windows went dark. Then the front door opened again and a bearded man in a peaked cap whom the agent identified as Captain Jacobi came out and walked away down the street with a rolling sea-dog's gait.

After half an hour, Falcoa's candle went out, leaving the building in darkness.

The next evening, the other police agent took his turn following Falcoa on his walk. The agent with the black eye led Ganelon across the street and through the front door. "Jacobi never lets us down," he said. Upstairs, the man picked the simple lock on Falcoa's door, lit the gas, and followed Ganelon, watching with obvious satisfaction as the detective examined both rooms without finding anything remarkable.

A copy of *The Count of Monte Cristo* lay on a small table beside the bed next to a candlestick and matches. At a table in the middle of the room, Falcoa had been repairing a marquetry box with damaged inlay. Among the glue pots, brushes, chisels, and other small tools, Ganelon picked up a small bottle filled with a clear, odorless liquid with a glass eyedropper for a stopper. Before he could taste it, the agent laughed. "It isn't soup, you know. Just water."

Ganelon reached over and picked up an awl from among the tools. He drew a fingertip along the spike and rubbed it across the ball of his thumb. Surveying the room once more, he indicated he'd seen enough.

They went back to their post across the street. When Falcoa returned from his walk, the other agent joined them. Events proceeded as the night before. But this time when Jacobi appeared and headed off down the street, Ganelon followed him.

The sea captain led him to the theater district and the crowded Café du Trac. Watching from outside, Ganelon saw Jacobi join a younger, clean-shaven man of good-natured appearance sitting at a table, his back to the wall. A fan of vaudeville, Ganelon recognized a number of performers still in their makeup at the surrounding tables, come to eat and drink before the evening's final performance.

Jacobi and his companion mixed a hearty meal with animated conversation. At the end, the sea captain rose, leaned over, and gave the young man a kiss on the cheek. The young man protested and rubbed his cheek. Smiling, Jacobi left the restaurant and headed back the way he had come.

Ganelon decided he might learn more by following the sea captain's dinner companion. So he took up his position across the street beside an advertising kiosk. As he waited, he noted that Victor the Human Goat was among the acts at the Theatre du Poche. Victor, a mournful, long-faced Hungarian, came on stage with a gunny sack filled with rocks and broken glass which he ate one after another with a cold appetite, devouring the gunny sack for dessert. Ganelon wondered what Victor would think of the Flower Diet.

Time passed, but the young man did not come out. When at last Ganelon started back inside, he was met by the rush of vaudevillians hurrying back for the final show. Ganelon stood aside, scanning faces as they passed. Last to come was the singer Marie Jardin who had made "Love in the Clouds" a sensation, accompanied by a boy with an awkward walk in rain cape and soft cap.

Ganelon searched the café but his prey had eluded him, perhaps through a side door. On his way home, the detective reconsidered the strange ending to the dinner. Had the young man been protesting the kiss, or was it the beard?

Ganelon arrived in London expecting the theft of the Perkins Steam Machine-Gun plans to be a simple matter. After all, he had access everywhere, the British government still considering itself in his debt. In 1839, Ganelon's arch rival, the evil genius Dr. Ludwig Fong, had kidnapped the young Queen Victoria and substituted in her place his niece Abigail, a look-alike from the English branch of the Fong clan.

A suspicious Lord Melbourne had asked Ganelon to investigate. The detective uncovered the substitution, traced the English monarch to the slave pens of far-off Timbuktu, and rescued her, frustrating Fong's plan to sell Victoria on the most perverse corner of the slave bazaar, where short English virgins were highly prized.

Those three weeks alone drifting down the Niger in an Arab dhow had been the happiest of Ganelon's life and, if he was to believe her, of Victoria's as well. Her later marriage to Albert of Saxe-Coburg-Gotha had shaken him profoundly. Had he known the Perkins plan was in a red dispatch box kept in the royal bedroom in Windsor Castle, Ganelon might well have refused his assignment.

The day of his arrival, Ganelon read that Prince Albert was in Liverpool dedicating a railway station. So he was not surprised that evening when a royal equerry arrived at his hotel. Ganelon traveled by closed carriage to Windsor, down a familiar secret passage, and into the arms of the woman he still loved.

He left at dawn with the Perkins plans, which he passed on to a discreet but slow copyist. Victoria would have to find other distant buildings for Albert to dedicate. This she did. But the day finally came when the original plans could be restored to the dispatch box. Despite Victoria's tears and pledges of love, Ganelon said goodbye, vowing to put her from his mind and heart forever.

During a turbulent channel crossing, Ganelon vowed many other things, including a pledge of celibacy. Indeed, with seasick logic, he pledged to father a line of celibate detectives to fight crime as the Teutonic knights of old battled the gods of the pagan forest. From Calais, Ganelon returned on wings of steam to San Sebastiano.

The money from the delivery of the Perkins plans allowed Ganelon to dine out of an evening at Chez Catulle, his favorite restaurant, and avoid, at least for the moment, coming under further obligation to his landlord's daughter, whose heart had grown fonder during his absence.

While Ganelon was in London, Medocq had staged a fake attempt to abduct Falcoa, implicating the secret service of San Sebastiano's principal rival, Sardinia. Then, by arguing Falcoa's need for protection, Medocq shifted the burden of the man's surveillance onto the general police budget. The two uniformed policemen with plumed hats and swords who now accompanied the shopkeeper about on his evening walks gave Falcoa the appearance of a national treasure. Polite applause often followed in his wake.

Not long after Ganelon's return, San Sebastiano's artistic crowd began carrying flowers about with them and scorned food. Eating, or at least eating in public, came to be thought vulgar. Among the toughs lounging on the street corners in the Duranceville district around the prison, the toothpick was no longer the touchstone of elegance. Some restaurants survived by serving Falcoa-salads of edible flowers, radishes carved to resemble roses, and carrot daisies.

Chez Catulle, Ganelon discovered, had taken its first small steps toward transforming itself into a bookstore. The large tasseled menus, relics of the great tassel craze of 1831 when everything from men's boot tops to fezzes were so ornamented, were replaced by thick octavo volumes presented to you by waiters with the wolfish look of literary critics who did not take your order so much as parse it.

In the following weeks, sizeable noses became a sign of beauty and depth of soul. Snorting and flaring nostrils crowded popular romantic fiction. Indeed, so many women with tiny, upturned noses despaired of marriage that a convent was given over to them on the site of the present parking garage on the rue des Soeurs Retroussés.

Of course, charlatans appeared hawking flower-nourishment schemes. Falcoa denounced them all, and if his name was used, took legal action. The most successful was Professor Dorhner's Apple Regimen School. For nine weeks his students ate nothing but a daily apple, the kind diminishing in size from large costard to tiniest crab. In week ten, they dined on apple blossoms. Afterward, Dorhner promised, they would thrive on the scent of flowers alone or their tuition would be refunded. The apple trees had just come into bud when the professor absconded with everyone's money.

At the close of Falcoa's first year in San Sebastiano the sluggish economy brought down the Giraffists, replacing them with a coalition, The Cabbage Rose Front under Eustache Novare, which tried to distract the population with military parades, band concerts in the park, and anti-Sardinian rhetoric.

Amid talk of war, Ganelon heard stories Falcoa had sold the army his Flower Diet and that secret production of the Perkins Steam Machine-Gun had begun in earnest. The second rumor surprised him most, for he had General Gaston's guarantee the weapon would only be used defensively.

Putting a certain message in the personal column of a certain evening newspaper, Ganelon was waiting on a certain park bench at noon the next day when General Gaston arrived at a brisk march, uniform and all, and sat down beside him. With a cavalry officer's innocence, Gaston felt all he had to do to assume a disguise was dismount and remove his spurs. Ganelon knew the man would be hurt unless they talked staring straight ahead and moving their lips as little as possible. So he did.

"Yes, we offered Falcoa a considerable sum for the Flower Diet," admitted Gaston. "Think of it, Ambrose, an army that didn't have to travel on its stomach!"

"Falcoa eats," insisted Ganelon.

"Well, no matter. The man refused to sell. Swore never to let it be put to military use." Gaston gave a prideful chuckle. "So here's what I did. During spring maneuvers, I had our soldiers spindle pippins on the spikes of their helmets. Our finny friends the Sardinians fell for it. They think we march to the Falcoa quickstep unencumbered by a plodding commissariat."

"And how do you know that?"

"They stockpile essence of upas-rhododendron oil and experiment with converting it into a gas. They mean to strike first, parading ashore behind a cloud they believe will destroy our army. Our Perkins Steam Machine-Guns firing from defensive positions will cut them to ribbons on the beaches." He wagged a triumphant finger over the word "defensive."

Ganelon stopped at the small café just outside the park gate, called for the afternoon newspapers and a glass of wine, and mused on how easily a useful fantasy can become reality. But his main question remained unanswered: What was in all this for Falcoa? The waiter returned and departed. Ganelon took a sip of wine and opened the first newspaper.

The Theatre du Poche's announcement of the return engagement by popular demand of that master marksman Monsieur Nano Gigante in his acclaimed role as the Musical Spider set Ganelon thinking how, even in tumultuous times, the public must be entertained. Then he paused. Hadn't the Musical Spider been on the same bill with Victor the Human Goat on the poster kiosk across from the Café du Trac? Coincidence enough to take him to the theater for the last show of the evening.

The candy-striped wallpaper and the sparkling gaseliers lent an element of fairyland to the crowded scene which the smell of orange peel and humanity struggled to contradict.

Spotting Captain Jacobi a few rows ahead of him, Ganelon decided he had been right to come. He sat through the contortions of the India-Rubber Family, a humorous recitation by a man in a farmer's smock, and the yapping of Yolanda and Her Dancing Dogs.

Finally a drum roll sounded and a flash of light and a loud *bang!* turned all eyes toward the topmost gallery at the back of the theater. The Musical Spider emerged from a cloud of smoke, a fantastic creature with eight furry legs, a papier-mâché head, bulging goblin eyes, and an iridescent jacket of greens, blues, and silver as though tailored from the skins of its fly victims. Too small to be a man, and too vigorous and threatening to be a child, the thing scampered out onto a web of wires stretched high above the audience.

On stage, the curtain parted to reveal a beam hung with sixteen bull's-eye targets. Now the creature unslung a rifle equipped with a drum magazine and began firing at the targets. Each bull's-eye made a silver bell ring. The tune he played was "Love in the Clouds." He played it again. But now a magic lantern threw the lyrics onto a scrim at the back of the stage. The audience began to sing along with the shots and bells.

Fresh magazines from the bandoleer across his chest allowed the Musical Spider to pick out other songs of the day, shooting over his shoulder using a pocket mirror, or blindfolded, or twirling in midair by his teeth. The audience joined in more enthusiastically with each song. Only Jacobi, Ganelon noted, sat silently, watching this extraordinary marksmanship with a critical eye.

Another drum roll and the Musical Spider swung down across the theater, skimming low over the heads of the audience. How the ladies screamed! Rifle in one hand, the creature fired, making the bells play "The Cabbage and the Rose Entwined," San Sebastiano's tunesome national anthem. The audience leaped to its feet as one, shouting out the lyrics. No need for the magic lantern here. Then, while the theater rang with cheers and calls to invade Sardinia, the Human Spider vanished back up its web.

Back out on the street, Ganelon bought a copy of the *Eclair du Soir* and discovered that on Sunday afternoon next, Luiz Falcoa would give an important lecture on the Flower Diet. He felt quite let down. Was that it? Was that all there was behind this complicated charade, charging people to come and hear you talk? Then Ganelon read further and discovered all proceeds would be donated to the soup kitchen run by the Abbey of the Holy Vernicle. Devil take the man!

When Sunday came, Ganelon, clutching a ticket sold to him by a shy monk in the lobby box office of the new Palais Polytechnique, took the famous ascending glass room which carried visitors from the ground floor Cave of Stalactites and Stalagmites display through the sputter and crack of the World of Electricity exhibits and up past the ingenious revolving cyclorama representing the Battle of the Cloaca Maxima when, during the Revolt of the Gondoliers in 1498, the gondola armada sheltered deep in the great sewer system beneath San Sebastiano was surprised and blown to kindling by Admiral Chapeau's galley fleet, which the wily old salt had equipped with shortened oars. When the great Apollonicon organ boomed out the battle's final cannonade, the whole building shook.

The auditorium was crowded. Falcoa began with a description of how the Flower Diet had come into his hands and changed his life. Then he spoke of the health advantages of living on the odor of flowers. By neither eating nor drinking, he insisted, man closes the door on disease. As for fluids, he added, they are easily obtained in a purified form through our pores, which he called "the skin's thousand tiny noses."

He spoke of the sinus passageways, that labyrinth where the Bull of Corpulence dwells, blocking flower nourishment from reaching soul and body. But this Bull, he told them, could be slain by inhaling a concoction of common chemicals, after which certain breathing exercises could reopen the sinuses to flower traffic.

At last he said, "I have traveled much, seen man at his very worst, and judged him not yet ready for the Flower Diet. But I have been deeply touched by the way you, the generous people of San Sebastiano, have welcomed me into your midst. In gratitude, I would like to make you a gift of the Flower Diet. I am ready to lead you all through the sinus labyrinth and teach you the secret chemical formula so that you may all slay your Bull of Corpulence.

"But I must warn you. You will need a well-considered and orderly plan if you are going to introduce the Flower Diet into your lives. I urge you to discuss it among yourselves. Once you have your plan, we can begin."

But Falcoa's final warning was lost in the next day's flurry of newspaper articles on San Sebastiano's happy future when the time and money spent on shopping, cooking, and eating would go instead for high-minded self-improvement.

That same afternoon three new companies to market the Flower Diet were traded on the Bourse, with schemes to buy it outright from Falcoa or with shares and royalties.

At a torch-lit rally that night, Paladins of Labor orators proclaimed the dawning of a golden age when factory owners no longer held the whip of starvation over the workers' heads. The next day, the owners claimed their own share of the Falcoa windfall by reducing wages another ten percent. Workers took to the streets in angry demonstrations.

Now land values plummeted, for how could flower-growing farmers stop people from flocking to the countryside at mealtime to gorge themselves downwind for free? Landowners called for laws to ban flower beds in public parks, to tax window boxes and require nose-restraining devices within 500 meters of flowers on private property. When the three Flower Diet companies merged, the Bourse went wild as people invested in the Consolidated Fragrances and secondary stocks like Excelsior Nose Fetters and the House of Greenhouses.

Amid the buying frenzy, Falcoa announced that he would never allow the Flower Diet to be sold. The stock market plummeted. Land values inched nervously upward.

Through all this to-and-fro, Ganelon walked the city wearing a baffled expression, shocking himself whenever he saw his reflection in a shop window. He had accused Falcoa of fishing in troubled waters; now he didn't know if the shopkeeper was fisherman, fish, water, or bait.

San Sebastiano didn't come to its senses until landlords tried to anticipate a future without kitchens or dining rooms by classifying each a bedroom and raising rents accordingly. Suddenly everyone remembered Falcoa's warning about the need for a planned and orderly transition to the Flower Diet economy. The debate began.

First Cavelli, the Giraffist leader, proposed that each year a tenth of the citizenry be chosen by lottery to learn the Flower Diet on the basis of one-man, one-chance. Outraged women stormed his house. From a window under the eaves Cavelli insisted that by "man" he meant woman, too, because, he smiled and told them, "Man embraces woman." Though not as old a joke then as it is today, it was old enough. The hellcat mob broke down his front door. Cavelli had to escape over the rooftops.

Next came the "Sinners to the Front of the Line!" people, who argued the most spiritually depraved, like the inmates of Duranceville Prison, ought to be instructed first.

"But aren't we all sinners, each of us in our own humble way?" asked middle-class leaders. "Surely Providence chose to situate one part of society in just the right place to learn the Flower Diet and then pass it along to society's two extremities."

The Paladins of Labor quickly declared it was the workers who had earned first claim to the Flower Diet by the honest sweat of their collective brow.

Meanwhile, on every editorial page someone wondered why this great gift, like all blessings from on high, shouldn't be distributed to the rich first, from whom, in God's good time, it would filter down to the commonality much as the deity provides for even the lowliest sparrow by feeding the mighty draught horse.

At Chez Catulle Ganelon cocked a democratic eye at this last image and almost cried out in disgust. Fortunately, a waiter recommending a book appropriate to read with veal to a diner at a nearby table caught the detective's attention and shook his head. Only because of Ganelon's long patronage was he allowed to read newspapers in the "Nonfiction" section of the restaurant where his favorite table now found itself.

Ganelon's spirits lifted when the Cabbage Rose Front's capable Minister of Education proposed that the Flower Diet be taught in the first two grades of elementary school, starting immediately. Here, many agreed, was a plan which could be expanded or restricted as the economy demanded.

But on further consideration, few parents liked the idea of chewing and swilling their way through a meal with flower-sniffing, spiritually superior children looking on.

And so the cry went out, "Sinners to the Front of the Line!" and the circle swung around again.

After a brooding dinner at Chez Catulle, Ganelon decided it was time for the detective and the shopkeeper to lay their cards on the table. He consulted his pocket watch. Falcoa would be on his way back from his walk. Ganelon would confront the man and tell him he knew about his Captain Jacobi identity and the business with the candle, how before he left for dinner he would make a downward-slanting hole with his awl in the side of the candle next to his bed, going as deep as the wick. Into this hole he would insert a few drops of water with the eyedropper. Later, when the flame reached the water and went out, anyone watching from the street would assume Falcoa had snuffed out the candle and turned in for the night.

Ganelon would threaten to broadcast Falcoa's deceptions if he didn't explain what he was up to. He would also promise to keep the man's secret if his intentions did not break the law.

While rehearsing all this, Ganelon had been trying to catch the eye of his waiter, whose nose was buried in a book. Finally he hastily threw some money on the table and left.

The streets were crowded. Ganelon remembered the "Sinners to the Front of the Line!" rally in the Parc de la Menagerie that night. He imagined people stepping forward with fervor to claim a place on the Rolls of the Depraved. And the Paladins of Labor were holding a torch-light march. Pointless to try traveling by horse trolley.

So Ganelon walked, passing an eminent doctor whose sandwich board advertised himself as a tree surgeon and a dentist hawking flavored gum for chewing from a tray emblazoned with the slogan: "Even obsolete teeth need exercise." On every corner, by shifting bonfire light, orators spoke on the Flower Diet question or men argued it among themselves. In every shadow lurked the Copper Fists, hired thugs who carried their wages in rolls of centimes in their fists, waiting for anyone to speak ill of the upper class.

Ganelon reached darker and quieter streets. Moving more quickly now, he could soon smell the harbor. The rue Vanesse was not far. Then he heard a gunshot followed by the rapping of a sword scabbard on the cobbles, a policeman's unmistakable call for assistance.

He arrived at the scene breathless and found Falcoa lying in the street before his shop with a policeman bending over him trying to stem a wound in his shoulder. The policeman recognized Ganelon. "The shot came from that warehouse roof over there," he said. "My partner will have the man for certain. There's only one way down."

Just then the old druggist from around the corner hurried up in felt slippers and a coat thrown on over his nightshirt and took over the wounded man's care. "I sent my boy for the ambulance," he told them.

Ganelon and the policeman stood scanning the dark rooftop until the other policeman shouted down to them. "Lost the bastard. Don't know how. Must've sprouted wings."

By the time the ambulance arrived, Falcoa was conscious and insisting he be allowed to recuperate at home. Only when a messenger from Prince Conrad arrived on horseback with instructions for the ambulance to drive the wounded man to the palace infirmary did Falcoa allow himself to be taken away.

Watching the vehicle trundle off, Ganelon understood Falcoa's reluctance to go to a hospital which offered him no secret opportunity to feed himself. But Prince Conrad's children were his little friends. What a game he would make out of them smuggling him food!

Next day, the news of the attempt on Falcoa's life and a rumor that he lay at death's door sent San Sebastiano pouring into the streets in angry crowds which marched off in too many directions for Medocq's police to control. The Sardinian embassy was set afire and its flag, the famous "Silver School and Sea" with its many shining fishes crowded onto a blue background, burned under the ambassador's nose. Workers destroyed the offices of the *Factotum du Matin* and wrecked the type for the late edition, including the editorial entitled "Why the Cream Rises to the Top." Copper Fists broke into the headquarters of the Paladins of Labor, beat up the occupants, and threw them and the furniture out the third-floor windows. The shops of the rue de Rigolo, long a bastion of middle-class style, were looted and burned.

By midmorning the *Admiral Chapeau*, armor-plated sloop and pride of San Sebastiano's navy, anchored in the Old Port and trained its guns on the Duranceville quarter. By noon, General Gaston was trying to maneuver cavalry through the narrow streets. A pall of smoke hung over the city. At the St. Felix Zoo, lofty coughs came from the giraffe house where long-neglected Anatole and Natalie lived.

In midafternoon a sudden tempering of crowd noises in the distance brought Ganelon to his garret window. Then curiosity sent him hurrying downstairs and out into the streets.

Suddenly there was Prince Conrad, riding alone down the Boulevard Tancredi dressed in the uniform and decorations of a Knight of the Order of St. Magnus the Great, his silent tut-tuts quieting the mob. In his wake, the story spread that Falcoa was out of danger and would be recuperating as a guest of the palace. When the prince rode back up the boulevard, cheers greeted him from all sides. The crisis had passed.

But the Palais Polytechnique was burning. Everyone flocked to see the fire, even the crew of the *Admiral Chapeau*. The fire brigade worked only to contain the flames. The building and its neo-contemporary style had never been popular. Too many remembered the fine old quarter demolished to make way for it. When at last, in the early evening hours, the floor under the giant Apollonicon organ collapsed, sending the instrument thundering down deep into the inferno, people gave out a happy roar as if a burden had been lifted from their souls. Then, slowly, the crowd dispersed.

Late that night, as he walked the smoky streets, Ganelon noted lights in the palace windows, as if the prince and his council of state were still at work. As he watched the traffic through the postern gate he recognized, among others, the chestnut team of the city's largest brewer and the dashing barouche of the president of the Bourse.

One morning a week later, Ganelon was strolling near the docks when he noticed ahead of him a man with a bright red, waist-length beard and Captain Jacobi's sea-dog walk. After buying an apple from a peddler's cart, the man turned off onto the rue Vanesse, polishing his purchase on the sling that held his left arm secure. He might have bitten into the apple if the detective hadn't just then drawn even with him. Instead he raised the apple to his nose.

"Leaving us, Monsieur Falcoa?" asked Ganelon, adding, "It's a terrible beard."

The shopkeeper turned and recognized the detective. "Yes, it is, isn't it? I'm told I look like a secret-police cadet. It's only till we're out of sight of land. If people thought I was being exiled, they might protest. Too many have already been injured on my behalf."

"But you are not being exiled," said Ganelon as they passed the dark window of the Shop of Far-Fetched Things.

Falcoa shook his beard. "I go willingly and promise never to return. Your grandees and altissimos consider me a disruptive presence. They have purchased my building and shop inventory and added a not-inconsiderable sum to hasten me on my way. They yearn for the quiet days before the Flower Diet." Here Falcoa looked over at the detective. "You knew I only pretended to lock the front door when I took my walks, and about Jacobi and my trick with the candle. You said nothing. Why?"

"To use a phrase of the moment, let's say I couldn't see the giraffe herd for all the legs."

They walked in silence until they reached the small bridge where the left branch of the Cornichon flowed into the Old Port. Instead of crossing over, Falcoa directed his companion down a flight of stone steps to a boat landing.

A young man waited there, seated on a pile of baggage with his back to them, watching the approach of the wherry and its crew from the steamer waiting beyond the harbor entrance. When he heard Falcoa's voice he turned and smiled. Ganelon recognized the young man that Jacobi-Falcoa had kissed in the restaurant.

"May I present my son, Fernando?" said Falcoa. "Or perhaps you know him better as Nano Gigante, the Musical Spider."

Ganelon was startled when the young man slid down from his perch and almost disappeared from sight behind the baggage. Fernando was a dwarf. His upper trunk and body were of normal size, his legs mere stumps. Yet the young man's eyes were frank and his voice a pleasant baritone when he shook Ganelon's hand. Then he set to helping load the wherry.

"And where will you go now?" Ganelon asked Falcoa.

"Paris, I thought. Perhaps I set my sights too high. But this cracked old pot of mine can't go to the well many more times. And I did promise Fernando's mother he would not have to spend his life performing in public. Unless he wanted to. I haven't enough money yet for that."

Falcoa touched the apple to his eye patch and to his wounded shoulder in a brief salaam. Then he followed his son into the boat and took a seat in the stern. From there he said, "A serious thing for a son to shoot his father, even for an expert marksman who only means to wound. Think of what must go through a son's mind as he takes aim. In Venice, Fernando missed. Fragments from the stone wall beside my head cost me an eye. But here he shot true."

As the wherry pushed off from the landing, Ganelon asked, "And in Paris, will it be the Flower Diet again?"

"No, that will have preceded me. I must use another name, tell another story. I'm not sure what. I will feel my way for a year or so. Perhaps a Frenchman was pointing out my path for me when he wrote: 'Common sense is the most widely shared commodity in the world, for every man is convinced he is well supplied with it.' "

As the distance grew between wharf and wherry, Ganelon thought of something amusing and called out a final, "What did you tell them in Venice, that you walked on water?"

But his smile faltered when the man bowed politely. This time, at least, Ganelon knew he had guessed correctly.

Unquiet Graves

O
N A CHILLY October evening in 1867 while the small Riviera principality of San Sebastiano lay beneath a hard, persistent rain, Ambrose Ganelon, founder of the detective agency that bore his name, worked late. For hours his short, stocky frame had been hunched over the ledger where for more than twenty years he had detailed the machinations of his arch-rival, the wily Dr. Ludwig Fong. Of late, when the business of the agency was finished, Ganelon had pondered a single curious question: why had Fong conceived so great a hatred for the fledgling Dominion of Canada? To find the answer he had even sent one of his operatives to the saintly and erudite Brother Cesari of Alexandria who lived in the open high atop a stone column and could only be communicated with by messages sent up in a basket.

All of a sudden Ganelon snapped the ledger shut and pushed it away from him across the Bokhara rug that covered his desk. He sat for a moment with hand over his weary eyes, feeling dull-headed and stale. It seemed to him that he hadn't been out of his carpet slippers for a month. Thinking that a long walk might do him good, he turned toward the window and for the first time he heard the dismal racket of the rain in the rue Blondin. With a fretful shrug he rose and started for the music stand where his oboe lay. Just then old Simon, his clerk, rapped on the door to announce Mr. Asher Benjamin, the dealer in antique jewelry from the Boulevard Tancredi who had been so helpful in the case the newspapers called The Portland Cameo Affair. Ganelon had just enough time to smooth down the lock of black hair on his high forehead and arrange the sour-tempered mask he used to face the world.

Mr. Benjamin arrived in the agitated state common to agency visitors. But Ganelon believed he detected a hint of elation in the man's distress, as though not all of his news was bad. Mr. Benjamin allowed Simon to carry off his dripping overcoat and hat to dry them by the fire in the outer office. Then he sat down in the chair Ganelon offered him and explained why he had come.

"I am president of our local Jewish burial society," he said. "So as you might imagine, I've found the Resurrectionist activity of late, all this ghoulish stealing of bodies to sell to medical schools, most unsettling."

Ganelon grunted sympathetically. San Sebastiano did, in fact, lag behind the Continent in the use of corpses for anatomical study. In the seventeenth century Princess Gloriana had given over the bodies of executed murderers for scholarly research and for two centuries this had been ample for the needs of science. But in more recent years, the demand for bodies had begun to exceed the supply, a shortage compounded by the marked decline in the number of murders in the principality after Ganelon opened his agency. Proposed laws to release the bodies of those who died in prison or indigent for medical study had encountered strong opposition because dissection still had a stigma the popular imagination associated with the fate of murderers.

"This morning a member of our community was laid to rest," continued Mr. Benjamin. "Two hours ago, for my own peace of mind, I decided to visit the cemetery. Leon, the caretaker, is conscientious enough after his own fashion. But I hoped I might impress upon him the need for vigilance. When I arrived I ordered the coachman to wait and hurried through the rain to the little lodge at the gate where Leon lives. An oil lamp was burning on the table but he wasn't there. So I went out into the desolation of the cemetery proper, calling his name. The teeming darkness made no reply. Alarmed, I hurried to where we'd buried the body this morning. Now here I should point out that our cemetery was laid out on low land. For this reason interment is above ground. Each coffin is placed inside a stone coffer and covered with a stone lid. Lifting a lid is a job for two men. But the coffer with the new body didn't seem to have been disturbed. I called Leon's name again. That's when I saw a light in a far corner of the burial ground. I ran toward it and found him lying dead beside his lantern. There wasn't a mark on his body and his eyes were wide and staring as if he'd died of fright. Next to him was an open coffer. The coffin inside was empty."

Having gotten past this terrible part of his narrative, Mr. Benjamin stopped to get his breath. Then he said, "I drove at once to police headquarters. A Sergeant Flanel returned with me to the cemetery."

"A peacock among policemen, Flanel," muttered Ganelon.

"He did seem … excessively dressed," observed Mr. Benjamin. "In any event, he declared the whole business to be the work of graverobbers. He said Leon had been 'burked,' that was the expression he used."

" 'Burked' as in the murderers Burke and Hare," said Ganelon. "They suffocated their victims and sold the bodies to doctors for dissection." Then he waved his hand as though scattering his words. "So what do you want of me?"

"I think Sergeant Flanel is mistaken," said Mr. Benjamin. "There's more here than murder in the course of a body snatching. Look into things and see if you don't agree that the events of tonight are of a different order entirely."

Ganelon cocked a wary eyebrow, recalling how quickly his few conversations with this man, however begun, had turned to the supernatural. Mr. Benjamin had a strong religious bent. Ganelon did not. Far from it. And he did not like chasing spirits around in the rain, be they imp or angel. "Are you quite sure the body buried today is still there?"

"Sergeant Flanel and I opened the coffer. The body was as we'd left it, in shroud and prayer shawl."

"And the stolen body, how long had it been dead?"

"Six weeks," replied Mr. Benjamin. "And vanished just like that."

Ganelon marked the note of elation in the man's voice. Scowling, he caught his lower lip between his thumb and forefinger and tugged at it thoughtfully.

They did not speak during the first few minutes of the trip to the cemetery. The dim interior of the carriage smelled of oats, harness leather, and that particularly dark red wine called Bull's Blood, a favorite among the principality's coachmen. Ganelon did not begrudge the man his wine on a night like this. The carriage moved ahead with a swaying, cradle-like motion, the sounds of the horse's hooves swallowed up by the drumbeat of the falling rain.

Then the dealer in antique jewelry spoke. "Did you ever meet the late Abel Peretz?"

"Peretz the furrier?" replied Ganelon. "Is it his body that's disappeared?" He had only known the man by his reputation as a subscriber to every worthy cause.

Mr. Benjamin nodded and said, "I knew Peretz almost from the day he arrived here, a young fugitive from some pogrom in Russian Poland with all he owned in a bundle under his arm and a fresh scar from a Cossack saber over one eye. He came into my shop looking for work. I had nothing but told him Mendelman down the street needed a cutter. Did he know the fur business? He winked like a rogue and left. Well, Mendelman hired him, but an hour later he snatched the knife from Peretz and shook it under his nose. 'You're no fur cutter,' he shouted. 'A fur cutter doesn't hold a knife like that. He holds it like this. Get out of my shop!' So Peretz left. But now he knew how to hold the knife, which was enough to get him a job with old Winkler the furrier around the corner, and by keeping his eyes open and his mouth shut he managed to hide his ignorance until he'd learned his craft. Yes, whatever Peretz set his mind to doing he did. Like winning the hand of Winkler's beautiful daughter. Now there was a happy couple."

The light from a lamppost shone in between the leather window curtains and touched Mr. Benjamin's face. He was smiling at the opposite seat as though the Peretzes were sitting there in the bloom of life. Then he frowned and said, "It was the typhus. The damned typhus carried off the young bride. From that day Peretz was a changed man. Oh, he'd always given his share to charity like the rest of us. But suddenly he couldn't give away his money fast enough. Every poor widow felt his generosity. Every threadbare scholar had a claim on his purse. He provided grave clothes for the dead and food baskets for the sick. The tin boxes of the charity collectors positively rattled with joy whenever Peretz passed by. So he lived and died."

"Why tell me all this?"

"Because whatever Peretz set his mind to doing he did," said Mr. Benjamin. "And in his final years his one desire was to die and be buried in Jerusalem. So this summer, when his health began to fail, he sold all he owned, house, business, his property in town, giving the money away to the needy and to establish a fund to provide orphan girls with marriage dowries."

"Quite admirable," began Ganelon, impatiently. "But ..."

"Peretz fell dead on his way to the dock on the day of his departure," said Mr. Benjamin. "As he lay there on the street some thief stole his wallet with the boat ticket to Port Said and the pittance he'd set aside to live until he died." He shook his head at the irony of it all, adding, "The police found the empty wallet in an alley nearby. And although it is not our custom, I placed it in his hands as a testimony to his many acts of charity when we arranged him for burial."

The pace of the carriage quickened. They had turned onto the broad boulevard that encircled the city where the ancient ramparts had once stood. Mr. Benjamin said, "When I first drove out here this evening something possessed me to pull back the curtain just as the carriage entered the street leading up to the cemetery. It was a most unearthly scene, the rain falling out of the darkness into the lamp light, the wind in the bare plane trees, the moving shadows on the rain-dashed cobbles. And there he was walking toward me in the middle of it all, a man in a long black coat and a broad-brimmed black hat. His beard was dark, full, and long, but I could not see the upper half of his face because he turned away as I approached. When the carriage had passed he faced forward again and continued on his way.

"Mr. Ganelon," said the dealer in antique jewelry, laying his hand on the detective's arm and choosing his words carefully, "I believe the man I saw was Abel Peretz. I believe his determination to be buried in Jerusalem proved stronger than the bonds of death."

Ganelon uttered an exasperated groan.

"I know what you're going to ask," said Mr. Benjamin quickly. "We buried Peretz in shroud and prayer shawl. Where did he get the clothes I saw him in? He found them among the caretaker's things. He and Leon were about the same size." The man nodded insistently and grew animated. "Imagine the scene. There is Peretz, with strength beyond our understanding, breaking out of the coffin and shouldering the lid of the coffer aside. And here comes Leon running to investigate the noise. What he saw was too much for his poor heart." Mr. Benjamin shook his head regretfully, adding, "With clothes to find and an omnibus to catch, I don't imagine Peretz even noticed his body."

"And what omnibus was that?" asked Ganelon.

"The one that stops at the bottom of the street. It would've gotten him to the station just in time to make the express to Marseilles. From there he'd take the early packet for Port Said."

"And I suppose he was going to pay for all this traveling out of that empty wallet you buried with him," said Ganelon, unable to keep the sarcasm from his voice. When Mr. Benjamin made no answer the detective asked, "You told Flanel all this?"

"Only the part about seeing the man walking in the rain. Flanel said he was probably just someone paying his respects to a dead relative. He said graverobbers usually work in groups of two or more with a barrow to carry away the body."

Ganelon laughed darkly. "My friend," he said, "Flanel is a fool. You are not. But Flanel's explanation of events is much simpler than yours. And Ockham's famous razor tells us the simplest explanation is generally the correct one." Ganelon folded his arms and settled back for the rest of the trip, adding just before he closed his eyes, "However, in this particular case, you're both wrong."

The old burial ground was surrounded by a whitewashed, stuccoed wall topped with a spiked railing. Mr. Benjamin stepped down into the rain, called up to the coachman to wait for them, and hurried to unlock a door in the wide iron gate. Ganelon followed in after him.

In a moment Mr. Benjamin obtained a lantern from the caretaker's lodge and lit their way through the dark necropolis until they reached a distant corner where cypress trees wept in the weather. "I had this one built for myself," said Mr. Benjamin, pointing to the open coffer beside which he had found the caretaker's body. "But I couldn't have Peretz buried in a pauper's grave." He held up the lantern so that the light fell on the coffin inside.

Ganelon stared down into the coffin for several minutes while the rainwater dripped from the brim of his hat. The empty pine box seemed to exude the chill of the beyond. Or perhaps the night was turning colder. "No, we're not dealing with graverobbers," he said. "They'd have taken a salable corpse, the one buried this morning, or Leon's, for that matter. Or both. But not Mr. Peretz's body in an advanced state of decay." Ganelon squatted down and made a quick examination of the muddle of footprints around the coffer, without distinguishing anything other than Flanel's fashionably pointed shoes. He straightened up and rocked back and forth on his heels for a moment. Then he said, "You'd had this one prepared for your own burial. Are there any other empty coffers nearby?"

Mr. Benjamin blinked and thought. "Over here," he said, leading Ganelon several coffers over. "Montefiore," he said. Then he pointed through the rain to another. "Solomon."

They set to work. The Montefiore coffer was empty. The Solomon was not. "Here's the explanation for your miracle," said Ganelon, a bit breathlessly from the effort of lifting the stone lid and carefully setting it on the ground. He took the lantern and leaned over the corpse in the coffer. The skin was the color of an old bruise and in places was beginning to take on a clumping, cauliflower-like texture. Someone had pulled the prayer shawl and shroud aside and made a deep, ten-centimeter cut across the body between rib cage and navel.

"But what's going on?" demanded Benjamin in a trembling voice. "This isn't Abel Peretz. I've never seen this man before in my life."

Ganelon turned his attention from the strange wound to the body itself. It was that of a man in his eighties with a full, white beard, a man who had spent some time in the Middle East, for his left cheek bore the scarring left behind by a boil called the Aleppo button which afflicted that region of the world.

"Leave me the lantern and go back to the lodge," said Ganelon. "Make some coffee to warm us up. And I'd be obliged if you'd put on the kettle. I'll be right along."

Shaking his head in wonderment, Mr. Benjamin disappeared into the darkness. When he had gone Ganelon reached down and picked up the small object that had glinted in the lantern light a moment before. Then he took a deep breath and did the job he had to do.

Ganelon crossed the cemetery with a slow, thoughtful tread. When he reached the caretaker's lodge he stood outside the door for several long minutes, oblivious to the rain. Then he stepped over the threshold and the warmth, the smell of the coffee on the stove, and the humble pleasure of suddenly being in out of the weather brought him back to reality. Casting off his sodden overcoat and hat, he took the kettle of hot water over to the wash basin on the corner table and began to scrub his hands vigorously.

Mr. Benjamin said, "This might help. The prayer shawl was of a coarse Middle Eastern weave. The man might have been Sephardic." As he poured the coffee he added, "But why desecrate a corpse like that?"

Drying his hands, Ganelon said, "A reason as old as the hills." He tossed the towel aside and drawing two small diamonds from a vest pocket, he passed them to Mr. Benjamin. "One of these was on the ground beside the coffer with the body. I found the other in the stomach."

Mr. Benjamin held each stone up to the light. "Perfect. Perfect," he murmured. Then he looked at Ganelon. "The stomach of the corpse?"

"I imagine they were both from a larger cache," said the detective. "In his haste the killer dropped one and overlooked the other."

"Well, if they were all like these it would be a fortune in diamonds," said his companion.

Ganelon took a swallow of coffee, choked, and swore. Mr. Benjamin shrugged apologetically and continued admiring the stones. "I'm a bit heavy-handed in the kitchen," he admitted.

"You make coffee by faith alone," said Ganelon, and collecting Mr. Benjamin's cup as he passed, he went to the door and threw the contents of both cups out into the night. Then he returned to the stove and started a fresh pot. As he worked he said, "So here we are. The killer forced Leon to take him to where Peretz's body was buried and help with the coffer lids. By then Leon had seen too much to live. So the killer brought him back to the first coffer and burked him."

"But why not just kill him there with the knife or the scalpel or whatever it was he used to get the diamonds?"

"The killer wanted it to look like the work of graverobbers," said Ganelon. "Yes, the burking's probably the only thing Flanel's gotten right this month. You see, both Flanel and the killer harbor the mistaken assumption that Burke and Hare were graverobbers. But people with nerve enough for murder don't have to haunt dark, rainy cemeteries to find their corpses." He poured the fresh coffee and watched carefully until his companion had sipped at his and nodded appreciatively.

"Drink up," ordered Ganelon. "Our killer is your man in the rain. We have visits to make. If we're lucky and he took the train they'll pick him up at the Gare St. Charles in Marseilles."

The arrival of Ambrose Ganelon and his companion caused a stir at police headquarters. An officer was dispatched to bring Sergeant Flanel from home. Another scampered off to get the current file of registration forms San Sebastiano's hotels must fill out for each guest. Ganelon and Mr. Benjamin exchanged glances when they came to David Elazar "late of Jerusalem" and traveling with Turkish papers, who was stopping at the Hotel de L'Angleterre.

Ganelon was pleased when their carriage pulled away from the curb seconds before Sergeant Flanel arrived in a hansom.

The concierge at the Hotel de l'Angleterre, a commanding figure, recognized at a glance that Ambrose Ganelon was a kindred spirit, a fellow tyrant, and replied to his questions as though addressing an equal. Mr. Elazar matched Mr. Benjamin's description of the man in the rain on the matter of beard, build, and height. Unfortunately he had checked out of the hotel that very afternoon. But the concierge's contact with the guest had been slight. He recalled only that the rack of newspapers which the hotel provided for its guests in the lobby had prompted Mr. Elazar to ask if they kept back issues, specifically those for the third week of August. The concierge informed him they did not, directing him to the office of the city's largest newspaper, *Le Factotum du Matin*. On parting, Ganelon and the concierge traded identical bows.

As they left the hotel Mr. Benjamin said, "But that was the week of Peretz's funeral."

"I suspected as much," said Ganelon, leading the way in the dash through the rain to the carriage. When they'd settled back in their seats he said, "An interesting development. A stranger comes to town to recover diamonds from a corpse in the Jewish cemetery. But it seems he only knows the week the man died, not his name. So he must consult the obituary notices."

"But the body in Solomon's coffin wasn't Peretz," insisted Mr. Benjamin. "And Peretz's coffin was empty."

"That part is puzzling, isn't it?" admitted Ganelon. Rapping on the sliding panel to the coachman's box, he ordered the man to drive them to the telegraph office. Then he asked his companion, "With quality diamonds to sell, where would you go?"

"To Amsterdam."

"Then a visit to the telegraph office should wrap things up for the night," said Ganelon.

"May I drop you there?" asked Mr. Benjamin. "I've one more trip to the cemetery tonight. The burial society has a dead stranger's remains to put to rest."

* * *

A week later, at Ganelon's request, Mr. Benjamin returned to the agency to be brought up to date on the mysterious case. Ganelon had already explained to him that the failure of the Marseilles police to arrest Elazar at the train station probably meant the man had traveled northward in slow stages, perhaps by carriage and river barge. Now Ganelon read him the reply to his telegram to the

Amsterdam police. They had located Elazar there. But when investigators arrived at his hotel the man had fallen to his death trying to escape across the rooftops. A quantity of diamonds was recovered from the body.

Next Ganelon read a communication fresh from his operative in Alexandria. "Sir," it began, "on receipt of your telegraphed instructions I proceeded to Jerusalem to inquire after Mr. David Elazar who, I learned, had recently been the center of a police investigation in the Jewish quarter attracting much attention here. Elazar was the servant of a wealthy old man of particularly tightfisted habits who, just before he died, converted all his possessions into cash. But after the funeral when the heirs gathered to divide the inheritance, they found the miser's strongbox empty. So they dragged Elazar before the police. Elazar denied knowing where the money had gone and was jailed on suspicion. After several days the police located a local diamond merchant who admitted selling diamonds in quantity to Elazar. So the servant was charged with robbing his dying master. On the eve of his trial Elazar broke down and admitted buying diamonds, but insisted he'd been acting on his master's orders and had been bound to secrecy in the matter. According to Elazar, the old miser wanted diamonds because he meant to leave nothing behind for spendthrift heirs to squander. So with his last breath he swallowed his fortune and expired.

"The court ordered the coffin opened and the body examined. And here things took a bizarre turn, for the dead man inside was a stranger, younger, with black hair, a saber scar over one eye, and clasping a worn wallet empty of all identification. (By some wild coincidence the wallet came from San Sebastiano's own Pepin & Fils leather-goods manufacturers.) This mix-up at the cemetery caused the charges against Elazar to be dropped. But he was kept under close surveillance. Two weeks ago, as he waited at dockside in Jaffa for the tender to take him out to the Port Said steamer and a trip abroad, the police arrived and searched him and his baggage. But they found nothing and had to let him proceed. Elazar hasn't been heard of since."

Ganelon joined his operative's report with the Amsterdam telegram and returned them to the file on his desk. "Well," he said, hoping to put a note of finality on the word, "with Elazar dead and the diamonds recovered for the heirs to squander as they see fit, I suppose the other details in the case are moot." He paused and started to rise, hoping Mr. Benjamin would agree that the matter was settled. When no agreement came and the man seemed firmly anchored in his chair, Ganelon cursed to himself, cleared his throat, and began to trace a complicated bit of rug pattern with the tip of his forefinger. "No doubt Elazar meant to recover the diamonds for himself after the funeral," he said. "But before he could act he was thrown in jail. He could have gone free by telling how the old miser had taken his wealth with him. But then he'd lose his chance at the diamonds. So instead he conceived a plan that would not only win him his freedom but get him the diamonds and out of the country to boot." Here Ganelon stopped. He worked at the rug pattern for several seconds. Then he took a deep breath and continued. "Elazar remembers a partner-in-crime from younger days, who's now a caretaker at a cemetery in San Sebastiano on the other side of the Mediterranean. So by telegraph he arranges for a devilish exchange. Elazar has Leon send him a coffin with a body in it. When it arrives he has accomplices substitute it for the miser's coffin, which they ship off to San Sebastiano. Once the diamonds are out of the country Elazar can tell the story of his master's final moments. Then he's free and comes here to recover the treasure."

Ganelon was about to launch into his description of the falling-out between Elazar and Leon: the caretaker's refusal to tell where he'd put the miser's coffin, Elazar's promise to give him a larger cut while planning to burke him later, et cetera, et cetera. But out of a corner of his eye he caught Mr. Benjamin shaking his head back and forth in the most pitying way. He looked up.

Mr. Benjamin smiled. "Why slander poor dead Leon's memory? Why concoct so complicated an explanation?" His face shone with joy. "Can't you see what happened? To grant the good man Peretz his wish for a resting place in Jerusalem, the Almighty miraculously exchanged his body for the miser's, its belly stuffed with diamonds. Realizing what has happened, Elazar tracks his master's body here and steals the diamonds, killing Leon in the process. It's that simple." He rose to take his leave.

Ganelon stood to shake the man's hand. "A miracle may be a simple explanation for you. It's a very complex one for me."

At the door Mr. Benjamin turned back, his smile clouded by wonder. "The only puzzle in this whole business," he said, "is how Elazar, knowing a miracle had taken place, could still go on to rob and commit murder."

As the door closed, Ganelon sat back down and stared at the spot where he'd traced the complicated pattern a few moments before. Then he smeared his hand across the rug as if to destroy what was left of his little tissue of lies.

Afterward he took his operative's report and reread the postscript, which he had not communicated to Mr. Benjamin because it had no bearing on the Peretz matter. His operative had written: "P.S., As I left Alexandria I received this answer from Brother Cesari to your question regarding Fong's antipathy toward the Dominion of Canada. He advised you: 'Remember the usurping Empress Wu.'"

Ganelon drummed his fingers on the desk. The usurping Empress Wu? The usurping Empress Wu? Then he remembered how the usurping Empress Wu, having taught a parrot and a cat to eat together out of the same dish, believed she had brought about the millenium. And was that why Fong feared Canada? Was he afraid that this yoking together of the French and the English, if successful, might bring about an end to time?

The Haunted Bookcase

O BOE MUSIC AND autumn sunlight filled the outer office of the Ganelon Agency. Old Simon the clerk was perched atop a stool at the high desk, recording expenses in a ponderous volume marked "1871". On a long wooden bench nearby sat three of the runners employed by the great detective, their hats on their knees. Whenever the bell on the wall clattered twice, the man closest to the door from which the woodwind strains were now coming would stand up, brush the crown of his hat with his elbow, and step into the inner office. This might prove the first leg of a journey across town with one of Ambrose Ganelon's visiting-card summonses or around the world to the floating Yangtze stronghold of the King of the Chinese River Pirates.

Beyond the low wooden railing in one of the upholstered client armchairs sat a long, lean gentleman in his fifties with large hairy ears and a knob of a nose. He wore a black stovepipe hat, a blue swallowtail jacket with less sleeve than he had wrist, and fawn trousers with straps under the insteps in the style of the generation before last. Clearly here was a man of business with better uses for his money than fashion nonsense.

But at the same time his steel spectacles rode his nose with a jaunty air as he passed the time with a back issue of the musical periodical *Vox Humana*, provided by Ganelon for just that purpose. And, in fact, if a newcomer had sat down beside him, offered a cigar case and asked what matter brought him to the rue Blondin, the man would have accepted the cigar with pleasure, thanked him for the light with his eyebrows as he leaned into the flame, and then told this baffling little story.

His name was Hippolyte McNab, a dealer in secondhand books whose shop filled three floors of a building on the rue General St. Cyr, his simple living quarters and large office occupying the fourth. McNab's particular skill was buying estate libraries. He claimed he could cast his eye over a room of books and in a twinkling detect an Estiennes, an Aldi, or a tall, untrimmed Elzevir Tasso lurking on the shelves. Sometimes in the case of the elderly or the sickly in need, McNab bought libraries and let the owners keep possession for the remainder of their natural lives. A book-lover himself, he could appreciate

40

the blow to a scholar or collector to lose his library. Besides, in this way he frequently outwitted Ponti, his particular rival in the business. Thus several weeks before, he had come into possession of the books of the Abbe Bonaventure, a popular confessor whose widowed sister, Madame Franck, tended McNab's shop, allowing the bookseller to concentrate on buying and on his sizeable business by mail. Madame Franck's son, Albert, had been pressed for gambling debts. Since Bonaventure's books were all he had of value to pass onto his nephew, he willingly sold them to McNab on the condition of lifetime possession. The priest then gave the money to Albert in place of an inheritance.

Bonaventure's modest estate took a long time to settle. When at last the library arrived, McNab was already behind schedule in preparing his quarterly catalog. Business before pleasure. All he had time to do was to stack the books in the bookcase cleared for that purpose and return to his work.

But the next day Madame Franck came to him all pale and agitated. She had had a terrible dream the night before. In her dream she found herself alone on a moonlit portion of the Quai Kellerman near a flight of stone steps down to the gentle Cornichon while the river fog licked at the topmost step in a most sinister way. Suddenly she heard her dead brother's voice crying out to her. She turned to see Scheherazade, their pet nanny goat of a childhood long past, emerge from the shadows, pulling a wicker goat cart which contained the little boy her brother had once been.

"Help save my immortal soul, Anna Marie!" cried the child in Bonaventure's mournful, adult voice. Then the apparition went on to admit to her that, although the Bishop forbade the practice, he had been among those confessors who sometimes required penitents to commit their confessions to paper. In this way he could submit their examinations of conscience to prayerful consideration and then return to them with spiritual counsel as well as absolution.

The day of his stroke he had been meditating on just such a confession, written on mauve letter paper, when there was a knock on his study door. He had slipped the document into a book at his elbow. His caller had taken him away from his rooms and before the priest could return he suffered the attack that killed him.

"Anna Marie," the voice pleaded, "by all that's holy, get me the time to find what I have lost! If someone finds that paper among my books, I will have broken the seal of the confessional and damned my immortal soul!"

With these words the goat cart reached the steps down to the river. But in the manner of dreams, the goat now became a grinning, thin-lipped man with chin whiskers and horns on his forehead and the shafts of the cart were Bonaventure's legs under the goat-man's elbows. Slowly and with pitiful cries, the priest was being dragged on his back down the steps into the fog and dark water.

Madame Franck's dream so distressed her that McNab willingly agreed to postpone examining his new acquisitions as long as she liked. After all, he expected to be overwhelmed with work for several weeks until the catalog was printed and in the mail.

McNab neither believed in ghosts inside dreams or out. But he did believe in keeping his word. So it was a couple of weeks before his eyes began to stray to the bookcase and its attractive contents. Surely examining the spines of the books could do no harm. He went over and, starting methodically at the left-hand corner of the upper shelf, he began to read the titles.

Now McNab's office was a veritable bachelor-antiquarian's den where no cleaning lady ever dared venture. The smell of leather bindings and old cigars occupied the air and dust lay thick everywhere, including the inch of shelf protruding from below each row of books in the bookcase. But to his surprise, McNab found the strip of shelf beneath the upper row of books swept clean of dust, as though someone had pulled the books out and then replaced them. And the same thing had happened to another foot of books on the shelf below. McNab scratched his jaw thoughtfully but could not resolve this mystery.

The next evening as he sat at his desk plying his pencil over the galley sheets of the catalog and eating a modest dinner of bread, cheese, and a half bottle of wine, he remembered the curious circumstances of the day before and went over to examine the bookcase again.

The dustless strip on the second shelf had grown by another foot!

That night before retiring, McNab checked the bolts on all the windows and the skylight in the corner of his office. Then he retired to his canopied bed, leaving the door between his office and his bedroom ajar, for he was a light sleeper at the best of times. Twice during the night when the bells of the Domo tolled a dark hour, McNab armed himself with a lighted candle and emerged from his bed, nightcap, nightshirt, hairy shanks, and all, to investigate the mysterious bookcase. But the strip had not increased in length.

Nor had it grown when he examined it by morning light.

McNab kept to his desk that day until it was almost three. Recently the Booksellers' Guild had decided to decorate its banquet hall with portraits of past presidents. Though McNab was not as active in the guild as he had been before his rival Ponti succeeded him to the presidency, it would have been ungracious not to make himself available for the sittings. Besides, he was familiar with the painter Rollin's distinctive style and had looked forward to meeting the artist.

For a week now at precisely three o'clock McNab had knocked on the door of Rollin's fourth-floor atelier, which, conveniently enough, was only in the next block. The painter had proven to be a bearded red-faced man with little breath and less conversation, who hid himself away behind his easel and seldom poked his head around the edge of the canvas. The bookseller usually passed the time looking out across the rooftops through the window the artist kept open because he said the fresh air helped his asthmatic condition. As chance would have it, McNab could see the bookcase in question, which stood beside one of his own rear windows.

So that day as he left for his sitting, McNab slipped a small brass spyglass into his pocket. Then he locked his office door and sealed the keyhole with a blob of red wax into which he impressed his intaglio ring.

Once again as McNab entered Rollin's building he remarked the man who was always lounging by the doorway and who observed him carefully over the top of a newspaper. At every opportunity throughout the sitting, McNab whipped out the spyglass and checked the bookcase. But no one came near it. When he ended the session, Rollin once again showed McNab the work in progress and once again the bookseller was impressed with the artist's unique vision.

When McNab returned to his office, the wax in the keyhole was intact. But the dustless strip on the bookcase had grown another foot. McNab slept on the situation and then early the next afternoon he presented himself at the office of the Ganelon Agency.

The oboe music stopped and was followed at once by the rude sound of moisture being blown from a woodwind reed. With a sigh, old Simon slid down from his stool and had already opened the wooden gate in the railing when the bell on the wall clattered once.

"Mr. Ganelon will see you now, Mr. McNab," said the old clerk.

When Simon led the bookseller into Ganelon's office, the stout little detective with the Napoleonic lick of black hair across his forehead stood with his hands clasped behind his back, scowling at a map of the world on which each of his operatives was represented by a white-headed pin and those of his nemesis, that manifold villain Dr. Ludwig Fong, with a black. The detective quickly pulled a cord which drew a curtain over the map and crossed to his desk. The departing Simon had laid the client's visiting card in the middle of the blue-and-grey Bokhara rug, a present from the emir of that province, which covered the desktop.

"Mr. Hippolyte McNab," he read aloud and, without looking up, he gestured McNab into an Empire chair whose obelisk legs rested on gilt sphinxes. The name identified the bearer as a descendant of the Jacobite refugees from whom

San Sebastiano's Prince Faustus the Fifth long ago recruited a famous regiment, The Prince's Own Scots Horseguards.

"I apologize for keeping you waiting, Mr. McNab," said the detective, taking his seat. "On busy days the oboe sharpens my powers of concentration."

"A cheery, bagpipey sound, sir," said McNab agreeably.

Ganelon fixed the man with a glower as dark as the pit, searching for mockery behind those innocent eyes. The bookseller met his gaze without blinking.

"Your story, Mr. McNab?" he demanded. After listening attentively to the details concerning the haunted bookcase, the detective said impatiently, "Mr. McNab, some say my fee is high. Others who place less value on the truth use the word 'excessive'. You are not the kind of man to throw money away because some books were moved. So there is something more to all this, isn't there? It's the coincidence that bothers you, correct?"

"You've hit the nail on the head, sir," exclaimed the bookseller. "I esteem Madame Franck very highly. If she had a dream and asked me not to touch her dead brother's books, I would not, even though I don't believe in ghosts. But when she has her dream and then the books start moving, why, that leaves me perplexed."

"Please describe this lady's character."

"I've never known her to tell a falsehood, if that's what you mean," said McNab. "Nor can her honesty be brought into question. Six years ago, when she started to work for me, I made several deliberate tests of that."

"A sensible woman, I take it?"

"Quite so, as far as the shop is concerned."

"And otherwise?"

McNab hesitated. "Well, I must admit she's overindulged her Albert. I made an effort to like the young man. In deference to her I even gave him work when he was in one of his financial straits. But he's a scoundrel, more suited for the horse whip than a mother's caresses."

Here McNab smiled sadly. "So there we are, sir. Madame Franck is a mother who loves her unworthy son. Hardly a crime." The bookseller paused. "I'll be honest with you, Mr. Ganelon. I had hoped someday to get the courage to ask her to marry this eccentric fellow I seem to have become."

"And now you doubt your intended?"

" 'Doubt' is a strong word, sir," said McNab. "But I am prepared to pay to learn the truth."

"Then so you shall, Mr. McNab," said Ganelon. "But I'm afraid we must begin with the most probable explanation: that Madame Franck is in league with someone to steal something from Bonaventure's library before you find it. Perhaps the son needs money again. Perhaps mother love has overcome her natural honesty."

"Perhaps," said the bookseller unenthusiastically. "But couldn't Ponti be the one in back of this?"

"You mean the president of the Booksellers' Guild is after some rare volume? I think not. He would only have to read the spines. No, someone is taking the books off the shelf. Why? To find something that isn't a book, like a letter file or a strong box disguised as a book. Or something tucked inside a book, like a will or a map or a baggage check or the combination to a safe. Something that might be found by a quick riffle of the pages. After all, the intruder doesn't have much time. How long were your sittings?"

"Forty-five minutes at most. Usually less."

Ganelon scowled thoughtfully and, without turning, sought the bell cord within reach of his chair. A second later a bright-eyed young man in a grey suit with a brushed hat in his hand was standing before his desk. "Ah, yes, ah—?" began the detective.

"Carnet, sir," said the young man.

"Very good, Carnet," said the detective. "And how is, ah—?"

"My mother, sir," said Carnet. "Much better, sir."

"Just back from—?"

"*Nunc fortunatus*, sir. I was in Lucknow."

"Ah, yes. I've dipped into your report. The close brush with the pariah dogs. The night trapped on the Tower of Silence with the carrion birds. And Suliman Sahib is dead?"

"Killed by his own Green Brotherhood, sir. And the Sacred Banner of Ali has been returned to the Mosque Inside the Mountain."

"No jehad, then. Good. You followed your instructions well. There'll be no holy war. We will talk more about this. And about the elephant rental among your expenses. Did the treacherous charms of the Princess Zenobia have to be experienced by moonlight?"

"A turning point of the investigation, sir."

"Two elephants, Carnet?"

"You warned me to keep my distance, sir."

Ganelon cocked a quick eyebrow. Then he said, "Time for a little change of pace."

As the Church of Saint Fiacre struck a quarter to three, Carnet was examining the lock on the door to the bookseller's office. Next he checked the window bolts. But as he moved a chair to put the bookcase stepladder in place beneath the skylight, something crunched near his foot. Carnet examined the grey powder on the floor and then mounted to the skylight. When he came down again, McNab was already standing with his pocket watch in his hand.

Five minutes later they were outside Rollin's building. McNab nudged Carnet as the man by the doorway observed them from behind his newspaper. Then, as they started inside, the bookseller laid his hand on his companion's arm. Across the street was a fashionably dressed young man heading back the way they had come. "That's Albert, Madame Franck's son. I've no doubt he's going to pay his mother a visit. Well, I could hardly refuse her that."

They took the stairs to the atelier. When the painter met them at the door, Carnet shook hands and bade McNab goodbye.

Early the next afternoon, old Simon ushered Mr. McNab and Madame Franck into Ganelon's office. The woman may never have been handsome but she had an erect carriage and an intelligent eye. Her mouth had a good-humored, if perplexed, shape to it.

The detective rose and offered them seats, stuffing a fistful of cablegrams into a leather folder. Then he sat back down and said, "Has Mr. McNab explained what this is all about?"

"I thought I'd leave that to you, sir," admitted the bookseller a bit sheepishly.

"Then to state the matter directly, Madame," said Ganelon, "someone has been going through the books that belonged to your late brother."

"I'm not surprised," said the woman. She turned and looked quizzically at McNab. "Nor can I see why it should surprise Mr. McNab. I told him about my dream."

"Ah, yes, your dream," said Ganelon. "Your dead brother's ghost in search of some penitent's written confession, else the seal of the confessional be broken?"

"Yes," insisted Madame Franck.

"You are a religious woman, Madame Franck? You are devout?" asked the detective.

"I like to think I am, sir."

"Are you prepared to swear before all you hold sacred that this dream was as you described it?"

"I am, sir."

Ganelon studied his plump pink fingers lying on the blue-and-grey design of the rug atop his desk. Then he looked up abruptly. "And are you prepared to swear that this dream was your dream?"

After a moment the woman sighed and shook her head. "No, Mr. Ganelon, I am not." When McNab groaned, she gave him a soft and comforting look.

Then she said, "No, Mr. Ganelon. My son Albert had that dream. My boy came to me in a terrible state the next morning. What were we to do? Mr. McNab would never believe anything Albert told him. He never wanted to set eyes on him again. So Albert asked me to go to Mr. McNab and tell him the dream as if it were my own. A white lie at best with my brother's soul in the balance."

"And did your son visit you yesterday while Mr. McNab was sitting for his portrait?" asked Ganelon.

Madame Franck nodded. "My son recently came into a sum of money from one of his many business ventures. He decided to emigrate to Canada, where they say ability does not need social standing to succeed. On the eve of his departure, it occurred to him, thoughtful boy, that I might be unhappy if he didn't let me contribute something to his going away. I had nothing to give but my wedding ring. He was pleased to take it. He sailed with the morning tide."

Ganelon and McNab exchanged glances of good riddance. Then the detective rose. "Thank you, Madame. One of my runners will find you a cab and accompany you back to the bookshop."

McNab, now also on his feet, said, "I respect your intentions in the matter— Anna Marie."

When the woman had left, Ganelon said, "Blind mother love has explained away your coincidence, Mr. McNab. Now as to the matter of the moved books, Carnet had no trouble discovering how the perpetrator entered your office. The intruder cut away the outside putty from one of the panes in your skylight and removed the glass. He could then reach in and unbolt the skylight. Once during the many times that followed when he did this, he accidentally broke off a piece of the inside putty, which fell to the floor where Carnet found it.

"In any event, by dropping down on a rope the intruder could rummage through the books and then go back up the way he came, replacing the pane of glass with soft mastic. But there were only two brief times when anyone could do this without your detecting them: on your way to the sittings and on your way back. But where your departures from your office were predictable, your return was not. From what you told me, that pointed the finger of suspicion in one direction."

Ganelon looked down to consult his large, old-fashioned pocket watch, which was the kind that up-to-date wits described as a mechanical turnip. There was a short knock on the door and a broad-shouldered, robust-colored man wearing the rosette of the Legion of Justice in the lapel of his dark suit brushed past old Simon and strode up to the detective's desk. His bearing was decisive and he threw the detective's visiting-card summons down onto the desk with an indignant gesture.

"Thank you for coming on such short notice, Judge de la Marche," said Ganelon. "May I introduce Mr. Hippolyte McNab?"

San Sebastiano's most prominent jurist, who had not noticed McNab when he strode into the room, now sagged abruptly at the sight of the bookseller. Judge de la Marche looked back at Ganelon and gave a shrug. "Apparently I am in your hands. Though I'm damned if I know how."

McNab leaped to his feet. "That's Rollin's voice!"

"Please sit down, both of you," said the detective. "As to the how, Judge, my man Carnet was in a doorway across the street when you left after the sitting, minus beard and painter's smock. His eye is trained for such things. He followed your cab to your house on the Place Scanderbeg. It was as simple as that. Now I'm sure you see no point in withholding those few facts that remain uncovered in this case."

Clearly the Judge did not. "All right," he said.

"Bonaventure and I were the best of friends in student days. Wild horses in tandem, some called us: he the high priest of atheists, I the tsar of all the anarchists. Thank God most young words and deeds as we uttered and did are written on the wind. Unfortunately, Bonaventure and I planned a book to outline our radical ideas.

"When I went to Paris for a year of study at the Sorbonne, we decided to make our book in the form of letters exchanged between friends. But even before I reached the French capital, Bonaventure had become bedfast with the illness which was his first step on the road to the seminary. Nevertheless, we began trading a quarto notebook back and forth between his sickbed and my student garret on the rue des Canettes.

"But Bonaventure's illness quickly turned his atheism into a pallid concoction. That only served to goad me to fresh heights of juvenile rhetoric. Even now I blush, remembering what I wrote. Then one day after delivering the notebook to the café from which the mail coach for San Sebastiano departed, I joined the crowd that had gathered to watch Louis Phillipe review the National Guard. I was nearby when the Corsican Fieschi's infernal machine discharged, striking down so many. Our book and my anarchy perished in the carnage, too. I returned to San Sebastiano a sober and chastened young man, bent on making the rule of law my life. Not long afterward, Bonaventure began his studies for the priesthood. We quickly drifted apart.

"Then several years ago I was on a hiking vacation in the Alps with some friends and we stopped at a small inn where a coach was changing horses. Among the passengers warming themselves around the fireplace inside was Bonaventure on his way to Vienna for medical treatment. We greeted each other a bit self-consciously after so much time and stood together by the fireplace. Perhaps it was to overcome the awkwardness that he asked me if I remembered the notebook. He told me he'd had it bound with a whimsical title of his own invention on the spine.

" 'Yes,' he smiled, 'few weeks pass when I don't dip into it. Having a little juvenilia at hand helps keep one humble.'

"I didn't bat an eye," continued de la Marche, "but inside I turned cold with fear. Were his words a veiled threat? My dealings with lawyers and politicians teach me to expect the worse. Who knew what kind of man Bonaventure had become? Was he telling me he had the means of making me the laughing-stock of San Sebastiano? Laughing-stocks are not appointed to our High Court, as I soon expected to be.

"Just then the coachman called his passengers back to their vehicle. With a smile and light handshake Bonaventure bade me goodbye. As my hiking companions chattered around me, I stared into the flames with my arm on the fireplace mantel. I am a serious man, gentlemen. My friends call me upright. Others consider me pompous. Personally, I like to think my life reflects credit on the law. I thought I could bear anything for the law. Anything but laughter, it now seemed. Was I completely in someone else's hands?

"I returned to San Sebastiano half convinced I would be approached by Bonaventure again, or by someone else in his name, with the price I would have to pay for my dignity. But no one came forward and I was appointed to the High Court. Bonaventure hadn't realized his power over me. Still, the man's delicate health meant the situation bore watching. It was a simple matter to put Albert, Bonaventure's nephew and heir, under obligation to me. His many scrapes with the law cried out for a benefactor in high places. When his uncle died, he would have willingly allowed me to select a book from the priest's library as a keepsake of an old friend from student days. Albert was not a young man to put much value on a book.

"Imagine my consternation after Bonaventure's funeral when I discovered his library was the property of Mr. McNab here? There was no way out but for me to steal the notebook myself. Delaying the settlement of the estate as long as I could, I extracted the details of Mr. McNab's habits and operation from the talkative Albert and examined the premises from the front and back.

"Then I went to Ponti of the Booksellers' Guild and offered to finance portraits of himself and living past presidents of the guild. For such a commission, Rollin willingly surrendered his studio to me for an hour each day, no questions asked. The moment Mr. McNab left for his sitting I would drop down from the skylight and give the books the three or four minutes I could afford them and then rush back across the rooftops to the atelier.

"The plan had only one weakness: how was I going to keep McNab from stumbling across the notebook before I found it? I paced. I wrung my hands. I tossed and turned in my desperate bed.

"In the small, frantic hours of the early morning the same day the books finally had to be delivered, I sat nodding in and out of a fitful slumber in my fireplace chair. Of course, I'd heard of Bonaventure's run-in with his bishop about written confessions. And reminiscing in student days, he had told me about the pet goat. As I dozed suddenly the whole concocted dream came to me in a single piece.

"A brilliant stroke! I would pay Albert to tell the dream to his mother as his own. In the next moment the coals in the grate flared up in a light with an odd mauve cast. Yes, and as an added touch I would say the confession was written on mauve paper. The sins of a woman. Albert's mother would appreciate that. And so here we are, gentlemen."

"But my portrait was a Rollin," insisted McNab. "And I saw it grow day by day."

"Our agreement," said de la Marche, "obliged Rollin to do your portrait. Each day he studied you on the street as you arrived for your sitting and when you left he set to work. So I always had progress to show you." Then he frowned. "But come, Mr. McNab. You have me. I offer a considerable sum for the notebook. If that isn't enough, I suggest you publish and be damned. I now see how ridiculous I've made myself trying not to become a laughing-stock."

"You mistake me, sir," said McNab coldly. "I sell books. Blackmail is not my trade. Come back with me to my office right now. Find your damned notebook and take it away with you. I'm afraid your view of your fellow man may be contagious."

Ganelon stood up. "Some calm, gentlemen, I beg you. Both of you go find this terrible volume and bring it back here. By then Simon will have the first fire of the season burning in the grate. We will destroy this damnable thing with a ceremonial glass."

Within twenty minutes McNab and the Judge were back arm in arm, de la Marche holding a brown leather book. "Bonaventure titled it *Two Babes in the Woods*," he smiled. "One peek inside and my ears are still burning with shame."

Without another word, he tossed the book into the fire, which was crackling to receive it. He was trembling with relief as Ganelon passed him his glass of vintage blue Veronica liqueur. Ganelon gave McNab a glass and poured one for himself. Then he turned to watch the flames feed at the edges of the book and made a toast. "To the follies of youth and old age."

"Amen," agreed the other two.

Then de la Marche said, "I'm in your debt, Mr. McNab."

"Easy enough to get out of that fix, sir," said the bookseller shyly, avoiding their eyes by looking into the flames. "I intend to ask Madame Franck to be my wife. I thought she would be most impressed if her beloved son's good friend on the High Court volunteered to give the bride away."

"With the greatest pleasure," said de la Marche, raising his glass again.

Here Ganelon lay a hand on the Judge's arm and turned him aside. "I hope you understand my fee for all this will leave Mr. McNab considerably out of pocket. I have a sizeable overhead." Ganelon's substantial charges were used to support his worldwide struggle against Fong.

De la Marche bowed. "Please have Mr. McNab's charges billed to me."

As Ganelon was acknowledging this instruction McNab shouted, "Look!"

The fireplace flames held the book in the grate in a firm grip now and, like live fingers, spread it open, revealing a folded sheet of mauve letter paper. As they watched, it seemed to defy the flames. But in the next moment a brown spot spread from one corner until it had consumed the whole. The paper disappeared in flames and its ashes rushed up the flue like a soul seeking heaven.

The Priest Without a Shadow

THE SECRET DRAWER in detective Ambrose Ganelon's desk in San Sebastiano contained a ledger bound in green buckram in which he recorded all the details of the many plots and continuing machinations of that evil genius, Dr. Ludwig Fong. The founder of the Ganelon Agency spent many long hours pondering this ledger, trying to decipher Fong's grand plan—and he was sure there was one—from these bits and pieces. If Ganelon's magnificent brain ever complained from weariness and needed to be spurred onward, the detective had only to turn to the inside front cover of the ledger where he had pasted the only known daguerreotype of his archrival.

The daguerreotype was enscribed: "To Ambrose Ganelon, a souvenir of Dr. Ludwig Fong who will never forget you. Christmas, 1855." Fong is shown standing with his elbow on a Doric column such as photographers provided before a backdrop painted to resemble the Rialto Bridge in Venice. Fong is a large man in a sealskin waistcoat, his watch chain strung with ornaments. His hair is oiled and wavy for he had not yet taken to shaving his round head to accentuate the roll of fat over the back of his collar. He wore his famous long black mustache turned up in the Prussian manner.

The manipulation of this mustache was the man's principle trick of disguise. By turning it down, curling the ends, or brushing it horizontally he was instantly Oriental, Mediterranean, or Latin American. But it was Fong's smile that held the eye, a magnificent thing, all teeth and curve. Only when you considered the state of the photographic art of the day and realized that Fong had to stand there motionless with that smile on his lips for thirty minutes did a chill touch your spine and the inscription ring with menace.

Now, twenty years later, Ganelon stared into the fireplace of the reading room of St. Petersburg's Aeolian Club and saw that smile again. He shuddered as if from the cold, threw aside the morning newspaper in his lap, stood up, and turned his back to the flames. His short stout frame took more of the heat than politeness would have allowed had the room's other occupants not been dozing in their chairs. The newspaper account of the Turkish adventures in the Balkans made it clear that Fong's hold over the capricious Sultan Abdulaziz had not diminished one tittle. Here were more entries for Ganelon's ledger.

As the detective brooded over these developments, his young friend Nicholas Andreyevitch came into the reading room dressed for the outdoors, his face as white as the snow on the tips of his shoes, his eyes wide and unseeing.

Ganelon, in the Russian capital to be inducted into the Imperial Society of Amateur Woodwind Virtuosi, had sought out this young composer, whose first opera had recently been published in a delightful transcription for the detective's instrument, the oboe.

Nicholas Andreyevitch stood for a moment as though transfixed. Then he saw the ormolu clock on the fireplace mantel and a puzzled look crossed his face. Abruptly he laughed out loud, setting the disturbed club members to muttering. "Ambrose Ivan-Yakovlevitch, the very man I need!" exclaimed the composer. With the color rushing back into his face he led the elderly detective from the room.

A report that Ambrose Ganelon had allowed himself to be led anywhere by anyone would have been met by incredulous laughter in San Sebastiano. There, on the rare occasion the detective left his formidable armchair in the rue Blondin he went well-armed with scowls and dark, forbidding looks. Nannies were known to scream if their young charges came within striking distance of his sturdy cane as he passed. But Prince Feinhart himself had requested Ganelon to try for a courteous tone during his visit to St. Petersburg lest he offend the Romanovs and provoke a war between the Russian Empire and tiny San Sebastiano, a conflict which might have a less triumphant ending for the Principality than the one with the Kingdom of Sardinia, popularly known as the War of Ganelon's Sneer. Remembering the word given his Prince, the detective allowed himself to be led.

As they crossed the hall to the card room where several tables of whist were already in progress, Ganelon said, "My young friend, just now you looked as if you'd seen a ghost."

Nicholas Andreyevitch nodded. "Or something very nearly like it," he said with a nervous laugh. Sitting Ganelon down in the wingchair in a quiet corner, he took off his overcoat and drew up a more modest chair for himself. "I pride myself in being a modern man," he said. "But what I thought I saw literally left my brain reeling. Let me tell you about it. A longish story. But there's a mystery to it."

"Good," said Ganelon for his St. Petersburg visit had been prolonged, leaving him restive and eager for a riddle to solve.

Taking a deep breath, the composer told his story. Since his appointment as Inspector of Naval Bands last year he and his wife had been looking for a house to rent. Last month they found the perfect place on the Moika Quai. A fashionable address, a reasonable rent, and most important, his wife fell in love with the house on the spot. He signed the lease. But several days before they were to move in a terrible murder took place in that empty house.

A workman of some description or another was stabbed to death, his head severed from his body and carried away. Fortunately neither Nicholas Andreyevitch's wife nor her aunt Marfa Petrovna who lived with them are drawn to such stories in the newspaper. Marfa Petrovna was a devout woman with a deep superstitious bent. She would never have considered passing a night in a house where she knew a murder had been committed.

The landlord blamed the whole thing on the house having been vacant so long. He replaced all the locks on the windows and doors. Remembering how much his wife loved the house, and not believing in ghosts or lightning striking twice, Nicholas Andreyevitch decided not to mention the murdered man. What they didn't know wouldn't hurt them.

So they moved into their new home. But, of course, as he should have expected, within a week on her way to market Marfa Petrovna made the acquaintance of a talkative neighbor woman who revealed the whole business. Marfa Petrovna returned home quite terrorized and refused to spend another night in the house unless the composer got a certain Father Egon to come that very night and exorcise the dark forces which she was sure possessed the place. Apparently this priest was known in the quarter for his success in such matters. The busybody neighbor couldn't say too much about him. She also mentioned that he never received visitors until after nightfall. This last seemed to make a great impression on Marfa Petrovna.

Nicholas Andreyevitch sighed. "And so, feeling sheepish and unmodern, I found myself mounting a dismal staircase with a rope bannister and no light to guide me but a candle stub on a cracked saucer provided by a filthy creature who proudly claimed to be the concierge. I found the priest's doorway on the topmost floor. When I knocked a voice told me to leave the candle on a shelf outside in the hallway and enter.

"The room was dark, the curtains were drawn. I did not close the door. From the hall light I made out the shape of a man in a conical clerical hat sitting at a deal table in the corner. He was bearded and had a mole the size of a twenty-kopek piece on his left cheek. As he offered me a seat I noticed his voice was weary and his accent from the South, perhaps Turkistan. Deciding to deal with him as I might a tradesman, I explained our predicament and asked for his rates.

"He said, yes, he knew of my house and the terrible crime committed there. Yes, he said, he thought he could cast out the dark forces within those walls, though it might take time. He would begin that very night. 'Tell your Marfa

Petrovna she has nothing to fear,' he said. Then he asked me to describe the location of the rooms in the house, explaining that he would have to construct a pentagram of prayer—his words not mine—on each floor.

"Finally this Father Egon gave me instructions which he insisted must be carried out to the letter. That evening at ten o'clock we were to unlock our front door and extinguish every light except the candle burning in front of the ikon in the music room on the first floor. Then everyone in the house was to gather in that room behind closed doors and wait until he told them they could come out. Telling myself I would go along with the man's mumbo-jumbo because I loved my wife and respected her aunt, I recovered my candle in the hall and found my way back down the stairs.

"Marfa Petrovna insisted on hearing every detail of my interview with the priest. I described my visit, adding in the hope of discrediting the man that for all his priestly airs he had forgotten to light the candle before his own ikon. But every detail of my story only added to her delight. 'Oh, I just knew it,' she whispered respectfully. 'Father Egon is one of them. One of the Doomed Saints.' "

Nicholas Andreyevitch cleared his throat with embarrassment. "The less fashionable folk tell stories of a breed of holy priests who have sold their souls to the devil in return for powers to heal and exorcise the minor demons, sacrificing their own souls to be of help to their fellowmen. Tradition has it that the devil takes their shadow to seal the bargain. Poor Marfa Petrovna believes Father Egon is one of these priests."

"And what do you believe?" asked Ganelon.

"I suspected treachery, of course," said the young man. "I moved the silver and my collection of Oriental enameled brass pieces into the music room where we were to stay. I also paid one of the policemen at the embassy next door to keep an eye on my entrance in case we were dealing with people who were after the furniture. That night my wife, Marfa Petrovna, Trifon the footman, and myself gathered in the dim music room. On the stroke of twelve I heard the front door open and close. For the next hour there were the sounds of someone walking about downstairs. Then I heard Father Egon's voice on the other side of the door. 'I have done much,' he said, 'but still have more to do. I will return at the same time tomorrow night. Please remain where you are until I have left the house.' We did as he asked. Marfa Petrovna would hardly have allowed it to be otherwise."

"And when you came out was anything stolen?"

"Not a thing," said Nicholas Andreyevitch. "Not that visit or any of the others. The next night we heard him in the hall and on the staircase. For the next three times after that he went upstairs. Last night when he spoke through the door he told us the end was near. I was happy to hear that. I confess I'd hate to have people learn I was letting an excorcist creep about the house."

Ganelon nodded. "Proceed with your story."

"Well, nightly hocus-pocus or not, I found my work going well. This morning I was so deep into my new composition that I lost all sense of time. Then a sudden drowsiness overcame me. Hoping to blow the cobwebs out of my head by a brisk walk in the weather I put on my things and set forth. The day was clear and cold. I hadn't walked far before my creative powers returned and I began to work on the composition again in my head.

"I don't know how long I walked and I was quite oblivious of my surroundings until a near accident with a cart brought me back to earth. I found myself standing almost at the door of Father Egon's dingy tenement. And who should I see coming down the street toward me all dressed up like a mujik, a common workman, in boots, red shirt, and sheepskin but Father Egon himself, cheek mole and all. In broad daylight. He passed by without recognizing me. As he did I looked down and discovered to my horror that the man had no shadow.

"I staggered away from that encounter with my beliefs in shambles. I knew I was only five minutes away from the Aeolian. I needed to tell my story to someone, so I came here. I was delighted to see your bodyguard, Sergeant Lucas, talking to the hall porter. I knew I'd find you in the reading room and—"

"—and when you came in you saw the clock. It said five minutes after twelve. You'd met your man at noon when even the humblest creature had no shadow."

"Such a tremendous relief," agreed Nicholas Andreyevitch with a sheepish grin. "Like having your sanity given back to you. But, of course, the question still remains: is our night visitor a priest or a mujik? Am I dealing with a man of the cloth, a saint or a scoundrel? Ambrose Ivan-Yakovlevitch, what is going on in my house?"

"The only way to find out is to invite me to wait with you when he comes calling tonight."

Early that evening Ganelon delivered a paper on the life of Marc-Anton Prattmann, San Sebastiano's great oboe maker, before the Tsarevitch Alexis and the fellows of the Imperial Society. It was after 9:30 when his droshky stopped before the house on the Quai Moika. Swathed in fur, the detective stepped down from the conveyance and his bodyguard, Sergeant Lucas of the San Sebastiano police, followed after him.

Ganelon stood in the falling snow on the sidewalk for a moment. Nicholas Andreyevitch's new home was one of a block of townhouses. Its immediate neighbor to the west was dark and possessed a hefty door and formidable shutters.

During his brief visit to the police that afternoon Ganelon had learned that it belonged to a notorious moneylender. An embassy bearing the coat of arms of Montenegro stood to the east. It was ablaze with lights, no doubt the result of the dangerous Balkan situation. Two policemen were stamping their feet before the doorway.

Sergeant Lucas looked at Ganelon and nodded up at the money-lender's attic. "They call St. Petersburg the Venice of the North, sir," he said. "Like its counterpart much of the city is built on piles. In Venice the dungeons and the strongrooms are in the attics."

Ganelon decided his promise to the Prince didn't apply to Lucas. He snorted and mounted the steps to his friend's house.

Trifon the footman took their coats and ushered them into the music room where the composer and his wife greeted them and introduced Marfa Petrovna, a fluttering, broad-faced woman on her way upstairs to extinguish the lights. Ganelon asked if he might accompany her.

If Marfa Petrovna seemed one of life's timid victims, Ganelon soon discovered she was made of flint whenever she thought her religious beliefs were being questioned. She would accept no other explanation of Father Egon but the supernatural one. As she reverently blew out the ikon candles in each room and closed the door, Ganelon inserted a short length of matchstick between door and door jamb. Each time Marfa Petrovna scoffed audibly.

They finished their business on the upper floors and took the staircase downward. In a French which suggested her tutor had come from Provence, she said, "You are not a believer, Mr. Ganelon. I mean no offense by that. But a man has been brutally slain here and his body desecrated. Until Father Egon has done his holy work the poor creature's soul will find no rest."

"I do believe in the existence of saints, Madam," said Ganelon, as they reached the bottom of the stairs. "And of sinners."

They entered the music room and took their places. Nicholas Andreyevitch's wife sat down at the piano and, as promised, began to play a new composition by a friend of theirs, a musical impression of some paintings by an artist their friend admired. Nicholas Andreyevitch sat on the bench beside her, turning the music in the meager light from the ikon candle. Marfa Petrovna knelt at prayer. Trifon sat erect in the darkness by the door, dozing with his palms on his knees.

As a churchbell marked the hour the street door opened and closed. The piano fell silent. Marfa Petrovna crossed herself. Sergeant Lucas, seated behind Ganelon's chair, half turned to face the door and slipped a hand inside his jacket. Footsteps—one boot had a creak—passed the music room. A board groaned on the staircase. Then there was silence.

"Please continue your delightful playing, Madam," urged Ganelon politely. But when his hostess insisted that the mysterious priest's arrival had broken her concentration, he wasn't unhappy. "Then with your aunt's indulgence," he said, "let us pass the time by considering mundane explanations for the riddle in which we find ourselves. I believe Lucas has a theory. Nicholas Andreyevitch?" The composer nodded. "Good. Now I find several peculiarities about this case and I would like to see how your theories dispose of them. First, there is the question of the severed head."

Marfa Petrovna interrupted. "But the poor man was killed for his gold teeth, I would have thought that was obvious."

Nicholas Andreyevitch said respectfully, "I think, Auntie, that a common laborer would hardly have gold teeth. Besides, the money scattered around would indicate that robbery wasn't the motive."

"Proceed," said Ganelon.

"Suppose it's like the Forty Thieves without Ali Baba," said the composer. "A gang of thieves have been using the vacant house as a den. Perhaps their leader has hidden their considerable loot in a secret place here, a place only he knows. There is a falling out over cards. The chief receives a fatal knife thrust. Fearing the police will recognize the dead man and realize what the house was being used for, the thieves carry off his head. They intend to return when the police investigation has died down and retrieve the hidden booty. But in the meantime we move in. Their new leader has to manufacture all this Father Egon humbug to get into the house."

Marfa Petrovna snorted.

Ganelon looked at her approvingly. Since snorting was forbidden to him he welcomed someone who could do it in his place. "Among other things, my young friend," said the detective, "your theory doesn't explain the identity card that the police found beside the body, a bit of information they withheld in the hope it would help them in the case. The card belongs to a man named Zelinov, a former Ministry of Transportation clerk who was dismissed for arrogant behavior toward a superior. According to his considerable police file, Zelinov turned to a life of crime, specializing in safecracking. This Zelinov hasn't returned to his rooms since the day the body was found. Perhaps Lucas has an explanation for the identity card."

Lucas' voice was sure of itself. "The attic was being used to tunnel through to the moneylender's attic strongroom next door. Zelinov was one of the gang. The way I see it they were almost through the wall when a derelict looking for a place to get out of the cold stumbled in on them and had to be killed. Zelinov knows the police are breathing down his neck and he thinks, now here's a chance to throw some sand in their eyes. He cuts off the man's head and exchanges identity cards. Then they conceal their work in the attic and leave until the heat's off. But when they come back you've moved in. So Zelinov becomes Father Egon, spends a night on the first floor for the sake of appearances, then tackles the end of the tunnel all on his own. Tonight he's up there throwing the gold down to his buddies out back."

"And what about the turned-out pockets?" demanded Ganelon.

"He was looking for a map to where the loot was hidden?" asked Nicholas Andreyevitch.

Ganelon looked at Marfa Petrovna and was gratified when she snorted again. He looked at Lucas.

"Zelinov went through the guy's pockets hunting for his identity card," said the policeman.

"If you're looking for something you stop when you find it," said Ganelon. "All the pockets were turned inside out."

"Then it was in the last pocket," insisted Lucas.

Ganelon shook his head. "The killer was looking for something else. He didn't find it. I also believe the victim was Zelinov."

"Why go to the trouble of cutting off his head and then leave the identity card behind?" asked Lucas.

"To conceal the man's assumed identity," said Ganelon. "Zelinov's known locally, but by another name."

"But why the darkness?" demanded Marfa Petrovna. "Why dig tunnels or search for hidden treasure in the dark?"

Ganelon bowed at the woman. "Gentlemen," he said, "there's the nub of the matter. Who can give us a plausible explanation of the curious fact that Father Egon insisted the house be in darkness?" Ganelon gazed around him. No one spoke. Nicholas Andreyevitch shrugged. Lucas spread his hands hopelessly. Ganelon looked back at Marfa Petrovna who wore a triumphant smile.

"Simple," she said. "Father Egon is who I say he is. He has no shadow. He goes in darkness for humility's sake. He doesn't want us to see how much he's given up for us. And also because the sight of his own shadowless form is a thorn in his heart, a constant reminder of his own damnation."

At that moment there was a step on the stairs. Then a boot creaked in the hall. A voice on the other side of the door said, "Praise be, the evil spirits have departed and the soul of our slain brother has been laid to rest. In payment for my services put whatever amount of money you deem fit in whatever poor box you choose. And pray for me. Please remain where you are for five minutes."

When that time had elapsed, Marfa Petrovna announced she was setting out at once for the local church whose sacristan would not dare refuse to admit her no matter how late the hour. When she could not be dissuaded, Nicholas Andreyevitch's wife insisted on going along as well. The composer ordered Trifon to accompany them.

When they had gone Ganelon said, "Your aunt is a shrewd woman who sees to the heart of things. But I didn't want to continue the discussion in front of her. Let her believe that Father Egon is who she thinks he is."

Ganelon lit a candle and led the way out into the hall and up the stairs. "Yes," he said, "as your aunt observed, darkness is the most important element of this case. Our fake priest is looking for the only thing you can and must look for in the dark. He was looking for light. Now let us see where he found it."

Ganelon made his way down the second-floor hallway, examining the rug at each door. He stopped and picked up a bit of matchstick on the right-hand side. Laying a finger across his lips, the detective opened the door, revealing a deep walk-in linen closet with shelves on all three walls. Handing the candle to Lucas and signaling him to shield the flame with his hand, Ganelon stepped in to the far wall.

He reached up and removed a stack of crisply folded tea towels on the topmost shelf. He replaced the stack and removed the next. A coin of light appeared on the ceiling about two feet back from the wall. Ganelon motioned that a chair be brought in from the hall. He climbed on the chair, raised himself on tiptoe, and squinted one eye. The small hole angled downward and outward through the wall.

He could see the corner of a black desk, a fringe of rug, and a low laquered cabinet against a wall. He could also hear muffled voices.

He replaced the towels, got down from the chair, and returned to the hall. Closing the linen closet door Ganelon said, "Nicholas Andreyevitch, I suggest you write your wife a note telling her you've been called away on my account and not to wait up for you. After that we shall all pay a visit to the Montenegrin Embassy."

A large army officer with a square jaw and a fierce black mustache matched Ganelon scowl for scowl before handing his visiting card over to a liveried attendant who vanished up the staircase with it. Almost at once the Montenegrin Ambassador, an elegantly dressed man with dainty feet, was hurrying down the steps with a smile and an outstretched hand to escort the great detective and his party up to his office. As they went the Ambassador expressed his pleasure at meeting a holder of the Order of the Black Wolf, his country's highest decoration which Ganelon had received for services to the royal house.

In the second-floor hallway people were hurrying from room to room. "We've been quite busy these last two weeks because of the Turkish threat to the Balkans," explained the Ambassador. "In addition, the fortnightly diplomatic pouch arrives by courier this evening and we must prepare the contents of the pouch that the couriers will take back with them tomorrow."

He ushered the visitors into his office. On the wall behind his large dark desk hung a full-length portrait of the current Prince of Montenegro, a dashing figure in a red waistcoat embroidered with gold, a red sash stuffed with pistols and cruel-looking yataghans, baggy blue breeches, a black cap embroidered with gold, and a long blue cape. The portrait's contemptuous and belligerent stare made the viewer avert his gaze which may be why no one had noticed that the left eye was a hole instead of canvas.

"Please have a seat, gentlemen," said the Ambassador. "Let me offer you some of our fine Montenegrin araqui." The low lacquered cabinet contained a fine array of bottles. The Ambassador toasted his visitors with the date brandy and took his place behind the desk. "Now what can I do for you and your friends, Mr. Ganelon?"

"Let me be of service to Montenegro as I have been in the past," said the detective.

The Ambassador frowned. "Please go on."

"You said a diplomatic pouch would be arriving this evening. Tell me how you will deal with it."

The Ambassador considered the request for a moment. Then he shrugged and said, "Captain Stanko whom you met downstairs will meet the couriers at the railroad station at eleven thirty and bring them here. The seal on the pouch will be examined to make sure it hasn't been tampered with. Then the pouch will be opened and the contents checked against the enclosed 'bill of lading,' so to speak. A matter of minutes. Then, considering the lateness of the hour, the contents will be placed in the safe to be dealt with in an appropriate manner in the morning."

Ganelon pointed at the lacquered cabinet. "That safe?"

Too astonished to deny the truth of Ganelon's words, the Ambassador said, "Why, yes," crossed to the cabinet, and opened it. He touched a button that made the back shelves of bottles reveal themselves to be clever facsimiles behind which was the steel door of a combination safe.

"I see it's a Lubke-Superwunderbar, a model as famous for its ingenious tumbler design as it is notorious for its thin walls. Well, at least that tells us something," said the detective.

"For God's sake, what?" demanded the Ambassador. "I don't understand."

"Nor do I completely," admitted Ganelon. "But we know the man has gone to the trouble of learning the combination when a small explosive charge in the dead of night might have done just as well."

The Ambassador shook his head. "No, I'm the only one who knows the combination. I have it memorized. It's never been written down."

"He read it over your shoulder."

"Impossible. I never open the safe with someone in the room." When Ganelon pointed out the missing eye in the portrait the Ambassador paled.

"A hole as accurate as that had to be drilled from this side," continued the detective. "Which means our man has access to the safe but chose getting the combination to blowing it open. In other words he wanted to be able to get into the safe without anyone knowing he had. Now tell me, is there anything important or out of the ordinary coming in tonight's diplomatic pouch?"

The Ambassador dabbed at his brow with an immaculate white handkerchief. "Yes," he said.

As a church bell struck the hour of one in the morning, Ganelon, Nicholas Andreyevitch, Sergeant Lucas, and the formidable Captain Stanko were waiting in the dark behind the door in the Ambassador's office. They heard a creaking boot in the hall. The office door opened and a rectangle of light fell across the rug and the desk. The shadow of a man stepped cautiously into this rectangle.

The shadow advanced into the room and stepped out of the light. A mild curse announced a knee had met an unexpected chair. Then a match flared, died, and a softer candle-glow took its place. The men standing against the wall held their breaths as someone carrying a pail with a mop in it crossed to the lacquered cabinet, opened it to the safe, and kneeling down, began to manipulate the combination dial.

Stanko was on the man in a moment, his great arm around his throat. The Montenegrin hurled the intruder into a corner and moved toward him, his fists huge and eager.

"That's him! That's Father Egon!" cried Nicholas Andreyevitch.

Ganelon ordered the Montenegrin back. Signaling Lucas to give the fake priest a chair, Ganelon poured a stiff araqui. As he handed the glass to the sweating fearful man the detective said, "Who are you and what is this all about?" When the man hesitated Ganelon warned him, "Your fate is in my hands. The Ambassador has agreed to whatever disposition I make of you. I could turn you over to the Russian authorities. Or I could give you to Captain Stanko here."

The man coughed on his drink. "My name is Major Hassan of Turkish Military Intelligence," he said hoarsely. "I have been sent here on a mission of the greatest importance. My orders were to locate the safe in the Montenegrin Embassy, discover its combination, and maintain access to it until further orders. To this end I approached an expert in such matters, an ingenious and as I was later to discover, an imprudent man named Zelinov. We agreed on terms.

"He soon reported that with forged references and under an assumed name he'd gotten a job as a night cleaning man at the Embassy. A week later he reported he had located the safe and intended to discover the combination by drilling a peephole through to the vacant house next door. Two weeks later he informed me he had the combination but insisted on a meeting in the vacant house that evening before he went to work.

"When I arrived he said the job was worth more than we'd settled on. Such demands are not that unusual in our business and I like to think I am a good haggler. But Zelinov suspected the extreme importance of the operation and his demands were extravagant. The argument grew heated. Now I am a short-tempered man when treated arrogantly and sometimes my hand is faster than my brain. Unfortunately, Zelinov's tongue was faster than his. He threatened to go to the Montenegrins.

"I could see he regretted his words before they were out of his mouth but by then my knife was in his chest. I cannot say whether he saw the regret in my eyes before he fell to the floor. On the chance he was carrying the combination on his person I went through his pockets. It was a fruitless search. I stood there with my whole mission dead at my feet and pondered what I was to do. Clearly I would have to find the peephole and rediscover the combination myself. No easy task for I didn't even know where the safe was kept. More immediately I needed to establish access to the safe.

"To this end, and so the Montenegrins wouldn't become suspicious when one of their night porters turned up dead next door, I cut off Zelinov's head and took it with me. If anyone cares, I dropped it in the Moika. Then I presented myself dressed for the part to the Montenegrin Embassy claiming to be Zelinov's brother-in-law. I said he'd gone back to his village to be at his mother's deathbed and had asked me to fill in until he returned. They weren't too happy. But I got the job.

"I didn't find the safe or the peephole that first night. But as I was putting away my mop and pail the next day, it occurred to me that where Zelinov would have concealed the hole on this side he wouldn't have had to have been so careful in the vacant house next door. All I had to do was rent the empty house and arrange for the Montenegrins to burn a little midnight oil. Then in the hours of darkness before I came to work I could search the house until I found the light from the peephole.

That morning I cabled Constantinople to get things underway. But I decided it best to wait a few days after the discovery of Zelinov's body before I approached the owner of the house. When I did, I discovered the house already rented. That very afternoon a Bosnian poet was assassinated and ten thousand Bashi Bazouks swept over the border into Serbia.

"Well, my people got me a report on the new tenants. I knew of the Doomed Saints. That would get me my darkness. I cabled Constantinople to keep up the good work. Then I had one of my female operatives meet the religious aunt on the street. Enter Father Egon. I found the peephole the second night. The telegraph lines between the Embassy and Montenegro were humming and the code book was coming out of the safe all the time. Over the next few days I was able to learn the combination.

"I want to see why," said Ganelon, holding out his hand.

Hassan's shoulders sagged. He drew an envelope from inside his red shirt. It bore the Montenegrin seal impressed in the wax on the back flap and diplomatic code numbers on the front.

"We have known for some time," said Hassan, "that the Prince of Montenegro had composed a letter in his own hand and was only awaiting the opportune moment to have it delivered to the Tsar Alexis by the Ambassador here. We were able to obtain the text of the letter, an impassioned appeal to the Tsar as the champion of the Slavic race to remember his past commitments to the people of the Balkans. It asks in the most flattering terms for assistance against the Sultan.

"Our version now in the safe is a perfect forgery including the coding on the envelope. Less than two dozen words have been changed or omitted. But now the tone is arrogant and demanding and the terms such that no Russian Autocrat could tolerate. When the Ambassador delivered that forged letter tomorrow morning a wedge would be driven between Russia and the Balkans, and Turkey would be free to crush those petty little countries without having to concern itself with its Eastern flank."

Fong was starting to repeat himself, thought Ganelon. It was the Ems telegram all over again. The detective knew Fong had been the one who had whispered into Bismarck's ear the scheme of editing that journalistic dispatch to provoke the French to war. "Tell me," said Ganelon. "In all your preparations did you every encounter a tall sallow-skinned man with a black mustache?"

"And a shaved head?" asked Hassan. He wet his lips. "When I was called in to be given my final orders there was someone else in the room. He was sitting behind me and I didn't see him clearly. But I'm sure of this: my superior whom I feared above all others was very afraid of this man. Once the man—"

"—laughed?"

"Yes," said Hassan, his voice made unsteady by the remembering.

Ganelon thought for a moment, tapping the envelope against the fingertips of one hand. "Thank you, Major Hassan," he said, honoring his pledge of politeness. "You may go."

Captain Stanko growled when the Turkish officer jumped to his feet. Ganelon waved him back.

"Thank you," said Major Hassan with a nervous smile. "Thank you, sir."

Ganelon shook his head. "No, it might have been kinder of me to give you to our Montenegrin friend here. You sold your soul to a devil incarnate, Major Hassan. And now you've failed in the task he set for you. You will find him a merciless pursuer. An hour from now his dogs will be on your heels. And no matter where you run to, his eyes will already be there. From this day forward I advise you to shun the daylight. Choose the path in the shadows."

Ganelon nodded toward the open doorway. Hassan stepped through it. For a moment his boot creaked in the hall and then he was gone.

AMBROSE GANELON II

The Gooseberry Fool

O N THE EARLY 1880s Europe was visited each year by a plague of assassinations at the hands of the same hired killer. The Continent's prefects of police christened this man the Gooseberry Fool because his annual itinerary approximated that of the hero in Andre Jurry's incomparable operetta of the same name.

Jurry's music told the legend of a nobleman from a northern clime whose passion for gooseberries sent him rattling southward in his carriage as soon as the roads were passable, startling crocuses from the ground and gilding willows along the way as if he were spring itself. Down the Danube valley, down the Adriatic coast to the very heel of the Italian boot he rolled and then was ferried, carriage and all, across to Corfu where Europe's first gooseberries hung ripe on the bush. Through spring and summer, the nobleman followed the maturing fruit northward in easy stages up into France and Germany, with a final cold, autumnal rush across the gooseberry fields of East Prussia.

But even though the police knew the which-way and the when—MURDER BY RAILROAD SCHEDULE, the newspapers called it—such was the Gooseberry Fool's skill and mastery of disguise that they could no more prevent his first assassination than stop the arrival of the first robin of the year. The hired killer came with a full order book and claimed his victims until the foliage turned.

Customarily, the police would have sought help from the fearsome Ambrose Ganelon, founder of San Sebastiano's famous detective agency. But age had dimmed those fabled powers, while his son and namesake remained an untried cub, a tinkerer among test tubes and flammarion flasks.

On a Saturday morning in July, 1885, Ambrose Ganelon II emerged from 18 bis rue Blondin, the family residence and the offices of the Ganelon detective agency, carrying a small suitcase. More than just a taller version of the father, the son's long legs, so becoming in his cavalry-officer days, now gave him a civilian elegance. Where the Founder, all scowl and armchair, brooded over cases like a python digesting a pig, until only the skeleton of truth remained, the son perambulated, preferring to talk things out on long walks about the city, his companions struggling to match his stride. At a later

date, his elegance and tenacity would earn him the nickname, the
Bouledogue des Boulevards.

A policeman with dandruff on his cape guarded the agency's doorway. One
had for years now, since the Founder's faculty of ratiocination was declared a
treasure of the principality. Acknowledging his salute, Ganelon went to stand at
the curb. He could almost hear the policeman ask himself why a Ganelon was
leaving town during Gooseberry Fool alert. Was San Sebastiano to go the way of
Paris, protecting itself from the assassin by following its prefect of police on
vacation for the month of August, leaving the city to waiters and American tourists?

But the Gooseberry Fool had not yet dared kill in San Sebastiano. Ganelon,
who did not want to remain forever in his father's shadow, wished he would try.
In any event, Ganelon was not going far. Young Baron Charles Sandor lived
only a few miles away across the Porpentine, the river which until twenty-five
years ago marked the eastern boundary of San Sebastiano just as the Tortue
marked its western limits (a fact which explains why the supporters of San
Sebastiano's busy coat of arms are that marriage made in heaven, the turtle and
the porcupine).

The Sandor money came from Vieux Gaspard's Ointment, a preparation named
after a local of the previous century legendary for his age and limberness of
joints. The current baron's grandfather, Baron Justin, an avid phrenologist (some
said he possessed an immense bump of credulity), had assembled for study a
collection of plaster heads of murderers.

Ganelon had written some months ago for permission to examine Baron Justin's
collection. Though impressed by the recent anthropometric work of the
phrenologist Bertillon, Ganelon considered the man's fourteen identification
measurements clumsy. He hoped to find his own cluster of three or four unique
to each individual on the skull near the sphenoid bone.

Having the patience of plaster, the baron's heads would be far easier to measure
than Ganelon's restless friends. He was beginning to believe the Sandors still
bore an ancient grudge against the Ganelons because the Founder brought one
of their servants to book for murder. Then yesterday evening he received a
hand-delivered invitation to spend the weekend studying the heads and to meet
the Hereditary Nawab of Jamkhandi and some of Sandor's business associates,
all come for the hunting.

The Nawab was renowned in his own land as a builder of hospitals, temples, and
schools, and famous abroad as a student of the human conscience, eager to promote
whatever might increase mankind's desire to do good and avoid evil.

The Sandor carriage arrived punctually, the crest on the door bearing the
same figure of the lean old man leaping in air to kick his heels which graced

each bottle of Vieux Gaspard's Ointment. Ganelon expected it would have first met the early train from Milan and was not surprised to find a passenger inside. His traveling companion looked up from a gilt-edged prayer book; his long, pale face was made longer and paler still by a flourish of black sideburns. The vehicle reeked of lavender cologne.

Ganelon introduced himself. The man closed the book on his finger, ready to flee back into it should the new arrival prove unedifying. "Lars Thorwald of Christiania," he replied, adding, "The great detective? I expected a much older man."

"You're thinking of my father," said Ganelon, as he had so many times before.

Thorwald bowed, then sniffed the air. "I must explain I do not use a scent. Signor Antonio Cipriani, who left aboard the same train which brought me here, spilled the contents of his atomizer onto the carriage floor while fortifying his handkerchief against the journey. The coachman promises to air things out when we're in the country and he can whip up the horses."

Thorwald looked grave. "Several days ago, in Milan, Cipriani and I toured Vieux Gaspard's new bottling works together. Though his cheeks were as bare as those cherubs which infest Italian art and his straw-colored vest dared to match his gloves *and* his spats, I judged him a superior type of individual. For a Neapolitan."

For many, Africa began at Naples. Englishmen swore by Calais. Ganelon understood some Scandinavians said at Lübeck.

The carriage started off. Thorwald gripped his bowler as if it were self-satisfaction itself. Was it the prospect of meeting the Nawab of Jamkhandi which made Ganelon think of the Solemn Order of Snarks? This secret terrorist brotherhood worshipped the fabulous Snark in its third incarnation:

"The third is its slowness in taking a jest.
Should you happen to venture on one,
It will sigh like a thing that is deeply distressed:
And it always looks grave at a pun."

Years ago, on the Nawab's first visit to Europe, a bomb had been thrown into his carriage in a Dresden street. The sputtering device passed through one window and out the other and bounced down some steps before exploding in a pastry-shop basement.

The Dresden police had reason to suspect Snarks. Some months before, the Nawab, dressed in the colorful costume of his native land, chose to dine at Aladdin's, a London restaurant of an Arabian Nights decor. As his party approached the entrance, an English gentleman emerged and, mistaking the

Nawab for the doorman, gave him sixpence and ordered he call him a cab. "All right, you're a cab," the Nawab replied. "But it will take more money than this to get me to call you hansom." The pun became famous throughout Europe. Yes, the Snarks hated the punster worst of all.

The carriage containing Ganelon and Thorwald left the city proper by the Porte de l'Est. Ganelon found something of historical interest to point out to Thorwald whenever his eyes crept toward his book. Suburban villas soon gave way to prosperous farms. Then they crossed the stone bridge with its ruined water mill and entered Transporpentine San Sebastiano.

In 1860, Sardinia ceded Savoy to France. Reviving Savoy's ancient claim to San Sebastiano, the French attacked at dawn across the winding Tortue river. The principality's outnumbered little army drove them back. Then, with San Sebastiano committed militarily on the west, the French cavalry appeared in force across the Porpentine. The bridge's few defenders barricaded themselves in the water mill, knowing no reinforcements could reach them through streets clogged with morning traffic.

The confident French, giving themselves over to brio, bugle blowing, and rushing about with messages, were astonished when San Sebastiano's crack sharpshooter regiment arrived, mounted behind the amazons of the women's chapter of the Club Vélocipède, who had darted there through traffic on their dashing penny-farthings. Brissac-Charbonelle's vivid paintings have immortalized the battle, the women in their broad pink-and-blue-striped jerseys, heads bent over the handlebars, the soldier-marksmen seated behind them firing left and right, the panic among the French horses. After the Half-Day War, as it came to be called, France was obliged to cede territory across the Porpentine which doubled the size of the principality.

Several miles onward, the easy slope of Mont St. Hugues and then the tower of the Sandor château appeared above the trees. The baroness, an attractive woman with an English wild-rose complexion, waited on the steps to greet them. Ganelon judged her several years older than her husband. They had met in England during the Sandor firm's failed merger talks with its principal rival, Old Father William's Supplifying Salve. Ganelon understood the baroness had been on the London musical stage.

When he and Thorwald stepped down from the carriage, she laughed, "What a smell of lavender! For a moment I thought dear Signor Cipriani had come back to us." Then she apologized for her husband's absence. The hunters were still in the field.

The baroness impressed Ganelon as a steadfast wife, one who judges others by whether they can help her husband or harm him. Had he only imagined that she seemed particularly grateful he had come? Ganelon had been taught to expect ulterior motive behind social invitations. Fashionable hostesses used to ask the Founder to their affairs to scare off jewel thieves.

The detective was given into the hands of LeSage, a middle-aged servant with an intelligent face who led him down several corridors. For Ganelon's convenience, his rooms would be in the tower Baron Justin built to house his collection. "It will also be quieter for you, sir," explained Le Sage. "The old moat has been excavated around the château proper for foundation repairs and installing the new drains. The masons will be back on Monday."

Reaching the tower, they took an iron circular staircase. The first two floors housed the plaster heads in cubby holes, the third the grandfather's old living quarters, which were well aired and bright. The study was dominated by a large marble head marked out phrenologically. A framed daguerreotype on one wall showed two men standing before a horse-drawn caravan.

"If the bald gentleman is Baron Justin, the other must be Gaston, the child-killer," observed Ganelon.

"Bonhomme Pickle himself, sir. In Paris. Usually they set up shop across from the Prison de la Roquette, where heads rolled like cabbages at harvest time. Their wagon held all they needed to make casts before returning the heads to the bereaved." LeSage pointed to a thick binder on the desk. "The registry, sir. Whenever you're ready to begin, I'll fetch the heads you'd like to see."

Ganelon got quickly to work with calipers and notebook while LeSage brought up four heads at a time in containers resembling hatboxes. After two hours of slow, careful measurements Ganelon heard the growl of iron on stone in the courtyard and went to the window. Gamekeepers were pushing a handcart heaped with dead grouse across the cobbles. Behind them came the hunters in an array of hats and buttoned gaiters.

Arriving with more hatboxes, LeSage joined Ganelon at the window. "There's his excellency the Nawab, sir," he said, pointing to a man with a round, café-au-lait face wearing a knickerbocker suit of the latest fashion. "And there, next to him, is Major Leland Sowerby."

Ganelon knew of Sowerby, whom the Nawab had graciously asked to join his permanent staff after he'd been driven from the Indian Army for gambling debts.

Next came the baron, his face open and boyish, proudly pointing out an aspect of the new drains to a lanky man in an old fringed-buckskin jacket. "Vieux Gaspard's North American representative?" guessed the detective.

"Mr. Caleb Hardacre, sir," nodded LeSage.

"And the duelist?" A slighter man marched behind, one jacket lapel tucked in across his shirt front as if to deny an adversary a white target in the meager light of dawn.

"Herr Franz Gruber of Leipzig, sir. Our Central European representative."

As the hunting party passed from sight, Ganelon returned to his work, which wasn't going as well as he'd hoped. The next few hours might prove or—as seemed more likely—disprove his thesis. He decided to work through luncheon, taking the meal on a tray. But in the meantime, his concentration became half-hearted. The parade of bald heads kept reminding him of Baron Justin who took "Know Thyself" as his motto and, long before Ganelon was born, had been a familiar sight walking about town thoughtfully reading the bumps on his shaven skull with his fingertips.

In the 1850s, Christian charity and phrenological inquiry led Baron Justin to establish an orphanage for the care and education of 153 street urchins (the legendary number of Scripture's miraculous draught of fishes), keeping the boys' heads shaven to better chart their phrenological development. Their uniform of baggy red trousers, blue short-coat, and red fez earned them the nickname the Petits Zouaves de Vieux Gaspard.

For recruitment, Baron Justin encased his servant, Gaston, in an immense green papier-mâché gherkin and sent him to the spices and condiments fair in the Place Madagascar, where he sold an excellent dill from a tray. A street urchin who let Bonhomme Pickle examine his head got a free dill and a chance at the coveted brass token, which meant entry into the orphanage.

The arrival of the young baron, now changed out of his hunting clothes, interrupted Ganelon's musings over this story, which would end so tragically. "Welcome, Monsieur Ganelon," said his host, smiling broadly and setting down the detective's luncheon tray. "May I intrude on your meal?" At Ganelon's urging the baron pulled over a chair, sat down, and beamed at the son of a national treasure of the principality. "You know, every birthday and Christmas my father gave me a Marchpane book." Austin Marchpane wrote popular accounts of the Founder's most famous cases.

"Until *Ganelon and the Pickled Boys?*"

"That *did* hit rather close to home."

Ganelon imagined that it had. "My father would never let a Marchpane book in the house," he said. The Founder denounced the many mannerisms the author concocted for him. Yet, Ganelon knew, his father had never uttered his loud accusatory "Ah-ha!" until Marchpane used it in *The Bridge of Traded Dreams*. And it wasn't until *Spawn of the Corsican Eagle*, where Marchpane touched on his hero's paternity, that the Founder began plastering a forelock down over his brow and posing, fingertips inside his jacket.

The baron's thoughtful smile lingered. Then he turned grave and leaned forward. "My dear sir, I need your help. One of the Nawab's cufflinks has been stolen."

When Ganelon cocked a disappointed eye, the Baron added urgently, "A large blue sapphire."

"And does this sapphire have religious or dynastic significance?" wondered Ganelon. "An eye from a temple goddess, perhaps, whose desecration must be washed away with human blood? Or does the loss foretell some doom for the Nawab or his house?"

The baron blinked. "Not that he mentioned. In fact, he urges me to forget the whole incident. Easier said than done. You see, it means I have invited a thief under my roof."

"Forgive me. I draw the line at stray cufflinks."

Sandor appeared crestfallen. In a moment he brightened. "Then how about lurking around a bit? You know, to make the thief think you're on the case?"

"You mean behind the potted palm?" The detective had to smile. Yet he could understand how the new baron might be unnerved by the thought of tarnishing his family name so soon. He put down his knife and fork. "Why don't you bring me up to date."

The baron pulled his chair closer. "The Nawab's manservant put the cufflinks away in the jewel case Wednesday night. Dressing his master for Thursday dinner, he found one missing."

"And who was here at that time?"

"Let me see. The Nawab arrived with Major Sowerby on Tuesday, from Rome, to see our orphanage with an eye to starting something similar in Jamkhandi. Mr. Hardacre and Signor Cipriani arrived Wednesday from Milan. This will be my first chance to meet the new Vieux Gaspard representatives my father chose just before his death last year. Of the other two, Herr Gruber didn't come until after dinner on Thursday. A pickpocket stole his wallet in Milan and lack of identification delayed him at the border. And, of course, Mr. Thorwald arrived with you this morning, bedridden in Milan with traveler's stomach until yesterday. I am sure the cufflink was stolen late Thursday afternoon."

When Ganelon asked why, the baron explained, "Because that was when my wife saw the Phantom Balloon." He smiled and added, "Who else but dear Louise?"

Ganelon understood. With Paris under siege during the Franco-Prussian War, the French evacuated the gold in the national treasury in hot-air balloons of a novel design. Each carried galvanic batteries to heat the air by means of a metal probe. When the balloon flotilla encountered fierce thunderstorms over the Massif Central, one balloon developed a loose battery connection. As it lost altitude, the crew dumped the precious cargo. When that failed to stop the descent, they escaped hand over hand along the tether line to their nearest neighbor. The damaged balloon was cut free and drifted southwestward, coming to rest in the forest north of San Sebastiano, where it became a local legend, rising into the air and coming to earth again at the loose battery connection's whim. It was said that the Phantom Balloon could pass overhead unseen until noticed by one whose heart was pure. Hence Sandor's "Who else but dear Louise?"

"When my wife rushed in with the news, the château spilled out onto the lawn, servants and all. I think that was when the thief stole the cufflink. We never saw the balloon, by the way. The wind must have shifted."

"I understand one of your guests left this morning."

The baron nodded. "Poor Cipriani. Oh yes, I know how it looks. But he couldn't have been the thief. With tears in his eyes and the carriage at the door, he begged me, for the sake of his honor, to search his person and his luggage. I reluctantly agreed. LeSage and I were thorough, I assure you. No cufflink."

Sandor stood up. "So there we are. After luncheon tomorrow I'm going to try a little parlor game suggested by one of our guests. If it doesn't get the cufflink back and you're done with the heads, may I put the matter in your hands?"

Ganelon returned to his measurements. But by late afternoon he had thrown down the calipers, closed his notebook, and turned away from the plaster head of Jean-Batiste Troppmann, the Kinck-family murderer. What he was looking for just wasn't there.

Time to turn his mind to the cufflink. Why steal a single sapphire cufflink when you could just as easily have taken both, a matched pair worth four times as much? Ganelon shook his head. You don't build a reputation catching stupid thieves. You needed someone like the Gooseberry Fool.

Or the murderer of the pickled boys. Some ten years after the Sandor orphanage opened, the corpses of four naked boys were discovered swirling slowly around in a solemn follow-the-leader in a sewer eddy beneath the Place d'Iota. Using his vast knowledge of the sewer system, the Founder calculated water flow and the modest Mediterranean tidal effect at that phase of the moon to pinpoint the exact sewer grating down which the bodies had been dropped. Brine in the victims' lungs led him to Bonhomme Pickle's warehouse only a hundred feet away. At first, old Gaston maintained boys from the neighboring Sandor orphanage had drowned stealing from his pickle barrels, their companions dumping the bodies into the sewer. But he could not explain the battering about the victims' heads. Taken into custody, Gaston would later confess to the murders and be sent to Duranceville prison for life. As for Baron Justin, his son took over the business and the old man never showed his poor, dog-eared head in San Sebastiano again.

No, they didn't make cases like the pickled boys anymore. But when Ganelon had voiced that same complaint on a recent visit to Father Sylvanus in his hermitage, the saintly priest had suggested that the Founder had solved his case by force of character alone, implying it was character not cases that Ganelon lacked.

As a boy, Ganelon had been sent to Father Sylvanus to learn the *via felix*, or the Happy Way, the forgotten medieval art of self-defence. An opponent was rendered horizontal with a hip lift and his body humors (blood, phlegm, choler, and bile) redistributed, producing a radical, if temporary, personality change. Ganelon's grammar had been a heavy board grooved with a maze in which four lead balls must roll but never collide. He practiced with it on his hip until he was as adept as his teacher. Now Ganelon wondered if the *via felix* could be self-applied. Might he stretch himself out horizontally, supported by a sawhorse in the small of his back, and redistribute his body humors until he had character or, at least, patience?

To business! If Cipriani wasn't the thief, and Gruber and Thorwald arrived after the cufflink was stolen, then Ganelon was left with two suspects: Sowerby and Hardacre.

As he concluded this reasoning, LeSage arrived to help him dress for dinner. While the detective stood before the mirror adjusting his white tie, LeSage said, "I think I should tell you, sir, you being a detective, that before your arrival I had the pleasure of caring for Mr. Hardacre's needs. While brushing out his vests, I discovered a business card. It read 'Jeremiah Wynne, North American Representative, Old Father William's Supplifying Salve.' "

"So he's been consorting with the enemy?"

"The Old Father William people are in financial straits and desperate to lay hands on our formula, sir. So I fiddled the lock on a curious flat leather box Mr. Hardacre brought with him. Inside was a full gray beard of the kind that hooks over the ears, and matching eyebrows. I never told the young baron. He'd be furious with my snooping through guests' things."

The guests gathered in the music room for a drink before dinner. "What a pleasure to meet the son of the great detective," said the Nawab of Jamkhandi. "I hope your father is well."

Ganelon lied and thanked him for his enquiry. Actually, the Founder was deep in the toils of oboe madness, an affliction common among woodwind players, whose compression of breath must eventually drive the upper palate into the very foundations of the brain. When the fit was on him, the Founder would rave about a love affair with a certain high personage whom he called Regina and see at every window the face of his nemesis Dr. Ludwig Fong, Eurasian arch-villain, chiropractor, and would-be master of the world.

Ganelon met the remaining guests. Suspect Sowerby had a flush face and a sad mouth made sadder by a turned-down moustache. Or was it the drink in his hand? Could Sowerby have stolen his benefactor's cufflink? Some people hate a benefactor most of all.

The duelist Herr Gruber, whose moustache-ends turned sharply upward, appeared something of a fire eater, his eyes aflash with the memory of his last such meal. After they met, Ganelon felt the man had been measuring him for an epée thrust.

Suspect Hardacre was mixing drinks. The American's weathered face suggested a sunburned neck beneath his collar and tie. "Pink-gilled," the English say, meaning "country bumpkin." But Hardacre was no yokel. Ganelon suspected he'd been among his countrymen who had lived in Europe during their Civil War as agents of the North or South. His French was fluent but encumbered, as though learned while he had the American habit of chewing tobacco. Could Hardacre be the thief? Surely a man who once chewed tobacco was capable of anything. And why the fake beard?

Louise Sandor took the detective by the arm, explaining, "Mr. Hardacre is mixing American cocktail drinks. Will you try one? Major," she asked Sowerby, "how do you find your …?"

"Tarantula Juice, ma'am," said Sowerby hoarsely, adding, "The name rather understates the taste."

Hardacre suggested a Lightning Bolt or Calamity Water. Ganelon chose the latter as sounding the least instantaneous. Then he raised his glass to Thorwald across the room. Thorwald wasn't drinking and replied with a bow. Was the self-righteous gentleman of the teetotal persuasion, too? Ganelon smiled to himself, remembering how Thorwald had shown no real interest in his running commentary during the carriage ride until the part about the Phantom Balloon only being seen by the pure of heart. From then on he missed no chance to sneak a glance skyward.

This reminded Ganelon of the lavender cologne. Could Cipriani's perfume atomizer have been used to smuggle the sapphire out of the château? He chatted his way over to the baron and asked if the atomizer had been examined. "Yes, I remember," said his host. "One of those blue glass things. LeSage took it all apart."

Just then a footman opened the dining room doors and everyone moved toward the table. The Nawab was given the place of honor on the baroness's right. Ganelon sat on his other side and offered his regrets for the stolen sapphire cufflink.

The Nawab dismissed the loss with a shake of his head. "My people believe that the Devil, that great aper of the Almighty, once tried to make an animal to match the horse in grace and beauty. But his best effort was the camel. And they say that when he saw how much we loved the beauty of God's flowers, the Devil hurried to his underground smithy and created precious stones, hoping their brightness would lure us from the righteous path. I have made a study of jewels. But they are the Devil's flower bed. We must never become attached to them."

"Some say a camel is a horse designed by a committee," replied Ganelon. "Could it be that the Devil is a committee?"

"He has faces enough to be many committees."

At the other end of the table, Thorwald had just pulled a bottle of Vieux Gaspard's Ointment from his coat pocket. "For Scandinavia, may I suggest one small change for the label?" he asked. "This old man smiles and kicks his heels in the air. But health is a serious business." As he spoke, Thorwald drew on the label with a pencil and sent the bottle around the table. "Conceal the smile thus. Now his eyes challenge us and say, 'I can do this. Why can't you?' "

When the bottle reached him Ganelon thought the penciled moustache on Gaspard's lip bore a striking resemblance to Gruber's. He handed it off to Hardacre, who burst out laughing. The German leaned over to look, turned red, and jumped to his feet. "Are you mocking me, sir?" he demanded of the American.

"Don't blow your stack, pard."

"Watch your words, sir," answered Gruber. "Your bowie knives and knuckle-dusters hold no fear for me. I eat uncouth boobies like you for breakfast!"

Hardacre was on his feet. "Watch what you try eating, friend," he warned, pulling up his coat sleeves. "Remember the Yankee oyster so big it took ten Germans to swallow it whole? I am that oyster, sir. I can handle shooting irons, too."

But seeing their outburst had distressed the baron, Hardacre sat back down. He forced a smile, rubbed the back of his neck, and added, "Not like another member of our hunting party."

Gruber barked out a laugh and sat down, too. "Yes, I hope the rest of the Indian Army shoots better than you do, Major."

"I believe I have already offered you gentlemen my apologies for the peppering," replied Sowerby.

"I forgave you when you ran off Cipriani," Gruber assured him. "Mollycoddles belong by the fireside, charming the ladies."

"Claimed I meant to murder him," protested Sowerby.

"You *did* shoot the hat off his head," said Hardacre.

The major scowled down at his plate.

"A borrowed hat," added Gruber. "Imagine tagging along on a hunt with a borrowed hat and stick."

"Stick or not, I think he shot as many birds as I did," observed the Nawab.

"It's your spanking-new hunting outfit that scares off the birds, your excellency," suggested Hardacre. "Our Henry Thoreau says beware of enterprises that require new clothes. Now, I'd happily sell you my old buckskin jacket."

As the table laughed, the Nawab wagged a mock-scolding finger and replied, "And I say, beware of enterprising used-clothes salesmen who quote Thoreau."

In the music room, after dinner, the baroness played the piano for their entertainment. There was talk of a game of whist. Thorwald chose to sit in a corner with his book. Gruber shook his head. "I shall retire shortly," he said, adding an ominous, "I am accustomed to rising before dawn."

While the card players were making up their game, Ganelon went over to turn the music for the baroness. "I always considered the Phantom Balloon cut from the same cloth as the emperor's new clothes," he remarked. "You have proven me wrong."

The baroness gave a sigh. "If you must know, I didn't see the blasted thing and never said I had. I was out on the lawn when Signor Cipriani burst from the woods, eyes like saucers, babbling about a great brown bag in the sky. It had to be our local phenomenon, the Phantom Balloon. So I raced back to the house shouting the news with Cipriani on my heels. Charles just assumed I'd been the one who'd seen it."

"And you never corrected his thinking?"

The baroness smiled without taking her eyes from the music. "Every wife wants her husband to believe her heart is pure, Monsieur Ganelon. Besides, Cipriani came to me later. His eyes must have been playing tricks on him, he said, and asked I not tell Charles, lest he be judged too excitable to be a Vieux Gaspard representative. I rather like dear, dithery Cipriani. I suspect he colors his hair."

Leaving the piano, Ganelon watched the men play cards for small stakes. He noticed that when Major Sowerby dealt, the Nawab got excellent cards, which he played very badly. After a bit, the detective bade the company good night and retired.

Thunder came. Then a steady rain began to fall. Ganelon sat on the edge of his bed and pondered how a cufflink could be worth an elaborate ruse like a Phantom Balloon sighting. He now became aware of a cold draft across his bare toes coming from under the carved highboy on the opposite wall. In his carpet slippers he tried to inch the heavy piece of furniture forward and was surprised when, with a click, it swung out into the room on concealed hinges, revealing an upward flight of stone steps.

Armed with a lamp, Ganelon mounted up into the darkness. The room beneath the conical roof was fitted with a cell with stout iron bars, whose door stood open. Crowded inside was an iron bedstead, a treadled potter's wheel, a box of hard rubber mallets and an ominous-looking bowl: a devilish grail of fire-scorched iron fitted about with large rusting screws. Cocking an eyebrow, Ganelon followed his footprints in the dust back down to bed.

Rising late the next morning, he found Hardacre playing pool alone in the billiard room. The man informed him that Gruber was off at pistol practice and the Sandors hadn't yet returned from church.

Ganelon said, "By the way, I recently met another American working in your line. Jeremiah Wynne?"

Leaning to make a shot, Hardacre laughed. "I reckon not. I'm Wynne." He straightened up and explained, "After the baron's father hired me on, I got wind the Old Father William people needed a North American man, too. So I paid them a visit in a fake beard. Hell, why not? Peddling both meant two salaries and double travel expenses. With the Big Drink between us, who'd be the wiser?"

"The baron deserves better."

Chalking his cue stick with care, Hardacre said, "A while back I found a thousand-legger—you know, a millipede—on my bedside rug. I stomped it good, and you know what? It was one of my own fake eyebrows. So the jig was up. I told the baron everything. He didn't mind. He said Old Father William would be bankrupt way before I got back home to the States.

In the music room, Ganelon found the Nawab deep in the *Times* of London and Sowerby playing Patience at a table nearby. And there, through a window, was Thorwald walking backwards across a muddy flower bed toward the château, his head thrown back on watch for the Phantom Balloon. He was coming dangerously close to the moat. As Ganelon moved to rap on the window glass, Thorwald reached the gravel path along the excavation work, turned, and walked away.

After a breakfast of coffee and a roll in the empty dining room, Ganelon asked LeSage to show him the hat and stick Cipriani had borrowed. LeSage led him back to the gun room and indicated a cloth hat with a peppering of small holes in the crown and a blackthorn from a rack of walking sticks.

"You also examined Cipriani's atomizer?" asked the detective, running his fingers over the stick.

"And needed several washings to rid my hands of the smell of lavender, sir."

"Could the blue bottle have hidden a blue sapphire?"

"The stone was much too large to pass through the neck of the bottle, sir," LeSage replied and took his leave.

The Nawab appeared in the doorway. "May I share a moral dilemma, Monsieur Ganelon?"

"You mean, should you admit you shot off Cipriani's hat, not Major Sowerby?" The Nawab's astonishment obliged Ganelon to add, "A great-aunt on my mother's side who was afflicted with flatulence late in life always kept an old cocker spaniel close by for scolding purposes should the need arise."

The Nawab understood. "Yes, Major Sowerby has very kindly taken upon himself my shortcomings with the shotgun," he admitted. "Yet I don't know how it happened. I knew Cipriani was there behind the bushes. I swear I shot high enough. Well, perhaps some day I will master the weapon."

"And whist, your excellency?" asked the detective.

The Nawab laughed at himself. "You can't become an English gentleman overnight. Still, I'd rather not call attention to my ineptitudes. But no one has ever left the table out of pocket because of the help Major Sowerby gives me."

Ganelon decided he needed a long walk in the open air to think things out. Leaving the château, he took the path toward the summit of Mont St. Hugues. If the perfume atomizer hadn't been used to smuggle out the sapphire, then nothing really made sense. Cipriani steals a single cufflink when he could have stolen the pair. To give himself an excuse to carry off his modest prize, he intrudes a borrowed hat on a borrowed stick into the hunters' line of fire, leaving telltale scratch marks of shot on the blackthorn. Sowerby, having been apologizing all morning for the Nawab, takes responsibility once more. Cipriani cries murder and decamps without the sapphire. No, it made no sense at all.

Up ahead, beyond where the path diverged, Gruber was sitting on a rustic bench, putting the finishing touches on cleaning his dueling pistol. Rising to go down to the nearby creek to wash the gun oil from his hands, he saw Ganelon and gave a polite bow. The detective bowed back before taking the upward path.

But the focused mind which came to Ganelon walking familiar streets eluded him in the country. Every step was a pleasant distraction. It would please the Nawab to know that wildflowers could hold him where the jeweler's window could not. He thought of the Doctrine of Signatures, which taught that plants of medicinal value bore a mark specifying their curative powers. He thought of Baron Justin trying to deduce character from bumps on the skull.

Reaching the summit, he stood beneath a blasted oak to admire the view. Beyond the Porpentine's curl he could make out a gray suggestion of the roofs of San Sebastiano, then the definite blue of the sea. Somewhere beyond lay the coast of Africa.

At the time of the Dresden bomb attempt on the Nawab, Ganelon had been serving in the Tripolitanian wars. One night, wrapped in his cape and staring into the campfire at the Sidi oasis, he wondered if the bomb thrower could have been Ludwig Fong. Killing doers of good deeds and thinkers of good thoughts was Fong's recreation, after all. Hadn't he himself set the fire that destroyed the convent where the blessed mystic, Mother Inez, communed with God? Hadn't he brewed the ink whose fumes killed the peacemakers about to sign the pact ending the Turco-Balkan War? And how many medical missionaries hurrying on some errand of mercy had taken a turning in the jungle trail and met a smiling Fong in the act of stripping off his goat-skin gloves?

But all that was idle speculation now. Fong was done killing with his own hands. During a recent medical missionary hunt he had contracted Zambezi, or Simpering Fever. Now even his felonious children fled his terrible doting smile. He shunned the light of day, living alone amid draped mirrors lest he stumble upon his smirk unawares. In an ironic intersection of crime and punishment his last victim, a world authority on Simpering Fever, had reportedly been on the verge of a cure.

The baron looked interested at luncheon when Ganelon mentioned his walk to the top of Mont St. Hugues. "That blasted oak was Grandfather Justin's favorite thinking spot," he said. "By then he'd turned to applied phrenology."

"Changing character by changing the bumps on the head?"

"Quite so. He designed the Sandor Corrective Cap, an iron skull-cap with adjustable screws to apply pressure where needed. He wore it himself for three years with nothing for his trouble but bad headaches. Then one night he was surprised by a violent thunderstorm atop Mont St. Hugues. As he stood hurling science's cool defiance into the teeth of wild nature, a bolt of lightning struck. Instantly, Grandfather's headache went away and he realized he must find a solvent to make bone malleable. Many thunderstorms later he hit on pickle brine. For hours he'd soak his head in brine, breathing through a straw, and then work at amending his character with a hefty rubber mallet. He was never successful. Perhaps he needed younger, more mutable bone.

"But by the time I came along he'd abandoned phrenology for pottery. I remember vividly his wild-eyed look when he talked of shaping base clay into splendid little receptacles."

Unwittingly, Sandor had told Ganelon why they never spoke of the pickled boys at home. The Founder suspected Baron Justin was the real killer. So did the young baron's father, who confined Baron Justin in the tower. And Gaston, given the choice of being the madman's keeper for the rest of his life or spending it in a quiet Duranceville cell, confessed to the murders. Ganelon found some satisfaction that the Founder had botched a famous case. But it still left him chasing after a stolen cufflink.

Once again, the table talk was Vieux Gaspard's Ointment. Barking his grim laugh, Gruber promised his shop owners would give the product prominent display or face him on the dueling piste. Hardacre, afraid his countrymen couldn't work their tongues around Vieux Gaspard, proposed a name change for the American market. Oil of the Limberlost, perhaps. Or Calaveras Frog Oil. A hop in every drop.

During dessert the Nawab turned to Ganelon. "After all I said last night about jewels, I find, on reflection, there is one I sorely covet, the Ararat Red, the legendary ruby which illuminated Noah's Ark during the forty dark days and nights of the Flood. It was stolen years ago from the Sultan of Turkey. I understand it may soon be on the market again."

The baron now asked his guests to adjourn to the music room for the parlor game he had promised. Ganelon was so shaken by the Nawab's words, he hardly heard him. The Ararat Red, he knew, was the pride of Dr. Ludwig Fong's fabled collection. Could Fong have used the ruby to hire an assassin to kill the Nawab? And wasn't it said that the Gooseberry Fool had a weakness for precious stones?

Pondering this grim possibility, Ganelon followed the others into the music room. The curtains had been drawn shut and seven armchairs set around the walls at ten-foot intervals. The baroness had taken her place at the piano. Ganelon wondered if the parlor game was to be musical chairs. He had been bringing up the rear and found the only chair left was between the baron and Gruber, directly across the room from the Nawab.

The baron cleared his throat and said, "In a moment the servants will take away the lamps and leave us in darkness. Then my wife will begin to play. With the darkness and the music to protect his identity, I beg the one who stole the Nawab's cufflink to return it. Place it in that bowl on the piano and the matter will be closed forever."

Ganelon shook his head firmly and went over and protested in the baron's ear, "I don't like this. The Nawab's life ..."

"But it was the Nawab who suggested this little bit of entertainment," replied the baron.

His words made Ganelon's resolve stumble. The detective went back and sat down in confusion.

"My dear baron," called the Nawab, who seemed to be enjoying himself, "I hope you're not placing a valuable bowl in harm's way. Major Sowerby knows silver. May he …?"

The baron agreed. Sowerby went and picked up the bowl, turned it over, and judged it a very fine piece.

"Which I am prepared to risk," said the baron.

Suddenly the Nawab's little manservant rushed into the room in considerable distress and whispered to his master. The Nawab smiled, patted his forearm reassuringly, and dismissed him. At the baron's signal the lamps were removed and the baroness began a vigorous polka.

Ganelon sat in the darkness for several minutes contemplating how very close he had come to making a fool of himself. Then he thought of what Father Sylvanus had said. Fool or not, at least he could have the courage of his convictions. Suppose the whole business about the cufflink had been leading up to this dark moment. What if the Gooseberry Fool was in the room?

Ganelon sprang up, stumbled to a window, and threw open the curtains.

The piano stopped. Everyone sat, blinking at the afternoon light. Except for the Nawab. He was quite dead in his chair, his head thrown back, lifeless eyes staring at the ceiling, the mark of the strangler's thumbs on his windpipe.

The baroness uttered a small cry.

Ganelon had failed the Nawab. But he resolved to do everything he could to find his murderer. "Send for the police," he told the baron. He looked around at the guests and added, "No one must leave this room until they arrive." Then he turned to Sowerby. "Can you clarify things, Major?"

Sowerby started to protest. Then the wind went out of him. "I didn't kill him, I swear to that. The Nawab was very embarrassed by the baron's fuss over the cufflink. So I proposed this little parlor game. He passed the suggestion on to our host. What his excellency didn't tell the baron was that he was going to give me the remaining cufflink to slip into the bowl. When the lights came back on, there it would be. The baron's honor would be satisfied. The Nawab would get the cufflink back and be no worse off than before."

"So that's what the Nawab's manservant came to tell him, that now the second cufflink was missing?"

"Correct."

Thorwald had gone to the piano. "But the bowl's empty," he said.

"Because you never put it there, did you, Major?" said Ganelon. "You palmed the second cufflink. Now you had the pair."

Avoiding everyone's eyes, Sowerby produced the two sapphire cufflinks and handed them to Ganelon, who passed them on to the baron. "Cipriani gave me the first cufflink the morning he left," Sowerby told them. "Said he found it. Said I could return it to the Nawab. Or, he said, I could suggest this little game and end up with both. Somehow he knew I was being pressed hard to repay certain gambling debts. As he pointed out, a matching pair would go a long way to settling things."

"But when the second cufflink went missing, wouldn't the Nawab have suspected you?" asked Hardacre.

"Not if Sowerby killed the Nawab to shut him up," said Gruber.

Sowerby shook his head. "Cipriani had the answer to that one, too. He knew how the Nawab liked his little ethical puzzles. He suggested I cloud the issue by wondering out loud what might happen if the thief actually tried to return the stolen cufflink in the darkness and discovered its mate in the bowl. Might he not consider the second cufflink a reward for his newfound honesty and keep both? This possibility intrigued the Nawab."

Suddenly Ganelon understood the part the perfume atomizer played. Having suggested the parlor game, the master assassin couldn't afford to be there in the room when the Nawab was found dead. So he said his goodbyes and left the château. His plan was to change out of his Cipriani disguise at the railway station and return as Lars Thorwald. But on the way he realized he wouldn't have time to wash off all traces of Cipriani's lavender scent. By dumping the atomizer on the floor of the carriage, he gave himself an excuse for reeking of lavender when he came back as Thorwald.

Here the baroness cried out again. There were faces at the window. Now a commotion broke out in the hallway. The doors flew open and Chief Inspector Flanel burst into the room followed by several of his men. Vain and slow-witted, the chief inspector's rise on the police force showed how much it had deteriorated as the Founder's reputation grew and the superior criminal found other places to practice his trade.

Flanel introduced himself to the astonished room. With a nod toward the corpse he said, "An hour ago, the prefecture received an anonymous message that the Nawab of Jamkhandi had been murdered and that his killer was still on these premises."

"Chief Inspector …" began Ganelon.

"Ah, young Ganelon," said Flanel. "Letting them get murdered right under your nose, eh? Well, never mind. Keep your eyes open and your mouth shut and you may learn something." Flanel turned abruptly and went to examine the body. Then he had the baron explain the chair arrangement and give him the names of the other guests, which he wrote down in his notebook. When he was done he looked much like the cat that had swallowed the canary.

"Chief Inspector …" Ganelon began again.

But Flanel lay a side of his forefinger across his lips. Then he addressed the room while pacing back and forth with the plodding, bearlike walk he had affected ever since Marchpane's *The Eye of the Snowstorm*, in which the author had the Founder comment on then Sergeant Flanel's prancing step. "I now intend to interrogate you one at a time, beginning with Herr Franz Gruber. Since this may be a lengthy process, you may all occupy yourselves as you wish until I need to see you. Be warned that I have men at all the entrances and on the grounds." At Flanel's signal the policemen began clearing the room.

Ganelon came over and said firmly, "Chief Inspector, the Nawab's killer is the Gooseberry Fool."

Flanel's jaw sagged.

Ganelon gave him a moment to let that sink in. Then he said, "And the Gooseberry Fool is …"

"Not another word," said Flanel, gloating like a peacock. "This is my investigation." Rubbing his hands together vigorously as though washing them in glory, the chief inspector turned to Gruber. "Actually I'm surprised to find you here, Franz Gruber."

"And why is that?" asked the German, clearly outraged at being questioned first.

"Because, sir, yesterday we received a report circulated by the Milan police that your body was found three days ago in a room at the Hotel Europa. You had been strangled and your face battered in. You are an imposter. You are the Gooseberry Fool."

Gruber barked a contemptuous laugh. No amount of badgering could shake the man's pickpocket story. After half an hour Flanel had him taken away to be held until the Leipzig police verified his identity.

The chief inspector scowled over his suspect list again, shrugged hopelessly, and looked in Ganelon's direction. When Ganelon mouthed Thorwald's name, Flanel had him sent for.

Now a stranger appeared in the doorway, a man with an air of serious purpose wearing a close-cropped beard in the style made popular by Cavour. "I must speak to Baron Sandor," he said.

"I am Chief Inspector Flanel, sir. Who are you?"

"My name is Antonio Cipriani, Vieux Gaspard's sales representative for Italy and Spain."

"How the hell did you get in here?" demanded Flanel.

"I had come expecting villainy," said the new arrival. "When I found men lurking around outside, I assumed they were up to something dark. I should have realized they were police. Villains don't lurk about with their hands in their pockets. In any event, when the man at the front door went into the bushes to relieve himself, I saw my chance and slipped inside.

"A week ago I was kidnapped on my way to visit the baron's new manufacturing facility in Milan and held in an old farmhouse north of Naples. From what my kidnappers said among themselves, I gathered I was being held so that someone could impersonate me here. I suspected the Old Father William people meant to steal our formula." The new arrival struck a kick-boxing stance. "No novice at the art of self-defence, I waited for my chance, knocked one of my captors down with a kick to the solar plexus, and escaped. But what was I to do then? Go to the police and they'd waste precious time confirming my story. So I decided to come directly here. In San Sebastiano I rented a rig, rode out here, and approached the château on foot. The rest you know."

Cipriani put on pince-nez glasses, drew the Friday edition of the Milan *Correro* out of his pocket, and said, "Oh yes, and this may interest you. It seems I wasn't the only Vieux Gaspard representative to be kidnapped." The article he tapped with his glasses read: "The police, acting on an anonymous informant, have determined the murdered man discovered Sunday last at the Hotel Europa and previously identified as Franz Gruber of Leipzig was, in fact, Lars Thorwald of Christiania."

Flanel snatched an invisible fly out of the air and shook it in his tight fist. "Got him!" he said. Then, as footsteps approached down the hall, he turned triumphantly to face the door.

But the policeman sent to find Thorwald had returned alone. "He's gone, sir, escaped from his room down a rope of knotted bed sheets."

"After him!" shouted Flanel, prancing out of the room. "He can't have gotten far! Lars Thorwald is the Gooseberry Fool!"

Ganelon stayed behind to explain to the amazed Cipriani how his identity had been used in the Gooseberry Fool's plan to murder the Nawab. When he had finished, Cipriani bowed and said, "I come at an inconvenient time. I will return tomorrow to put myself at the baron's disposal."

Ganelon pointed to the window where Flanel and a crowd of shouting policemen were dashing across the lawn. "Don't leave yet. You'll miss all the excitement."

"It looks like they've picked up his trail," said Cipriani. As the pursuers entered the trees he added a worried, "If that's the way the villain went, and he holds to that course, he should emerge from the woods near where I tied my rig." Ganelon made no reply. "But he'll get away!" Cipriani insisted, starting toward the door. "Somebody has to warn the police."

"No need. Thorwald's still here in the château. As for the trail, I saw him fake those footprints this morning. At the time, I thought he was looking for the Phantom Balloon."

"The Phantom Balloon?"

Ganelon sighed. "Please, let us avoid these needless explanations, Mr. Fool. Or may I call you Gooseberry? You are a regular one-man band. First you were one Cipriani, then Thorwald. And now you are another Cipriani, sneaking downstairs like you'd just arrived fresh from the arms of your kidnappers."

The master of disguise gave a resigned smile. Then his eyes turned cold, he shifted his feet, and asked, "What gave me away? After all, if we don't profit from our mistakes, why make them?"

"You'd thought everything through so carefully I knew you'd have a safer escape plan than dropping from a rope of knotted bed sheets into the rubble of an excavated moat and then limping off across country with the police close behind."

The assassin shifted his feet again. "I really am a kickboxing expert, you know. And you, I understand, are a master of the *via felix*, the Happy Way. Or is that your father?"

"You were right the first time. Shall we find out which martial art is the better?"

"I'm tempted. But tell me, does the *via felix* actually change your opponent's character?"

Ganelon nodded. "By redistributing the bodily humors. But the effect is only temporary."

The assassin grimaced. "Then I'm afraid I am your prisoner. Temporary or not, a human chameleon must treasure his own personality, his inner core, above all else."

"Come along, then," ordered Ganelon. "We'll hunt up your rig where you really left it and drive in to the prefecture. I hope we don't meet Chief Inspector Flanel along the way. You are my prisoner. Besides, an afternoon's run in the woods will do his character no end of good."

The Verbatim Reply

O N A JUNE afternoon in 1894, a tall unshaven man in dusty boots and a ragged grey-green jacket with dark-green facings in the German style appeared at the porter's lodge of the British Embassy in Sofia, Bulgaria. "Hello, Iosep," he smiled in answer to the porter's disapproving gaze.

The porter's simple brow unfurled. "Mr. Ganelon, sir! Welcome, sir!" he cried eagerly. Carrying his prosperous stomach out of the lodge, Iosep the porter took up the new arrival's threadbare carpet-bag. Ambrose Ganelon, the second to bear that name, refused to surrender the flat wooden case with brass corners which he carried under his arm.

With his free hand outstretched, Iosep showed the way across the modern courtyard. "His Excellency is in London, sir. He will be distressed he missed your visit." Ganelon, son of the founder of San Sebastiano's famous detective agency, was an old friend of Ambassador Millington and, as Iosep knew to his profit, a generous guest during his previous stays at the Embassy.

"Then I'm in the hands of Mr. Brownlow?" asked the detective.

"Ah, sir," replied the porter sadly, "last night our poor chargé d'affaires was struck down by a carriage in the street. He is in the hospital. Mr. Horner is taking his place."

Horner? Ah, yes, Ganelon had a favorable memory of Gervaise Horner, the young Embassy clerk he'd met on his last visit. "A young man of bottom" were the words Millington had used to describe him, meaning he possessed character, solidity, and staying power. The Ambassador also predicted a fine future for Horner in the Foreign Service, high praise from a man who judged his subordinates severely.

The chattering Iosep ushered Ganelon into the Embassy. Recently Sofia had swept away much of the trappings of the Turk and replaced them with buildings such as the British Embassy, more in the current European style. As they started up the black-marble and steel-filigree staircase to the second floor, Horner emerged from the anteroom to the Ambassador's office carrying an envelope. He was a fair-haired, athletic-looking young man whose cheeks had not quite lost their down. In a diplomat's dark cutaway and striped trousers, he appeared a bit like a child caught playing grown-up.

"Has the carriage arrived, Iosep?" he asked. Then he saw the porter's shabby companion and he smiled. "Mr. Ganelon, what a pleasure to have you back with us again."

"Am I intruding?" asked the detective.

"Of course not," insisted Horner. "The more witnesses the better. A callow twenty-three-year-old is about to deliver an ultimatum to the Bulgarian Foreign Minister. I'd give my right arm for poor Brownlow's beard."

"And how is he, your chargé d'affaires?"

"He was delirious when I stopped by the hospital last night to collect his valuables," said Horner gravely. "This morning the hospital sent round to say he had fallen into a deep coma." Then he said, "Will you excuse me from making you welcome until I've returned from my visit to Foreign Minister Krumm?"

Ganelon bowed and continued up the stairs. While speaking to Horner, he had noticed through the anteroom doorway a very world-weary-looking gentleman lounging in a chair with his legs out-stretched, his ankles and arms crossed, and his eyelids teetering on the edge of sleep. Or so they seemed. The English are admonished not to eat as if they are hungry. It seemed to Ganelon that some of them approached life the same way. He asked Iosep who the gentleman was.

"Viscount Vyvyan, sir. He came to us recently from the Paris Embassy." The porter's voice grew confidential. "A question of gambling debts and scandals of the heart, sir."

Yes, Ganelon thought he detected something of the diplomatic languor about the man. The British still operated their Foreign Service in tandem, the Diplomatic and the Foreign Office. The primary prerequisite of the former was an income of 400 pounds a year. Though the Foreign Office examinations were more competitive, at least its clerkships were salaried. Ganelon understood that young Horner had given up Sandhurst to enter the Foreign Office when the death of his father made him the sole support of a mother and three sisters.

Iosep left Ganelon alone in the small suite of rooms on the second floor where he was accustomed to stay. As he prepared to shave and take his first real bath in several weeks, he heard a carriage enter the courtyard and stop below his window. After a minute or two, it clattered off again. Ganelon smiled. The beardless lad was off to beard the formidable Dr. Krumm in his lair at the Foreign Ministry.

Ganelon allowed himself a long soak in the tub. It seemed to him he had been going full speed for the past two months. And part of it was his own fault. Yes, a small alarm bell should have gone off in his head two years ago when his archenemy, that manifold villain Duhamel Fong, was elected to the French Academy.

Europe had not found it strange that Fong should be among the Immortals, as the Academicians were called, for it only knew the man as the West's greatest authority on hypnotism. At the time, Ganelon had simply chalked it up to another example of Fong's incredible ego. But Ganelon had been mistaken. With the Immortals under his hypnotic spell, Fong accelerated their revision of the great French Dictionary, which for years had been bogged down in the mid-Cs. By the time the ancient frenzied scholars reached the Ms, people were remembering the legend that the end of the world would occur on the day the French Academy finished its Dictionary.

Fear gripped the Continent. And everywhere Europeans spoke out loud in their sleep in fear of the approaching Zs. Stock markets tumbled, property values plummeted, and whatever was tangible went for a song. And Fong was the buyer. Then, when he'd bought his fill, it amused him to stop work on the Dictionary and dispatch his immortal colleagues against Ganelon. Being attacked by a gang of assassins was one thing. But having one's life threatened by a military genius one day and the world's foremost toxicologist or a master of the psychological novel the next was quite something else again. For days the shadows across from 18 bis rue Blondin were crammed with the lurk of Academicians in their green-brocaded uniforms and rang with the clink of their ceremonial swords.

Ganelon dealt with each Immortal in turn as gently as the situation would allow. But the cumulative effect was draining. One day after a ninety-five-year-old theologian, an authority on the medieval mystics, tried to garotte him on a public street Ganelon decided to drop out of sight for a bit until the learned onslaught had abated.

That same afternoon, he kissed his beautiful wife, patted his son, heir, and namesake on the head, and vanished in disguise through a hidden passage in the basement, carrying a large camera and tripod over his shoulder. Whenever he felt the world was too much with him, Ganelon would take a roam through Europe disguised as an itinerant photographer, snapping pictures of the Continent's major criminals. It was healthy outdoor work and not that difficult. The streak of vanity runs deep in criminals and their sense of security when on home ground is almost endearing. Sometime during the photo session, Ganelon would bring out a mirror which he described as a light reflector and set it at an angle close to the subject's head. These shots showing full face and profile simultaneously were much prized by the police forces of Europe.

But on this particular trip, Ganelon began hearing things—a whispered word here, a word not spoken there, a careless boast. And when he added these scraps together, he decided a quick trip to Constantinople might frustrate one of Duhamel Fong's darker designs and pay him back in part for the plague of murderous Immortals. So Ganelon had shipped his photographic gear home by train and come to the British Embassy in Sofia for a brief rest-stop before finding a new disguise and slipping over the border into Turkey.

Ganelon emerged from the tub to discover the housekeeper had laid out one of the Ambassador's tweed suits and provided a pot of coffee and a box of Millington's excellent Russian cigarettes. Ganelon drank a coffee and smoked a cigarette while he dressed. Then he heard a carriage in the courtyard again.

He went to the window and watched as Horner descended from the vehicle, looking not unpleased with himself. Apparently the young man had delivered his government's message without any breach of protocol, like getting his foot caught in the Foreign Minister's wastepaper basket. Ganelon smiled down on the budding diplomat, for he had once been young himself. Then he lit another cigarette and stood at the window, thinking of the task that lay ahead in Constantinople.

After a while, he roused himself. He'd had another reason for stopping at the Embassy. He was anxious to have the fruits of his photographic labors sent back to San Sebastiano in the safety of a diplomatic pouch. Picking up the flat box with the brass corners, he went downstairs to find Horner.

The young Englishman's desk in the anteroom was empty. Through an open inner door, Ganelon saw Horner sitting in the Ambassador's chair. The safe in the wall behind him stood open. Ganelon sensed the young man had been sitting there motionless for a long time, staring with unseeing eyes at the papers all spread out on the desk. His face was white, his hair unkempt. Rarely had Ganelon seen anyone so cast down in so short a period of time.

"Anything wrong, Horner?" he asked from the doorway.

The clerk jumped and stared. "No, no," he insisted and hurriedly began gathering up the papers. "How can I help you, Mr. Ganelon?" asked Horner, failing in his attempt to muster a laugh. When Ganelon had explained about the diplomatic pouch, Horner said he would be happy to oblige. He accepted Ganelon's box and added it to the wall safe along with the papers, taking his time, with his back turned, as though trying to compose himself.

"You're sure nothing's wrong?" asked Ganelon again. "You looked a rather tragic figure a moment ago."

Horner shut the wall safe hard to lock it and turned around. "I was thinking of my family," he said. "A touch of homesickness, I suspect."

Ganelon judged the first remark to be true and the second false. "Of course," he said. "Well, thank you about the box." He was halfway across the anteroom before Horner caught up with him.

"Mr. Ganelon," he said, "I know from the Ambassador that on more than one occasion you have been of great service to our government. The recovery of the plans for the Prentice-Jenkins land torpedo, for example."

Ganelon bowed and waited for the young man to decide if he was going to speak his mind. The detective suspected he was going to be called on to recover something. Otherwise Horner wouldn't have specified that highly impractical Prentice-Jenkins battlefield device which was essentially a naval torpedo slung between two motorized bicycles.

After a moment's agonizing, the young man looked Ganelon straight in the face and blurted out, "An hour ago a private train left Sofia traveling at full speed on a non-stop trip to the Black Sea coast. Is there any way you could get on board and replace a letter in a dispatch case with another that I would give you?" He gave the detective a woeful look. "You see, if you cannot, then I am a ruined man." Horner fell into his seat, put his elbow on his desk, shielded his eyes with his hand, and shook his head hopelessly.

Ganelon dragged over a chair and sat down nearby. "Tell me," he said.

After a moment, Horner rallied himself and sat up straight. "Perhaps you know that several weeks ago the Bulgarians requested a clarification of my government's position on the question of warships in the Black Sea," he said. "Ambassador Millington was recalled to London to assist in drawing up our reply. Yesterday afternoon London cabled us in cypher to expect an answer today. That very evening Mr. Brownlow had his accident."

"Today my government's reply arrived by cable and in cypher. Thus the responsibility of decyphering and delivering the reply fell to me. I don't have to tell you how nervous I was. Dr. Krumm is quite a fire-eater and I knew he wouldn't care for my government's position on this question—all the more so when it was delivered to him by a young cub. Nevertheless, I unlocked the Ambassador's wall safe, took out the cypher, and set to work. When I was done, I returned the cypher to the wall safe. My next task was to recast my verbatim version of London's reply, rearranging the sentences and changing the phrasing. Need I say why?"

Ganelon shook his head. Of course the British would assume the Bulgarians had intercepted the encyphered cable. If the reply was decyphered and delivered verbatim, the Bulgarians would only have to compare the cable and the reply to break the British diplomatic cypher.

"I have been well schooled in the redrafting procedure by Mr. Brownlow," said Horner. "It isn't that difficult. However, in so sensitive a matter I worked with care and, I think, a good measure of success. Mr. Millington requires us to make fair copies of both the verbatim reply and its rephrased version so he can judge our handiwork."

"I had just finished this when Viscount Vyvyan arrived. You might say that Vyvyan's on the entertaining side of our business and he keeps entertainer's hours. I'm on the working side and schedule myself accordingly. I don't mind. Vyvyan isn't a bad chap, really. But he came to us under something of a cloud and the Ambassador still isn't quite sure what to do with him. He hasn't even given him a key to the wall safe yet. In any event, Brownlow thought highly enough of Vyvyan's penmanship that he set him the job of transcribing the final drafts of any messages going beyond the Embassy walls. Vyvyan has been very obliging in this regard. So when he arrived, I sat him right down with pen and paper and dictated my recast version of London's reply.

"Just as the ink dried, I heard Iosep's voice and thought the carriage had come to take me to the Foreign Ministry. I jumped up and in a bit of a rush I put the verbatim reply and my copy of the redraft in the wall safe and Vyvyan's copy of the redraft into its envelope and came out into the hall. But it was only Mr. Ambrose Ganelon. After I left you, I came back in here and chatted with Vyvyan until the carriage finally arrived.

"At the Foreign Ministry, I was shown into Dr. Krumm's office at once, where I found him in hat and coat, putting documents into a dispatch case. The Foreign Minister apologized for receiving me in that manner but said he had been summoned to Odessa to meet with his Russian counterpart on the warship question. Adding my government's reply to his dispatch case, he assured me he would read it before he reached the coast. With further apologies, he escorted me to where our carriages waited, his to take him to the railway station, mine to bring me back to my Embassy.

"I returned here intending to draw up a cable informing London of the Russo-Bulgarian meeting, but when I unlocked the wall safe to get the cypher I discovered Vyvyan's copy of the recast message staring up at me from a shelf. And the verbatim reply was missing. That could mean only one thing: like a blundering fool I'd put the verbatim reply in Dr. Krumm's envelope by mistake. In effect, I had hand-delivered the British diplomatic cypher to the Bulgarians."

"I imagine there is a procedure you follow to warn London of a compromised cypher," said Ganelon.

Horner nodded, avoiding the detective's eyes. "A code word. I haven't sent it yet."

"Ah," said Ganelon.

"I had to be sure, you see. I went through the wall safe with a fine-tooth comb."

"And now?"

"Mr. Ganelon," said the young man in earnest dismay, "when London learns of my blunder I'll be dismissed from the Foreign Service." When the detective said nothing, he continued: "Think about it. We've been rephrasing our messages for years. What do you really think the chances are the Bulgarians are still checking them against the encyphered cable?"

The desperate young man waited for an answer and then said, "Damn it, Mr. Ganelon, in ten days London will be issuing the new six-month cypher. In ten days this whole blasted question will be moot!"

"You propose to do nothing to rectify the situation, then?" asked the detective.

"I'm just trying to explain why I haven't rushed to cable London," insisted Horner. Then he said, "Please, is there any way you can help me?"

Ganelon checked his pocket watch. "You know," he said, "my father kept up-to-date schedules of the entire railway system of Europe in his head. He could travel from Edinburgh to San Sebastiano without leaving his armchair, naming every station he passed through and calling out the time all along the way. He even turned queasy on the Channel steamer. But my mind's made of lesser stuff. Do you have a timetable?"

"I believe Iosep does," said Horner.

The detective nodded. "All right, I'll do my best to help you, Horner. Don't get your hopes up. But hold off sending your cable until I get back. Now where's Vyvyan's copy of the reply?"

Night was falling on Sofia by the time Ganelon returned to the Embassy carrying several mysterious parcels tied up with string. The sound of the detective's step on the staircase brought a grave-faced Gervaise Horner to the anteroom doorway. "Mr. Brownlow died half an hour ago," he said.

"He was an honorable man," said Ganelon.

"I've been thinking about just that," said Horner. "I'm glad you're back. I asked you to do the impossible. Now it's time for me to cable London about the cypher. I've already been a fool. If I delay any longer I'll be a scoundrel, too."

"Bravo," said Ganelon. As he rearranged his parcels to free one arm, he added, "There are times that try men's souls and incidents that test an individual's character." He drew an envelope from his inside coat pocket and handed it to Horner.

Inside the envelope Horner found the verbatim reply. He uttered a bewildered, "But how—?"

"If anyone asks," said Ganelon, "please tell them I boarded a high-speed, non-stop train that had left the station an hour before me, entered the compartment of a wide-awake Bulgarian Foreign Minister, and switched diplomatic messages right under his nose. That should add considerably to my legend. Unfortunately, the truth is more banal. Come along. I'll tell you what really happened while I change. There's a Bulgarian police inspector coming at any moment to drive me on the next leg of my journey to the Turkish border."

As Horner followed after him up the staircase, Ganelon began his story.

When he'd left the young Englishman, the detective had paused to consult Iosep's railway timetable in the porter's lodge. Then he hailed an up-to-date cab and drove away on India rubber tires to police headquarters. When he gave his name, he was promptly ushered into the office of an inspector on the happy list of regular recipients of the fruits of Ganelon's photographic wanderings. This grateful police official listened to Ganelon's needs and quickly supplied the names of two of Sofia's underworld specialists along with a blunt note to each advising full cooperation with the visitor from San Sebastiano.

An hour and a half later, Ganelon and a man with a splendid blue-black mustache and a leather suitcase were standing in a doorway across the street from the apartment building where Vyvyan lived. The detective consulted his pocket watch and a moment later the Englishman emerged and set off on foot down the boulevard. Ganelon and the man with the suitcase followed at a prudent distance.

Any doubt Ganelon had that Vyvyan was his man vanished as the imposing walls of the new railway station loomed ahead of them. They entered the building just in time to see the Englishman buy a platform ticket and pass through the turnstile. Ganelon and his companion did likewise, parting company on the platform amid the bustle of passengers and the steamy racket of modern transportation. As Ganelon crossed to the railway buffet, he noted the sleek and luxurious lines of the Green Train standing in the station.

The gloom of the café restaurant allowed the detective to slip into a corner table unobserved. Vyvyan had taken a seat in a window booth already occupied by Wolff Tuchmann. Ostensibly a wagon-lits porter on the Green Train, this man was actually one of Duhamel Fong's couriers, making regular pick-ups and deliveries between Berlin and Bagdad and back again. This bit of knowledge had served Ganelon so well in the past that he hadn't bothered to move against Tuchmann.

As the detective watched, Vyvyan passed an envelope across the table and then rose quickly and hurried out of the buffet. Tuchmann put the envelope in his inside breast pocket. Then he sat in the booth for a few minutes, his hand on a concealed revolver, his eyes darting about suspiciously as if he sensed he was observed. Finally he stood up and started to leave.

But as he passed through the doorway, the man suddenly looked back over his shoulder with a hard stare as though trying to pierce the dark in the very corner where Ganelon sat. At that moment, Tuchmann collided with a hurrying passenger with a splendid blue-black mustache. He might have fallen if the traveler hadn't had the presence of mind to grab him. Ganelon's corner was forgotten as the red-faced Tuchmann shook the helping hand from his lapel indignantly and reached inside his jacket to reassure himself that the envelope was still there before hurrying away in the direction of the Green Train.

The story begun on the staircase came to an end in Ganelon's room. "So there you are," said the detective as he untied the last of his parcels. "Thanks to a master pickpocket, the verbatim reply is back where it belongs."

"But why did the Bulgarians give it to Vyvyan?" demanded Horner.

Ganelon paused in the act of holding up the last part of his new disguise to examine it in the light. "My dear fellow, you still don't understand. Well, in a way I'm pleased you don't. All right, quite simply stated, there never was any mixup on your part—none at all. You delivered the correct copy of the message to Dr. Krumm."

"But that can't be," insisted Horner. "I found Vyvyan's copy in the wall safe and the verbatim reply was missing. And I'm the only one with the key."

"What about Brownlow's key?" asked Ganelon, as he began changing into his disguise—the outfit of a master of the Dancing Dervish brotherhood.

"I put all of Brownlow's valuables in the wall safe. I saw his key. It was on his watchchain."

"But did you examine it closely? Did you try it in the lock?" asked Ganelon.

"Of course not," said Horner. "What are you getting at?"

"There were two reasons to stage Brownlow's accident," said Ganelon. "It left you in charge and it gave them a chance to replace his key with another—a lookalike prepared from Vyvyan's direction. That's what you saw on the watchchain." Ganelon slipped the long, bell-skirted dervish robe over his head and continued. "This afternoon, when you'd left for your appointment with Dr. Krumm, Vyvyan opened the wall safe with Brownlow's real key. He pocketed the verbatim reply and, using your fair draft of the rephrased message, he wrote it out again in his elaborate hand. Then he put Brownlow's key back on the watchchain and closed the wall safe."

Horner shook his head. "If Vyvyan could open the wall safe, then why all the rigamarole? Why not just copy the whole cypher?"

"Such modesty in a young man is certainly refreshing," said the detective. "My dear fellow, they didn't go to all this trouble for a cypher with a mere ten days of life left on it. The prize they were after was Gervaise Horner."

While that was sinking in, Ganelon looked down at the embroidered dervish slippers and wiggled his toes. "A bit tight," he said. "I am cursed with big feet." Then he continued. "You see, I know how these people work. Brownlow's accident with the Ambassador away was a little too neat for my liking. They made you believe that you'd compromised the cypher, knowing there were two things you could do: cover up your blunder or cable London. If you chose the cover-up, I rather think you would have soon been approached by someone in possession of the verbatim reply. To explain how he came by it, he would probably hint he was with Bulgarian Intelligence. In return for some information of a trivial nature, he would agree not to expose what you had done. Since you were already a scoundrel, you would agree. Then there would be other modest demands, which you would also agree to."

Ganelon put on the high brown-felt flowerpot of a hat and went to stand in front of the mirror above the fireplace to judge the result.

"Oh, you can be sure for the first few years you would not groan under the small favors he would demand of you. As a young man destined to rise high in the Foreign Service, you would be too valuable to squander. But each of these small services would bind you closer to this man and to his master, Duhamel Fong. Fong is a patient man. But one day he would reap a bountiful harvest for having you in his power.

"But either way, Fong would win," continued Ganelon. "If you'd cabled London and owned up to your blunder, you would have been dismissed from the Foreign Service. In that case, Vyvyan would probably have inherited your key. So at the very least Fong would end up with the new cypher when it came out and perhaps a few other choice items before Vyvyan ruined himself or was unmasked."

"The Ambassador will have my full report on Vyvyan when he returns at the end of the week," said Horner.

"Oh, I wouldn't give the Viscount more than forty-eight hours," said Ganelon. "You see, using that example of his handwriting you gave me, a very skilled forger composed an insulting and highhanded letter at my dictation in which Vyvyan appears to announce his resignation from Fong's despicable service. I must say that letter allowed me to get a few things off my chest. I hope I didn't overdo it. This communication was in the envelope my pickpocket substituted for the one he took from Tuchmann. Since Fong reads his mail promptly, I'd say Vyvyan can count his life in hours."

Carriage wheels ground across the courtyard cobbles. The Bulgarian police inspector had arrived.

"On the other hand, you could tell Vyvyan what I've done," said Ganelon. "With a bit of a head start, he might find someplace on the far rim of civilization to crawl into for the rest of his life. The decision is yours."

Ganelon was ready to go. To see if he had left anything behind him, he spun around like the dervish he was, with his arms outstretched, the right hand with upturned palm as if to claim the blessing of the Almighty, the left palm inverted to show that what he received would be handed on to others. Then he gathered up his carpet bag and he and Horner left the room.

A Pocketful of Noses

A T THE TURN of the century, before the Protocols of London outlawed espionage activity in San Sebastiano, there existed in that principality a modest district of not more than half a dozen narrow winding streets famous as the spy mecca of Europe. Bounded by the rue Marc-Anton Prattmann, the railway freight yards, the rue Poucette, and the slant of the Marius Aqueduct, the Quadrilateral (as the district came to be known) boasted shops catering to every need of that ingenious, argus-eyed breed, from button-hole cameras, fatal fountain pens, knockout drops, and clothes of the most inconspicuous color and cut to shoes with hollow heels.

Today nothing remains of all this except the shop with the blank sign and the bare window, the place of business of the maker of the finest invisible ink ever concocted. But in the Quadrilateral's heyday, when spies at work, on vacation, or between situations flocked there, the sidewalks buzzed with foreign tongues, the cafés rang with songs of other fatherlands, and the restaurants smelled of spicy elsewheres. No safer streets existed in the Principality than those of the Quadrilateral. In fact, a murder within those precincts was so rare as to be a matter not for the police but for San Sebastiano's Intelligence Service.

On a moonless October night in 1901 a monocled and titled exhussar officer now in the pay of the Danes and a professional seductress fresh from the Balkans were strolling around the district's perimeter when they heard a short cry of pain and fleeing footsteps in the darkness on the other side of the aqueduct. Exchanging glances, the strollers turned back in search of the policeman they had passed only moments before. Had they waited they would have seen the prostrate figure of a man with the hilt of a knife protruding from his back crawl out of a dark street and into the half light of one of the ancient archways. Face down and grunting with effort, the man worked his way across the cobbles and up onto the sidewalk beneath a street light, a tortured journey that brought his death less than a minute later to the attention of the Intelligence Service.

Ambrose Ganelon, the second to bear that name, did not care for Nino Briquet's opera *The Revolt of the Gondoliers*, and since his wife and young son were away on a visit to the Tower of London, he had given his box to friends. They were delighted when he arrived unexpectedly and smiling, took a seat behind them. A handsome man with the erect carriage befitting a former officer in the Tripoline Lancers, Ganelon wore evening dress well, while the white gloves covered the acid stains which work in the laboratory left on his large hands.

When the house lights dimmed and the orchestra struck up the overture, Ganelon immediately turned his opera glasses to the dress stalls below where a slightly goggle-eyed man with a trim black mustache and a head of airedale ringlets sat at the side of one of the principality's most striking ballerinas. The world hailed this man, Duhamel Fong of the French Academy, as its greatest authority on hypnotism. Ganelon knew him as the archmalefactor of the West and Europe's most sinister spymaster.

Though the Ganelons and the Fongs were old rivals, it had been years since the mad, high-pitched sound of Fong laughter had been heard in the streets of San Sebastiano. Fong had arrived yesterday. Thanks to the statute of limitations and some fancy legal footwork, no valid warrants were outstanding against him in the Principality. He was free to walk the streets, appear in public, and snap his fingers in Ganelon's face. Yet the detective wondered if Fong's visit might not have some other purpose, something to do with the theft last week of the plans for the new Austrian naval range finder. Both the Russians and the Japanese were prepared to pay handsomely for the device. Ganelon hoped it did. He would be pleased to give Fong a taste of prison. To this end he decided to keep a personal eye on the man.

A hand touched Ganelon's shoulder. Police Inspector Marleau's upright silhouette filled the doorway. Ganelon joined Marleau in the small retiring room behind the box where a gaslight burned. Beneath a photograph of Prince Feinhart inscribed to Ganelon and decorated with two crossed blue and pink bicolors stood a gilt table and two gilt chairs upholstered in crimson Utrecht velvet.

Ganelon sat down on one and offered the other to the policeman. But Marleau declined. A sad-faced individual whose black alpaca suits, high stiff collars, and dark narrow ties contributed to his nickname, "The Archbishop," the police inspector was formal to the point of stiffness and in fact did not seem to bend in all the usual places.

"My people just rang me up, sir," he announced in his hushed cathedral voice. "The body of a murdered man has been found in the Quadrilateral."

Ganelon gave a nod of mild interest. In addition to operating the famous detective agency his father had founded, Ganelon headed the Principality's Intelligence Service. There were those who said he *was* the Intelligence Service.

Marleau cleared his throat before continuing. "My people tell me that contrary to standing orders they proceeded with the case as if it was a police matter and moved the body to the Morgue." As if to forestall a display of indignation the policeman added quickly, "May I observe on their behalf that they could be said to have followed the spirit of the order." He scowled disapprovingly at the word "spirit." "Though most certainly not the letter."

"And how was that?" asked Ganelon.

"The attack on the victim did not occur in the Quadrilateral. The man had to crawl a good hundred feet to die there."

Ganelon's interest evaporated. "My dear fellow," he said, "you were quite right. I should have been consulted. But since it doesn't seem to be an Intelligence matter, why, no harm's done." But this remark didn't have the palliative effect Ganelon hoped for.

"Did I mention what they said about the pocketful of noses?" ventured Marleau hopefully. "Don't you find it intriguing that the man was carrying five artificial noses?"

"I most certainly do," said Ganelon calmly, getting to his feet. "I'll follow your investigation with great interest."

Marleau thought for a moment before saying, "It occurred to me, sir, that perhaps the man crawled into the Quadrilateral deliberately, to bring you into the case."

"A very clear supposition," lied Ganelon who found the idea a romantic and highly unlikely one. But at least he now understood Marleau's problem. In rebuking his men for moving the body he had no doubt hit upon this fanciful explanation to show why they should have obeyed the letter of the law. Now if Ganelon chose not to investigate, Marleau would lose face with his men.

Early in his career Ganelon decided he could never compete with his father in the area of armchair ratiocination or black insociability. Instead, he turned to the crime laboratory and to heighten the contrast, worked hard to make himself a gentleman in Cardinal Newman's sense of the word: one who never inflicts pain. So there was nothing else he could do. A brief appearance at the Morgue was required to set Marleau right with his men. Fong wasn't going anywhere for a few acts.

Achmed, Ganelon's Berber chauffeur, must have seen the police inspector arrive for he stood at the bottom of the Grand Staircase with his master's coat, silk hat, and cane, and had brought the robin's-egg blue Voltigeur electric landaulette around to the front of the Opera.

"The dead man's name was Dagrutin," said Marleau as they stepped up into the vehicle and Achmed closed the door behind them. "A Serbian. His passport was stamped at the railroad station this morning which probably means he arrived on the Occident Express."

The Voltigeur glided off, Ganelon with his cane between his knees and a hand ready to tip his hat to anyone he knew, while Marleau sat upright, proud to be seen with the great detective.

When they reached the Morgue they quickly discovered the case involved six artificial noses instead of five. Like the others, the one the corpse wore was made of hollow India rubber and attached to the inside of the nasal cavity with a patented toggle. This nose was white where the others were various fleshy shades. Ganelon turned the nose over, admiring the workmanship and noting the name "Newnose" incised on the inner edge. Then out of respect for the dead he replaced the nose on the corpse.

The dead man had been in his late thirties. His thick black hair was pomaded, his closely shaven cheeks smelled of cologne and his mouth of wintergreen. His fingers were manicured. His chest bore an old circular scar with the puckering associated with broken bottles twisted in wounds. Perhaps the man received that mark in the same fight that had cost him his nose. Ganelon pulled the sheet up over the corpse's face.

He and Marleau returned to the basket containing Dagrutin's personal effects. In addition to the noses there was a suit and shirt made in Vienna, Serbian silk underwear and socks, Italian pointed shoes, two diamond rings, and a gold pinkie ring. ("He was quite a dandy, our Dagrutin," observed Marleau with disapproval.) There was also a tin of wintergreen breath pastilles, a room key from the Hotel Sebastopol, and a billfold containing several hundred francs.

"It certainly wasn't robbery," insisted Marleau so loudly that Ganelon knew one of the Inspector's men had returned from the corridor where he'd gone for a smoke.

"I couldn't agree more," answered Ganelon in a stage voice. He picked up the key from the basket and rattled it. He still had no reason to believe the case involved Intelligence. But the Hotel Sebastopol was on his way back to the Opera.

Dagrutin's room revealed very little until Ganelon discovered a smallish cardboard box and a sheet of crumpled wrapping paper in the waste basket by the washstand. The paper was addressed in long hand to Dagrutin care of Poste Restante, San Sebastiano. The stamps were Italian, the postmark Genoa. A rubber stamp declared the box had been opened for customs inspection. "My dear Marleau," said Ganelon, handing the box and paper to the police inspector, "it appears you've been right all along."

Marleau, who had grown downcast, brightened. He puzzled over the box and the paper. Then he threw up his arms helplessly. "I'm afraid I don't follow you.

The man received a box. All we know about the contents is that they were harmless enough to pass customs inspection. There's no return address. We don't even know who sent it."

"Compare Dagrutin's name on the paper with the signature on his passport," said Ganelon.

Marleau did as he was told. "It's the same!" he exclaimed. "The man mailed the box to himself."

"From Genoa yesterday according to the postmark," said Ganelon. "Now why mail a small something ahead when you could bring it in your baggage? It could well be an Intelligence matter. To put the question in a more interesting way: why is it all right for the customs people at the post office to see the contents of the box and not those at the railroad station? Let's go downstairs to the desk. I have a phone call to make and so do you. I'd like two of your best men to pick up a bit of surveillance for me at the Opera."

Within the hour the Voltigeur pulled up in front of the San Sebastiano railroad station sending a galvanic quiver from flank to flank down the line of horses at the hack carriage stand, a telegraph of the shape of things to come. A young man with an intelligent forehead was waiting for Ganelon and Marleau in the customs office. When he had introduced the police inspector, Ganelon said, "Sorry to bring you back to work at this hour. I hoped you might remember this man. We believe he arrived this morning on the Occident Express."

The customs man looked at the passport photo. "We searched everyone getting off the Occident Express," he said. "I searched this one personally. An apprehensive sort and in something of a hurry. We watch out for that."

"I'd like to know if he was carrying five artificial noses."

The customs man shook his head. "No. I'd have remembered that. Even though they'd be duty free."

Ganelon thought for a moment. Then he added, "You searched everyone. What was that all about?"

"A telegram said a passenger named Adler would be carrying contraband in a secret compartment in his suitcase."

"Adler?" demanded Ganelon. "Victor Adler? Tall with red hair and a squint?" Victor Adler was an enterprising freelance spy who had made his reputation several years ago by stealing the specifications for the British Submersible.

The customs man nodded. "We went through his things with a fine-tooth comb and turned up nothing." Ganelon wasn't surprised. Since the time Adler was apprehended carrying a copy of the official report on the French summer maneuvers of 1893, he'd been careful to pass whatever he stole to an accomplice.

"So we searched everyone else as well," said the customs man. "That's standard procedure. Smugglers have been known to use anonymous tips like that telegram to get us looking one way while they slip something past us another."

Nothing more could be done that night. Out on the railroad-station steps Ganelon asked Marleau where he could drop him. The policeman chose home. As the Voltigeur sped silently through the dark streets Marleau said, "I'd be less than frank if I didn't admit I'm up a tree on all this."

"You're being modest," insisted Ganelon.

The police inspector pursed his lips thoughtfully. "All right," he said, "we've got a dead man with a pocketful of noses. But when he went through customs earlier today he didn't have them. From this I conclude they were in the box he mailed to himself from Genoa yesterday."

"Very good," said Ganelon.

Marleau turned stiffly to look Ganelon in the eye with wonderment. "But why?" he demanded.

"Dagrutin was carrying something very important across the border hidden inside the artificial nose he was wearing," said Ganelon. "He knew if he was searched the other noses would give away his hiding place. So he mailed the extra noses ahead."

"And was that 'something very important' what he was killed for?"

"No doubt," said Ganelon.

"And this fellow Adler was involved?"

"His being on the train could have been a coincidence," admitted Ganelon. "On the other hand if I had to make a list of people I thought capable of stealing the plans for the Austrian naval range finder, Adler's name would most certainly be on it. Let's meet tomorrow morning at the Central Post Office and see if we can't clear up some of the loose ends."

When Marleau arrived at the post office the next morning he was greeted by Achmed and the landaulette at the curb and Ganelon emerging from the building.

"According to the man at the customs counter, Dagrutin's box contained six used artificial noses and nothing else," said the detective. "The man insisted he gave each nose a careful inspection."

"Where does that leave us?" asked Marleau, adding, "Oh, by the by, after the opera my people followed Fong to the ballerina's apartment where he spent the night. He didn't get back to his hotel until two hours ago. He's still under surveillance. Now what?"

Ganelon led the policeman over to the newspaper kiosk beside the post-office entrance. The Principality customarily granted kiosk licenses to army widows.

Ganelon had found it informative to secure certain kiosks for women with active minds and powers of observation. Madam Albert was one of these. Her husband, who had served under Ganelon in the Lancers, had died in the charge at Lejah in the shadow of Mount Lebanon.

Ganelon passed Dagrutin's photo through the woman's small window. "By any chance did you notice this man yesterday morning about ten o'clock, Madam?"

"I recall him quite well," said the woman. "He was carrying a suitcase and was in something of a hurry. On his way inside he asked if I had the day's *Echo de Beaulieu*. But the turf sheets hadn't come yet. They arrived in the next five minutes and I was outside untying the bundle when the other man, the tallish carrot-top, pulled up in a cab across the street. Then the first fellow came out of the post office and bought his paper. He opened it to the personal column and hurried down the steps reading all the way. At the curb he hailed a cab. He'd barely driven off when the other fellow sprinted over and said, 'Give me one of what that man got.' Then he dashed back to his cab which drove off in the same direction as the first."

As they headed for the Voltigeur, Marleau said, "Well, now at least we know where Adler picked up Dagrutin's trail."

"Ah, we know much more than that," said Ganelon, following the police inspector into the vehicle. "We know that Adler and Dagrutin were working together. Adler was too familiar with Dagrutin's ways for that to be otherwise." Ganelon spoke to Achmed in Arabic and the Voltigeur started on its way. The detective continued, "As you said, he picked up Dagrutin's trail at the post office. But he didn't follow him there. That meant he knew where Dagrutin was going. In other words, he knew about the noses and the business of mailing them ahead."

Ganelon offered his cigarette case to the policeman and when Marleau declined, he lit up a Royal Beauty. "Imagine something along these lines and the story won't be too far wrong," he said. "Adler steals the plans and immediately passes them on to Dagrutin. Adler is well-known to the Austrian authorities, after all, while Dagrutin is—what?—an obscure ex-bartender whose only asset was a nose he lost in a street fight. In any event, Adler knows there's a fortune at stake and doesn't intend to take any risks.

"Their destination is San Sebastiano where he has arranged to meet the buyer. He and Dagrutin travel separately on the same train by leisurely stages from Vienna down into Italy. Dagrutin's job is to carry the plans past any customs on the way inside a rubber nose, mailing the others ahead for the reason I've explained. But Dagrutin plans to double-cross Adler and has been in contact with the same buyer on his own account.

"Dagrutin is the one who sends the telegram from Genoa, hoping to delay Adler at customs long enough to drop out of sight. But because he and all the others are searched as well, he doesn't get the head start he counted on. Adler picks up his trail at the post office. He kills Dagrutin at his convenience and recovers the plans." Ganelon tossed his cigarette away. "And that brings us to the question of the missing nose."

"It seems to me six is a surplus," said Marleau.

"There are six at the Morgue," observed Ganelon. "And he mailed himself six. But that meant he had to be wearing a seventh when he went through customs at the railroad station."

Here the Voltigeur stopped before a shop with a large red ear hanging over the door and artificial arms and legs arranged neatly in the window. Ganelon dispatched Achmed to the offices of the *Echo de Beaulieu*. Then he and Marleau went inside the shop. Glass eyes arranged by color in apothecary jars stared at them from the counter as they entered. Manufactured ears seemed to cock themselves in wall display cases on either side. Peglegs of every shape and design stood up straight in umbrella stands along both walls.

A small well-kept man in a frockcoat appeared silently in a doorway behind the counter. His polite smile of greeting turned to sadness as he looked them up and down. Ganelon knew the man had dismantled them limb by appendage, rebuilt them entirely with his own wares, and was imagining how much better they would look. "How may I help you gentlemen?" asked the shopkeeper.

Delighted that someone in the principality did not recognize him, Ganelon chose to keep himself in the background. "My friend Police Inspector Marleau here would like some information on artificial noses," he said. "Newnose, to be precise."

"An excellent choice, sir," said the man, addressing Marleau gravely. " 'Newnose is good nose,' sir," he added, turning to a drawer behind him. "That's their slogan. But why judge them by that? It's a fine product. We sell them singly"—without turning back to them he set a single nose on the counter—"or in sets."

"Inspector Marleau would like to know if they are sets of seven."

The man turned and placed a narrow box of seven noses ranging from white to purple on the counter. "Precisely," he said, smiling at Marleau's cleverness. "Solving the dilemma of the changeable complexion. The patented attachment available only with the Newnose product enables a gentleman to switch noses quickly if he feels himself about to turn white with terror or pink with embarrassment, et cetera, et cetera."

Ganelon surveyed the set for the one missing from Dagrutin's collection. "He'd like to know about the purplish one," said the detective.

"The nose of conviviality, sir," explained the shopkeeper, looking Marleau straight in the eye. "All work and no play is said to make Jack a dull boy."

"The Inspector has a final question," said Ganelon. "These noses aren't quite the shape of the ones he is inquiring about."

"These are the Mediterranian model," said the man.

"And could you tell him, is there a Serbian?"

"I would have to order it for the Inspector."

"Thank you. Perhaps he'll get back to you on that," said Ganelon, leading Marleau toward the door.

"Thank you, gentlemen. I trust I may be of service to you in the future," said the man in a voice that was sincerity itself.

Outside on the street Ganelon said, "You carried that off admirably, old man. Now, if I were you I'd send my men around to all the bars and other dens of conviviality on the far side of the Aqueduct and see if anyone remembers Dagrutin. If luck's running with you, someone might even remember Adler lurking in the background. That would make your case against him."

Just then Achmed arrived in the electric with a copy of yesterday's *Echo de Beaulieu.* Ganelon opened the paper to the personal column and read. After a moment he said, "Ah, this looks like it. 'Nostradamus: the Mask Market tomorrow morning at 11:00. You'll know where to stand,' " Ganelon looked at Marleau. " 'Nostradamus'— a cruel code name for Dagrutin. I think I know who came up with it."

The annual wholesale Mask Market took place six months before each Mediterranian carnival season in the remains of the old Roman arena. Retailers flocked from Nice, Cannes, and Menton to see what the master mask and carnival paraphernalia makers of San Sebastiano had invented for the new season. Stalls covered the entire ground where the Seven Hundred and Seventy-Seven Christian Martyrs of San Sebastiano had met the lions and tigers from the menagerie of the animal-loving proconsul, P. Cornelius Lucullus.

Every kind of carnival ware and gaudy paper goods from masks and dominos to Japanese lanterns, colored streamers, and confetti were on display. The fine day had drawn a large number of visitors and the masks magnified the scene. The arena's many ancient gates and the gaps in the walls made it an ideal place for a meeting.

Ganelon stood in the first row of stone seats, holding a banana purchased from a fruit seller. Looking down on the scene, he quickly found Adler standing in front of the booth specializing in nose masks with glasses, eyebrows, and mustaches attached. 'You will know where to stand.' Yes, he was a very cruel man, was Duhamel Fong.

Adler, arms crossed, displayed the nose between the thumb and forefinger of one hand. Clearly, he didn't want Fong to have any doubts about who had the plans and who expected the money. As the crowd ebbed and flowed around Adler, Ganelon wondered if his plan would work. He could easily have prevented the exchange by having Adler arrested. But he wanted to catch Fong with the plans in his possession. Keeping his eye on the red-headed man, Ganelon peeled his banana, handed the edible part down to a passing organ-grinder's monkey, and folded the skin so he could hide it in his hand.

At five to eleven Marleau marched up to announce, "My men are in position, sir." Then he added, "And I'm obliged to report that Fong gave us the slip at the hotel a half hour ago. The man watching his suite outsmarted himself. When he saw Fong head for the elevator he stepped in ahead of him. That's sometimes a very effective bit of surveillance business, as you know. But Fong veered away just before the door closed and took the stairs. Our man in the lobby said several people came down the stairs but swears Fong wasn't one of them."

Ganelon knew Fong to be a consummate quick-change artist, a little-known weapon in his arsenal of deceit. By the first turn in the stairs Fong's hair would be straight and white or hidden beneath a skin cap of baldness. By the second turning his nose would be retroussé or puttied into a hawk's beak. By the third, wadding from the shoulders of his reversible jacket would be stuffed into his cheeks. The man could have crossed the lobby as anyone.

So Fong was already here. No doubt he had spotted Ganelon strolling about up in the seats. No matter. Ganelon was sure Fong would take any risk to pull something off right under his archrival's nose.

As Ganelon and Marleau watched, the traffic of people jammed up in front of the counter where Adler stood. When it cleared away the nose was gone, leaving Adler to stuff an envelope into his inside coat pocket. "Now," said Ganelon.

Marleau blew a whistle and a uniformed policeman appeared in each gateway. If the crowd failed to notice, Ganelon was sure there was one who did. He counted on Fong's confidence in his disguise and in his cool arrogance. The man would not make a break for it. He would wait until the suitable moment and then stroll out of the arena like any other visitor. Ganelon knew that right now, down in the crowd somewhere, Fong was watching him, curious to see what he was up to and what he thought a few policemen could accomplish.

Ganelon turned to Marleau. "Follow about ten feet behind me, old man," he ordered. "And keep an eye peeled for a suspicious face in the crowd."

Ganelon strolled with his cane down the empty aisle of stone seats, wondering if Cardinal Newman would ever forgive him for what he was about to do. He opened his hand, and still holding onto the banana peel by the stem, he let it fall to its full length so that anyone watching could see what he was doing. Then he dropped the banana peel on the stones behind him.

Marleau, stiff, erect, and proper with his eyes intent on the crowd, approached the peel step by heavy step. When he reached it, a foot went out from under him and high-kicked up into the air. The man's whole body seemed to be dragged up after it and hung in the air for a fraction of a second.

Then Marleau fell to the ancient stones with a thud that jarred his bones from head to heel. Fifty yards away at a stall selling skull masks and skeleton costumes an old clerical gentleman threw his head back and laughed that hideous, piercing laugh that Ganelon knew so well.

Vaulting down to the floor of the arena, Ganelon dashed between the tables of merchandise toward the laughing masterspy. Fong saw him coming, turned pale, and ducked into the crowd, heading in the direction of the far wall. Ganelon fought his way through the crowd with hardly an apology, using his height to keep the top of the archvillain's head in sight. When they broke into the open, Ganelon was a stride closer to the breach in the wall that was Fong's destination.

He blocked the man's escape as four policemen converged on them. Fong's eyes bulged with rage from behind his clerical disguise. He cursed and flung the artificial nose down on the ground at Ganelon's feet. It took one of those crazy bounces that India rubber noses take, making Ganelon lunge far to his right to pin the thing to the ground with his cane.

In that instant Fong slipped by him and disappeared through the opening in the wall. Ganelon knew there was no point in pursuit. By the time anyone reached the street, Fong could be a hundred different persons. But they would meet again …

"Not at all, sir," said Marleau who was sitting up on a stone bench, nursing his distressed head. "It was an excellent ruse to make the man reveal himself. Don't worry about me. When it comes to hard knocks, being proved right is the best ointment."

" 'Proved right,' Marleau?" asked the detective.

"My original deduction, sir," said the police inspector. "About Dagrutin crawling into the Quadrilateral to get you involved in the case."

"Ah, yes. Of course," said Ganelon, as he turned to watch Adler being hustled out to the waiting police van. By way of amends to Marleau, Ganelon did not mention his own conviction that the noseless Dagrutin, vain to the last and feeling his life ebb away, had crawled into the Quadrilateral in search of a street light where he could select the white nose from among the others and dress himself for death.

AMBROSE GANELON III

Harps of Gold

L ATE IN THE afternoon of December 24, 1916, the rain falling over the trenches of Flanders turned to a wet snow that clung to the barbed wire and lay on the ground for an instant as if reluctant to disappear into the stinking mud of the battlefield. Behind the lines the dense flurries were crowded with dark marching shapes and muttering voices.

Where two communication trenches converged, a pair of officers stood in the weather watching the army move forward. The younger of the two, Captain Ambrose Ganelon III, wore a kepi bearing the cabbage-and-rose insignia of the principality of San Sebastiano and, beneath his trench coat, the sky-blue tunic and grenadine-colored trousers of the Tripolitanian Lancers. His face showed the abundant small scars and innumerable flat, shiny spots that mark the bare-knuckle boxer, one, the eyes suggested, who hadn't won a fight for a long time. After the three-day bombardment of Chastigny, Ganelon had been found crouched under a ruined field kitchen, chuckling thoughtfully to himself. And it was his eagerness to get back into action that convinced the doctors he had become slightly *dégommé*, or unstuck. He'd been reassigned to the Canadian First Division as liaison with the French forces on their right flank.

The other officer with the narrow cane and red-tabbed lapels was Brigadier General Lester ("Whacko") Bridges, on a morale-boosting visit to the Canadian troops who were to lead the assault. Whacko Bridges was something of a legend among the Canadians, having seen combat at Ypres and St. Julien. The men liked the company of survivors.

Just as the snow began to fall, Ganelon and the general had managed to get themselves lost in the crisscross of communication trenches, abandoned saps, and old footpaths behind the lines as they were making the passage between Company C and Company D of the first brigade of the Sydenham Rifles, which was to be their final stop before the attack. The Sydenhams were a prison regiment, half the rank and file having obtained release from prison for agreeing to serve in the army.

The place where the two officers stopped to get their bearings had probably once been an orchard. But all the trees had fled, leaving stumps and shattered bits of wood to mark their places. Soldiers passed in the white gloom with their heads bowed under the burden of the weather. To Ganelon the new metal helmets gave them a coolie look.

When the general had his cigar going to his satisfaction, he continued what he'd been saying. "No, son, I'll tell you what this is all about. Last Christmas with the Germans and our boys out in no man's land playing football together and singing carols and exchanging presents scared the hell out of the brass. You can't run a war like that. So they dreamed this up. We won't gain an inch and there'll be heavy losses. But the survivors will be too bone weary to play football tomorrow." Bridges laughed. "And they call *me* crazy."

Ganelon hadn't been around the general long enough to hear anyone call him crazy. But he knew the man claimed to have been born with a lucky caul, which might account for his reputation for foolhardiness.

A soldier with a leather dispatch case and a young lieutenant carrying a full kit appeared out of the snow on their way, as luck would have it, to Company D. "I'll have you with the Sydenhams in three shakes of a dead lamb's tail, sirs," promised the dispatch runner.

The lieutenant's name was Sutton. He had a short fair moustache that looked as if it had only been started in officers' training school and bright blue eyes. "You a new man out, Lieutenant?" asked the general as they hurried on through the mud.

"No, sir. I transferred from the RCR. I was with them at Mont Sorrel."

The general grunted and gave Ganelon a glance from under his heavy eyebrows. Ganelon knew an officer wouldn't leave a fashionable unit like the Royal Canadian Regiment for the Sydenhams unless he hadn't been given much choice. He wondered how the young officer had disgraced himself.

Sutton looked up at the snow. "The men say the Germans have some machine that makes the weather."

"Then they bungled it today," the general assured him heartily, "keeping their own spotter airplanes on the ground. We may surprise them yet." Bridges had been less optimistic earlier that afternoon. "God, I'm sick of beating the drum for this madness," he had told Ganelon. "But if the men have to do it, it's better they do it with a will. A month ago the Frenchies sent a regiment to the attack bleating like sheep. We don't need anything like that."

"You related to the Chatham Suttons, Lieutenant?" asked the general. "I knew Albert whose brother shot himself after the Petrolia Gas and Oil scandal." Before Sutton could answer, a jingle of harness announced two horses and a transport sergeant coming back from delivering hot rations to the front line. Ganelon saw the general stare and go pale. When the man and horses had passed Bridges whispered, "Did you see him, son, the fellow walking with the sergeant? It was

Henderson. He winked. He gave me that 'come-on-in-the-water's-fine' look of his. It's the second time he's come to beckon me over since he got himself killed at Ovillers a year ago."

"I only saw the sergeant, sir," replied Ganelon uneasily.

Bridges smiled. "No, he won't leave me alone. Ghosts love haunting battlefields. Why not? They're out of the filthy business."

When they reached Company D the dispatch runner and Sutton went off looking for Captain Herbert, the company commander. The front line was as sloppy as a run-off ditch, a deep, narrow thing of weathered sandbags crowded with scaling ladders and soldiers in full packs brought up from the reserve trenches for the initial assault. The sergeants were expecting the general's visit. They roused the off-duty men of Company D from their ingenious dugouts and lean-tos of canvas, corrugated metal, and old doors built under the trench parapet. Bridges spoke briefly on the upcoming engagement with the help of an oilcloth map which Ganelon produced from a trench-coat pocket. Bridges indicated specific objectives with a slap of the crook of his cane, adding a "Whacko!" to each blow. Then he gave them his pitch about the advantage in fighting a war on the attack. Nine chances out of ten, he told them, trench wounds were to the head and fatal. What any sensible soldier wanted was a nice clean arm or leg wound to put him in hospital, or better yet on a ship back home. And those he'd only find out of the trenches and advancing on the enemy. The men smiled at the general wistfully as if they'd like to believe him and cheered at the end when he ordered them a double ration of rum before tonight's action.

Then it was "stand-to." Twice a day at dawn and dusk, the hours when an enemy attack was most likely, the men on the front line on either side of no man's land mounted the firing step and waited in readiness.

Bridges and Ganelon headed for company headquarters, a dugout built into the side of a trench connecting the support line and the front line. The general pulled back the gas blanket over the entrance and waved his aide through. At the bottom of fifteen steep steps Ganelon found the familiar dim, low-ceilinged, twelve-by-twelve-foot room, bunk beds with chicken wire for springs and empty sandbags for mattresses along the far wall, in one corner a broken-down easy chair, next to it a portable phonograph on a stack of munitions boxes, and next to that a small, potbellied coal stove that vented out the dugout door. A tinsel Christmas star hung from the ceiling beam in the middle of the room and beneath it on a small, roughly made table was a bottle of whiskey, glasses, a black-handled bowie knife, and a candle on a small tin lid. General Bridges lit the candle and smiled at the bottle appreciatively. "A good host, Captain Herbert," he said, pouring them both a drink. "Though a terror if put into a temper, I'm told. Happy to have him on our side."

The general sat down at an upturned box at the table and fell silent. Respecting his superior's quiet mood, Ganelon leaned back against the wall and stared at the tinsel star. It sent his thoughts above ground. Ganelon imagined stand-to on this of all nights, two lines of armed men facing each other across a graveyard of landscape and barbed wire that stretched from the Channel to Switzerland. And they would stay there watching until utter nightfall made attack unlikely. Then the Sydenhams would send out work details to cut their own wire and open the way for the bloody work ahead. But Ganelon felt strangely abstracted from everything. Being a general's aide was a lot like Bridges's friend Henderson on his Cook's tour of hell. Ganelon was here but out of it. Tonight he would sleep in a warm bed back at Division. He finished his drink and poured another.

After a long while Captain Herbert and Sutton arrived fresh from stand-down, bringing the evening chill in on their trench coats. Herbert was a stocky, florid-faced, middle-aged man with hard, quick eyes and a blunt manner which, combined with the temper of which Bridges spoke, may have accounted for why he was only a captain. "Glad you didn't wait for us, General," he said, pouring whiskey in a glass and passing it to the young lieutenant. "Brought Sutton here back for a welcome drink."

"Quite so," said Bridges. "Do you know Captain Ganelon, my aide?"

"The famous detective-agency family," said Herbert, shaking Ganelon's hand. " 'We never sleep,' right, Captain?"

Ganelon corrected him. "That's Mr. Pinkerton."

But Captain Herbert had moved on to more important things. "Sutton here says they tried a night attack at Festubert," he told the general in a worried voice.

"The Germans got their flares up before we were through the wire, sir," said Sutton. "The ones that come down slow on parachutes."

"Well, the poohbahs back at Division expect this time we'll catch them dreaming of Christmas in Hunland and all that sort of heehaw," said the general with a short, grim laugh. Then he frowned and asked Herbert earnestly, "Didn't you serve with Captain Wales?"

"He saved my life once and my bacon more times than that," said Herbert, adding, "Things happen when they leave a man in the trenches too long. I hear they moved his court-martial back to tomorrow. I've sent for Poynter."

The general asked, "Poynter? The witness? Is he still here?"

"Not for long," said Herbert. "Goes back to Division tonight. Too damned precious to die in battle."

Ganelon saw the general grow thoughtful at this news.

Then Lieutenant Sutton said, "Excuse me, sir. Will I have time to write something home?"

"Go ahead," said Herbert. "We'd best keep out of the way for a while. The men get the jitters with officers fussing about. I've got a letter, too. Somewhere." Herbert slapped his pockets, found an envelope, and dropped it on the table. "Maybe the general will take them back with him."

Sutton moved the candle to the corner of the table next to the nearest lower bunk where he sat, chewing on a pencil and concentrating on his letter.

"Beautiful woman, Wales's mother," remarked the general. "Old Henderson lost his heart to her completely. I'd hoped Wales would get off with broken to the ranks. But there's talk of a firing squad."

"God!" exclaimed Herbert, slamming his fist on the table. "I should've broke Poynter's filthy little neck when I had the chance!"

Ganelon knew Captain Wales's story. He'd married on leave in England. Soon there were stories about his wife and another man. One night Wales's raiding party had come back without him, the men reporting they'd become separated from him in the dark and then heard shots. Wales was arrested at Calais trying to cross to England using the leave papers of an officer killed in the shelling two days before. Poynter bore the captain a grudge. He saw him going through the dead man's things and, when Wales went missing, put two and two together and tipped off the military police. Division looked on the robbing of the corpse of a fellow officer as a crime as terrible as desertion in the face of the enemy. Poynter's testimony was expected to blacken Wales's character enough to warrant the death penalty.

Artillery shells fell nearby. Then the barrage moved closer, making the gas blanket belly in.

Touching the knife thoughtfully, the general asked, "Where'd you find the pig-sticker?"

"Took it from a German raiding party last night," said the captain, passing him the whiskey. "Ugly thing, eh? A blackjack or a leaded stick isn't good enough for them anymore. I figured Division would want a look."

The general smiled. "No, they'd only cut themselves." Bridges handed the bottle to Sutton. The lieutenant, who was sharpening his pencil with a pocket knife, passed it on to Ganelon without pouring himself a drink or losing his thoughtful expression. As Ganelon tilted the bottle he smiled to himself, imagining Sutton and the girl he was writing to walking together through Maria Chapdelaine country.

Three more shells hit nearby. A moment later a large corporal and a small private ducked into the dugout, hurried down the steps, and came to attention in front of the captain. "You're a lucky devil, Poynter," Herbert told the clerkish-looking private. "You get to miss the show. You too, Corporal. You get to escort him back to Division."

The eyes behind Poynter's steel-rimmed glasses told Ganelon that this was disturbing news. The man was clearly not the corporal's favorite person. And he knew it.

"I hear you had trouble finding us, General," said Herbert. "The corporal here can show you the way back."

"I've come this far, I might as well go along on your little stroll in the country tonight," replied the general.

"Sir ...," protested Herbert.

"General ...," said Ganelon.

Bridges shook his head at his aide. "It's back to Division for you, son. That's an order. You're still dragging your wing. I brought you along to remind you how bad things can get up here. Don't rush the mending. And you, Captain Herbert, can rest easy." The general took out a letter. "I couldn't tell the people at Division what I meant to do. They've been winning too much of my money at cards to let me go. This'll put them in the picture." He added his letter to Herbert's. "The way I see it, either the people running this war are crazy or I am. If I'm killed I'll be dead right. If I make it to the enemy wire alive then I'm a raving lunatic. And if I'm captured, well, the Germans will have a crazy general on their hands."

Here Lieutenant Sutton gave a quiet curse. He was bleeding from the nose, spattering blood down the front of his trench coat. "It's nothing," he insisted, trying to stem the flow with a khaki handkerchief. "I get them now and then since Festubert. It'll pass."

A pair of legs appeared on the steps. A voice said, "Our wire cutters are back in the trench, Captain." The legs disappeared. Herbert swallowed his drink and stood up. As he did, there was a sudden artillery barrage that seemed to come down in the direction of the front line. The dugout shook and the dust fell. The general muttered, "The bastards are early and they're firing short."

"Those are German guns," said the captain. "Either they're working on our troop concentrations or ..."

"... or great minds thinking alike, the Germans came up with the same filthy idea we did," agreed the general.

Suddenly a cluster of shells landed almost on top of the dugout. The candle fell to the floor. The darkness was palpable. Ganelon felt it leap around him. But at least it hid his fear. The bombardment continued, each long minute worse than the one before. The air smelled like a freshly dug grave. Just when Ganelon was sure the shells would never stop coming they slackened and seemed to move away.

Now he heard other noises around him, the sound of leather and metal and low laughter which he suspected was his own. The smell turned to tobacco smoke on damp uniforms, cordite, and the ever present chloride of lime.

"Get the candle, somebody," ordered Captain Herbert.

"Got it," said the general. "It's the damn matches I can't find."

"Here they are, sir," said Sutton. A match flared and the young lieutenant, who was still on his knees on the floor, lit the candle.

"Good God!"

Ganelon followed the general's astonished eyes to Poynter's bloody body sitting on the bottom step with his legs spread out in front of him and the hilt of the bowie knife protruding from his throat. The corporal knelt down by the body, turned quickly, and said, "He's dead." He held up his bloody hands as proof of his words.

Remarking to himself that those hands had been bloody before the corporal knelt down, Ganelon took the man's place beside the body. A front pocket of the victim's uniform jacket had been torn loose and hung down like a flap on his chest. One trouser pocket was turned inside out while the other was not, suggesting a hurried look for something which had been found. "Somebody came a very long way to murder," observed Ganelon over his shoulder.

"Hell, we all did," remarked Herbert in a hard, grim voice, adding, "Well, Captain, it looks like you get to practice the family trade. But we can't hang around to watch. We all have tonight's work to do. You know where to find me if you need me." Herbert looked at Sutton. "Lieutenant," he said.

Sutton scrawled a quick line to his letter home, sealed the envelope, added it to the others, and followed in Herbert's careful footsteps around the corpse and up the steps. At the gas blanket Herbert turned back and said, "Get back to your platoon, Corporal. You've gone and let your ticket out of this mess get himself killed."

The general put a farewell hand on Ganelon's shoulder and nodded at the corpse as though he was leaving his aide in good company. "Right up your alley, son," he said. "Good. It'll keep your mind off things. Henderson and I will be watching to see you figure out who done it." General Lester ("Whacko") Bridges stuck his cane under his arm and took the steps two at a time.

As the corporal moved to follow him, Ganelon said, "I know this wasn't your work, Corporal. You had a hundred better places to kill Poynter between here and Division."

"Yes, sir. Even with you along, I'd have found a way to get us separated in the dark. I'd have fixed him good."

"But you did take something from his body."

"He kind of fell into my arms in the dark," said the corporal. "I knew he was dead. I only took back what wasn't his. You see, sir, we have this sweepstakes thing before a big push. Everyone pools their money. The survivors divvy it up afterwards. The dead don't care. The wounded figure they're well out of it. And besides, the medical orderlies would only rob them along the way. Anyway, before I could give the pool money to the padre to hold, Poynter stole it from my kit, figuring to get away with it because he was being sent back to Division for the court-martial. He didn't like me much. I served under Captain Wales, sir, and proud of it. I never let Poynter forget that. He wasn't very happy when I pulled escort duty."

"A thief, was that why he's with the Sydenhams?"

The corporal shook his head. "Shady bookkeeping, sir. Remember the Petrolia Oil and Gas business? That was Poynter. No, you wouldn't know about that. But it was pretty big in our part of the country. Hit a lot of our better people in the pocketbook. Speaking of that …" He handed Ganelon a leather coin purse. "I'd be obliged if you hold this for me, sir." Then the corporal was gone.

Ganelon sat back down at the table. He couldn't leave while there was still whiskey in the bottle. Besides, he had his family trade to practice. He poured himself a drink, looked over at the dead man, and considered asking the usual parlor-game questions. Who had the motive and the opportunity to murder Poynter? Motive? It was almost refreshing to see a man killed for a reason again.

From outside he heard the officers' whistles and knew the attack had begun. He imagined the men mounting the ladders and doubling up to move through the gaps in the wire. Now they were forming up into a loose line on the other side. He heard the distant tock-tock-tock of the German machine guns and knew the flares were up. So much for surprise! He heard his own voice telling the men to close up and maintain the distance. "Not so fast! Steady on the left! Easy! Easy! Keep the line straight!" Ganelon remembered what it was like to be standing on ground crawling with wounded.

With a terrible roar shells exploded all around the dugout. Ganelon crouched forward over his glass, and in his grab to save the bottle he knocked the candle to the floor again. The blackness around him bucked and heaved. To keep from going mad he focused his mind on the murder. As for motive, both the general and Herbert had reason enough to kill Poynter, the witness who could send Wales to the firing squad. And suppose the lieutenant was one of the Chatham Suttons, victims in the Petrolia Oil and Gas embezzlement? Suppose he'd had himself transferred here on purpose but arrived by one door just as his prey was about to leave by another? So all three had motive.

In his mind's eye Ganelon placed them where they'd been when the candle went out. Herbert, standing at the table, was closest to Poynter and could very easily have picked up the knife, taken two steps, and plunged it into the man's throat. The general, sitting at the other end of the table, was only two more paces away. And Lieutenant Sutton on the lower bunk was almost as close. All three could have killed Poynter ten times over before the candle was relit. But which one actually did?

Like a thunderstorm, the artillery barrage moved away as quickly as it came. Ganelon didn't bother to light the candle. He sat in darkness. After a while he heard the stumbling and curses as another wave in the attack moved up from the reserve trench. He didn't discover his hand was shaking until he raised the whiskey to his lips. Darkness covers a multitude of cowardices. Ganelon thought about that for a moment.

Suddenly he was down on his knees, feeling about on the floor for the candle. The man who stabbed Poynter in the dark knew he risked being spattered with blood. His guilt would have been apparent to everyone as soon as the candle was lit. Unless he bloodied himself beforehand.

Ganelon found the stump of wax and lit it. Sutton's letter was addressed to a Mrs. Curtis Sutton of Chatham, Ontario. He tore it open. The several pages inside were blank except for a single line. No, Sutton hadn't been writing his lady love. His mind had to focus completely on his spur-of-the-moment plan to kill Poynter. The single line he wrote in his letter read, "Mother, I have found the bastard and he is mine!"

Ganelon stood up, buttoned his trench coat, and set his kepi at the angle at which they are worn in the Tripolitanian Lancers. Stuffing the letters in his pocket, he moved past the murdered man and up the steps. The trench was crowded with troops standing in the wet snow waiting for their turn to go up to the front line. The stretcher-bearers had started crawling out in ones and twos to drag in the wounded who lay close to the parapet. Ganelon may have been ordered back to Division. Nobody said he couldn't bring a wounded man or two to the aid station on the way.

He followed a stretcher-bearer through a hole in the wire. Thirty yards brought him to the place where the wounded groaned among the dead. A hand gripped Ganelon's arm. He grabbed the man under the armpits and dragged him toward the trench. Overhead, beyond the whispering of the machine-gun bullets, the sky was bursting with bright celebration. The falling snow might have been its gay debris. Ganelon made many trips out into the battlefield. Once during an intense barrage he took shelter in a shell hole, and when the next flare lit up the scene he found himself face-to-face with the body of a young officer with a moustache and a revolver who looked no more like a murderer than Sutton had. At last, muddy, exhausted, and with his arms and legs heavy with fatigue, Ganelon found a spot among the snowy human shapes on the firing step and fell into a deep sleep.

He didn't know how long he slept. He woke, cold and stiff, to an echoing silence. For a happy moment Ganelon was a boy again, nodding off during Mass in San Sebastiano's damp old cathedral. Then he was back there on the firing step, listening for the sound that had awakened him.

Someone lit a cigarette, and in that bright moment Ganelon saw that the men around him were awake and listening too. A man across the way said, "I thought you were dead, mate," and chattered on, bringing Ganelon up to date. The Sydenhams had taken the trenches opposite. But the Germans, having intended their own offensive that night, were able to counterattack in force. They drove the Canadians out, pursuing them back across the battlefield. Reinforcements allowed the Canadians to turn and stand their ground. After a bloody hand-to-hand, both sides had fallen back to the trenches they started from.

The man stopped to listen. Ganelon heard the sound too, and knew it was the one that had awakened him. Was it a congregation at prayer? Was it a choir of many voices singing a low, sad hymn? "What the hell's that?" he demanded.

"The wounded," said the talkative soldier. "Been coming and going like that for two hours."

Ganelon understood. From the blasted ground and barbed wire of no-man's-land, where the wounded lay the thickest, voices were crying out for help in English and German.

"They won't let us go fetch them in," said the soldier. Another said, "Got to save ourselves for the attack tomorrow." "The knockout blow," said a third bitterly. Someone else cursed and then another. Men were getting up onto the firing step to peer out toward the terrible sound.

Just then Ganelon heard something else, a strange noise of men and metal coming up the communication trench. But they weren't reinforcements. Ganelon strained to see through the darkness. Suddenly he heard a military band strike up a lively march from the German trenches. Now another on the left flank struck up a French march. At that same moment the Sydenham Rifles' regimental band appeared out of the snow. As Ganelon watched in bewilderment, the bandsmen halted, raised their instruments, and began to play. He moved closer, doubting his eyes and ears. Was it some kind of damn band competition? Here? Then the answer came to him. Great minds were still thinking alike. The powers-that-be on both sides were afraid a night listening to the wounded would leave the men unfit for the next day's hostilities. So they'd sent for the bands. Let music drown out the battlefield. Ganelon counted the sounds of three more bands on the night air. He wondered what the opposite word for "miracle" was, for he was surely witnessing it.

And there among the Sydenhams' bandsmen stood a man whose daguerreotype face Ganelon recognized from the padded covers of the old album on the piano back home. His great-grandfather held him with a long and mournful look before shaking his ghostly head and turning back to his clarinet.

Ganelon moved quickly down the communication trench, telling himself the aid station would still need help carrying the seriously wounded back to battalion hospital. But in fact something told him he must get the hell away from that place. As he hurried on he wondered what sins on earth had placed his great-grandfather, the amateur oboist, in what for him would have been a real purgatory among the single-reed instruments.

Then Ganelon came face-to-face with another ghost. The corporal stepped out from the parapet wall. "Yes, sir, I made it," he said, grinning vaguely. "Not many did. Not the captain. Not the general. So he wasn't crazy after all. And I reckon I saw that new lieutenant what's-his-name dead in every other shell hole." Ganelon heard the corporal's quiet laughter. He took the man's arm and tried to lead him to the aid station. But the corporal shook his hand away firmly and politely. Hefting the purse Ganelon had returned to him, he explained, "Got to wait for the others to divvy up, sir," he said. "There's got to be others."

Just then Ganelon caught a snatch of Gilbert and Sullivan amid the jumble of band music. The tune sent him staggering recklessly through the darkness, deaf to the curses of the sleeping soldiers he jostled in his flight. Now he knew why he had to get away. Sooner or later the bands would run out of marches. Then the Germans would switch to Waldteufel and Strauss, the French would strike up Offenbach, and the British and the Canadians would play *Penzance* and *Pinafore*. Hymns and Christmas carols would be next.

Ganelon meant to be long out of earshot before the angels bent to earth to touch their harps of gold.

The Zoroaster Grin

THE FIRST WEEK of August, 1925, brought rumors that Ambrose Ganelon III, who had recently taken over San Sebastiano's famous detective agency, was going to be murdered. Ganelon maintained his trademark lopsided grin in public, concerned only that his father, now semiretired and away on a private investigation, would hear the story and return to be of help.

Somewhat shorter than his scientific father, Ganelon was broader in the shoulders. Six years in the trenches and a few more going toe-to-toe with the principality's underworld had given him a battered-about face and a scrappy, two-fisted reputation.

Talk of his impending murder persisted into the second week amid rejoicing in the streets, for San Sebastiano was celebrating Reiteration Days, its merry commemoration of the Battle of the Tortue in 1625, when Prince Leonard, the Laughing Cavalier, defeated Captain-General Martin Corbeau and his Puritan pikemen to restore the House of Tancredi to the throne.

Since every skeleton in the Tancredi closet had a couple of spare funny bones, the festivities emphasized organized hilarity and hi-jinks as well as street dances, costume balls, and nightly fireworks. It would all conclude in two days' time with the Shaggy Dog Awards, given for the funniest story written to a punchline announced the year before.

Tradition excused the Ganelons from these events. Custom called for those around the prince to wear the cap and bells. And no one had been brave enough to suggest that Ganelon's terror of a grandfather wear such headgear.

Late one afternoon, as the detective sat brooding over the agency books, Madam Hortense Gadebois, their secretary-receptionist, knocked and paused, as if to give any murderer time to escape by the window, before pushing her large jaw through the office door. "London on the line," she announced. "It's the Sweeney." Madam Gadebois took her vacations in London, where Cockney rhyming slang paired the CID's famous Flying Squad with Sweeney Todd.

This particular Sweeney was Inspector Haverstick, who had served with Ganelon during the War. The Englishman sounded relieved to hear his voice, for the rumors had reached London, too, and newspapers were updating Ganelon's obituary. "By the bye, I just gave your prefecture a jingle regarding some strange goings-on at this end. The owners of small translating services have been dropping like flies. No sign of foul play. But from Frau Gruber to Signor Pecci, the corpses wore the same grimace of horror, a ghastly ear-to-ear grin. You'll never guess what our medical brass hats think we've got," he added confidently.

"Ho-Ho fever," guessed Ganelon.

Haverstick was amazed. "Right on the bloody noggin. But don't hang up. There's more. We found the name 'Dr. Underhill' in a victim's appointment book. Our only one of those is an Old Persian scholar at the British Museum." Ganelon tightened his grip on the neck of the telephone.

"Anyway, we entered his apartment with a warrant, to be greeted by another grinning corpse, one Dr. John Bolton, a colleague of Underhill's. Dead for several days, just about the time his wife reported him missing. No sign of Underhill anywhere. Then, three days ago, he was spotted at Croydon aerodrome boarding a Paris-Lyons-Marseilles-San Sebastiano flight. Heading your way. Thought I should fill you people in. We need a little chat with Underhill. Well, keep the old head down."

Hanging up the telephone, Ganelon sat rubbing the small triangular indentation on his left temple. Old Persian and hideous smiles brought to mind Clyde Mustapha, the man who had given him that scar.

Thief, archaeologist, fluent in ancient languages, Mustapha seemed born to break into the dusty strongbox of time and rummage there at will. He had come to San Sebastiano to steal the priceless toadstone amulet which St. Magnus had taken from the corpse of the Great Worm of the Cloaca Maxima, the dragon whose lair the Romans had disturbed when digging San Sebastiano's sewers. The amulet, which today hangs above the saint's tomb in the Abbey of the Holy Vernicle, is reputed to make the wearer as transparent as the great polar ice worms are. How Mustapha stole the amulet and Ganelon recovered it are set down in *Ganelon and the See-Thru Thief* by one of Austin Marchpane's stable of authors who later found more success in food packaging.

There were certain people whose movements Ganelon followed with interest, feeling better when he knew a continent or two separated them. Mustapha was one of these. So last month, when he heard of the man's death at an archaeological dig near Qum, he requested details from the Persian gendarmerie.

Ganelon located their reply in Mustapha's file and read it again. "Honored sir," they wrote, "the circumstances of Mr. Clyde Mustapha's death follow. If we are to believe Osman, the labor foreman at the dig, Mr. Mustapha had just uncovered an electrum tablet inscribed, as ancient riddles are, with much writing on the front and a short answer on the back. Before he could examine it closely, a foreign visitor arrived, a man with a limp who seemed to be a partner in the expedition. The two men withdrew with the tablet into Mr. Mustapha's tent. Soon after, Osman heard a roar of laughter and Mr. Mustapha staggered outside, red-faced with hilarity, and fell dead, a terrible grin on his face. When the workers at the dig saw it, they threw down their tools and fled, shouting about the Mark of Zoroaster, a silly local superstition that need not concern civilized men such as ourselves.

"Our Captain Aslan visited the site, where he found the body, as described, but both the visitor and the tablet had vanished. Without a sign of foul play, our investigation could go no further. Death is attributed to acute Ho-Ho fever, a disease named after the Chinese twins who invented the abacus and are said to have died laughing with delight at their discovery. This affliction is rare here, but not unknown.

"Our humble greetings to your illustrious father. The memory of his visit amongst us so long ago remains golden, and our astonishment at his solution to the disappearance of the great turquoise called the Peacock's Footstool continues unabated. ..."

Ganelon closed the file and returned to the agency books. But they put him in so bad a humor that after dinner he decided to visit the Cellars, low drinking haunts where, he understood, the furtive gentry were already celebrating his demise.

He left 18 bis rue Blondin on foot. His father had taken the roadster, leaving nothing but the old robin's-egg-blue electric Voltiger laudauette whose operation only Achmed, their Berber chauffeur, knew. Bedridden up in the attic now, old Achmed slept his days away unless his dreams drove him out along a dangerous run of the coastal highway when he might suddenly sit bolt upright, eyes feverish, and seek the steering lever with a withered hand.

At the end of the street Ganelon noticed a woman with bobbed blond hair sitting in a parked sedan. She was working in a cross-word-puzzle book with a yellow pencil by evening light. When the woman raised her pretty head, something about her made him wary. Or was it the fact that she ignored him, looking down the street the way he'd come? Smiling at his own conceit, Ganelon walked on until he reached the Cellars, a resort for San Sebastiano nightlife since the time of Captain-General Martin Corbeau.

After driving the effete Prince Florisant and his extravagant court into exile, the Captain-General had ruled the principality with a heavy hand in a very solemn glove. Buckles were banned from shoes and hats, to laugh in public was a felony called "incitement to frivolity," and no one was allowed on the street after compulsory evening prayers.

So nightlife fled underground to a mazy, interconnected world of cellars, passageways, and elaborate tunnelings from which the principality once quarried stone and dug the clay to build itself. Meanwhile, overhead, the night watch patrolled, long-necked cobble-horns in their ears, skimming along the street listening for underground blaspheming or slap of playing cards.

For his first stop Ganelon chose an unsavory den called Au Tombeau du Chasseur, which took its name from the mural behind the bar, the ever-popular Hunter's Funeral theme: the sportsman's coffin on the tumbrel followed by a wolf in priest's stole and other denizens of field and forest smirking behind their mourning while a crocodile sold bottles of his own tears from a tray.

But a careful eye will notice the acolyte rabbits taking up the rear carrying an armchair with an oboe on it. Yes, this is the funeral of Ganelon's grandfather, founder of the detective agency. Notice the wolf-priest's resemblance to the deceased's archenemy, the evil genius Dr. Ludwig Fong. See how the animals in the cortege carry the tools of the petty criminals' trade, from burglar's jimmy to coin-parer's knife. Note the ace peeking from the sharper's sleeve, or how the wild boar in stovepipe hat hung about with crepe winks out at you as he picks his neighbor's pocket. There behind the crocodile is the bucket from which he fills his fraudulent bottles.

Ganelon was halfway down the flight of stairs from the street when the noisy room below him fell still. He got a drink at the bar and chose a table where he could watch the faces of the new arrivals fall as they caught sight of him. In truth, none here would ever rise high enough in crime to merit his family's attention. Take Buvis there. The big man scowling down into his drink through thick lenses had started out collecting debts for the bookies. Once, with youthful enthusiasm, he had had his neck tattooed with a dotted line and instructions to the guillotine operator: "Cut here!" Today, gone to fat and chartered accountancy, Buvis cooked the books for criminal enterprises and wore turtlenecks to hide the tattoo.

Then, as if to contradict Ganelon's very thoughts, old Piccolo came limping down the steps leaning on his thin Malacca cane. A hired assassin, master of the dart-gun until gouty feet forced his retirement, Piccolo had avoided locking horns with the Ganelons by working abroad. When the old man saw him, he grinned broadly before vanishing into a smoky corner. Ganelon wondered what had brought him out on bad feet.

Piccolo's grin reminded him of the Mark of Zoroaster. After the letter from the Persian gendarmerie, he had tried to look it up in the one-volume office encyclopedia. He learned that the Persian seer Zoroaster was the only human born laughing, that he was a popularizer of the ideas of the Greek Pre-Socratic philosophers in his corner of the world, that he had some mysterious power over the surrounding kings and ruled them much as great Solomon ruled the djin. But he drew a blank on the Mark of Zoroaster. Well, whatever it was, it had spread to London.

By his next drink, Ganelon found himself thinking once more about Blanche Gautier, the beautiful young woman, with a face like the moon in a sky of black hair, who now rented the spare second-floor room at 18 bis, which she used for her modest palm reading and Tarot consultations business. She was studying for her spiritualist's license while supporting herself by leading and playing tambourine in the Palace All-Girl Orchestra.

He had taken Blanche out several times, most recently to a matinee to see *A King in Exile*, the latest bittersweet adventure of Auguste, the sad-faced star of the Czechoslovak silent screen whom everyone called "Auguste Elephant" because of his protruding ears. Later they walked in the Parc de la Menagerie, the topiary garden on the site of the royal stable of rare animals, discussing the film and arguing about the symbolism of the one-legged hurdy-gurdy player who appeared at critical points in the story. Blanche had a mind of her own, expressing herself with flashes of spirit which hinted at a formidable temper.

Newspapers had tried to link Ganelon romantically with Ludwig Fong's Irish granddaughter, Lady Emerald Fong. But the women he met professionally weren't the kind you'd start a family with. Blanche was something again. And it wasn't just the advantage for a man in his line of work to be married to a woman with second sight. She made him think about the future.

Thanks to Ganelon's father and grandfather, criminals of genius were avoiding San Sebastiano. To survive, the agency would have to expand abroad. Ganelon saw it sending operatives all around the world. Ganelon men, people would call them. G-men for short. He saw them wearing some distinctive piece of apparel, he hadn't decided what. The rough-and-tumble aspect of the business seemed to exclude crested blazers, while cub newspaper reporters had already preempted the porkpie hat.

Trenchcoats sounded promising enough for him to visit an army-surplus warehouse. But in the last months of the War manufacturers had added belts, loops, and buckles, as if such things alone could bring victory. Seeing them hanging there on racks, Ganelon thought they looked more like empty straitjackets than detective-wear.

A short cry of pain and dry gasping interrupted his thoughts. Piccolo hopped out of the gloom on one leg, a hand clutching a gouty foot, the other clawing at his wheezy throat. Then the old man pitched forward onto the linoleum to begin the long writhing crawl toward death which characterized the slow poisons into which he dipped his darts.

Ganelon watched helplessly as the master assassin died. Had Lady Emerald Fong hired Piccolo to kill him? Had he finally convinced her his intrusions into her affairs reflected no romantic interest on his part, only a determination she should never regain control of the San Sebastiano waterfront? Or was her jealous brother Sean Fong, he of the red pompadour, behind the attack?

The Irish Fongs got their San Sebastiano foothold while Ganelon was away in the trenches and his father was concocting mind games for Allied intelligence to use against the Central Powers. The struggle to drive them out had been long and hard. And in the end they had gone no farther than the S.S. Mrs. Henry W. Nesbit, an old Great Lakes collier converted by the Fongs into an off-shore gambling boat and whippet dog-track just beyond the three-mile limit.

And if it was the Fongs, what had saved him? Had someone accidentally stepped on Piccolo's foot, making him inhale the dart himself? Or had it been deliberate? Did Ganelon have a friend in this place? After a long look around the room he finished his drink. It was, he decided, time to go put a damper on the festivities at another cellar, perhaps the Élysée des Rats.

By the time Ganelon returned to the moonlit rue Blondin, the city lay in official darkness. Each day's festivities closed with a blackout to commemorate Petitpas's Manifesto.

During the Captain-Generalcy, the students of the École Normale Pantomimique marched to Sunday services in a solemn body and listened to the sermons so attentively that Corbeau decided they were giving sanctimoniousness a bad name and suppressed the school. Among the students cast out to starve, mimes without diplomas, was young Petitpas who, one gray market day as shoppers and merchants haggled half-heartedly over wilted bunches of gray turnips, leaped up onto a vendor's barrow and mimed a message, urging everyone to march against the stiff wind of tyranny, shatter the shrinking glass box of oppression, and pull together on the rope of common purpose—here he smiled and twirled elegant invisible moustaches—by rallying to the Laughing Cavalier.

Pikemen seized Petitpas and threw him into the deepest dungeon of the Château Gai prison where he met death, legend said, valiantly miming wind, glass box, rope, and moustaches in the utter darkness.

As Ganelon crossed the rue de Pau, a narrow pitch-black alley, he thought he heard hobnailed boots on cobblestones. Some said the ghosts of Corbeau's pikemen were walking abroad again. He stopped to cock an ear. The darkness seemed to cock an ear back at him. After a moment he moved on.

Half a block from home he stopped again. The bruiting about of his murder had made him cautious. On the opposite curb stood a man in smoked glasses with a cane which shone white in the moonlight. The figure was hunched up in a dark overcoat with a turned-up collar and a slouch hat pulled down to meet it. He seemed to lurk. If a blind man could lurk. If the man was blind.

The detective watched him slash his cane around on all sides as if making sure he was alone. Only then did he pull cotton wool from one ear and lean into the street, listening to hear if it was safe to cross. Cramming the cotton wool back in place, the man stepped off the curb.

A car engine roared to life. Ganelon had forgotten the blonde with the bobbed hair. The dark sedan rocketed past him with the woman at the wheel. The man in the street never heard it coming. The sedan hit him squarely and tossed him up onto the sidewalk at Ganelon's door. As the detective sprinted toward the fallen man he saw the car's registration number in the moonlight when it sped off around the corner. He reached the body, kneeled down, and found no pulse. The dead man's smoked glasses had been lost in the impact. His eyes were taped over with moleskin.

According to his passport, the man was Everest Underhill. He had arrived by air two days before. In the passport was a slip of paper with Ganelon's address.

When the coroner's wagon and the police had left, Ganelon went upstairs to the family living quarters. He undressed and sat on the edge of the bed and smoked a cigarette. He didn't know why Haverstick's Underhill had been coming to see him decked out like he'd been, or why the blonde in the sedan had killed him. Tomorrow, he swore to himself, he would find out.

As his head hit the pillow, the first boom of the nightly display of fireworks sounded from the barge beyond the harbor. Ganelon fell asleep amid this man-made thunder and dreamed he lay, uniform caked with mud, on the sloping side of a shell hole, his arm around a length of pipe protruding from the mud. He remembered being separated from his raiding party and tumbling into the hole in the dark. Exhausted with trying to get out, he dreamed he'd fallen asleep at last with the pipe tucked in his armpit.

Stiff and cold, he was awakened by a subterranean *tap-tap-tap* and thought German sappers were tunneling over to his lines. But when he put an ear to the pipe the tapping became the beat of a small orchestra. The music stopped. After a smatter of applause came laughter. Then a man who sounded like he wore a funny hat said, "Two Greek shepherds walking along the road. The fat one says to the thin one, 'Hey, Anaxamander, did you hear about Thales?' 'Why, no, Anaximenes, what's Thales done now?' Anaximenes says, 'He was out stumbling around in the dark looking at the stars when he fell into a well. So some wiseacre says, "If Thales had been looking in the well he might've seen the stars but looking at the stars he didn't see the well." ' "

Here Ganelon awoke abruptly into morning sunshine. When his feet hit the floor he smiled and shook his head. His war dreams were less frequent now and leavened with other things. That Thales story, for example, had arrived anonymously a few days before in a letter with a London postmark.

Suddenly he remembered Underhill and his smile vanished.

Later, heading down to the office, he smelled Blanche's delicious coffee. Under other circumstances, he would have stopped. She was always happy when he did. But he had Underhill's murder to look into. As he started past her door it opened. She seemed to know it was pointless to invite him in. She smiled and warned him, "If you go to the Café Americain today, avoid the *soupe du jour*."

"Why?" he wondered.

She shrugged. "I don't know."

"Anyway, your long-distance powers are improving. The cafe's a good six blocks away."

"Seven if it's an inch," she insisted, adding, "No news of your father?" When he shook his head she closed the door.

Ganelon continued down the staircase, wondering if he'd had something to do with his father's trip. To prepare him for a future announcement about his marital intentions, Ganelon had mentioned taking Blanche to the moving pictures to see Czechoslovak star Auguste Elephant. He had forgotten that prominent ears were a mark of the Tancredis. The next day his father left for Prague.

In the 1850s Beaumont-Zoltan, San Sebastiano's Prince Royal, was already exhibiting clown tendencies, painting his face white and appearing at functions with immense shoes poking out from under his ermine robes. In those days Europe gave its princes double-barreled nicknames like Tum-Tum, Plon-Plon, and Fi-Fi, the Prussian one. So Beaumont-Zoltan became Bo-Zo, who, at his majority, renounced the throne in favor of his younger brother and ran off to join the Cirque de la Lune, accompanied by his loyal guardian General Gaston, who mastered the silver cornet so he could play in the circus band.

Until World War I, whenever the circus appeared locally the Tancredis attended incognito, proving, perhaps, that what circus people say is true. Time spent wearing the red nose is not subtracted from one's span of years.

But wars hate circuses. The 1914 one drafted bareback riders into the cavalry, sent their dapple grays to drag artillery pieces through the mud, and marched the clowns off into the various general staffs. Somehow the Cirque de la Lune survived intact before vanishing on the Eastern Front. Some say Bo-Zo lost his memory and his bright red nose amid the horror of the Pripet Marshes. Others claim he had been sighted in Vladivostok with the Czech Legion in 1918. Ganelon's father had pledged to investigate every lead until he found the lost prince, dead or alive.

When Ganelon reached his office, he telephoned the prefecture. The inspector investigating Underhill's murder told him they had traced the sedan to a car-rental agency on the Quai des Matelots. A young Englishwoman named Felicity Bolton had rented it. She was, the policeman reminded him, the wife of the same man London thought Underhill had murdered. Near dawn a fishing boat returning from a night's work had found Mrs. Bolton's body floating near the harbor entrance. She had been strangled with the strap of her shoulder bag.

At the car-rental agency the dead woman had given her address as the Hotel Sebastopol. But in fact neither she nor Underhill were registered at any hotel in the principality, all of which were booked up weeks ahead during festival time.

Hanging up the telephone, Ganelon decided to visit Emile Lang, the principality's own Old Persian scholar. Strange outfit or not, Underhill hadn't looked like he'd been living on the street for two days. Perhaps he'd been staying with a colleague.

Coming out onto the street, the detective discovered someone had carved a large intertwined "VR" on his front door with a heavy, pointed object.

When a cannon ball took off the Captain-General's head at the Battle of the Tortue, his pikemen had thrown down their arms and disappeared back into the city. Among the crowds who welcomed the Laughing Cavalier the next day were some who brought more effort than conviction to their cheering.

Through the years the pikemen's descendants had added a grumpy, if silent, ballast to the carefree city. But when England's Queen Victoria made her pronouncement that she was not amused, they began secretly writing "VR" in letters large and small everywhere to announce that they were not amused, either.

Ganelon set out for the Academy, where Lang had his office. When the clown stilt race blocked his way he detoured by the Café Americain, whose outside menu announced "alphabet" to be the *soupe du jour*, whatever that was. It hardly sounded menacing. Now he doubled back to the crowded Boulevard Tancredi, where entire blocks were given over to humorous cartoon work in bright chalk by pavement artists from around the world.

He was halfway up the Academy steps when he noticed a piano-movers' truck pull up to the curb. Blanche and the Palace All-Girl Orchestra regularly performed at the Shaggy Dog Awards. The prince liked to warm up the audience with a few jokes of his own and used rim shots and a healthy shake of tambourine to signal for laughter. Was the truck delivering their piano? Then why, he wondered, had it been following him since he left the rue Blondin?

As Ganelon walked into the Academy, one of the uniformed concierges, a portly man with large flat cheeks, stopped him to ask who he wished to see and then fell in step with him as his escort. "Seeing it was you, sir, I thought you'd come about last night's odd little break-in," he said. "Turns out nothing was taken. Unless you count the burglar making himself a cup of the Director's tea. May I show you something and ask your professional opinion?"

When Ganelon nodded, the concierge ushered him into a small staff common room. "Now the police say the burglar got in through that window over there. They say someone left it unlocked. And I admit I do open it on my break. I must, you see. We don't allow smoking in the building." The concierge demonstrated by putting his head and shoulders out the window and lighting a cigarette. After a puff he pulled himself back inside, keeping his hand with the cigarette out in the fresh air. "But I'm always careful to lock the window when I'm done. So how could someone use it to break in? Does that lock look forced to you?"

It did not. "Perhaps someone used it to break out," said the detective. Then he left the concierge to finish his cigarette and took the stairs to the third floor. The door to Lang's office stood open. The room seemed burrowed out of a great pile of books and scholarly journals.

Ganelon knocked on the doorjamb. Lang peered around the side of a heaped desk like an RFC pilot trying to navigate his large-engined Sopwith Gnu, the devil-may-care tilt of his horn-rimmed glasses adding to the effect. Then Lang stepped into full view, a brisk little man who swept two chairs clear of papers, took one, pointed Ganelon to the other, and asked, "How's Underhill?"

"Dead."

Lang's eyes swelled with surprise. "The Mark of Zoroaster?" he asked, making his face into a terrible grin.

Ganelon shook his head. "Hit by a car." He described Underhill's death, adding, "Didn't you see the papers?"

"Newspapers, those kindergartens of callow words squirming and mewling about on the page? Never read them. I prefer my language dead as a doornail."

"Can you fill me in on this Mark of Zoroaster business?"

Lang pulled his chair closer. "They say Zoroaster came up with a joke so funny that if you heard it you'd die laughing. And with this terrible rictus on your face, this immense grin. The Mark of Zoroaster. Zoroaster used his fatal joke to kill Ghilghulnebber, King of Mesopotamia, and after that got pretty much his own way in that neck of the woods. Legend has it that just before he died he wrote his joke down somewhere."

Lang raised a finger. "Let's move forward a couple of thousand years. Enter Theo Gideon, a dealer in antiquities and backer of shady archaeological excavations. Ten days ago Gideon offered Underhill a substantial sum to translate a rubbing from an Old Persian tablet."

"Zoroaster's joke?"

Lang shook his head. "A mildly humorous story about two shepherds. That's as much as Underhill would tell me."

Ganelon cocked an eyebrow.

"Here's the funny part," continued Lang. "Gideon came by for the translation with John Bolton in tow. Bolton's another Old Persian man. Gideon said he wanted a second opinion, which was all right with Underhill, though he found it a bit odd because he'd heard Gideon, who is something of a ladies' man, was involved with Bolton's wife. Anyway, Gideon asked Underhill to read his translation aloud. When he did, Bolton burst out laughing and literally laughed himself to death, Mark of Zoroaster and all."

Ganelon interrupted him. "Let me see if I've got this straight. Underhill translates this joke and nothing happens to him. But when he reads it out loud, Bolton dies and Gideon doesn't."

"Right," said Lang. "And there's more. The next thing Underhill knew, he was being taken to Bolton's house at gunpoint. Gideon and Mrs. Bolton locked him in a small bedroom. But he overheard parts of their plans. Gideon had things to do in London. Then he'd come here and kill you. On his return they'd kill Underhill, staging it to look like Mrs. Bolton had shot an intruder. After that, somehow or other, they'd be living on easy street.

"Underhill was finally able to escape out a water-closet window. He hid in London for a day or two before deciding to fly here to warn you. But stepping off the plane, he spotted Gideon and Mrs. Bolton waiting at the gate. Underhill managed to slip out another way. But he was too afraid to go to your place. Terrified. Wouldn't tell me why. Said it was better I didn't know. He holed up with me in a terrible state of nerves."

While Lang spoke, Ganelon was watching a grand piano being hoisted up past the office window behind the man's shoulder. A Canadian instrument, though whether a Heintzman or a Sherlock-Manning, he would need a better look at the underbelly before he could say.

"Of course, I advised Underhill to phone you," Lang continued. "But he said a wild story's better told face-to-face. Yesterday I got back here around dinnertime. He'd hopped it. Painted one of my canes white and fled over the rooftops."

The Old Persian scholar sat back in his chair. "Well, there you are. Now you know as much as I do. No, hold on. I'm lying. I didn't tell you that Gideon paid me a visit. Here. Late yesterday afternoon."

"What about?"

"Asked me to give Underhill a message. Come to think of it ..." Lang slapped his jacket pockets, pulled out an envelope, and passed it to the detective.

Inside, Ganelon found a blank sheet of paper. He shrugged and added the sheet to the pile on Lang's desk and got to his feet. "You say this Theo Gideon's here in town. What's he look like?"

"Ordinary garden-variety sort. Never knew what women saw in him." Then Lang brightened and added, "Limpish. Got a bad break once jumping out a bedroom window when some husband arrived back unexpectedly."

Ganelon left Lang's office and started down the staircase. Things were getting clearer. Gideon had been the other man in Mustapha's tent at Qum. And the tablet Mustapha found that day hadn't been a riddle. It had been Zoroaster's joke with the punchline on the back. Gideon watched Mustapha read the front of the tablet without cracking a smile. Then he saw him turn the tablet over, read the end of the story, and die laughing, his fatal grin proof positive that Mustapha had found Zoroaster's deadly jest.

So Gideon took the tablet and fled. Just as Zoroaster extorted obedience from kings, Gideon planned to extort money from the wealthy. He would send them the first part of the story anonymously just as he'd sent it to Ganelon. Then he'd use the threat of the punchline to bleed them for the rest of their lives.

Back in London, he made rubbings of the tablet. He had Underhill translate the front and Bolton the back. Underhill's translation killed Bolton because Bolton knew the ending. But it didn't kill Gideon, who had carefully pocketed Bolton's translation unread.

So the joke worked in English. But Gideon's dream was international. He hired translators in all the major languages and repeated what he'd done with Underhill and Bolton, using their English version of the joke. The unlucky ones he gave the punchline to all met Bolton's fate.

Ganelon wasn't a millionaire and didn't know his part in all of this. But now he understood the terrible risk Underhill had taken to come and warn him. Without ever reading the punchline himself, Gideon still had a thousand ways he could use it to kill Underhill. He could hire someone to whisper the fatal words in his ear in a crowd or shout it from a passing car. Or have it placarded on every bus or sandwich-man in the city.

Or spell it out in alphabet soup. Yes, Ganelon knew the first part of the story, too. So he was as vulnerable to the punchline as Underhill.

Outside, on the Academy steps, the detective paused to ponder his next move. Feeling a tackiness under his foot, he looked down and found a red cross painted on the stone. Then he noticed that people coming up the steps were making a wide circle around him and staring up over his head where, five floors above him, a nine-foot Heintzman grand piano hung on broad leather straps.

He sprinted back inside the Academy and followed the concierge's directions to the stairs leading up to the roof. During school vacations Ganelon had toured with his reformed-jewel-thief, active-concert-pianist mother, spending much of it stretched out comfortably beneath grand pianos as she practiced or performed. This familiarity with piano underbellies came in handy during the war. The German Zeppelins carried the Fong Armaments bombsight. The Fongs boasted it could drop a grand piano down Buckingham Palace's chimney. In the War's first months, the Zeppelin masters used confiscated Belgian instruments to try to do just that, hoping to demoralize the British. They failed, but inspired the Woodbine cigarette people to issue a series of grand-pianos-of-the-world trading cards. The British tommies Ganelon met in the trenches collected these cards avidly and were so impressed by his ability to distinguish a Heintzman from a Sherlock-Manning that they gladly followed him on his night raids into no man's land.

Ganelon burst out onto a roof strewn with bodies dead of gunshot wounds. One—Ganelon recognized him as the driver of the piano delivery truck—lay over by the parapet close to the Fong Armaments bombsight and the hammock of straps holding the piano aloft, a machete clutched in his dead fist.

Standing at the parapet, Ganelon gazed out across the rooftops to where the Mediterranean hung blue in a blue sky. The coroner's people had come and gone. He had asked the police if a Theo Gideon was registered at a hotel in the principality. They had just gotten back to him. Gideon was not.

Overhead an ancient tri-wing Prentis-Jenkins Hedgehog lumbered across the sky dragging a banner. "See Napoli and Die," it said, referring to the city's largest undertaker. Words to mute the festivities, perhaps. Some said the Napolis came from pikeman stock.

The airplane's message could just as well have been from Gideon, leaving Ganelon lying dead on the roof wearing the Mark of Zoroaster. His only chance to survive was to locate Gideon. The punchline would have to be somewhere close by so others could use it to kill for him. If Ganelon could find out where, maybe Gideon would be the one who ended up wearing the fatal grin.

A trip to the morgue might point him in the right direction. Mrs. Bolton had been Gideon's lover before he murdered her. If they'd been staying together somewhere, Gideon might still be there.

The tourist traffic was heavy and he was delayed by the parade of comical automobiles carrying the participants in this year's zany hat competition. At long last he reached the morgue.

Among Mrs. Bolton's effects, he found a yellow Padishaw lead pencil. Ludwig Fong saw early that to rule the world he must control communications. To that end, he acquired China's vast graphite deposits and soon dominated the pencil market. So it was not strange to find a Fong pencil in any pocket or handbag in Europe. But under a pocket-glass this one revealed faint scratches on the Manchu yellow paint as if once clutched in a hand armed with razor-edged mandarin-length fingernails. Mrs. Bolton's nails were sensibly short. Lady Emerald Fong's were not.

At her late Uncle Parnell's wake—Fong of the Silver Tongue, they called him, and said he could flatter pigs into climbing trees—at his wake, when the time came to close the lid of the coffin, which stood in the corner like a five-day clock, the corpse argued silkily against the shutting and might have carried the day had not Lady Emerald Fong severed the living tongue from the cold flesh with her fingernails. They lay the still-chattering appendage in a gilt casket filled with poppy juice. Even Fongs hoped for Heaven and meant to rouse the tongue from its drugged slumber to plead their case before the Judgment Seat while high in the trees of Paradise pigs snorted and snuffled agreement.

Wherever Mrs. Bolton and Gideon had been staying, the pencil suggested Lady Emerald Fong had not been far away. Ganelon thought of the Fong gambling boat out beyond the three-mile limit and checked his watch. He had sneaked aboard the boat several times during his struggle with the Fongs. If he hurried, the same disguise might serve him again. He hailed a cab to take him back to the rue Blondin.

Later, another taxi deposited a brown-robed monk of the Order of the Holy Vernicle on the Quai des Matelots. He took his place among the other monks waiting in the quai-side launch. No one recognized him. Simply by taking off his shoulder-holster and Hrosko automatic Ganelon shed his trademark lopsided grin. He'd had a small skin-colored skullcap made up to serve as a monk's tonsure and complete his disguise.

By the time of his death, St. Magnus and his monks had driven off the local dragons as well as a plague of devils who rode about the San Sebastiano countryside in suits of armor, claptrap boiler-plated contraptions of clacking cogs and wheels resembling windmills on horseback. Then the monks fell under the influence of St. Boniface, who had them find secure hospices for Holy Land pilgrims as far as the walls of Acre. Later they became inn-masters whose establishments, the Sign of the Saracen Dog, with the head of an Egyptian wolfhound over the door, came to symbolize hospitality across Europe.

The monks survived the suppression of the monasteries during the Captain-Generalcy by bartending in the Cellars. They have been dispensing spirits and spiritual counseling ever since. Many worked the bars of the S. S. Mrs. Henry W. Nesbit.

The launch arrived alongside the gambling boat. When the others headed for the locker room and their black bartenders' trousers and pinstriped vests, Ganelon, who already wore his beneath his disguise, set off in the direction of reception, throwing his robe into the next chambermaid's basket.

The young man behind the desk, one of those pretty Irishmen, the devil's cherubim the Ganelons called them during the Fong troubles, with eyelashes a whore would die for, consulted the register. Yes, a Mr. Gideon was staying with them; he gave Ganelon his stateroom number.

Ganelon descended to Gideon's deck. Once, hearing someone coming, he slipped into an unlocked cabin and peeked out to glimpse a man carrying a suitcase and a raincoat over his arm disappear down a gangway. When Ganelon started out again, more voices sent him ducking back inside. This time it was Sean Fong, pompadour and all, with several highbinders, one carrying a bucket that smelled of rat ambrosia, a substance so irresistible to rodents that exterminators use it to bait their poisons. He watched them take the gangway, too.

At last he reached Gideon's stateroom. The door was unlocked. He slipped quickly inside, certain he would find the punchline. But he triggered something and a narrow sleeve of iron bars dropped from above to surround and hold him. Instinctively Ganelon grabbed two fistfuls of bars. A bird-lime substance caught and held his hands. When he set his feet on the crossbar for leverage to free himself, his feet stuck, too. He was straining to break free when the cabin lights came on.

Lady Emerald Fong sat at a desk facing the door: four Chinese highbinders on her right, four stocky little Irish spalpeens, the pug-nosed sweepings of Killarney and Kildare, on her left. Highbinder or spalpeen, there wasn't a profile in the round-headed lot.

Their mistress's skin was perfect ivory, with a dusting of freckles which lent a pixie air even her unsmiling Irish eyes could not contradict. Drumming a yellow pencil on the desk blotter, she spoke, her voice mixing the lilt of Ireland and the sing-song of Old Cathay. "You have brought your handsome clay pot to the well of the Fongs once too often, Ambrose. You invent these reasons for our paths to cross. Back in Sligo we'd call boys like you 'lamp-lighters,' flirts who get the girls interested and then walk away." Her smile was brief, suggesting childhood memories which were short on happy days.

"I tried to kill you twice today and should crush you like a bug," she continued. "But something about you touches my mothering side. So I offer you a partnership. Marriage. A brood of wee ones running about. The name Fong-Ganelon dances on the tongue. Yet I must be mistress. Only a Fong rules a Fong hearth."

As he struggled to free himself from his inelegant situation, Ganelon cursed her through clenched teeth.

Ludwig Fong's granddaughter raised one long fingernail. A highbinder with a fat paintbrush began applying rat ambrosia to Ganelon's trousers from the belt downwards. "Before you refuse, consider the alternative, Ambrose," she suggested.

At her next signal, the spalpeens shoved two stout wooden poles through the bars of Ganelon's cage, picked it up, detective and all, and carried it like a sedan chair out into the hall. They set the cage down next to an elevator. Then their evil mistress came closer. Tapping her pencil on the bars, she said, "My brother Sean has gone below to whet the appetites of your welcoming committee. The rats will go quite wild when they hear the elevator, knowing dinner's on the way. A slow ride down. Lots of time to think over my offer."

When Ganelon opened his mouth to defy her she shoved her pencil between his teeth, eraser end out. "If you change your mind, just push the Stop button. It's the only button that works. But when you do, Ambrose, it means you've agreed to a little training course to bend you to my will."

The spalpeens trundled Ganelon into the elevator and set the cage down. Then they stepped back out into the passageway. The door slid shut. The elevator began its trembling descent. Ganelon spat the pencil out and made an open attack on the glue holding him captive. Back there in the cabin he'd felt it give. But elasticity was its strength. It gave but didn't break. As the elevator settled into the bottom of the shaft he regretted spitting out the pencil which could have helped him play for time. He was thinking of Blanche Gautier when the door slid open.

Even war in the trenches hadn't prepared him for the carnage that met his eyes. Blood dripped everywhere. The last of the rats were scurrying through it, back into the closing slot in the wall. Three red skeletons in sodden rags made a pile by the door, which was streaked with bloody finger marks. A fourth, a skeleton flayed clean of flesh right up to the scalp line, leaving only the red pompadour intact, was hanging in a death grip from an overhead pipe. How long, Ganelon wondered, before gravity had dragged Sean Fong's legs low enough for the rats to leap upon them?

There stood the rat-ambrosia bucket, the wood licked white as new. Ganelon remembered now hearing an odd rapping as the elevator door opened, the sound of a ladle against another bucket summoning the rats back home. He had no doubt the summoner was Gideon. Had he been the man going down the gangway? Did the suitcase and raincoat mean the punchline was leaving the ship, perhaps even the principality?

It cost Ganelon time and skin to free himself from the bars. Then he pushed the dead remains away from the door with his foot and was not surprised to find the door was now unlocked.

He hurried upward until he came out on the evening deck. San Sebastiano glowed in the distance. The ship's crew were rushing about. His escape had been discovered. Without a second thought, Ganelon dove into the dark water.

Never a strong swimmer, he was happy to see the fireworks barge. He rested there, hanging in the water. Then he completed his swim and, sodden and his teeth chattering from the cold, was picked up by a passing police car. They had been looking for him everywhere. The prefecture had received a bomb threat against the life of Prince René.

The close relationship between his family and the House of Tancredi demanded Ganelon be by the prince's side when he was in danger. Fortunately René had only one public event left on his schedule, bringing Reiteration Days to a close with the Shaggy Dog Awards. So head cold, raw nose, cap and bells and all, Ganelon was there at Academy Hall the next day. He spent the morning supervising the police in their inspection of the hall, a steep rise of seats around three sides of a small stage. They checked under the seats row by row, crawled beneath the stage, and clambered up the narrow iron ladder to examine the space between the roof and ceiling. They found no bomb in place. Perhaps it would be carried in and thrown by someone in the audience.

That afternoon, just before the ceremony, Ganelon was waiting at the main entrance to the hall, eyeing the last of the crowd as it filed in. Twice he sneezed, making his own little racket of bells. Finally the reception-room doors flew open and the prince emerged with the judging committee, whose chairman carried the famous embroidered bag with the winning entries. Then came the members of the Academy, including Emile Lang, in rank on rank and all properly capped and belled.

The prince came over to commiserate with Ganelon about his head cold and inquire into his marital prospects. (The Tancredis were growing anxious for a Ganelon heir.) He was delighted when Ganelon hinted he might have met the right woman.

As if she read his mind, Blanche chose that moment to signal the Palace All-Girl Orchestra to strike up the overture to Scalamandre's operetta *The Man from Poet and Peasant*, the colorful life of Francesco Lazaire, San Sebastiano's first Minister of Culture and Agriculture. The prince led the way into the hall with Ganelon close by and forty Academicians marching behind them in solemn sway.

The crowded hall was a cliff of faces, many belonging to hopeful Shaggy Dog contestants. The procession mounted the stage by a flight of steps over the orchestra pit while the cinematographic people cranked their cameras and the newspaper photographers jostled to capture the image of a Ganelon in cap and bells on film. The detective felt his nose immense and as red as Prince Bo-Zo's. He imagined it in splendid magnification up on the newsreel screen.

René took his place on the small throne near the front of the stage, with the judging committee and Ganelon nearby. The Academicians stood at the back. Then the children from the orphanage came on stage to start things off with a touching synchronized pantomime rendition of Petitpas's Manifesto, wind, glass box, rope, moustaches, and all. Ganelon was happy to get through the patriotic silence without a sneeze.

Now the prince and the judging committee approached the podium. Ganelon stood more toward the back, scanning the upper seats. The close quarters were ideal for a bomb thrower. Or perhaps the assassin might take the suicide route and slip in among the award winners with a bomb hidden on his person.

René began with a few jokes, decorated with rim shots and the rush of Blanche's tambourine. Then the awards began. Ganelon moved closer to the podium, hand inside his jacket on the butt of his Hrosko automatic. The funniest Shaggy Dog stories written to last year's punchline were judged in three categories based on length: standard, miniature, and toy. The prince read the winning story in each category aloud. Amid the applause each winner came up to receive his prize.

The last winner was returning to his seat when suddenly, from the uppermost row, a woman dressed in widow's weeds with a glittering tiara rose and began shouting, "We are not amused!" She kept it up until the police got to her and carried her away. Ganelon had edged backwards to keep an eye on the protester. Now he joined in the relieved laughter. It looked like they'd made it through the awards with no attempt on the prince's life.

But he had forgotten the final part of the ceremony. Prince René still had to read the new punchline for next year's stories. The chairman of the committee took the envelope from the ceremonial bag. The Prince opened it and drew out a sheet of paper.

Here Ganelon felt a sneeze coming on. He made his upper lip as long as he could to fight it back.

"And Anaxamander says …" read Prince René.

Anaxamander? The shock of the name unleashed Ganelon's sneeze. As a man, the forty members of the Academy turned toward him in a cacophony of cap bells and hissed, "God bless you!" Whatever Anaxamander said, Ganelon didn't hear it.

Suddenly Ganelon understood. The foiled attempts to murder him, the threat against the prince's life, everything. Gideon wanted Ganelon to die here with the Zoroaster grin on his face and the newsreel cameras catching it all on film. After that, what millionaire could resist the man's extortionist demands?

And that explained Gideon's visit to Lang. It got him inside the Academy. He hid there until it closed, found the punchline envelope, steamed it open with the Director's teakettle, and substituted his deadly one. Then he let himself out the concierge's window in the staff common room.

Something was happening at the podium. The puzzled committee chairman had stepped forward and was whispering in the prince's ear. René showed him the punchline. The chairman glanced at it and shook his head decisively. The prince apologized to the audience. He had been given the wrong envelope. Then he surrendered the podium to the chairman, who recited the correct punchline from memory.

But Ganelon's attention was focused on what Anaxamander said, on the piece of paper the prince had crumpled up into a ball and now held between thumb and index finger. When the chairman's recitation ended and the prince signaled for a rim shot, the ball of paper flew out of his hand and down into the orchestra pit.

Ganelon caught Blanche's eye, nodded, and hoped she understood. But the ceremonies were over and he had to follow the prince out of the hall.

When Ganelon raised his hand to knock, Blanche called for him to come in. She sat at the small table where one day her crystal ball would go. A smoothed-out sheet of paper lay there now. "Something told me this would interest you," she said. Picking it up, she began, "And Anaxamander said—"

Ganelon stopped her. He explained about the Mark of Zoroaster, Gideon's grand plan, and how he'd had Underhill and Bolton killed and murdered Mrs. Bolton and the London translators.

"I see," she said. "Yes, I'm afraid I do see."

Ganelon nodded. You didn't need second sight to understand that he and Blanche had no hope of a future together. Sooner or later, they would have a fight and, Blanche's temper being what it was, she would let slip Anaxamander's words. Even if she never did, those words would always be there, hanging over the relationship.

For a moment, neither of them spoke. Then Ganelon said, "The scented stationery," referring to a box of lavender notepaper he'd given her when the Valletta case had taken him to Rome.

He smiled when she asked if he wanted it back. "No," he said. "But we might still do Gideon a bit of mischief. It just might work. At least it's worth a try. You see, he fancies himself a ladies' man. I was hoping you would write a letter for me." He nodded at the piece of paper. "Leave off the 'Anaxamander says' part. Sign it, say, 'A Secret Admirer.' Something like that." Ganelon handed her Gideon's home address. "I got this from my friend Haverstick."

"The Sweeney?" she asked.

"That's the one. We'll let him mail it. An innocent London postmark would be best."

At Willow-Walk-Behind

I N A WINDY March afternoon in 1929, a piebald day, now cloudy, now sunshine, Ambrose Ganelon III drove his white Terrapin convertible with the top up along the narrow, twisting road that tunneled through the Old Forest, the dense stand of trees covering much of Transporpentine San Sebastiano. His destination was Willow-Walk-Behind, a religious retreat house run by the monks of Saint Magnus.

As the trees hurried by, Ganelon recalled his father saying that when Hannibal's elephants crossed the Alps people thought they were seeing a forest on the march, a Birnam Wood in search of some southern Dunsinane. And, speaking of trees, he remembered reading somewhere that even the oldest of families seldom outlive three oak trees. Grim food for thought, he being the third of his name to operate the principality's famous detective agency. True, his archrivals, the descendants of the evil Dr. Ludwig Fong, were in their third generation, too. But they had prospered since the War, particularly the English branch of the family led by Dorian Fong-Smythe, while the private detective business had never been worse.

The sudden slapping of rubber interrupted Ganelon's gloomy musing. He had a flat. An impatient frown crossed his battered, street fighter's face as he pulled off the road beside some ancient apple trees. In a clearing behind them stood an orchard of younger trees in full blossom, their trunks wrapped in white cloth like the legs of racehorses. He got out his jack and spare and changed the tire. Then he leaned against the car and lit a cigarette.

Suddenly a cloud crossed the sun and a voice close-by said, "Some say it was this time of the year when Adam and Eve were created."

Ganelon swung around. An old man was leaning against one of the dotard apple trees. Brown and gnarled, he might have been carved from its wood. "I didn't mean to startle you," he apologized. Then, glancing back at the apple blossoms, he continued. "Let's hope Paradise lasted longer than just the time between the flower and the fruit."

"You said it," agreed Ganelon.

The old man smiled. "Came to help you with your tire. Can't move as quickly as I once did. Are you going far?" When Ganelon said Willow-Walk-Behind, the smile vanished. "Be careful in those woods, brother," said the old man. "Something has gotten into the trees."

With a smart *beep-beep*, a low-slung bright blue roadster with an attractive young woman behind the wheel rushed past them. Ganelon watched the driver disappear around a corner. "Maybe it's only the wind," he answered absently, his mind still with the pretty lady.

"Something strange, I mean," insisted the old man.

The retreat house was an ancient stone mill to which substantial additions had been made. The parking area in front was crowded. Ganelon noted the bright blue roadster whose registration number said it was from northwestern France.

Father Boniface, the portly, red-faced retreat master, came out to welcome Ganelon, who was a frequent visitor because his friend and teacher Father Sylvanus lived in a nearby hermitage. "Looks like business is booming," said the detective.

"Not the religious retreat end of things," the priest told him. "No, but Prentiss-Jenkins Aviation draws a lot of people who need a place to stay."

Ganelon recalled that a large area of woods in the neighborhood had recently been cut down to provide a runway and a storage area for the British company, which was buying up surplus fighters and bombers from the War, flying them here, and storing them under canvas for resale.

"Yes, it's all 'Come Josephine in My Flying Machine' around here," said Father Boniface, who'd been a song plugger and a ballroom dancer—some said he was the original "Willie" in "Waltz Me Around Again, Willie"—until the carnality of the Turkey Trot and the Grizzly Bear drove him to a late religious vocation.

"As if things aren't hectic enough," continued the retreat master, "one of our guests wandered off after dinner last night. Probably got himself lost in the woods. We only discovered him missing at breakfast. We've had people out looking for him all morning. I've called the police. All this on the feast of Saint Magnus, our founder. And a very special Saint Magnus Day, at that."

Before Ganelon could ask what was special about it, Father Boniface winked and held out his hand. "I'd better put it in our safe," he said, cocking his head apologetically.

Ganelon had forgotten to leave his Hrosco automatic at home. Now he unstrapped holster and weapon and handed them over. As they disappeared inside Father Boniface's habit, one corner of the monk's mouth turned downward and the other up in a perfect replica of Ganelon's trademark cockeyed smile.

Picking up Ganelon's suitcase to take it to the detective's usual room, the priest turned back to say, "When you see Father Sylvanus, ask yourself if perhaps he's been alone in the woods too long."

As Father Boniface entered the retreat house, Ganelon's old friend Captain Alain Jerome came out the same door. Jerome possessed an aviator's confident air and a dashing moustache. During the War he commanded San Sebastiano's tiny air force with its cabbage-rose roundel, operating from an airfield just behind the lines where Ganelon's regiment saw action. Jerome's unit had taken "Love in the Clouds" as their theme song, a melody dating back to the giraffe craze of the 1840s when Anatole and Natalie were the most popular animals in the San Sebastiano zoo. His pilots even painted giraffe markings on their sturdy little Prentiss-Jenkins Hedgehog IIIs as a kind of ur-camouflage.

The last time Ganelon saw Jerome was three years ago as the man set out on a surveying job for something called the Cairo to Cathay Railroad.

"Your march through Syria, Arabia, Persia, and beyond, you said it sounded like fun. Was it?" asked the detective.

Jerome laughed. "As far as it went. When I reached Teheran I found a telegraph telling me I was let go. My employers had run out of money.

"As luck would have it, Riza Khan, who had been Persia's Minister of War and had just become the Shah, heard of my arrival and invited me to dinner to discuss the railroad project. I found him a down-to-earth and ambitious leader.

"When he told me he meant to bind his unruly country together by increasing the army three-fold, I recalled the words of the British staff officer in Constantinople when I described my surveying trip. The Brit said they couldn't guarantee my safety. But if the Bedouins did capture me, he promised to send out planes and bomb the beggars until they let me go.

"I heard myself suggesting that the Shah might do the same job with an air force and at a fraction of the cost. How better to put down tribal revolts and maintain order in remote corners of the country? With warplanes a glut on the market he could buy all he needed for next to nothing. And there were plenty of aviators who'd jump at the chance to fly them.

"The Shah said he'd study the idea," said Jerome. "But I could tell he liked it. Now for the long and short of it. A month ago I received his letter authorizing me to put together a Persian air force. Needless to say, there'll be a tidy commission for yours truly when I do. So here I am, looking over what the Prentiss-Jenkins people have in the way of aircraft and interviewing pilots. My old friend Wing Commander Timmons is here representing a British team. Not to mention our old nemesis Baron Waldteufel on behalf of his German flyers. Even the Soviets are interested." Jerome looked at his wrist watch. "An hour ago the Shah's man General Massoudi arrived in San Sebastiano by British flying boat from Alexandria to see what I've put together."

As he spoke, an old open touring car turned in at the retreat-house gate. It made a complete circle of the parking lot as though Father Carlus, the driver, who was done up in motorcycle goggles and a white duster, was reluctant to end the journey. Three visitors and their baggage sat behind him fresh from San Sebastiano's old port where Imperial Airways had a quay-side hangar for their giant amphibious aircraft.

"That's Massoudi, the one in the military uniform," said Jerome. "The other two are my old Cairo to Cathay employers, Major Ibrahim and Mr. Wang." He indicated the tall man in a white suit, with a long jaw and a red tarboosh, carrying a horsehair fly whisk, and an Oriental gentleman who seemed uncomfortable pent up in western dress. "They're here to discuss fresh financing for their railroad with Miss Khalila Assad." With a nod toward the blue car, Jerome went to greet the passengers.

Waving to Father Carlus, who had stopped to admire the Terrapin, Ganelon continued on his way to the back of the retreat house where a flagstone walk and a dozen sturdy willow trees circled a good-sized pond. Centuries before, a stream on the property had been dammed up, creating the pond and a millrace to drive the mill's waterwheel, long since fallen to ruin. The unharnessed overflow still found its way down to the sea, where its brown water vanished like chimney smoke into the sky-blue Mediterranean.

It was Friday. Two young monks were out on the pond in a rowboat trying to net carp for dinner. Ganelon recalled Father Boniface's complaint, "English monks always chose salmon rivers when they built their cathedrals. We must do with carp."

Suddenly a monk gave a shout and jumped into the water. His companion followed. Wading across to a large willow, they struggled, trying to extricate something from the submerged tangle of the tree's roots. As Ganelon reached them they were dragging the body of a man in a dark suit up onto the grass. One monk hurried off to fetch Father Boniface.

Ganelon knelt to examine the body, noting the wound from a heavy blow to the back of the head. The other monk said they'd seen the dead man's heels floating beneath the willow branches. The detective found that the most interesting thing, the torso and head floating below the feet, so deep in the water.

"It's Mr. Elmer Shypoke, the missing guest," said a woman's voice.

Ganelon looked up. The beautiful driver of the blue roadster was standing there. He was sorry he'd surrendered his Hrosco. The cockeyed grin it gave him charmed the ladies.

"Strange the way he was floating," she added, pushing her black hair out of an alert and intelligent face.

"You've a good eye," said Ganelon.

A male voice with an English accent said, "A shoulder money belt filled with gold guineas will do that to you." The speaker was a tall, fair-haired man wearing a blazer and a Royal Flying Corps tie. He had a twisted chin and an indentation like a deep thumbprint low on one cheek. A *casse-gueule*, as the French called those who brought face wounds out of the War. The man introduced himself. "Timmons," he said.

Ganelon opened the dead man's jacket to reveal the bulging shoulder money belt. Well, the killer's motive hadn't been robbery. "You the one who led Jerome around in the hospital when he couldn't see?" he asked Timmons. Jerome had been caught on the ground during one of Baron Waldteufel's aerial gas attacks. Temporarily blinded, he'd been led away in a crocodile of like-injured. During his long recuperation in a San Sebastiano hospital, Jerome and Timmons had become fast friends.

"My jaw was all wired up," said Timmons. "It was the dumb leading the blind. Have you met Miss Khalila Assad?"

"So you are the famous private detective," said the young woman. "Please call me Khalila. May I help you in your investigation? I am not without experience in such matters."

Ganelon remembered something from one of the magazines he subscribed to—was it *P.I. Tidbits?*—about a Levantine religious youth group solving crimes in the city of Nancy. "Better leave this to the police," he said. He could tell she was disappointed. But he had his reasons.

Jerome and Father Boniface came hurrying down the path. While the priest knelt to pray beside the body, Khalila told Jerome, "Mr. Ganelon says this is a police matter. That's fine with me. I don't work well with men who talk to trees."

"You were driving fast," protested Ganelon. "This old man came out of the orchard to help me change a tire."

Khalila frowned at him, put her arm in Jerome's arm, and led him away. As he went the pilot shot Ganelon a puzzled look over his shoulder.

Ganelon watched the woman go. "Something of a coquette," he said to Timmons.

"Don't ask me," replied the Englishman.

"The money belt, how come you knew about it?"

"We flew over from Croydon to Paris together, Shypoke, Baron Waldteufel, and I. Shypoke bragged about the gold and showed off what he called his shooting iron to keep it safe."

Then he added, "If you ask me, Standard Oil sent the man to fish in troubled waters. Anglo-Persian Oil's agreement is with a local warlord. The Shah could invalidate it."

"I hear the country's oil production could one day equal that of the U. S.," said Ganelon.

"So they say," said Timmons. "Perhaps Shypoke thought the gold might help him with the Shah's man Massoudi. Shypoke's arrival certainly spooked the Anglo-Persian people. Instead of waiting for Massoudi, they left this morning for Teheran to deal with the Shah directly."

"And Waldteufel was on your Paris flight, you say?"

"Yes, our plane was a tri-engine Prentiss-Jenkins Gladiator, the 'box kite,' as they call them. A noon takeoff followed by a leisurely lunch on a wide table in a spacious cabin made it a very popular flight. Waldteufel was on board, but just barely. We were powering up when a chauffeured Daimler drove out onto the field to deliver him and his baggage."

"The Daimler driver, did he have a club foot?" asked Ganelon, describing Eustace, Dorian Fong-Smythe's chauffeur. Timmons hesitated. "I didn't notice," he said.

Ganelon set out for Father Sylvanus's hermitage again, taking a path beside the nearby retreat-house chapel which led deep into the woods.

It was perhaps ironic that a private detective of the two-fisted school would be a student of the art of nonviolent self-defense called the *via felix*, the Happy Way. Invented by Saint Magnus for his monks' use in protecting the holy places of Europe during the early Middle Ages, it involved a hip lift and the redistribution of an adversary's body humors (blood, phlegm, choler, black bile), changing him temperamentally, from, say, a homicidal maniac into a hail-fellow-well-met sort. An adept practiced using a heavy wooden planchette grooved with elaborate channels and four colored balls. Ganelon had just mastered a very difficult maneuver called Navigating between Presumption and Despair which was the door to a higher level of the Happy Way.

The detective followed the narrow path for some distance before he reached a small clearing where a fat blue-green cedar tree built of galvanized metal stood. During the War, Fong Armaments manufactured these sniper boxes and observation posts for the German army. Ganelon remembered the festive note they added to the forward saps and no-man's-land at Christmas. After the Armistice, the Fongs sold some off as outhouses, toolsheds, and, in Father Sylvanus's case, a hermitage.

Ganelon's father once described Father Sylvanus as the very image of El Greco's famous portrait of Saint Ildefonso, the patron saint of dart players.

Curious, Ganelon had looked the painting up in an art book. The saint had been sitting at a small table reading his breviary. As El Greco captured him, he is holding up a dart which probably served as his bookmark and is about to let fly at a dartboard somewhere off the canvas.

Father Sylvanus certainly had the saint's high forehead, long aristocratic nose, and whimsical smile. But today he was solemn and preoccupied. He invited Ganelon in and congratulated him after watching his work with the planchette. "Your father had not come this far." Then his eyes went to the open door. "The trees are restless," he observed.

"You're the second person to tell me that today. It's the wind."

The hermit shook his head. "I grew up near woods like these. When I was a boy people used to say: 'Elms do grieve. Oak he do hate. Willows do walk if you travels late.' "

"Willows walk?"

"Indeed," said Father Sylvanus. "Uproot themselves at night and stalk unwary travelers muttering all the way."

"Then Willow-Walk-Behind didn't take its name from the willows and the walk behind the retreat house?"

"It was called that and shunned locally long before our order bought the old abandoned mill and ancient willows around the millpond. We wanted the property because our founder and his early followers lived as hermits hereabouts."

In a voice as casual as he could make it, Ganelon said, "Father Boniface thinks you have been in the woods too long."

"And he may be right. When the winter wind works their twigs and branches I've started to believe I can read something of what the trees are dreaming. They are not happy dreams. The willows may be the unhappiest, though I haven't yet learned the cursive script of their branches. The trees fear for something. I think it is the Cairo to Cathay Railroad."

"I don't understand."

"The Chinese say a train journey of a thousand miles begins with a single wooden railway tie," said the priest. "Railroads devour forests. Oh, trees are as innocent as children. When they saw their first woodman's axe they said, 'Look, look, part of it is one of us.' But like children their anger, when it comes, can be a terrible and mindless thing."

Father Sylvanus stopped. "Leave me now," he said. "I have much to do."

On the threshold of the hermitage Ganelon turned back to ask, "What did Father Boniface mean when he said this was a very special Saint Magnus Day?"

"Our founder rose from his deathbed, went outside, stuck his head in a hollow tree, and shouted a last prayer. Ever since we've had stories of monks meditating alone in the woods on Saint Magnus Day hearing a muffled voice speaking to them. From records kept we have discovered that this phenomenon occurs once every seventy-five years. Today is such a special day."

As Ganelon approached the retreat house he saw a man in a tweed suit and hat, leather gaiters, and a narrow Malacca cane under his arm hunkered down examining Shypoke's body as Father Boniface looked on. Inspector Nestor Flanel, a third-generation policeman, had a personality so grating his superiors gave him every suburban assignment just to get him as far from the prefecture as possible. This explained the gaiters and cane, useful for investigating crime scenes in long grass. Flanel saw Ganelon and made a cold what-the-hell-are-you-doing-here face.

Ganelon's two-fisted image would suffer if Flanel suspected he was a student of the Happy Way. The detective decided to pretend he'd come to Willow-Walk-Behind for spiritual refreshment. He turned abruptly and entered the retreat house chapel.

The little church was famous for its unusual windows. The one toward the retreat house depicted Saint Magnus Preaching to the Trees of the Forest in bright stained glass. The window's mate on the forest side was of clear glass, as if inviting the trees to peek in.

Ganelon paused as he had many times before to admire the stained glass. There was the saint shaping his fingers into the twiglike runic characters the forest understood. Crowded around him were trees of every size and description. Even the oak had come and brought his friend the pine. Conveniently, the window had an inch-wide border of clear glass so he could also keep an eye on Flanel at the millpond.

When Ganelon's eyes grew accustomed to the chapel's dim he discovered he was not alone. Khalila stood nearby, staring up at the stained glass.

"Sorry to intrude," he said.

"My people told me to be sure not to miss seeing this famous window," she said without turning. "It's very impressive. And, oh, I know now why you didn't want to get involved in Mr. Shypoke's murder. Inspector Flanel is a very unpleasant person. He made it quite clear he didn't want amateurs or private detectives interfering with his investigation."

"There's more to it than that," said Ganelon, explaining how, over the years, his family had driven every competent criminal from San Sebastiano. So its police force no longer attracted minds of high caliber. Men like Flanel blame their lackluster careers on the Ganelons and spurn their help. He didn't tell her that his family's reputation had driven his own business away as well. Sometimes, after reflecting on his father's and his grandfather's brilliant achievements, there was nothing left for Ganelon to do but visit some low bar and pick a fight with the biggest and meanest guy in the place.

Then he heard himself say, "I'm surprised your people would trust the Cairo to Cathay business to—" He hesitated over the right words. "—someone so young and good-looking."

She laughed. "I thought you were going to say to such a flirt," she said, using the word *allumeuse*, which went back to gaslight days. Then it meant a female lamplighter. Today it was a woman who lights the boys up and walks away.

"Being friendly does help me with my task," she admitted. "I've been sent here with a tentative proposal for the Cairo to Cathay principals. But my people also want to know if Persia is stable enough for a railroad to be built across it. I think the guests here at Willow-Walk-Behind can answer that question. Being friendly helps."

"Why the interest in the railroad?"

"My people are reclusive, industrious, and astute in the way of business. They must think it a solid proposition," she said, adding with a smile, "though China has always fascinated my people. If I repeated some of the China stories our elders tell you'd have to laugh."

Wondering if she'd found Shypoke an unsettling presence, Ganelon asked, "Did you see Shypoke last night?"

"Now you sound like Inspector Flanel."

"Flanel can make a real shambles of things. When he's around, a parallel investigation never hurts."

"I saw Shypoke at dinner," she said. "That's it."

"What did you do last night?"

"I took a walk with Captain Jerome," she said. "Along the way we met with Ivanov, the Russian pilot. He walked with us for a bit. After that I went to my room. I came down later to Father Boniface's office. He lets me use his telephone to keep my people in the picture. But somebody else was using it. I believe it was Baron Waldteufel. So I went to bed."

Having answered his questions, Khalila left the chapel.

Ganelon remained where he was, watching Flanel oversee the loading of Shypoke's body onto a coroner's gurney. Then Khalila appeared at the millpond. A moment later Jerome and Timmons came around a corner of the retreat house, standing aside as the gurney trundled by.

Suddenly an excited monk came running out of the woods, shouting and pointing back the way he had come. Flanel and the others followed him back into the woods.

Ganelon came out of the chapel to find out what was happening. As he passed the millpond Baron Waldteufel stepped from behind a willow tree. "Still lurking, are we, Baron?" he said. In aerial action over the trenches the German liked to creep up on an enemy aviator by flitting from cloud to cloud until ready to pounce.

The Baron stared at Ganelon through his monocle before giving a smart click of his heels and a short bow from the neck. Then he said, "Two monks on a work party in the woods discovered a second body in a crashed airplane. The others have gone to investigate." He pointed to the path they had taken.

"Then I think I'll join them," said Ganelon. "Care to come along?"

The Baron shook his head. "It's the Russian, Ivanov. Yesterday he buzzed the retreat house, no doubt hoping to impress General Massoudi with loop-the-loops and barrel rolls. He didn't know Massoudi had been held up in Alexandria by a sandstorm. This morning the Prentiss-Jenkins people had us all over at their facility for a champagne brunch and a walk-around to show off some newly arrived aircraft. Miss Assad was invited, too. Ivanov stayed on after we left. No doubt he meant to repeat his aerial display for Massoudi today."

Then, as if he knew Ganelon's next question, Waldteufel said, "Inspector Flanel asked when I saw Shypoke for the last time. I said at dinner. But on reflection I think I heard him later that night. I was using Father Boniface's telephone. I'm pretty sure somebody was outside listening at the window next-door where the Anglo-Persian Oil people and Timmons were meeting. I believe it was Shypoke."

Striding off into the woods, Ganelon soon caught sight of the others. When Jerome saw him he dropped back. "I hope our dead man isn't Ivanov," he told Ganelon. "That would complicate things. Massoudi brought word the Shah favors a Russian team. I rather think he feels the Russians have their hands too full with their tin-pot revolution to pose any threat to his country."

"And the British would bring too much of an imperial agenda to the task," said Ganelon. "Which leaves Waldteufel and his Germans."

Jerome nodded. Then after a few moments he said, "By the way, the old guy you talked to back there by the orchard, I'm sure he was only a fruit farmer. But when I was a boy, they told stories about the Old Apple-Tree Man, a tame tree spirit who warned people when it wasn't wise to go into the woods."

"Then he should have warned Shypoke," said Ganelon. "And speaking of Shypoke—"

"Let's see," said Jerome. "I saw him at dinner. Afterwards I went for a walk with Khalila, who had some questions about the feasibility of the Cairo to Cathay Railroad. A very smart girl. And oh, yes, we ran into Ivanov. Later I was standing at my window when I saw Shypoke again. He was coming around the side of the retreat house."

"Was anyone following him?"

"Not right behind him, no," said Jerome, adding, "Look, I'm sorry. I still take these drops for my eyes before I go to bed. I chose just that moment to put them in. Remember the story of the blind man cured at Bethesda? At first he said he saw men like trees walking. That's what I saw, a blurry shape just like a tree walking come out of the retreat house and head off in the direction Shypoke had gone."

Ganelon sighed to himself. That's all he needed, a walking tree. He imagined his grandfather laying his oboe aside to give his full attention to so intriguing a development. He saw his father bouncing his fingertips together thoughtfully as he considered the truth hidden behind so unscientific a story. Ganelon found himself wondering where the nearest bar was.

He and Jerome walked on for another fifteen minutes until they reached the crashed Russian biplane. Nicknamed a Pasternaki from its tapered, parsniplike fuselage, it had come down across a clearing and smashed into the base of a large tree. The dead pilot, a round-faced blond young man, wore a green uniform with red markings.

With a nod at his partner standing by the airplane, the monk who'd guided them to the crash explained, "Brother and I had been sent to clean the brush away around what we hope is Saint Magnus's Tree. As Father Boniface put it, 'There'll Be a Hot Time in the Old Town Tonight' if we're lucky enough to hear our founder's voice speaking to us across the centuries. Anyway, as we were starting back we heard the plane go over. Then its engine cut out and we heard it crash."

Flanel examined the body and announced the pilot's neck had been broken in the crash. After walking slowly around the airplane, he stood rocking back and forth on his heels and tugging at his lower lip, doing a fine impersonation of a man deep in thought.

Khalila toured the wreckage. When she reached the gas tank she rapped on it. Then she came over next to Ganelon. "Sounds empty to me," she murmured.

Ganelon had wondered why there'd been no fire or explosion on impact. Nice detective work. You bet, business was slow at the agency. But having a beautiful junior partner around might make the time go faster.

At Flanel's signal the monks emptied a scythe and two rakes from their wheelbarrow, loaded up Ivanov's body, and trundled back to the retreat house with everyone following behind.

Two dead bodies or not, it still wasn't Ganelon's case. Maybe that was just as well. He was here to get to the next level in the Happy Way. With that in mind he left the others when they reached a small side path that led to Father Sylvanus's hermitage.

Ganelon found the hermit sweeping the dirt floor of his galvanized dwelling with a broom of twigs. "Any chance of squeezing in a lesson, Father?"

The priest gave him a sad smile. "Let's leave that for the new Father Sylvanus," he said, adding, "Did I ever tell you I was born on Saint Magnus Day seventy-five years ago? I came in with our founder's prayer and I have a strong premonition that I will go out with it. So I have much to do, including the naming of the new Father Sylvanus from among those I have trained. I had high hopes for Father Carlus before he chose the byway of speed-demonry."

The old priest looked around at the forests as if for the last time and said, "Saint Magnus was much in awe of trees, the way they stood half in heaven and half deep in the earth, much as we humans do. Meditating on this set him to wondering if the vast underground network of tree and seaweed roots could be used as a long-distance communication system. Stick your head in a hollow tree, shout your message, and someone with his head in a tree at the other end would hear what you said. Imagine sending a message from one end of Australia to the other using the roots of the shady coolabah tree.

"Fortunately Saint Magnus confided this wild idea to no one. Otherwise he might have been judged mad and unfit for canonization.

"But my predecessor and teacher, Old Father Sylvanus, as they called him, found the saint's secret diary among some ancient manuscripts in our library. By translating it he was able to calculate the precise hour when the saint's prayer, having circled the world, would return to where it had started. Tonight we will find out if his calculations were correct.

"Of course, the original tree has long since fallen to dust. But any hollow tree of the same kind would surely do. Though reasonable men may disagree on what kind of tree it was."

Father Sylvanus returned to his sweeping for a moment. Then he said out of nowhere, "Some say the next great battle between Christianity and Islam is nigh. I hear some Germans are telling the French that when that day comes their Mr. Hitler will be the new Charles Martel, the hero-warrior who will defeat the Arabs once and for all.

"Be that as it may, a small religious group called the Druze believe that when this conflict ends and the victorious side, whichever it is, stands bloody and exhausted, then a vast Druze army will march out of China, defeat the victor, and rule the world."

"A Druze army in China?"

Father Sylvanus nodded. "The Druze believe that for centuries their male dead have been reincarnated in China for just this purpose."

"And how better and faster to move such an army than by rail?" added Ganelon.

"Indeed, so you may live to see exciting times. Well, I leave all that to you. Goodbye, Ambrose." Ganelon went down on one knee to receive the old priest's blessing. Then Father Sylvanus went back into his metal hermitage.

Ganelon returned to the retreat house with a troubled mind. Since the death of China's president Sun Yat-sen several years ago he'd heard rumors that Fong-Smythe had forged an alliance with the country's most powerful warlords, for what purpose he hadn't discovered. If an army did come out of China, would it be Fong-Smythe's?

Ganelon started dressing for dinner early. Knotting his tie at the window, he noticed Timmons and Massoudi below him on the flagstone walk in animated conversation as the twilight deepened. He couldn't hear anything. But then he saw Timmons hold his hand out, thumb and fingers pointing down at the knuckles, making the Dragon's Claw, the sign of the Fongs, the thumb buried deep wherever the clan leader was and each finger in one of the world's four corners. Massoudi shook his head at the claw in disbelief. But clearly it left him unsettled. If Timmons connected the Baron with the Fongs he'd have gone a long way to disqualifying Waldteufel for the Persian job.

Ganelon watched as Massoudi and Timmons went their separate ways. Then he saw Waldteufel, ever the lurker, step from behind a nearby willow and glare in the direction the Englishman had gone.

As the detective finished dressing there was a knock. Timmons stood in the doorway with a bottle of scotch under one arm, a gazogene under the other, and carrying two glasses. "What'd you say to a drink before dinner?" he asked.

Ganelon invited the Wing Commander in.

As he made the drinks Timmons said, "You know, there's much more involved here than jobs for redundant aviators or the sale of surplus aircraft or how a Persian strongman controls his trackless empire." He passed Ganelon his drink and gestured at the wall as if it were a map of Asia. "They used to call it the Great Game. Persia lies athwart Britain's road to India and it keeps the Russians away from their long-sought-after warm-water port." He lit a cigarette. "The British have much history in the area. And the Russians. Before nineteen seventeen the Persian army was officered by Russians who trained the Shah himself."

"Sounds like you know what you're talking about," said Ganelon.

"A friend in high places filled me in on things when he heard I might be heading to that neck of the woods."

Ganelon nodded as if he accepted Timmons's explanation. But all it did was convince him that the man was British Secret Service. "By the way," he asked, "when did you see Shypoke for the last time?"

Timmons shrugged. "Last night I met with the Anglo-Persian Oil people. I hoped they might persuade General Massoudi to favor my people for the flying part. I thought I heard someone outside the window. When I looked I saw Shypoke listening at Father Boniface's window. Why, I don't know. It was none of my business."

As soon as Timmons left, Ganelon hurried off to the dining room hoping to get the chair next to Khalila at the Cairo to Cathay Railroad table. The four of them made a jolly bunch. When different nationalities gather they often find common ground by telling humorous stories about the English. When Ganelon's turn came he quoted Alphonse Allais' remark, "Queer people, the English. Whereas we in France name our public places after famous victories—Rue de Rocroy, Place Iéna, Avenue de Wagram—the English insist on naming theirs after famous defeats—Trafalgar Square, Waterloo Station, and so on." Khalila's laughter rang silver in his ears.

Then he saw Jerome at a corner table throw down his napkin and leave the dining room and noticed for the first time that the pilot's friend and table companion Timmons wasn't there. Excusing himself, Ganelon rose and went after Jerome.

As he fell in step with him the pilot said, "I went by Timmons's room on my way to dinner. No answer. I figured he'd gone down ahead. When he wasn't at our table I decided he'd been side-tracked. But not for this long. There's one man who really likes his rations."

At Timmons's room Ganelon turned the knob and the door swung open. The Englishman lay stretched out on the floor amid a wreckage of bottles and glasses, dead from a blow to the back of the head. The killer must have been waiting behind the door when Timmons returned from Ganelon's room.

Noticing something odd about the dead man's large aviator's wrist watch, Ganelon checked it, hoping it might have stopped during the assault, giving a clue to the time of death. But the watch was still running. It had just lost its crystal.

Grim-faced, Jerome looked down at the dead body. "My friend deserved better than this," he said.

Inspector Flanel arrived quickly, gaiters and all. He interrogated Ganelon and Jerome. Then they left him hunkered down viewing the crime scene from multiple angles and turning things over with his stick.

After compline, a procession of monks carrying fat candles set out for the hollow oak Father Boniface had decided was St. Magnus's Tree. Those guests who wished to come along fell in behind, dressed for the cool night air. They included Khalila and her Cairo to Cathay people, the Baron, General Massoudi, and Ganelon and Jerome, who arrived at the last minute.

They entered the woods and proceeded to Father Sylvanus's hermitage. After a bit, when no one appeared, the retreat master said, "I guess the good Father still doesn't believe my tree is the kind our founder used. He may regret not joining us." Then he ordered the procession to continue.

They started out on the same path they had taken that afternoon to the crash site. But for Ganelon the trees loomed larger now on either side and seemed to fall in behind them as they passed. He chalked this up to the darkness, the candlelight, and Father Sylvanus's stories. But he didn't remember so many tree roots in the path. The stumbling monks uttered gentle appeals to this saint or that as their candle flames sketched abrupt patterns on the darkness. More forceful expletives came from the guests in a Babel of languages to which an owl or two uttered replies. Just beyond the wreckage of the Russian airplane a breeze sprang up, guttering the candles. Protective hands cupped the flames, dimming the light even more.

At last the procession reached a place where the bracken had been scythed and raked away around an ancient oak standing alone some twenty feet off the path. It had a large waist-high hole in its trunk. The monks turned in and gathered in a semicircle about the tree.

Father Boniface produced a pocket watch. "The hour of our blessed founder's prayer approaches," he said. "Forgive us if we of his order listen first." Then he directed the monks, in alphabetical turns, to put their heads in the hollow oak, tapping each on the shoulder when his time was up. So the minutes passed. None heard the expected voice. Pulling his own head out of the tree, Father Boniface shook it sadly and signaled the guests to take their turns. Ganelon went last. The hollow in the tree was silent as a tomb. Then the hour had passed.

The downcast procession returned, more strung-out and stumbling than before. As the lights of the retreat house came in view they discovered that Baron Waldteufel had gone missing somewhere along the way. Arming himself with a candle, Jerome volunteered to go back and try to find him.

When the others reached the millpond they found a monk with his head and shoulders inside a hollow willow near the one in whose roots Shypoke's body had been entangled. When Father Boniface touched him and said Saint Magnus's hour had passed, the body slid from the willow and onto the grass. It was Father Sylvanus. The dead priest's face wore a smile of final contentment.

Ganelon asked, "Does the smile mean he learned Saint Magnus's prayer?"

"Oh, the prayer is no secret," said Father Boniface. "No, his joy must mean he heard it spoken in our founder's very voice. You see, late in life Saint Magnus turned mystical in an attempt to discover the unknowable side of the Almighty, the *deus abscondus*, the hidden God. He rose from his deathbed and had a disciple help him to a hollow tree nearby, and in a 'Hello, Central, Get Me Heaven' kind of thing, he stuck his head inside and shouted: 'God, Whoever You are, I love You.' "

The monks carried Father Sylvanus's body into the chapel. The guests returned to the retreat house, except for Ganelon and Khalila. Ganelon followed the body out of respect for his teacher. Khalila came, too, saying, "The Cairo to Cathay people have accepted our terms. I leave for home in the morning. But I'd like a chance to see the famous window by candlelight."

Half an hour later Ganelon and Khalila left the monks to their vigil over Father Sylvanus's body. As they came outside they saw Inspector Flanel heading in their direction.

"I hear Baron Waldteufel wandered off and Jerome's gone back to find him," said the policeman. "When he does I intend to arrest the baron for murder. He was killing off his rivals for the Persian air force job. He had the motive and the opportunity to siphon off Commissar Ivanov's gasoline. And I have proof positive he killed Wing Commander Timmons. During my careful examination of the broken glass in Timmons's room I found this, the baron's monocle." Flanel opened his hand triumphantly to reveal the crystal from Timmons's watch.

Just then Jerome emerged from the forest darkness. He was alone. "I went as far back as the last spot I remembered seeing Waldteufel with the procession. No baron."

Examining the night, Flanel decided it was too late to start a search. He promised to return in the morning.

Ganelon walked Khalila back to the retreat house. "Flanel's a very lucky man, being right for so wrong a reason," he said. "He may make Chief Inspector yet." Then he added, "We have to ask ourselves, what's so important about the Persian air force job to make it worth killing two people?"

"Three, counting Shypoke," said Khalila.

"Shypoke was a mistake all round. The man wanted to eavesdrop on the Anglo-Persian Oil people's meeting but got the wrong window. The baron thought

Shypoke was listening in on his telephone call to England. That's why he killed him. Know the name Dorian Fong-Smythe?"

When Khalila shook her head, Ganelon told himself she soon would if she came into partnership with him. Then he said, "He's Waldteufel's employer. So why's it so important to Fong-Smythe that the baron gets the Persian job?"

Early the next morning Ganelon and Khalila led Flanel on the route the procession had taken and described the events of the night before. On the way the inspector looked for traces of the baron's wandering off. They had not expected to get as far as the hollow oak. But that was where they discovered Waldteufel dead next to the tree, the blade of a scythe driven through his body.

Flanel waved them behind him and studied the scene, stroking his chin.

As Ganelon looked at the wooden-handled scythe he suddenly remembered Father Sylvanus's remark about what the trees had said about the woodman's axe: "*Look, look, part of it is one of us.*"

After a bit Flanel said, "Here's what happened. On the way back to the retreat house the Baron got separated from the procession. In the dark and half blind—for let us not forget, I found his monocle at the crime scene—he was beset by his guilty conscience and panicked. He started to run. As often happens in these cases, he went around in a circle and came back to the hollow oak, plowing headlong into a lower limb. See the mark of a blow to his head. Stunned, he accidentally fell on the scythe a careless monk left behind after clearing the bramble around the tree. Case closed."

"A wound toward the back of the head is tough to come by running full tilt into a tree limb," observed Ganelon.

Flanel gave a dismissive laugh. "As he ran he heard one of the owls you spoke of. Wild-eyed, Waldteufel looked back over his shoulder toward the sound. Bang!"

Ganelon and Khalila exchanged glances. Then, promising to send two monks back with the wheelbarrow, they left Flanel hunkered down examining the scene of the crime.

They walked in silence for a long distance, neither wanting to bring up the terrible murder. At last Khalila said, "I can't imagine Jerome a killer."

"That scythe sure didn't walk back there on its own," said Ganelon. "I saw it at the crash site on our way to the tree. It was right where the monks left it when they emptied their wheelbarrow to load up Ivanov's body. Look, when the procession started back Jerome got Waldteufel to hang back on some pretext and hit him a good one, leaving him for dead. On the way back Jerome had second thoughts about whether he'd killed him or not. He volunteered to find the baron so he could finish the job, picking up the scythe on the way."

"Still—" protested Khalila.

"Waldteufel and Jerome spent the entire war trying to kill each other off. Those are things you can set aside in peacetime. But it's something else when an old enemy kills your best friend."

Later that morning Ganelon was waiting, suitcase in hand, beside the blue roadster when Khalila came out of the retreat house dressed for travel in a cloche hat and a coat with a fur collar. A monk followed behind carrying her suitcases.

She was surprised to see him. "I thought we'd said our goodbyes," she said while her baggage was being loaded.

They had. But Ganelon had something he couldn't ask her until he'd gotten his Hrosco back from Father Boniface. He gave his cockeyed grin. Would she, as a professional courtesy, one private detective to another, give him a lift back to San Sebastiano? "I promise you a good lunch, a tour of our little city, and a business proposition you might find interesting."

"But what about your big white car?" she asked.

"I'm leaving it here," said Ganelon. "Tomorrow's the feast of Saint Fiacre, patron saint of taxi drivers, when the monks do the Blessing of the Automobiles. Afterward Father Carlus will drive the Terrapin into town for me. His assistant will follow in the touring car to make the Imperial Airways pickup. Carlus will go back with him."

"Isn't Saint Fiacre patron of gardeners?" asked Khalila suspiciously.

Ganelon grinned again, a bit more urgently this time. "Some saints wear two halos," he said. "So is it a deal?"

She raised an amused eyebrow. "A deal," she said and slid behind the steering wheel. Ganelon got in on the passenger side, stowing his suitcase behind the seat.

As they sped off toward San Sebastiano, Ganelon said, "By the way, I spoke to Jerome just now. He asked General Massoudi to let him put together the Shah's air force using the San Sebastiano pilots he'd led during the war. Massoudi agreed."

Talk of Jerome still bothered Khalila. But Ganelon knew that any army coming out of China on the Cairo to Cathay Railroad would need control of Persian airspace. Intentionally or not, Jerome had frustrated Fong-Smythe's grand design. And anyone who could do that, Ganelon considered his friend.

As the roadster passed the new orchard an old man working among the trees waved a brown arm at them. When Khalila pretended not to see him and smiled down into her fur collar, Ganelon leaned over and gave the horn a smart *beep-beep*.

AMBROSE GANELON IV

Coins in the Frascati Fountain

T HE AGENCE GANELON, San Sebastiano's celebrated detective agency, operated on the old vaudeville maxim: never follow one banjo act with another banjo act.

Ambrose Ganelon I, who founded the agency in 1840 when the tiny principality reigned as the Riviera's most fashionable watering place, had been a detective of the armchair school. In fez and carpet slippers he would sit making oboe reeds while the rich, the humble, and the perplexed Inspectors of Police filed by. They told their tangled stories and departed, comforted by soulful notes from the detective's oboe. Those wood-sounds fell sweetly on the ears of law-abiding citizens, but they set the Underworld's teeth on edge. Criminals shunned the rue Blondin whenever Ganelon was solving a case.

Ambrose Ganelon II, who took over the agency in 1881, had been a pioneer in the field of scientific investigation. He was the author of classic works on pathology and criminal psychology, along with a number of handbooks of a more practical nature: *A Policeman's Guide to Human Hair*, for example, and *Footprints and What They Tell Us*. But there was a hidden side to his life. Among the family's most treasured possessions was a letter of commendation from Prince Rene written in invisible ink. Yes, Ganelon had been the mysterious "G," founding head of the Slyboots, as San Sebastiano's feared and respected Intelligence Service is still popularly known.

In 1922 Ambrose Ganelon III brought a new style to the agency, combining the mental powers of his predecessors with a rough-and-tumble approach to detection. He and his two-fisted operatives interviewed clients while wearing fedoras on the backs of their heads and stretching their feet on the desks. Bottles of Scotch and voluptuous blonde secretaries were standard office equipment. Outside of business hours, however, Ambrose Ganelon III neither spoke out of the side of his mouth nor leered at beautiful women. He was, in fact, a gentle, sober husband, preoccupied with bringing up his son in all the traditions of the Ganelon family.

How proud he had been when little Ambrose, at the age of three, had interrupted his reading aloud from Great-grandfather's memoirs (the chapter entitled *My Most Baffling Case*) and identified the fat old sailor as the mad strangler ten paragraphs before Great-grandfather revealed the solution. How proud again when at the age most children were just learning to read, little Ambrose had stood at his Grandfather's knee and broken the Italian naval code.

Watching the boy grow to manhood, Ambrose Ganelon III realized that he had sired the greatest sleuth of his line, perhaps in the history of detection. There was only one question in his mind. "My dear boy," he once wrote to his son who was away adding to San Sebastiano's Olympic gold medals, "Your Great-grandfather worked from an armchair, your Grandfather from a laboratory. I, as you know, belong to the two-fisted school. You will be the greatest detective of us all. But of what style, I wonder?"

Beyond the harbor entrance the luxury yacht La Pomodora rode at anchor, huge and immaculately white. Ambrose Ganelon, the fourth of that name, sat in the approaching motor launch with his right leg crossed carefully over his left. On leaving his office, Ganelon had discovered pink flesh peeking through his threadbare left knee. There had only been enough time to ink in a dark blue spot on his kneecap. Ambrose Ganelon IV had a style of his own: he was the first of his family to be a detective of the impoverished school.

Even in his father's day the agency had experienced a marked decline in business. "I am happy to report that this year, as last, we have not had a major case," wrote the two-fisted detective that summer to his vacationing son touring the Underworlds of London, Paris, and Amsterdam disguised as a brass-knuckles salesman. "After three generations I think the Agence Ganelon has taught the criminal to shun our beloved principality."

But it wasn't until his father's tragic death that Ganelon IV came to understand the real meaning of these words. Interrupting his study of Mafia involvement in the opium trade, he flew home to take over the agency, leaving the Hong Kong police with irrefutable proof that behind the plastic surgery Mao Tse Tung was actually a Sicilian named "Peaches" Carboni.

For the next few years Ganelon watched the family money melt away as he struggled to keep the agency's door open. He reduced his staff, then reduced it again. At last he moved quietly from the sumptuous first-floor quarters to a cramped little one-desk office and shabby bed-sitting room under the eaves. But at least the bronze plaque with the name *Agence Ganelon* remained on the building on the rue Blondin. Ganelon knew that if that plaque ever disappeared, the master criminals of the world would descend on the prosperous little principality in force.

Apollo Apollinaris, a chubby little man in dark glasses and a yachting cap heavy with gold braid, was waiting at the top of the gangway. "Welcome aboard La

Pomodora, Monsieur Ganclon," he said with unconcealed awe. "The best I dared hope for was one of your top operatives."

"In matters involving our leading citizen I prefer to handle things myself," said Ganelon. Apollinaris owned half of San Sebastiano, including the Casino. But that was only a small part of his vast financial empire. Apollinaris-Arabian Petroleum, for example, shipped oil on Apollinaris Line tankers built from plate supplied by Apollinaris Steel using ore from Apollinaris Mines in Labrador.

As he led Ganelon the considerable distance to the afterdeck, the multimillionaire said, "Your dynamic father once saved me from slow arsenic poisoning at the hands of my wife of the moment, a beautiful woman with a passion for Spanish chauffeurs. Your father's death saddened me. Most unfortunate."

One day at the agency, Ganelon's father had stepped in to break up a fist fight at the water cooler. (Several years of inactivity had frayed the tempers of his hard-hitting staff.) Suddenly, operatives were pouring out of their cubicles, all aching for a good melee. They fought each other until exhausted and, bloody and grinning, got to their feet, smoothed the dents out of their fedoras, and discovered Ganelon's father at the bottom of the pile, dead of a broken neck.

"May I present Miss Billie Baxter and Miss Mitzi Latour of my secretarial staff?" said Apollinaris, when they reached the afterdeck. Two bikinied sunbathers wriggled their bodies in a languid greeting. "And over there is the notorious Jo Jo Mouton of Marseilles," said the multi-millionaire.

Leaning back with his elbows on the rail was a burly, red-faced man in a homburg and dark glasses. In spite of the heat he wore a camel's-hair overcoat which almost hid the bulge of a pistol. Ganelon guessed it was a Hunsecker-Bowles DeLuxe which came with a barrel extension, silencer, telescopic sights, and a holster that doubled as a shoulder stock. "Jo Jo is with the Strongarm Corporation," explained Apollinaris.

Ganelon frowned. The Strongarmers described themselves as international trouble-shooters in the areas of industrial security, labor relations, and lobbying. In other words, they provided their clients with good old-fashioned protection, gangs of strike breakers, and a mercenary army to overthrow uncooperative governments. Whatever business the Strongarm Corporation had with Apollinaris, its presence in San Sebastiano was an affront to the Ganelon escutcheon.

The multimillionaire sat the detective down at a canopied table and called for drinks. "Ah, have you injured your arm?" he asked with a solicitous frown.

"It's nothing, I assure you," said Ganelon who had twisted his arm slightly to hide the frayed sleeve.

"Only a flesh wound, eh?" said Apollinaris. "Ah, how I envy the exciting life you lead! Crime, violence, the world of deep passions!"

"It all becomes quite humdrum," said Ganelon, more interested in the cigarette that Apollinaris was about to offer him from a jewel-studded gold case. For reasons of economy the detective hadn't had a cigarette for two days.

Apollinaris stopped in the act and snapped the cigarette case shut. "No," he insisted. "This is the humdrum life." He made a gesture with the cigarette case that took in the yacht and perhaps even included Miss Billie and Miss Mitzi. "A multimillionaire, Monsieur Ganelon, is a man who no longer has dreams, because whatever he wants he can have. Paradoxically, he is condemned to live out the dreams of others. At this very moment we are riding at anchor on one of the dreams of any number of ambitious young men. In many ways it is more their dream than mine. For when the sea rises and falls they don't get seasick. They may dream of dining on fine food from plates of platinum, but I'm the one who gets the indigestion."

Apollinaris leaned forward with the open cigarette case. "Does that sound like self-pity?" he asked. Before Ganelon could take a cigarette, Apollinaris snapped the case shut as if to punish himself. "Yes, I suppose it does," he sighed. "But you know, Monsieur Ganelon, I wasn't always as rich as Croesus. I have known hunger and deprivation. At seventeen I was making a meager living as a tourist guide. Then came the fateful day! I found myself guide to a dour old Scot who felt he wasn't getting his money's worth unless I could answer questions about every building or statue we passed. I was not, I might add, above inventing stories just to satisfy him.

"We had just visited our colorful old market where you can buy those delightfully embroidered pincushions in the shape of our patron saint and were proceeding to the Herpetological Museum by way of the Place Frascati. Now in those days the fountain was quite neglected and overgrown with moss. Apart from some vague legends connecting the fountain with death, I knew nothing about it."

"Undaunted, I told my inquisitive Scot that according to legend, if you made a wish and threw a coin in the fountain, your wish would come true. To my astonishment he unsnapped his leather change-purse and threw in a coin. Such are the effects of legends on a man from a country full of ghosties and ghoulies and things that go bump in the night.

"I tried the story out on other tourists. Invariably it evoked a coin. By going back later to collect the money I was soon able to lease the fountain from the puzzled city fathers for a small annual fee.

"With the lease in my pocket and some small financial backing from the adjoining cafés I had postcards made, picturing 'San Sebastiano's Famous Wishing

Fountain' and describing the legend. These I gave away free to the postcard vendors. By the next season I was able to commission a hungry song writer to set the legend to music. An arrangement of *One Coin in the Fountain* for mandolin and accordion became quite popular. And so the story spread and the fountain began to be included in the guide books.

"Not long after, a lady novelist wrote a best seller about a poor American governess who throws a coin in the famous Frascati Fountain and then marries her employer, a dissolute Italian count who, under her saving influence, turns to writing wholesome tracts for the edification of the working class. The movie version, by the way, starred Mary Pickford.

"I could go on and on. Today, as you know, thousands of tourists come each year to throw their coins in the fountain. If they wonder about it at all, I suppose they think the coins go to some worthy charity. In actual fact, the coins go to me. Or at least they did. Monsieur Ganelon, someone is stealing from the Frascati Fountain! I am losing as much as three hundred francs a day."

Ganelon had hoped for a case worthy of his scintillating powers of deduction. The disappointment showed on his face.

"Perhaps the baffling nature of the crime will intrigue you," said Apollinaris. "After all, how can the coins be stolen? A policeman guards them from eight in the morning until twelve thirty at night. Each evening the fountain is floodlit. And since I noticed the shortage, I, Apollo Apollinaris, the multimillionaire, put on hip boots and personally clean out the fountain with a broom each night at twelve fifteen. You see, those coins are especially precious to me because the fountain was the first step to my fabulous fortune."

"How can you be so sure you are being robbed?" asked Ganelon, stifling a yawn.

"My accountants have worked out an interesting corelation between the number of tourists who visit San Sebastiano and the amount of money that will be thrown into the fountain," said Apollinaris. "Within a franc or two it's amazingly accurate." The multimillionaire's face brightened. "How about this?" he said, hoping to kindle the detective's interest. "The shortages began two months ago, the same day the body of an unidentified man was found floating in the fountain."

"Cause of death?" asked Ganelon crisply.

Apollinaris looked crestfallen. "Pneumonia," he admitted. "And a month before that it was an unidentified woman, dead of a liver condition." He shook his head sadly. "The police found no evidence of foul play in either case."

Apollinaris leaned forward confidentially. "I'll come clean, Monsieur Ganelon," he said. "I have another reason for wanting you to take this case. For some time now, the Strongarm Corporation has been pressing me to let them represent my interests here and abroad in matters such as this. In fact, they have been quite insistent."

Apollinaris glanced over at Jo Jo Mouton who was staring up at a pure white gull hanging in the air above the yacht. Apollinaris smiled slyly. "I hit upon a very clever way to stop all their pestering," he said. "I told them that I would contract for their services on one condition: that they can end the mysterious thefts of coins from the Frascati Fountain before the Agence Ganelon can." Apollinaris struggled to swallow a laugh. "And they fell for it," he giggled. "Please accept the challenge, Monsieur Ganelon, and rid me of these larcenous leeches."

Ganelon knew of the Strongarm Corporation's unpleasant habit of devouring those who employed it. Once it got its teeth into Apollinaris, it would pick him clean. Suddenly, more was at stake than a few coins in a fountain or even the Apollinaris multimillions. San Sebastiano could not be allowed to fall into the hands of the Strongarm Corporation. "You have convinced me," said Ganelon.

"Good," said Apollinaris. "Just between the two of us, I find Strongarm's methods a bit—" A pistol shot rang out and a white, feathered bundle fell to the deck. Mouton scratched his nose and returned the Hunsecker-Bowles to its holster. "—a bit sudden," Apollinaris finished.

Former Inspector Hector Jouvet spent his retirement at the Café de l'Esperance, always sitting, melancholy and erect, at the same sidewalk table. He rose respectfully and wiped his mouth with a napkin as Ganelon stepped from the little green car. The old police inspector revered the Ganelon family, particularly Great-grandfather Ganelon, in whose honor Jouvet had once taken up the oboe. But an ultimatum from his landlady had cut short his musical studies. Jouvet was now modestly proud that his idol's Great-grandson had called him for information.

"My dear Monsieur Ganelon," he said, "won't you join me? The tripe is delicious."

Ganelon declined, preferring to conserve what little operating capital he had. "About the bodies in the fountain," he asked.

"As for the woman," said Jouvet, taking up his knife and fork again, "the information is a bit thin. Estimated age: sixty-five to seventy; cause of death: chronic liver condition. Clothes worn but well kept. No identification papers. The body was buried in Poitier's Field. As for the man—" Jouvet stopped. "I believe we are being observed."

A bull-necked man with a broken nose, a narrow forehead, and a scowl was sitting two tables away. Like Mouton, he wore a homburg and a camel's-hair coat.

Ganelon nodded. The man had followed him in a black limousine.

"Do you think he can read lips?" asked Jouvet.

"I'd be surprised if he can read anything," said Ganelon. "And now about the body of the man."

"I think I can be a little more help to you there," said Jouvet. "As you may know, I give a weekly workshop on identification methods at the Police Academy. As luck would have it, I used that very body as a classroom project.

"Here's what we had to go on. Estimated age: seventy to seventy-five; cause of death: pneumonia. Clothes worn but well kept. Shoes cheap but recently resoled. No identification papers. Well developed torso and heavily callused hands. A curious ring of light calluses in the socket of the right eye. Bronze filings under the fingernails.

"I gave the shoes to my cadets and sent them off. Here we were quite fortunate. A shoemaker in the rue Scribe not only identified the repair work as his own, but knew the dead man by name. In fact, they had been in the baby-shoe bronzing business together for several years. Customers would leave the baby shoes with the shoemaker and then the dead man—he called himself Dupont but spoke with a marked German accent—would pick them up and return them bronzed. A vanishing craft in our time. In all San Sebastiano I know of only one other place— a little watch-repair shop near the Bourse—that bronzes baby shoes."

"To get back to Dupont," said Ganelon, a bit impatiently.

"Apparently this Dupont was something of an eccentric," continued Jouvet. "Hard of hearing, short-spoken, and preoccupied with his own thoughts which were of a rather moralistic nature. If the shoemaker asked him how things were going, for example, Dupont would shake his head and mutter, 'War is wrong' or 'Sloth doesn't work.' Or sometimes he'd smile and say, 'Temperance is good' or 'Justice has been done.'

"This evidence of strong religious convictions may, I believe, explain how Dupont's body came to be in the fountain. That very morning, when the shoemaker arrived at seven thirty to open his shop, he expected to find Dupont waiting for him, as he always was except when the weather was bad. 'My Fair-Weather Friend' was the shoemaker's nickname for Dupont. Instead, he found a parcel of bronzed baby shoes on his doorstep. I think we can assume that Dupont, feeling death approach in the night, felt compelled in conscience to leave his sickbed and make his final delivery. Perhaps he stopped on his way home to drink of the fountain's life-giving waters, died, and fell into the pool."

Jouvet looked pleased with himself as he pushed his empty plate aside. Ganelon tensed. But instead of pulling out his cigarettes the old sleuth ordered a slice of

Camembert. "But who was this Dupont and where did he come from?" Jouvet went on. "I believe I can answer these questions in a manner not unworthy of your Great-grandfather himself.

"Dupont was actually a Prussian nobleman—note the accent and the callus marks around the eye, the marks of a monocle. For generations his family had served the Fatherland in the artillery—note that Dupont was hard of hearing, an occupational hazard of that branch of the military. Following the ancient practice, the family supplied their own cannon, a bronze heirloom, more a symbol of their readiness to serve than anything else.

"Then, during the First World War, this Dupont, this Baron von Whatever-his-name-was, sees the flower of Europe's manhood destroyed in the carnage of the trenches. Revolted by war, he gives up his titles and estates and experiences a religious conversion à la Tolstoy. Meditating on the evils of war, pondering the other great moral issues of our time, he wanders from country to country dragging the family cannon behind him. For he has made a vow: he will not rest until he has melted down that instrument of war and death into symbols of life and hope—into bronzed baby shoes to inspire proud parents with joyful memories." Jouvet stopped, his voice thick with emotion.

The silence roused Ganelon from his thoughts. "You mentioned a watch-repair shop that bronzed baby shoes," he said. "Are you free to undertake a small assignment for the agency?"

Back at the rue Blondin, Ganelon parked in front of the drug store and waved gratefully to Georges, the pharmacist, who had volunteered his little green car when the business of inking in the kneecap had put Ganelon behind schedule. The driver of the Strongarm limousine, which had followed him doggedly from the café, scowled thoughtfully.

Under the eaves again, the detective dined on his last two eggs (hard-boiled), searched unsuccessfully through his wardrobe of disguises for a stray cigarette, and spent the rest of the evening poring over his files on Apollinaris and the Strongarm Corporation. Ganelon didn't feel particularly challenged by Strongarm's Board of Directors: Allister Fong, Hans Brunner, and Blacky S. F. X. Ryan, though each had their reasons for hating San Sebastiano and the Ganelon family. But he didn't underestimate Strongarm's Chairman of the Board, Count Myshkin, the frail, white-haired old man who had already matched wits with two generations of Ganelons.

In 1906 Myshkin, then a young officer in the Czar's Intelligence Service, had attempted to realize Russia's centuries-old dream, a naval base on the Mediterranean. From the bowels of the pocket battleship Vladivostok, then on a courtesy visit to San Sebastiano, two Cossack regiments, horses and all, were to spill out and occupy the defenseless principality—defenseless because the wily Myshkin had secretly under-written an American tour for the San Sebastiano Opera Company, featuring its celebrated production of *Aïda* in which the principality's entire army appeared as spear carriers.

Only Grandfather Ganelon and the Slyboots stood in the way. They knew that Myshkin was in San Sebastiano posing as the recreation officer of the Vladivostok. But they did not know why. Or why the battleship was taking on such large quantities of oats—65.3 times more than was needed for the Russian sailors' kasha. Then the Slyboots' Russian Room, which monitored the Czar's troop deployment on a large pin-filled map, reported the disappearance of two Cossack regiments. Putting the oats and the Cossack horses together, Grandfather Ganelon suddenly realized the audacity of the Russian scheme.

Fortunately, Myshkin's timetable was delayed by a three-day run of luck at the Casino. When, at the insistence of his Cossack companions, he cashed in his chips and left, his carriage was followed by another. At that time of night the Central Post Office Building was empty except for Pierre Boulanger, the ancient telephone operator. Boulanger had guaranteed himself a job for life by removing all identification from the jacks and holes of the switchboard, the nerve center of San Sebastiano's communications with the outside world. With Boulanger dead, Myshkin would signal the attack with a flare gun.

Grandfather Ganelon and his Slyboots dashed upstairs to find Boulanger mortally wounded on the floor. (From his hospital bed he was later to blackmail San Sebastiano into giving him a State funeral before he would teach a successor how to run the switchboard.) The Cossacks turned and snarled, but they were no match for the Slyboots. In desperation Myshkin tried to fire the flare gun through the window but missed. As the room exploded into phosphorescence he jumped from the window into the Cornichon, the principality's gentle little river, and vanished beneath the surface, dragged down by the weight of his Casino winnings. Or so it was thought. As for the Vladivostok, she waited two more days for a signal that never came. Finally the Cossacks mutinied and forced the captain to put out to sea so that they would be home for Russian Christmas.

In later years Myshkin popped up again, always the mastermind behind some devilish plan, always a worthy and menacing adversary. And of late there were stories that he was the secret kingpin of Soviet espionage in the West.

What if San Sebastiano should now fall into Communist hands? Could the free world afford to lose the tiny principality which a gracious American Secretary of State had once described as "that most precious jewel in the diadem of the North Atlantic Treaty Organization"?

At 11:30 Ganelon set off to witness the collecting of coins from the fountain. Across the street, Georges, the pharmacist, was about to drive off in his little green car. He waved to Ganelon and stepped on the starter. The car exploded, vanishing in a cloud of thick smoke. Georges staggered from the wreckage in tatters and started kicking furiously at what was left of the right front tire. "It isn't supposed to do that!" he shouted indignantly.

Ganelon hurried on his way, followed by the bull-necked Strongarm man on foot. The great detective knew the bomb had been meant for him. Apparently the Strongarm Corporation was prepared to kill to win its race with the Agence Ganelon.

Ganelon led his heavy-footed pursuer down one narrow street after another as he revolved the case in his mind. What did he have so far? Two bodies in the fountain. Was the first connected with the second? Was the second—Dupont's— connected with the thefts? Or was it only coincidence that his body was found there on the very day that the shortages began? And who was Dupont?

Ganelon shook his head. Poor Jouvet. Ganelon's Great-grandfather always liked to compare an armchair detective with a landscape painter. The genius of both, he insisted, resided in the seat of the pants. Both must know *where* to sit. Strange words from a man who seldom left his armchair. But of course in his own case he meant taking up the correct position before an interior landscape of supplied information.

Jouvet had set up his easel so close to the calluses in the dead man's eye socket that they gave his picture a very Prussian cast, complete with antique cannon, war in the trenches, and an earnest vow.

Stepping back a bit, the landscape became less coherent and considerably less romantic. Dupont was an old baby-shoe bronzer with a stock of commonplace aphorisms. ("Sloth doesn't work," though undoubtedly true, was hardly profound.) And Dupont's build and callused hands—which Jouvet insisted were the result of dragging around a bronze cannon—certainly evidenced a more strenuous profession than baby-shoe bronzing. Perhaps Jouvet's visit to the watch-repair shop would shed more light on Dupont.

Ganelon walked on until, from behind him, he heard the unmistakeable sound of a silencer being fitted onto the barrel of a Hunsecker-Bowles. Turning the next corner quickly, Ganelon ducked into a courtyard doorway. The bull-necked pursuer, Bruno, hurried by, heading straight into San Sebastiano's Armenian quarter, the home of rug merchants like the notorious Leon Barbarian who sat in front of his shop until all hours, begging each passer-by to come in and rob him blind because his wife needed a brain operation. This remark never failed to infuriate Mrs. Barbarian who would burst out of the shop, wild-eyed and incoherent with rage. Barbarian would give a sad little shrug, his point made.

Ganelon retraced his steps in the direction of the Place Frascati.

The Frascati Fountain occupied one side of the cobbled square. Cafés lined the other three. Under the watchful eye of a policeman in summer whites, Ganelon joined the small knot of tourists in front of the floodlit pool.

At the end of the Eighteenth Century the wealthy Frascati family had torn down the simple stones of the original fountain which dated from Phoenician times and commissioned an itinerant fountain sculptor and clockmaker named Mathias Swartzwald to construct a monument worthy of the family name. The theme of the sculptured figures was "The Wedding of Neptune and the Cornichon." The Sea God and a matronly woman representing the River Goddess were the central figures and of heroic size. Beneath their clasped hands water cascaded down from a grotto into the fountain's oval pool. At Neptune's back were a dozen man-sized demigods of the sea mounted on plunging dolphins, seahorses, and ponderous terrapins. The River Goddess was attended by nereids carrying distaffs, butter churns, stalks of wheat, and other objects representing the various activities of San Sebastiano.

Behind the statuary rose an eighty-foot clock tower. Below the clock face were two doors through which, as Swartzwald described his conception to the Frascatis, was to appear the most dazzling display of mechanical figures ever designed by man. As the clock struck four, for example, the Four Horsemen of the Apocalypse, done in life-size, would emerge from the right-hand door and, making appropriate gestures, ride slowly across to the door on the left. At seven o'clock the Seven Deadly Sins would appear. At nine, the Nine Muses. And so on. At high noon, in addition to the Twelve Apostles there would be a mechanical re-enactment of the Battle of the Cornichon when the army of San Sebastiano led by Guido Frascati threw back the Moors under Akbar the Cruel.

Swartzwald labored for years. Finally, San Sebastiano gathered in the square to witness the wonderful display of mechanical figures. The clock struck high noon. The right-hand door opened but instead of the Twelve Apostles and the Battle of the Cornichon, the figure of a shepherdess appeared, complete with crook, and crossed slowly to the other door. Surely that couldn't be all. The crowd waited. Even when the sky clouded over no one left the square.

At the stroke of one the door opened again and the figure of a man in a slicker and nor'wester appeared. As he did, rain began to fall. Every hour on the hour from that day forward, the shepherdess appeared if the weather was fair, the man in the slicker if it was foul.

Of course this was much less than the Frascatis had paid for and they tried to lay hands on Swartzwald. But he was nowhere to be found. The most popular version of what happened was that Swartzwald had squandered much of the Frascati money speculating in copper and tin, then fled the city with his family to avoid prosecution ...

Ganelon turned as Mouton and five other men in homburgs and camel's-hair coats emerged from a limousine with much slamming of doors. Mouton lined his men up in front of the fountain. He busied himself adjusting a hat here and a tie there until they were all replicas of himself in various sizes.

At 12:15 a second limousine arrived. The policeman saluted smartly as Apollinaris stepped out, in the company of Miss Billie and Miss Mitzi. "Ah, Monsieur Ganelon, have I kept you waiting? Am I late?" said Apollinaris as he opened the trunk compartment of the limousine. Sitting down on the rear bumper, he pulled on a pair of hip boots and added thoughtfully, "Though perhaps I should be late more often."

"Why do you say that?" asked Ganelon.

"It's an odd thing," said Apollinaris. "A few weeks ago I fell asleep at a testimonial dinner given in my honor by the Friends of the San Sebastiano Zoo. The speeches were particularly long and boring. People tend to go overboard when they want you to give them an elephant. In any event, that night I didn't get here until twelve forty-five."

"You mean the policeman had gone off duty and the coins had been left unguarded?" asked Ganelon.

Apollinaris nodded. "But oddly enough, that was the only time in the past two months that there wasn't a shortage." Ganelon's expression prompted him to add, "Do you find that interesting?"

"Perhaps," said the detective cautiously.

"Well, here we go," said Apollinaris, taking a long-handled broom and stepping into the pool. First he worked across the back of the fountain, carefully overlapping each push of the broom as he waded forward into the water. Then he waded around to the front of the pool and pulled with the broom, raking the coins into the shallow water. There they were scooped into a wire basket and emptied into canvas bags.

Meanwhile, the bull-necked Strongarm man had come into the square carrying a bright red and yellow carpet over his shoulder. "I got it for a song, Jo Jo," he said proudly. "The old geezer's wife needed a brain operation."

"I told you to give You-know-who the business, Bruno," snarled Mouton with a glance in Ganelon's direction. Bruno hung his head and joined the circle of glowering Strongarm men who were placing canvas bags filled with coins in the trunk compartment of the multi-millionaire's limousine. When the trunk was locked, two of the Strongarm men got up on the rear bumper. Ganelon and Mouton joined Apollinaris and his party in the limousine. Bruno and the rest of the Strongarm men pulled up behind in their car.

At 12:30 the floodlights on the fountain went out and the policeman headed homeward. A moment later the caravan of cars set off for the Banque Apollinaris.

"Here is something I forgot to mention, Monsieur Ganelon," said Apollinaris. "Tomorrow in Chicago the Strongarm board meeting will be turned into an early-morning Think Tank devoted to our mysterious thefts of coins, with all the directors spitballing ideas back and forth and generally gray-celling the whole shenanigan. They will have Jo Jo's reports, photographs of the fountain from every angle, and even a scale replica of the Place Frascati. And of course Jo Jo will be in touch with them by phone. I might add that Strongarm's Mr. Fong called me this morning regarding the grille I installed over the outlet pipe in the pool so coins wouldn't be washed into the sewer. He—"

"Hey!" protested Mouton.

"No, Jo Jo, fair is fair," said Apollinaris. "Your Mr. Fong jumped the gun a bit, starting to spitball before Monsieur Ganelon had agreed to accept the case. The grille is six feet square, made of half-inch bars covered with a substantial mesh and bolted to the floor of the pool. Since the outlet pipe is only two feet in diameter, Mr. Fong wanted to know why the grille was so large. I explained that the pool drops off sharply as it approaches the outlet pipe. The larger grille makes it more convenient for sweeping out. Unless I miss my guess, Mr. Fong thinks our thief is getting at the coins from the sewer system."

They arrived at the Banque Apollinaris where two armed guards with an escort of Strongarm men carried the money directly to the counting room. The others waited in the limousine.

"Of course Fong's mind would run to sewers," thought Ganelon. Fong's Grandfather, the infamous Dr. Ludwig Fong, Eurasian arch-criminal and would-be world dictator, had once attempted to blow the crowned heads of Europe to smithereens as they gathered in San Sebastiano for the coronation of Prince Adalbert II. Becoming curious during one of his solitary walks about the abundance of water rats in the flag-decked streets, Great-grandfather Ganelon had entered the city's sewer system where, after a lengthy search, he located Fong just about to set a match to the fuse of an immense explosive charge while the *Coronation March* thundered down from the mighty cathedral organ overhead.

The warped genius led the detective on a wild chase through the strange, dank world of subterranean waterways and dripping passages. Cornered at last, Fong had grappled with the aging detective on a ledge above the main sewage canal. Both had lost their footing, fallen, and been carried out to sea by the rushing water. An ironic way for an armchair detective to meet his end.

A guard approached the limousine and handed Apollinaris a piece of paper. The multimillionaire read it and spread his hands. "We are short nearly three hundred francs," he said.

Ganelon declined Apollinaris' offer of a ride home, choosing to walk in order to collect his thoughts. But he had hardly gone half a block when he heard the heavy-footed Bruno behind him. The detective turned off onto the Boulevard Tancredi whose street life and crowded cafés would frustrate Bruno's evil designs for the moment and give Ganelon time to speculate.

Ganelon was interested by the fact that the fountain had not been robbed the one evening Apollinaris arrived late. Somehow, by arriving at 12:45 instead of 12:15, Apollinaris had frustrated the thief. Therefore the thefts must take place after 12:15—between the time Apollinaris collected the money and the time he delivered it to the bank. For if the thefts took place earlier, then the money would be missing whether Apollinaris arrived late or on time. That was logic speaking—the voice of Ganelon's Great-grandfather.

Unfortunately, Ganelon had just witnessed the collecting and the delivery to the bank. The money was not being stolen after 12:15—the evidence of his senses told him that. Amid the flammarion flasks and retorts of his laboratory (where he frequently mixed up batches of rum nougat for his grandson), Ganelon's Grandfather always insisted that logic by itself was like a bear in a zoo. Unable to roam the forests and streams of real objects and sense experience, cut off from the bee trees of technology and the berry bushes of statistics (Grandfather had a sweet tooth), logic lost its vigor and played tricks to please the crowd.

Ganelon's ancestors kept arguing inside his head. As for himself, the detective decided to sleep on the case. Crossing the Cornichon by the Pont des Oreilles, he entered the Dureville section, the dark, narrow streets of San Sebastiano's criminal quarter. Behind him, Bruno's footsteps quickened and once again came the sound of the silencer being fitted on the Hunsecker-Bowles. Ganelon smiled and turned down the rue Crevecoeur.

Here, as for centuries, a Lady of the Evening stood in each doorway. As Ganelon passed by, each made him an offer in a businesslike but not unpleasant manner. The detective politely declined them all. The annals of San Sebastiano are filled with tales of the generosity and heroism of its Ladies of the Evening. Ganelon's own father—who, under the code name "Casanova," had led the Nightshirts, the principality's dreaded Resistance fighters during the Second World War—had much praise for the ingenuity with which the brave Ladies of the Evening hid downed Allied flyers from the Gestapo. Neatness and matronly decorum characterized the Ladies of the Evening; in return they expected to be treated with civility.

Ganelon heard indignant voices behind him. Apparently Bruno had made a coarse reply to one of the Ladies of the Evening. Angry women were crowding around the Strongarm man. Someone was calling for soap to wash out his mouth. Ganelon paused at the end of the street to let the beleaguered Bruno see where he was going. Then he entered a dimly lit Underworld hangout, the Café Noir.

The patrons knew him well. Legerdemain, the pickpocket, dropped his drink. Tartine, the petty forger, quickly sneaked the cap back on his fountain pen. Big Charlot, the mugger, tried to look inconspicuous. The rest cursed the detective and his family under their breath, while secretly dreaming of some day pulling off a job big enough to merit a Ganelon's attention.

A large, nattily dressed burglar with pomaded hair blocked Ganelon's path. Babar the Elegant. Babar looked hopefully at the detective and then glanced down at the end of a diamond bracelet hanging, as if by accident, from his breast pocket. Ganelon knew the bracelet well. Ten badly cut, flawed stones in a mediocre setting, it was the property of a lonely spinster who paid burglars to steal it because she found Inspectors of Police charming. Ganelon smiled, shook his head, and passed by.

"Ah, Maurice, my friend," said Ganelon, addressing the proprietor in a loud voice, "I've come to ask you a favor. Scotland Yard informs me that Mad Dog Watkins has escaped from Wormwood Scrubs again and is headed our way in a stolen homburg and camel's-hair coat. He's perfectly harmless. Old Mad Dog hasn't gone berserk or run amuck in years. Still, Scotland Yard would like to have him back. So keep your eyes peeled, eh?"

Maurice grunted noncommittally. Ganelon waved and walked on through to the back door. He had scarcely closed it behind him when he heard the uproar of voices, the overturning of tables and breaking of bottles which meant that Bruno had burst into the café still frothing at the mouth from his encounter with the Ladies of the Evening.

Ganelon awoke early the next morning. He stuffed his cheeks with cotton batting and put on a white cap and jacket and a black eye-patch. A few minutes before 8:00 he was trundling an ice-cream cart into the Place Frascati. The day was warm and the sky blue. Ideal ice-cream weather. Still, he had misgivings. Along with the vanilla and chocolate, he had been talked into buying three cartons of fudge-and-date ripple. "An American flavor sensation that's sweeping the Riviera," the wholesaler had insisted.

Two men approached the fountain from different directions. One was a policeman who took up position beside the pool and leaned on his saber. The other, a fair-haired young man with a mustache, stopped directly in front of the fountain and looked up at the clock. At that moment the clock struck eight. As pigeons circled the square, the figure of the shepherdess emerged from one door and glided mechanically across to the other. "Fair weather," thought Ganelon gratefully, as he watched the young man walk away.

A few old men drifted into the square to sun themselves on the benches or play calanque, San Sebastiano's national game based on which of three regulation-size crumbs of bread would be eaten first by the pigeons. Next came the souvenir vendors and the street urchins with big eyes and shoeshine kits. By 8:30 the tourists had started to arrive to throw in their coins and make their wishes.

"Ice cream!" shouted Ganelon as Mouton and his grim-faced men burst out of the Strongarm limousine. All were equipped with small walkie-talkies. Mouton stationed two men in the cafés to the right and left of the fountain and two others, wearing binocular cases, in a fourth-floor window of the Hotel de la Fontaine. Mouton himself, accompanied by Bruno who wore a noticeable bruise under one eye and a swollen lip, took a table in a café directly across from the fountain.

At 8:59 the young man with the mustache entered the square again. As before he looked up at the clock until it struck and then walked briskly back the way he had come. Not long after, the first of the tour buses marked "San Sebastiano By Day" pulled up to the fountain. Ganelon watched as the passengers were herded over to the pool where they threw in their coins and were then quickly herded back into the bus.

Meanwhile, Mouton had entered the phone booth in the middle of the square. Ganelon pushed his cart over to the door where Bruno stood guard. "Ice cream?" asked the great detective pleasantly. Scowling, Bruno pushed Ganelon aside and reached down into the cart. He rummaged through the cartons and pulled out an ice-cream bar.

"That's fudge-and-date ripple, sir," said Ganelon meekly. "A popular new flavor."

Bruno eyed him suspiciously and bit into the ice cream. He cursed, spat, and grabbing Ganelon by the throat, reached for his Hunsecker-Bowles.

"Bruno!" snapped Mouton, sticking his head out of the phone booth. "Myshkin's still in the sack. But the Think Tank's starting to spitball anyway. Fong says check out that outlet pipe to the sewer. Maybe somebody's getting at the money that way."

So Myshkin had overslept. "Sloth doesn't work, my dear Count," thought Ganelon, recalling one of Dupont's aphorisms. Then Bruno, who was still holding him by the throat, gave the detective a shake and threw him to the ground. Muttering to himself, the Strongarm man stuffed his pockets with chocolate ice-cream bars and hurried away.

Ganelon got to his feet. His frightened look was just part of his disguise. As a youth Ganelon had spent a year at a Carthusian hermitage mastering the *via felix* the Happy Way, that almost-forgotten art of medieval self-defense based on redistributing an opponent's body humors (blood, phlegm, choler, and black bile) to produce an instantaneous change in temperament. With a hip lift and a deft twist of the wrist Ganelon could change a homicidal maniac into a simpering milquetoast or the most civil and obliging of men. His teacher, the venerable Father Sylvanus, had made him swear to use this terrible power only in the cause of justice.

More buses arrived, and more tourists appeared on foot and in cars. "Ice cream!" shouted Ganelon as coins flashed through the air and into the water. He was beginning to understand what a gold mine the fountain was for Apollinaris. But he was no closer to solving the riddle of how the money was being stolen.

The policeman, for example, bored as he looked, always had one eye cocked for the tourist whose hand might stray into the fountain, or for the aging pensioner hoping to eke out his allotment with a wad of chewing gum on the end of his walking stick, or for the bright young urchin taking advantage of the new steel coinage to rob the fountain with a magnet on a string. Nevertheless, Ganelon decided to investigate.

The policeman accepted the vanilla bar as his due. "This must be interesting work," said Ganelon.

"Dull as dishwater," said the policeman.

"But I'll bet you get a bit of excitement now and then," said Ganelon. Perhaps the thief was staging diversions—fake car accidents, fist fights, runaway horses.

"Dead as a graveyard," said the policeman, turning to pose for two lady schoolteachers with cameras. At that moment the young man with the mustache arrived at the fountain again. The clock struck ten.

"A regular visitor, that young man," said Ganelon.

"Tourists," said the policeman bitterly. "We pose for their snapshots. We give them directions. But laugh at their stupid jokes?" He shook his head. "That's where I draw the line."

Ganelon made a sympathetic noise.

"Listen," said the policeman, "I'm here on night duty and it's raining and it's dark. Suddenly that nut with the mustache pops up out of nowhere with a string of the oldest jokes on God's green earth. Why did the chicken cross the road? Just to be polite I laugh. Next thing I know he's coming back every night, same time, same tired jokes."

The policeman had finished his ice-cream bar. Ganelon offered him another. This could be the diversion the detective was postulating. "Did all this start about two months ago?" he asked.

"More like three," said the policeman, stripping the wrapper from the ice-cream bar. "Back when we had all that rain. Funny thing, this guy only made with the jokes if it was raining. Two months ago, when that dry spell hit us, he stopped. Now he shows up on the hour, but no more jokes."

The policeman bit into the ice cream. It was fudge-and-date ripple. He grimaced and demanded to see Ganelon's peddler's license. Fortunately the policeman was distracted by the first of the sleek tour buses marked "See the Riviera in Twelve Hours" which dashed into the square, paused long enough for its passengers to rain coins into the fountain from the windows, and then dashed off again.

Ganelon pushed his cart over to the telephone. Time to call Jouvet. As he arrived at the booth, Mouton stepped out and snapped fresh orders from the Think Tank into his walkie-talkie. Apparently Blackie S. F. X. Ryan suspected that the street urchins were a gang of midgets in disguise.

Ganelon smiled. Only Blackie S. F. X. Ryan would think of counterfeit urchins. Ryan had once forged and antiqued a document deeding San Sebastiano in perpetuity to one of his ancestors, an Irish court jester, as a reward from the Emperor Charlemagne for having introduced the pratfall into France. His masterful forgery had defied the experts. Today Ryan would be sitting on the throne of San Sebastiano if Ganelon's father had not detected one flaw: following the medieval practice, Ryan had dried the Emperor's crude signature by sprinkling it with sand—a fine, gritty sand familiar to all hot-dog lovers and indigenous to only one place in the world, the beach at Coney Island.

Ganelon also learned that Myshkin, refusing to spitball on an empty stomach, had stopped for breakfast on his way to the Think Tank. The Chairman of the Board was a notorious trencherman. "Gluttony doesn't work either, my dear Count," thought Ganelon as he dialed the Café de l'Esperance.

"Ah, Monsieur Ganelon," said Jouvet sheepishly, "from some celestial archair your Great-grandfather is laughing up his sleeve at simple old Jouvet and his Prussian baron."

"You visited the watch-repair shop then?" asked Ganelon.

"Yes," said Jouvet. "Apparently, bronzing baby shoes was only Dupont's sideline. Our Dupont was also an expert freelance watch-repair man. According to the owner of the shop, he could fix anything that told time. Give him a leaning hourglass or a burned-out electric clock and he'd bring it back to tiptop working order. The owner also remarked that recently Dupont had been driving himself hard and muttering 'Sloth doesn't work' under his breath all the time. He also developed a bad case of Watch Repairman's Eye—calluses in the eye socket from using a jeweler's loupe."

Ganelon grunted. Were Dupont's hands those of a watch-repair man?

"One more thing," said Jouvet. "The morning Dupont's body was found, a young man came into the shop, put a parcel on the counter and left without saying a word. The parcel contained all the watches and baby shoes Dupont was supposed to have delivered that morning."

"If this young man had fair hair and a mustache," said Ganelon, "I will have further need of your services."

Back at the fountain the street urchins were turning ugly, misjudging the intentions of the men in homburgs and camel's-hair coats who were patting their cheeks to check for the stubble of a beard. One Strongarm man had retired to the sidelines with well-kicked shins. A second was being followed around by a band of shoeshine boys.

Just before eleven Jouvet arrived at the fountain. The young man with the mustache made his appearance at 10:59. This time Ganelon examined him more closely. An altogether undistinguished chin, eyeglasses in steel frames, a sturdy green suit with wide cuffs. Why did he visit the fountain on the hour? What was his connection with Dupont? And what about the business of the jokes? When the young man left the square again, Jouvet followed at a discreet distance.

There was a mild commotion and turning of heads as Bruno crossed the square in the direction of Mouton. The wind shifted and from some distance away Ganelon could tell that the Strongarm man had been investigating the sewer. So could Mouton. He waved Bruno back. They conversed through the walkie-talkies. Bruno was shaking his head. He had found out the hard way what Ganelon already knew: the outlet pipe from the fountain narrowed to an impassable one-foot diameter before it reached the sewer. Ever since Great-grandfather Ganelon perished in its main canal, a detailed knowledge of the sewer system had become a part of every Ganelon's training, should he in turn ever have to chase a villain beneath the city streets.

At 11:59 the young man returned. Jouvet was not far behind. A sergeant relieved the policeman for lunch. The Strongarm men downed plates of cold cuts and bottles of beer and scowled at the fountain. Ganelon chewed listelessly on a fudge-and-date ripple and shouted his wares.

For the rest of the afternoon tourists poured into the square, the young man made his on-the-hour, every-hour appearances with Jouvet on his heels, and new orders arrived regularly from Chicago. Eaves-dropping by the phone booth, Ganelon was pleased to learn that Myshkin had stormed out of the Think Tank in a rage because they had started without him. As Chairman of the Board he claimed the right to throw out the first spitball. "You shouldn't lose your temper, my dear Count," thought Ganelon. "Anger doesn't work either."

A little before 3:00 a dark shadow fell across the square. Ganelon looked up, half expecting to find the immense head of one of the Strongarm men peering down over the rooftops to examine the fountain as if it was the scale replica on the Think Tank table. Instead, a shelf of dark clouds had appeared low in the sky. As the clock struck the hour the figure of the shepherdess appeared to announce fair weather under a darkening sky.

The clouds moved closer and the wind turned cold. By 4:00 Ganelon had to admit that fudge-and-date ripple had been a complete failure. Once, earlier in the afternoon, an American had shouted to his wife, "Hey, Madge, they've got fudge-and-date ripple!" The delighted tourists had eaten two apiece while visions of Saginaw, Michigan, danced over their heads. But the local people distrusted fudge-and-date ripple. The French tourists laughed at it in scorn. The Germans shook their heads gravely: fudge-and-date ripple had tried to sweep Baden Baden the season before.

"Ice cream!" shouted Ganelon as a crowd of angry old men chased a Strongarm man out of the square. When they tottered back, Ganelon approached their leader, a distinguished gentleman wearing the green rosette of a Master of the Pigeons. Each square in San Sebastiano had a Master of the Pigeons, who is the final arbiter in games of calanque.

"Trouble, sir?" asked Ganelon.

The old man was breathing heavily from the chase. "Why, that scoundrel kicked his way through three games of calanque," he said indignantly. "The pigeons will be upset for hours." Suspecting that possibly the thief had trained cormorants to dive for coins and disguised them as pigeons, Chicago had ordered the birds checked out. The idea was Hans Brunner's. Ganelon found it unworthy of the man who had once used a specially designed denture to bite the stones out of ladies' rings as he kissed their hands. So equipped, Brunner had pillaged San Sebastiano's social functions until Ganelon's father, waiting at the end of a bejeweled reception line, had apprehended him, his cheeks stuffed with diamonds and emeralds.

The detective looked up at the sky. "The games were going to be rained out anyway," he said, adding, not without bitterness, "in spite of your celebrated weather figures."

The Master of the Pigeons arched an eyebrow at this slight on the Place Frascati. "Ah, my dear Rosenkranz," he said, speaking to a russet-colored pigeon at his feet, "this gentleman mocks our weather figures. Remind him that up until a few weeks ago they had given us two hundred years of faithful service."

Ganelon's pulse quickened. "By 'a few weeks' would you mean two months perhaps?"

The old man smiled. "This gentleman connects the breakdown of the weather figures with that body in the fountain, my dear Rosenkranz. Does that mean he believes our local legend that Mathias Swartzwald, the dishonest clockmaker, was cursed to wander the earth, returning every seventy years to drown himself in despair at the scene of his crime? But you and I know the facts. The weather figures broke down one month ago, not two. Liberation Day, to be exact."

In 1944 the Nightshirts had taken to the streets and driven out the Germans. Liberation Day commemorated that event.

"If you will recall, my dear Rosenkranz," said the old man, "after weeks of not a cloud in the sky a sudden thunderstorm canceled the parade to the Tomb of the Unknown Nightshirt. As I hurried home across the square the clock struck and there was the shepherdess out in the downpour. Since that historic day one month ago, only the shepherdess appears, rain or shine." The pigeon strutted away and the old man followed him.

Light rain was beginning to fall as Jouvet followed the young man into the square and, as previously instructed, gave up the surveillance. Without penetrating Ganelon's disguise, he bought a fudge-and-date ripple bar—it would later appear on his expense account—and stood watching the fountain. Ganelon quickly pushed his cart out of the square. The ice-cream strategy had been a fiasco.

Fifteen minutes later, Ganelon had changed into his blue suit and was seated beside Jouvet in a café near the fountain.

"I've kept the square under surveillance," said Jouvet. "Nothing odd to report." He grimaced. "Unless you count an ice-cream bar I bought. It quite upset my stomach."

"What about the young man?" asked Ganelon quickly.

"The subject," said Jouvet, "is a bird lover. Except for his hourly visits to the fountain and time out for lunch, he spent every minute in our Museum of Natural History examining the bird displays. He had lunch at Chez Viviani, a small Italian restaurant on the rue Babette. I also dined there, so as not to attract attention.

Mussels and canneloni. Delicious." Jouvet smacked his lips. "Only ten francs, wine and gratuity included," he added quickly.

"Quite reasonable," said Ganelon gruffly.

"Money well spent," insisted Jouvet, "for I struck up a conversation with the waiter. It seems that the young man is Swiss and has been taking lunch there for the past three months. The waiter regards him as a bit of a tragic figure. At first he appeared several evenings a week in the company of a pretty girl. The waiter called her the Girl in the Yellow Raincoat, because she always wore one. After about a month they must have had a lovers' tiff because the girl stopped coming with him. Now the young man returns one evening a week, but he is always alone."

"Thursday evenings?" asked Ganelon.

Jouvet nodded in amazement and assumed the eager expression of a little boy about to be taught a magic trick.

Ganelon sighed. "You say he is a bird lover," he said. "Yet each trip to and from the museum and the fountain he passed our zoo with its excellent aviary. Obviously he is a lover of stuffed birds. This was confirmed when you mentioned Chez Viviani. As you know, many of our cafés are official meeting places for coin collectors, chamber-music lovers, Doberman pinscher breeders, et cetera. On Thursday nights the Royal Taxidermy Society of San Sebastiano meets at Chez Viviani."

"A brilliant deduction!" said Jouvet, pulling out his cigarettes. Ganelon tensed. But the old man absently put them away again. "They would only taste of—what did the scoundrel call it?—fudge-and-date ripple," he said. "Yes, a brilliant deduction. But as much as I admire your Great-grandfather, perhaps my temperament is more suited to the scientific approach. I fail to see, for example, what stuffed birds have to do with the case."

"Probably nothing at all," said Ganelon. The great detective closed his eyes and for several moments was lost in thought. "Listen," he said at last. "Three months ago the body of a woman was found in the fountain. More or less simultaneously the Swiss arrived on the scene, plaguing the night policeman with jokes and visiting Chez Viviani with a girl.

"Two months ago Dupont's body was found in the fountain and the thefts began. At more or less the same time the girl disappeared and the Swiss gave up telling jokes in the rain and began to visit the fountain on the hour.

"Then one month ago the weather figures broke down."

"What do they have to do with it?" asked Jouvet.

Ganelon shook his head. "But I know that somehow the weather is involved," he said.

"Something along the lines of your Grandfather's fine study into the influence of the lunar cycle on Underworld activity?" asked Jouvet, referring to the book written by Ambrose Ganelon II—*The Tides of Crime* (London: Stoat and Sons, 1921).

"Not quite," said Ganelon. "In any event I have another assignment for you."

"I hope it involves test tubes and microscopes," said Inspector Jouvet. "I think I've been bitten by the scientific bug."

Back in his apartment Ganelon was tempted to change into his derelict's disguise and go stand in the soupline operated by the monks of the Abbey of the Holy Vernicle. Instead, he stacked his money into little steel piles. Of the 25 francs invested in ice cream, only 17 remained. But enough for one more venture into the world of commerce.

Not long after, he was back at the fountain with a new pushcart that sizzled in the light rain. From behind a fake black beard Ganelon shouted, "Hot chestnuts!" at the few people hurrying homeward across the deserted square.

The rain persisted. Buses marked "San Sebastiano By Night" pulled up within throwing distance of the fountain. Dry and cosy, the tourists weren't in the market for hot chestnuts. Even the young Swiss failed to appear. But then it was Thursday, get-together night for the Royal Taxidermy Society.

Ganelon cursed the weather and, as the clock struck the hour, he cursed the figure of the shepherdess as well. At least some of the pieces would fall into place if the weather figures had broken down two months ago instead of one. But he had no reason to doubt the Master of the Pigeons' story.

Bruno and another Strongarm man approached the fountain, grumbling over new orders from the Think Tank. Muttering against the rain, they scanned the seagods and nereids. Maybe the thief had painted himself gray and blended in with the statuary.

They also let drop that Myshkin had been coaxed back to the spit-balling session. But first he was going to take two fashion model friends to lunch. "Why does the old geezer strut around with young dollies on his arm?" wondered Bruno out loud.

"Pride, my dear fellow," thought Ganelon. Sloth, Guttony, Anger, and now Pride. Myshkin was well into the Seven Deadly Sins for so early in the day, Chicago time.

For the next hour Ganelon stood in the cold rain and pondered. How was the money being stolen? So far, his day in front of the fountain hadn't supplied the answer. And he didn't expect much more from what little time remained.

The secret had to be hidden somewhere in that night when Apollinaris arrived late. If he collects the money at 12:15, he is robbed; if he collects it at 12:45, he is not. Now, what happens in that extra half hour? The policeman leaves and the floodlights are turned off. The fountain is dark and unguarded. Ideal for a thief. But nothing is stolen. Why? Couldn't the thief operate while the policeman was there? Why not?

As if on cue, the night policeman approached to warm his hands over the coals and help himself to a handful of hot chestnuts. Ganelon smiled ingratiatingly and thought on. But he could discover no way that the presence of the policeman— the man's appetite for chestnuts was insatiable!—would *favor* the thief.

All right then, was there some reason why the thief couldn't work in the dark? Why would he need light? To see the coins? To see his way?

"Hey, Madge, I can't find the ice-cream guy. How about hot chestnuts?" Ganelon looked up. The American couple from Saginaw, Michigan, had braved the rain for more fudge-and-date ripple. As Madge shook her head, the clock struck and the floodlights came on, illuminating the figure of the shepherdess as it glided out into the rain.

"Fair weather," laughed the husband. "You just can't depend on this foreign stuff, Madge. This morning it called the shot and now it's on the fritz."

Ganelon stroked his false beard thoughtfully. The American assumed that the weather figures had just broken down. Why? Because this morning the shepherdess has been correct. But even a broken watch is correct twice a day.

The Master of the Pigeons said the weather figures broke down a month ago, on Liberation Day. Why? Because on that day the shepherdess had appeared in the rain for the first time. But that particular rainstorm had ended a month-long dry spell. So, in fact, the breakdown could have occurred two months ago. It just wouldn't have come to anyone's attention until the first rain. Good!—that gave him some answers (bizarre as they were), including why a watch-repair man had callused hands. Think big, Ambrose IV.

Just then a long, red hook-and-ladder pulled into the square and up to the fountain. Misses Billie and Mitzi were in the cab beside the driver. Perched high on the rear steering seat was Apollinaris, wearing the full-dress uniform of an Honorary Grand Fire Marshal, complete with plumed helmet, epaulettes, bottle-green tunic, and silver-voiced trumpet. Mouton hurried over.

"I thought I'd stop by on my way to the Fireman's Ball," said Apollinaris, without leaving his seat.

"Anybody tries for the money and it'll be the last thing they try for," said Mouton, tapping his Hunsecker-Bowles.

Apollinaris cleared his throat. "Jo Jo, mightn't there be some question as to the legality of such drastic measures, considering the small amount of money involved?"

"Strongarm likes to keep it nice and legal," laughed Mouton, handing the multimillionaire a piece of paper.

Apollinaris studied the paper. "As I understand it," he said, "this is a permit to exterminate pigeons at the Frascati Fountain."

"It's a license to kill," said Mouton. "If the thief tries anything, we start exterminating."

As Mouton returned to his post, Apollinaris looked around the square expectantly. Then, with a disappointed shrug, he was about to signal his driver to proceed, when he sniffed. Looking down, Apollinaris discovered Ganelon. "Ah," smiled the multimillionaire, "the simple pleasure of hot chestnuts!"

The agency's reputation demanded that it show itself. "Mr. Apollinaris," whispered the detective, "I'm Agence Ganelon Operative Number Twenty-five. Please pretend we are haggling over the price."

"I knew you people would be around here somewhere," beamed Apollinaris. "What a clever disguise! Anything to report?"

"We know *who*," said Ganelon. "*How* still remains a mystery."

"But not for long, I'll bet," smiled Apollinaris. He sniffed again. "Hot chestnuts. What an old-fashioned treat for everyone at the Fireman's Ball! Give me all you have."

Ganelon hastily scooped the chestnuts into paper cornets, adding up the cost as he went. Thirty francs. Burdened down with the many little packages, Apollinaris found he couldn't reach his wallet. He winked. "Just put this on my bill," he said, as the hook-and-ladder pulled away.

Ganelon pushed his cart into a dark alley. Like the ice cream, hot chestnuts had been another disaster. Fortunately he had a spare disguise—dark glasses with a false nose attached, a white cane, and a soft, peaked cap. Ganelon tapped his way across the square and sat down beside the telephone booth. Spreading out his few remaining coins in the upturned cap, he drew a carpenter's saw and a violin bow from under his coat. *Red Sails in the Sunset* (scored for the musical saw by Ganelon himself) filled the almost deserted square.

Thus employed, Ganelon turned his mind once more to the question of why darkness foiled the thief. Why did he need light? Ganelon looked at the fountain. The floodlights had brought the statuary out of the shadows and turned the cascade to gold. But they also made the surface of the water shine. Enough to hide the presence of the thief beneath the water? Could that be the answer to the riddle?

At that moment a tour bus rumbled into the square. As the hail of coins from its windows broke the surface of the pool, Ganelon detected taller spurts of water. The Strongarm guns above the street were working over the pool foot by foot. The Think Tank had thought of a diver, too.

Ganelon had the receiver off the hook before the end of the first ring. "Jouvet here," said Jouvet. "The records show the following unidentified bodies found in the Frascati Fountain and buried in Poitier's Field: men—1801, 1833, 1868, 1906, and 1937; women—1803, 1829, 1871, 1910, and 1925." Jouvet paused. "Insufficient data to permit a scientific conclusion. How many bodies, for example, were found in the other fountains during the same period? Is there a corelation between the bodies and solar storms or barometric pressure or stock-market fluctuations? Et cetera. Et cetera. Further studies are mandatory." Jouvet sighed. "An old man is foolish to get involved in the scientific approach. It could take years."

"In the meantime," said Ganelon, "could you represent the agency at the collecting of the coins tonight and then accompany Apollinaris from the fountain to the bank?"

In the next hour the rain slackened. A few gamblers on their way to the Casino dropped coins in Ganelon's hat for luck. Enough for a sandwich. *Waltzing Matilda* evoked coins from some late-arriving Australian tourists. Enough for a few cigarettes.

As the tiny stock of money grew, Ganelon tussled with logic. Evidently the thief needed light. Yet he didn't operate in the daytime. Evidently he needed artificial light. And this brought Ganelon back to the floodlights again. Why would they have to be on before the fountain could be robbed?

Mouton held his palm out the phone booth door and snapped his fingers. Bruno gave him a 50-centime piece from Ganelon's hat. "God bless you, sir," said Ganelon.

"It's cocktail hour for Myshkin," said Mouton, when he'd made his call. "But Fong and Brunner have an idea. Maybe the thief has fitted a trained sewer rat with special teeth so it can nip through that grille and carry off money in its cheeks."

"Aw, come on, Jo Jo. The Think Tank's getting punchy," said Bruno, as he pocketed the coins remaining in Ganelon's hat. ("God bless you, sir," said Ganelon.)

"The sewer's your department," said Mouton. "Check it out."

Ganelon struck up a Gilbert and Sullivan medley as they left. His bow arm moved automatically across the flexing saw blade. Behind the dark glasses the great detective was deep in thought. That, of course, was it. The thief didn't need light. But he did need the floodlight—plus the grille across the bottom of the pool.

It was now 12:15. Mouton and his men converged on Apollinaris and his hook-and-ladder as it arrived for the collection. Jouvet appeared at the same time, wearing a fedora and a belted raincoat. Ganelon shook his head. Apparently the old Inspector had decided to try the two-fisted approach. Shouldering two Strongarm men aside, he introduced himself to Apollinaris and patted Miss Billie and Miss Mitzi on the knees.

When the multimillionaire had swept out the fountain, everyone drove off to the bank. A minute later the floodlights went out and the policeman headed home. Ganelon picked up his empty cap, tucked the bow and saw under his arm, and tapped his way out of the square.

Fifteen minutes later a shadow slipped across the square. Passing under a street light it became, for an instant, the figure of a man, naked except for a loincloth. It was Ganelon in the briefest of his disguises—dark-gray body-paint from head to toe. He stepped into the pool and pulled himself up on the back of an unoccupied stone dolphin. Neptune now had another demigod of the sea.

Ganelon didn't have long to wait. First came the squeak of old hinges. Then someone passed from behind the cascade and slipped into the water. A moment later a head bobbed to the surface in the middle of the pool. It vanished and reappeared several times.

Then a figure emerged from the water about a foot from the motionless Ganelon: a young woman in a bikini and bathing cap, carrying a wicker basket filled with coins. She went to the edge of the fountain where the young Swiss with the mustache came out of the shadows to meet her. They embraced and spoke in whispers. Then the Swiss walked out of the square and the woman returned behind the cascade. She had exchanged her wicker basket full of coins for a bag of groceries.

Ganelon started to dismount to follow her when the wind shifted. He froze, his eyes searching the shadows of the square. Bruno had returned from the sewer. The Strongarm man stepped out of the darkness. With a quick glance at the cascade he strode after the young Swiss.

Dripping with water from the cascade, Ganelon crossed a dark room piled with scrap metal toward a vaguely lit stone staircase. The steps led to a second room containing two large four-posters, a wooden cradle with rockers, and an iron stove. Sounds from above led him up two more flights, past a workroom smelling of acetylene.

The fourth room was crowded with bronze figures: medieval soldiers and Moors, haloed saints, the Four Horsemen of the Apocalypse, representations of various virtues and vices, the Nine Muses, the Ten Commandments, and others, all set into a spiral track on the floor. The woman—she now wore a yellow raincoat over her bikini—was working on one of the figures with a file. "Miss Swartzwald, I presume," said Ganelon.

She swung around and stared open-mouthed at what looked like a fugitive from the fountain statuary.

When Ganelon had introduced himself, the girl regained her composure. "Yes, I'm Heidi Swartzwald," she said defiantly. "Put me in jail and throw the key away. But the money's mine. It's my dowry, willed to me by my father and six generations of Swartzwalds."

"So Mathias Swartzwald didn't run away," said Ganelon.

Her laughter walked a line between anger and tears. "Granted he had a poor head for business," she said. "Granted his man-hour projections per mechanical figure were unrealistic, his cost estimates absurdly low, and his choice of subcontractors—they kept going bankrupt on him—poor. But old Mathias was still a great craftsman and the fountain was his lifework.

"But the Frascatis said, 'No more money. No more extensions. Finish the mechanical figures by a certain date or go to jail for breach of contract.' Old Mathias knew he couldn't finish his work and redeem the family name in prison. So the night before the impossible deadline he and his wife moved in here.

"When Wilhelm, his son, was graduated from clock school in Switzerland he came to live in the clock as well, bringing with him a Swiss wife. Father and son hoped to complete the work in a few years. But then old Mathias died."

"And they put his body in the fountain," said Ganelon.

"How could he be buried legally without his identity becoming known?" asked Heidi. "After that a fountain burial became a kind of Swartzwald family tradition.

"Working alone, Wilhelm completed all the parts for the figures. As his father had done, he gave each part a number and wrote the number in a book plus where each part went. But before he could begin the assembling work, some plague or other carried him off. His son Wolfgang, also a clock-school graduate, had to hurry back from Switzerland with his family.

"That's when tragedy really struck. Wolfgang's little son—my great-grandfather—decided to re-enact Napoleon's retreat from Moscow with his toy soldiers. A stickler for realism, the little tot simulated a blizzard by tearing the book with all the numbers into little pieces.

"Suddenly we had thousands of parts—wheels and cogs, nodding heads, pointing fingers, shrugging shoulders, legs that marched, legs that minced—but we didn't know which went where. Three generations of Swartzwalds broke their hearts trying to puzzle out the whole mess.

"Just look at this, Monsieur Ganelon," said Heidi, putting her hand on the bronze figure of a portly man sitting cross-legged in a chair and gazing up at the ceiling with his fingers laced behind his head. "This is the one that drove my father to despair Sloth, one of the Seven Deadly Sins. It's full of all kinds of moving wheels inside, but nothing happens. 'Sloth doesn't work!' my father used to sob."

Suddenly a beam of light fell across the wall. It came from a peephole in the door through which the shepherdess made her hourly appearance. "The floodlights," said Heidi in a puzzled voice. "Someone's turned them on."

Ganelon jumped to the peephole. Below, men in homburgs and camel's-hair coats were spilling out of the Strongarm limousine. Mouton and Bruno opened the trunk compartment. Bruno reached inside and pulled the bloody head of the young Swiss into view.

"They've got Jean-Jacques, my fiancé!" said Heidi who had come to share the peephole with Ganelon. "Who are they?"

Ganelon explained about his detective-criminal race with the Strongarm Corporation. "Will Jean-Jacques talk?" he asked.

"I'm sure he will," she said. "He's really a very chatty and outgoing person. And just full of funny stories."

In fact, Jean-Jacques seemed to be talking so freely that Bruno had to hit him on the head and close the trunk compartment to shut him up.

"They shouldn't do that," insisted Heidi. "Jean-Jacques has claustrophobia. That's why he didn't come in here to live with us when mother's death brought me back from clock school. Oh, at first it wasn't too bad. On rainy nights when I didn't have to play shepherdess, Jean-Jacques would distract the policeman so I could slip out of the fountain and be with him. But since father died, the best we've been able to do is steal a few sweet moments together when he brings the groceries and exchange loving glances when I make my appearances on the hour."

At a command from Mouton, Bruno had stepped into the pool and was now almost chest-deep in the water, heading straight for the cascade. Abruptly he pitched face first into the water. The surface of the pool churned for a moment. Then Bruno reappeared, struggling to his feet. He strained to move forward again, fell over sideways, and disappeared under the water once more.

"The Strongarm people wear steel caps on their shoes," said Ganelon. "Convenient for kicking a man when he's down, but clumsy for walking across an electromagnet."

Bruno came to the surface again, splashed to the edge of the pool, and crawled out in stockinged feet, gesturing furiously.

"Getting me my dowry cost my father his life," said Heidi. "First he tried the baby-shoe bronzing business. But there was just no money in that. Then he caught pneumonia from the hours he spent in the water wrapping the crossbars on the underside of the grille with wire and hooking into the current from the floodlights."

"A very ingenious man," said Ganelon.

"Yes," said Heidi proudly. "When the fountain was swept out, some steel coins stuck to the grille."

"Except for the time Apollinaris arrived late—after the floodlights and your magnet had been turned off," said Ganelon.

A banging echoed up the stairs. Mouton's men were trying to force their way in. But Ganelon had bolted the cascade door behind him. "We'll be safe enough here until morning," he said. "When the policeman comes on duty I'll have to turn you over to him."

Heidi nodded. "It's ironic really," she said. "Except for a final touch or two, the mechanical figures are ready to work and the Swartzwald name will be redeemed. And pretty soon, Jean-Jacques and I would have had enough money to set ourselves up in business. He is a master taxidermist and I am a master clockmaker. Together we planned on revolutionizing the Swiss Cuckoo-clock industry which has been resting on its laurels for three centuries. Little toy birds indeed! We intend to design a series of clocks whose form and function determine the bird. For example, an alarm clock would contain a rooster; a ship's clock, a salty old parrot; a Grandfather clock, a bald eagle or a coot. Real birds, each one a masterpiece of the taxidermist's art."

Heidi looked at her wrist watch. "Time to get ready to play the shepherdess," she said, crossing over to a costume of bronzed cloth.

"Miss Swartzwald," protested Ganelon, "step out that door and you're dead and the national security of San Sebastiano is in gravest peril."

"Well, don't blame me," said Heidi. "All this was old Mathias" idea, not mine. Maybe he wanted to give the Frascatis something for their money. Maybe he was inordinately proud of a rheumatic condition called Swartzwald Elbow that runs in our family and forecasts the weather with extraordinary accuracy. All I know is that a Swartzwald has gone through that door on the hour for two hundred years." She took a firm grip on her shepherd's crook. "Don't try and stop me."

Ganelon chewed his lip, remembering the words of Father Sylvanus: "Alas, my son, not even the *via felix* can make a woman reasonable."

"All right," said Ganelon, "what does the Swartzwald Elbow say, weatherwise?"

Heidi grabbed an elbow and closed her eyes. "There is a high-pressure ridge moving in from the north-northeast, bringing generally cloudy conditions and intermittent showers to the San Sebastiano area," she said. "Temperatures will range from seasonable to below seasonable. Morning fog in the low-lying areas will make driving conditions hazardous."

"Technically speaking then, it's man-in-the-slicker weather," insisted the detective. "So if someone has to go out there like a duck in a shooting gallery, it will be me. But let's see if we can't confuse the issue a bit."

As the clock struck the hour, Mouton and his men raised their guns to greet the shepherdess. But Pride swaggered out the door instead, followed by Covetousness bowed down by material possessions and his hand in Pride's hip pocket. Next came Lust (out of respect for the women and children in the audience, old Mathias had represented him as a Peeping Tom with a stepladder), and then Anger who threw his bronze hat down and jumped on it with a gnashing of teeth.

Strongarm jaws dropped as Gluttony waddled out, alternately raising a bronze leg of lamb and a bronze bottle to his fat lips. Envy followed, eating his heart out as he watched Gluttony eat. Sloth came next, followed by Ganelon in a bronzed slicker and nor'wester.

"I am Hopeless Resignation," he thought. "The Eighth Deadly Sin."

"Come on, you guys. Check them out!" shouted Mouton.

Bruno sprang to life. His first shot struck Pride's inflated chest. The men cheered the satisfying *bong* and raised their guns again. Bruno waved them down. His next shot got Covetousness between the shifty eyes. Lust, going up and down the ladder, was more elusive. Bruno missed it twice before scoring a direct hit just as the figure passed through the other door.

For a brief moment Ganelon thought he might get across alive. But Bruno snapped off two quick shots—*bong, bong*. Anger and Gluttony were checked out. Envy was easy and Sloth a sitting duck—*bong, bong*. Ganelon was still too far from the door to try a dash for it.

"All together on this last one!" shouted Mouton impatiently. Ganelon faced the upturned guns with a mechanical shrug. "Ready!" shouted Mouton. Ganelon wondered if tradition didn't call for him to be offered a final cigarette. "Aim!" shouted Mouton. Ganelon braced himself for the shots.

Instead, two policeman on bicycles glided out of the shadows. "Your papers, gentlemen, if you please," said one of them sternly. The camel's-hair firing squad lowered its guns. Ganelon passed through the other door which closed behind him with a bang.

Once inside, Ganelon put his eye to the peephole. Down below the police were examining Mouton's license to exterminate pigeons. Satisfied, they saluted smartly and pedaled away.

"Miss Swartzwald," said Ganelon testily, "do you expect me to repeat that little performance on the hour until morning?"

"I didn't start the stupid tradition," said Heidi who was fussing over the damage the bullets had done to the Seven Deadly Sins. "But if you don't go, I will. I told you—the show must go on."

"That's why we must take the offensive," said Ganelon. "That's why we have to invite them in."

He opened the door and stood back.

The Strongarm men scuffed out their cigarettes when Bruno returned, at the wheel of the hook-and-ladder. Mouton was the first one up the ladder and onto the platform across which Ganelon and the Seven Deadly Sins had paraded a few minutes before. Wary of a trick, Mouton waited until the others had joined him before moving cautiously toward the open door.

The whir of machinery greeted his approach and four bronze figures in medieval costume jerked into view. They arranged themselves shoulder to shoulder and raised trumpets to their lips. Behind them, the little army of San Sebastiano filed out the door, led by Guido Frascati bearing his famous two-handed sword, Invictus. Mouton and the Strongarm men bunched together uneasily.

Then the door behind them sprang open and the Moorish host under Akbar the Cruel squealed out beneath infidel banners. The Battle of the Cornichon was about to be re-enacted. Mouton's men formed a circle around him, some firing into the Christians, others into the Moors. But both armies advanced with slow relentlessness. The firing became wilder. Mouton shouted for everyone to break for the ladder. But at that moment both armies raised their weapons and charged.

Mouton and his men disappeared in a forest of clashing swords and scimitars, spears and battleaxes, mechanical arms, legs, knees, and elbows. When the Moors, conforming to history and to old Mathias' cogs and wheels, turned and ran, they left a battlefield littered with dented homburgs and unconscious Strongarm men. Only Mouton and Bruno escaped. Battered and bruised, they retreated on all fours along with the vanquished Moors fleeing back through the door from which they had come.

Once inside, Bruno was the first to untangle himself from the Saracen feet. His mouth was bloody where he'd been struck by the flat of a sword, and one eye was swollen shut. He spat out a tooth, cursed, and made a staggering lunge at Ganelon. The detective sidestepped agilely. He caught his attacker around the waist and applied a quick hiplift that brought the Strongarm man's body parallel to the floor. Ganelon tipped him this way and that in a skillful redistribution of his four body humors. Then he sat Bruno down. The bull-necked man looked up from the floor with a shy grin.

"Thanks a lot, there," he said good-naturedly. The *via felix* had triumphed again. The Strongarm man pumped Ganelon's hand. "Bruno's the name, Mayhem's the game," he said. Blushing, he added, "But my mother always called me her Little Cabbage. Been years since anyone called me that."

Before Ganelon could oblige, Mouton stepped forward, waving his Hunsecker-Bowles. The ripe, blue lump on his forehead had come from the studded mace which Robert, Bishop of San Sebastiano, had wielded instead of a sword because the Church forbade the shedding of blood by Men of the Cloth.

"Stand over there with the girl, Ganelon," Mouton ordered. "Now here's the story. Bruno and I catch the girl stealing. She grabs a gun and tries to escape just as you arrive—better late than never. She shoots you. I shoot her. Bruno will back me up. Right, Bruno?"

"Hello there, Jo Jo," said Bruno who was following the proccedings with childlike interest from the floor.

"As for the guy in the trunk of the car," said Mouton, "we stick his head in a bucket of cement and drop him off a pier. Right, Bruno?"

Bruno winked at Ganelon and Heidi. "Whatever you say, Jo Jo," he smiled, adding in a stage whisper, "Old Jo Jo isn't really a bad egg. Underneath it all he's got a heart of gold."

Mouton whirled. "Have you gone nuts, Bruno?" he demanded. "Who says I've got a heart of gold? Who says I'm not rotten to the core? Are you going to back me up or not?"

"All the way, Jo Jo, old buddy," said Bruno agreeably. "Provided it's okay with our friends here. So what's your complaint? Come on. Admit you're not a bad egg, not really."

Mouton lashed at the smiling face with his pistol. But Bruno grabbed his arm and wouldn't let go. "Admit you've got a heart of gold," he coaxed. "Call me your Little Cabbage."

Before Mouton could get his arm free, Ganelon had applied another hiplift. In a moment the Strongarm chieftain was on the floor beside a grinning Bruno. Mouton sat there pensively for a second or two and then turned to his companion.

"Bruno," he said benignly, "have you ever wondered what life is all about? I mean *really* all about?"

Ganelon, still wearing the bronzed slicker, stood at the edge of the fountain beside a beaming Apollinaris. "Since Miss Swartzwald and her fiancé have agreed to return the stolen money, I hope you will see your way to dropping the charges against them," said the detective. "One can't help admiring a family that has lived inside a clock for six generations."

"Agreed," said Apollinaris. "As a matter of fact, in return for a controlling interest in their little business enterprise, I intend to finance it myself. Apollinaris Stuffed Clocks, Unlimited. How does that sound?"

"By the way," said the multimillionaire, "your Inspector Jouvet was a godsend. I invited him back to the Fireman's Ball with us. As luck would have it, he and Miss Billie were taking a bit of air on the terrace when he noticed the Strongarm people stealing the hook-and-ladder which I had just that evening donated to the Fire Department. A fine person, Inspector Jouvet, and a great one with the ladies."

"Apparently so," thought Ganelon. Jouvet, who was over by the multimillionaire's limousine letting Miss Billie and Miss Mitzi feel his muscles, had just presented his expense account. It seemed the the young ladies drank nothing but champagne cocktails.

Apollinaris looked up at the clock and rubbed his hands together with delight. "Do you know what I'm going to do?" he asked. "Inspired by the television industry, I am going to dress up some of those marvelous mechanical figures in sandwich-boards and rent the space out for advertising. Sloth, for example, might be used to promote one of those patent medicines for iron-poor blood." The clock struck the hour and the Four Horsemen of the Apocalypse appeared. "Pestilence, War, Famine, and Death," said Apollinaris enthusiastically. "Any insurance company would jump at the chance to sponsor them."

The multimillionaire offered Ganelon his bejeweled cigarette case. The detective snapped it open. There were no cigarettes, only an inscription: *To Ambrose Ganelon IV from a grateful Apollo Apollinaris.*

"I noticed how much you admired my little cigarette case," said the multimillionaire. "Take it instead of your fee. It is fourteen-carat gold and those, of course, are matched sapphires and rubies."

Ganelon sighed inwardly. Even without the inscription he could not sell or pawn the case without revealing the secret of his poverty.

Weary and dejected, Ganelon set out for home. As he passed the phone booth in the middle of the deserted square the phone rang. On impulse Ganelon picked up the receiver. "Jo Jo Mouton, please," said the operator. "Chicago calling."

"Tell Count Myshkin that Mouton is in jail for stealing a hook-and-ladder and assaulting eight policemen," said Ganelon. (The effects of the *via felix* had worn off as the eight policemen were putting Mouton and Bruno into a patrol car.)

A new voice broke in on the line. "Monsieur Ganelon?" it rapsed. "Myshkin here. How much like old times having my designs frustrated by a Ganelon!" Myshkin paused. "I assume my designs *have* been frustrated."

"You'd better believe it," said Ganelon.

"I do, I do," said Myshkin. "But multimillionaires are like buses—there's always another one along soon. My dear Ganelon, tell me: did the solution to our little riddle have anything to do with the floodlights and the grille on the bottom of the pool?"

Ganelon explained about the electromagnet.

"Alas," said Myshkin in mock despair. "I was on the verge of the truth earlier this evening. I had gone to Aristotle's, a pleasant Greek night club where the sound of the basouki and breaking glass stimulates my mind much more than those idiotic spitballing sessions. There I was, fitting ideas together this way and that when I became intrigued by the floodlights and the grille. But before I could finalize my thinking, the Incredible Tamara, a bellydancer of no small skill, began her number and I quite lost my train of thought. I'm afraid I have too many vices to be a real villain. Ah, well, until the next time."

The streets were silent. San Sebastiano, the free world, and Apollo Apollinaris slept in peace. The Strongarm Corporation had been deafeated. Ganelon headed homeward, his mind already elsewhere. Perhaps, if he pried loose a jewel from the cigarette case, Babar the Elegant could fence it for him.

"My dear Babar," thought Ganelon, rehearsing the conversation in his mind, "I have a service to ask. A friend has a small stone—quite honestly come by, I assure you—that he wishes to dispose of through unconventional channels."

Why doesn't he take it to a regular dealer? Why, indeed? Ganelon racked his brain.

"A good question, Babar. To answer it we must cast our minds back one hundred years to when the Khyber region lay at the mercy of a secret society of Pathan assassins whose leader ruled by virture of a sacred dagger encrusted with matched rubies and sapphires ..."

The Bird-of-Paradise Man

L ATE ONE HOT summer afternoon a large unmarked truck drove out of San Sebastiano's rue Rivarol and turned westward at a snail's pace onto the Quai des Matelots. The man in the passenger seat raised a bullhorn and as the truck inched along, his magnified voice proclaimed, "New refrigerators for old! New refrigerators for old!"

The loiterers enjoying the harbor breeze along the stone wall of the embankment turned around. The women leaning on their windowsills above the street craned to see beyond the fluttering curtains. Again the man with the bullhorn announced he would trade everyone on that block a brand new refrigerator of the latest design for their old refrigerator.

At this part of its length, the Quai des Matelots overlooked the fishing-fleet basin of the Old Port. The street floors of the narrow stucco buildings were occupied by sea-related shops: a small ship-chandler's, the branch office of a maritime insurance company, a diving-equipment dealership, a sponge importer. The inhabitants of the upper floors were sea-related, too, and knew worldly goods to be slippery, elusive things which, once caught, must be held onto tightly. Their eyes went round with surprise and then narrowed suspiciously.

Madame Faustine, the wife of a wholesale scrimshaw knickknack man, was the first to step forward. She'd been meaning to replace her old refrigerator anyway.

The man with the bullhorn ordered the driver to stop the truck. Two giants in blue coveralls jumped down from the back. He signaled them to follow after Madame Faustine, who indicated her fifth-floor window. The crowd laughed nervously as the two giants exchanged unhappy glances. When Madame Faustine reappeared several minutes later, the two men were right behind her, sweating under the burden of an ancient, once-white machine now as brown as the summer polar bear at the St. Felix Zoo.

Madame Faustine smiled around at her neighbors as if to say, Well, at least I've got the damn thing down for the trash to take away. Then she gave the man with the bullhorn a flat stare.

He did not hesitate. At his signal, the two men hoisted the old machine up onto the back of the truck and out of sight. Madame Faustine licked her lips nervously and looked down at the ground. Suddenly the crowd sucked in its collective breath. Madame Faustine looked up and her heart fluttered. The two giants emerged from the darkness of the truck interior working a magnificent new refrigerator out into the sunlight. The machine was as broad as a wardrobe, with two fine doors and a spigot for ice water. It was of the color called avocado. The women in the crowd groaned with envy.

As quickly as they brought the old refrigerator down, the two giants manhandled the new one across the street and through Madame Faustine's doorway. When they reappeared empty-handed, the crowd cheered and rushed to surround the cab of the truck. The man set his bullhorn down and proceeded calmly to business, repeating that he would give a new refrigerator for every old one offered.

By the time the five o'clock whistle blew at the fish-salting works in the next block, the man had given away four refrigerators and left one woman crying because his new machines were too wide to get up her staircase. Then the man announced it was quitting time. But he promised the truck would return the next morning at ten o'clock. And it would be business as usual. New refrigerators for old.

Like Haroun al Raschid, Caliph of Bagdad, who delighted in wandering the narrow streets and exotic bazaars of his city incognito, Prince Raoul of San Sebastiano sometimes felt the need to rub elbows with the simple folk of the principality, whose lives he suspected to be more real and marvelous than his own. When this fit was on him, he would kiss Princess Dixie, his beautiful American wife, on the cheek, toss little Wallace Adolphus, the Prince Royal, up into the air so he could catch him again, and leave by his private entrance in the palace wall. Then, bowing modestly to the applauding citizens or saluting policemen, he would hurry to the rue Blondin where his good friend Ambrose Ganelon had his detective agency and living quarters. There he would let Ganelon apply a scar or a full beard at the makeup table and they would disappear into the night in disguise.

Ganelon did not mind playing faithful vizier to Raoul's caliph now and then. The rulers of San Sebastiano and the four generations of Ambrose Ganelons were always close. But that family of brilliant detective minds had almost eliminated ingenious crime from the principality. Cases were few and fees far between. A modest trust fund was all that kept the agency plaque on the downstairs doorway and the wolf pack of international crime at bay. Invariably, Prince Raoul chose the end of the quarter when Ganelon was counting every franc for one of his little jaunts. Since royalty never carried money and Ganelon was expected to pick up the tab for these adventures, he favored visits to the derelicts in the soup line outside the Abbey of the Holy Vernicle. They did not, he knew, tour the underworld hangouts of the Duranceville Quarter or the cosmopolitan dance halls of the Quadrilateral as much as the prince might have liked.

In the week before the quarterly check, Ganelon often made do by dropping in on professional acquaintances and accepting their invitations to lunch, which sometimes became his only meal of the day. He had just such a plan in mind this morning when he turned onto the rue Morgue. There was the Coroner hurrying down the steps. Ganelon called and gave the man a cheery wave. The Coroner frowned at him and stepped into his car, leaving Ganelon on the sidewalk watching his lunch drive away.

He tried to get to Counter Intelligence headquarters and Colonel St. Cyr who was always honored to pick up a luncheon check. But though he hailed them, no police car would give him a lift as tradition demanded. Frustrated and hungry, the detective spent the afternoon browsing among the paintings of the Marbeuf Museum where the guards greeted his well known smile with blank stares.

At the end of his tedious and perplexing day Ganelon mounted the fourth and last flight of stairs up to his office and bed-sitting room beneath the eaves of 18 bis rue Blondin to find Prince Raoul sitting on the top step with each elbow resting on a large laundry bag.

"Ah, Ambrose," said the prince with a disappointed smile, "I'd hoped you'd be free for a little excursion with Buzz Haycock." Buzz Haycock was the name the prince used when incognito, the hero of his favorite juvenile adventure books. "But I see you're on a case."

"And how do you deduce that?" asked Ganelon, who had been tutoring the prince in detective ways.

"Elementary, my dear Ambrose," said the prince. "You're wearing a false mustache."

Ganelon touched his upper lip and cursed to himself. Now everything was clear. Just before he reached the rue Morgue that morning, Ganelon had encountered a man on a street corner who was handing out sample four-packs of a new brand of cigarettes. The detective had accepted his windfall. Then he turned the corner, applied the mustache he always carried in his wallet in case of an emergency, and strolled back for another. He was so pleased at his good luck and cleverness that he forgot to take off his disguise. "The case is solved," said Ganelon, stripping off the mustache. "Where would you like to go?"

"We've been ignoring the fairer sex on our outings. Let's try that new Chez Lundi laundromat on the rue Rivarol and hear what the ladies are saying about our management of affairs of state. I brought along the royal napkins to add purpose to our presence."

"Good enough," said Ganelon, calculating the cost of the royal wash.

A half hour later, they were sitting in the bright plastic interior of the new Chez Lundi with suds and laundry spinning around on all sides, Prince Raoul lurking behind a black eye-patch and Ganelon trying to see around a putty nose. The women tending the wash discussed nothing but the wonderful event of that afternoon on the Quai des Matelots. Raoul eavesdropped outrageously, a hand behind his ear. At intervals he would look back at Ganelon with a bright smile as if to say, Yes, this is daily life, isn't it?

When the women fell silent and the prince began eyeing the candy and soft-drink machines, Ganelon decided to protect his money by suggesting a stroll around the corner to the quai. They were caliph and vizier, after all, and new refrigerators for old had an Arabian Nights air.

On the way Ganelon remarked, "But let's rule out anything in the Aladdin line like an old refrigerator with a genie in furs and mittens inside ready to grant any wish provided it involves frozen food." When Ganelon added a smile, the blinking prince saw it was a joke and laughed gaily.

They turned the corner onto the quai and found the block crowded with people and old refrigerators. To speed things along, a committee of the stronger residents were carrying down the old refrigerators now. Tomorrow they intended to help carry up the new refrigerators, too. Some machines stood throbbing at the curb powered by extension cords run out through the second-floor windows. Other owners were giving away food from their thawing machines. Bottles of wine and glasses had appeared and the whole block had taken on a busy carnival air.

"Drat!" said the prince. "There goes my best idea. This little old lady is out shopping, you see, and stumbles onto an exchange of microfilm between two members of an espionage apparatus. Little does she know her package of frozen petit pois contains the plans for the ultra-secret nuclear death-ray. Desperate, the spies follow her back to the quai, et cetera, et cetera."

"I'm shot down, too," admitted Ganelon. "I asked myself why a refrigerator and decided it was because it would take two men to get it up the stairs and into an apartment. I was thinking of the meeting of the leaders of a rival gang, or a man on a hit list, or a miser with a priceless collection of jade. But this throws everything out the window."

"Suppose someone's hiding in the refrigerator," asked the prince. "When the apartment's asleep, he emerges and does some dirty deed."

Ganelon shook his head. "No one gets a new refrigerator without looking inside." He spoke absently, for he was more interested in hearing what the residents had to say about new refrigerators for old. The consensus seemed to be that it was a publicity stunt.

But a dreamy-eyed woman with a meager pyramid of curls atop her large head believed otherwise. "This rich American millionaire is after my little Queen of the Alps, the prettiest little refrigerator in the world," she insisted. "An oldy but goody, and maybe mine's the only one left in captivity. He collects refrigerators, this millionaire. He's got one of every kind, except for a Queen of the Alps. So he sends agents all over the world, peeking into respectable people's windows. At last he finds mine on the Quai des Matelots. But Mr. American Millionaire is afraid to make me an offer for it. What if I squeeze him dry? So he devises his grand scheme. Well, so be it. Let no one say I stood in the way of my neighbors getting new refrigerators." The people about her muttered and walked away.

But Ganelon stepped forward with a sudden thought. "An interesting idea, lady," he said in a counterfeit voice. "But tell me something: is there anyone who isn't going to trade?"

"Some who would, can't, poor souls," said the woman. "These new wider models won't go up all the stairs. And we have the clumsy ones like Mr. Andre there." She nodded toward the brawny young man in shirt sleeves sitting on the curb crying wetly into his hands. The woman explained that Andre and his brothers-in-law had gotten his old refrigerator stuck on a turning on the stairs on the way down. The machine seemed wedged in permanently.

Ganelon's attention was drawn from the crying man to a bow-legged, underslung, and faded old woman with a scowl, picking her way around the refrigerators and extension cords. She strode along, carrying a black-oilcloth shopping bag from which protruded a loaf of bread and the top of a bunch of celery. "Hardly the look of a woman who's about to get a new major appliance," observed the detective.

The Queen of the Alps owner laughed. "That's Madame Rosalie, the piano teacher, heading home in time for her seven o'clock class. Oh, she'll get her refrigerator, all right. But she wanted two. That's her house there standing by itself at the top of the street. She rents out her fourth-floor front furnished and wanted to trade in that refrigerator, too. But her tenant won't let anyone into the apartment for any reason."

When Ganelon made a disapproving noise, the woman nodded. "They say this Captain Maurice rented Madame Rosalie's apartment because it looks out to sea. Though he's no seafaring man. An indoor face if I ever saw one. I was there the day he arrived. Legless from the knees down, the poor old fellow. The taxi driver lifted him out of the car like a baby and carried him up to the apartment, and then his luggage and the wheelchair. That very same day a locksmith fitted the apartment door with a heavy bolt and a fat chain. No one's ever seen the man since, or the inside of the apartment. Even the grocery boy leaves everything outside the door."

Madame Rosalie's narrow, five-story house stood alone at the very end of the block where the rue Nicholas intersected the quai, an abutting building having been demolished some years before. The dusty shop of a dealer in nautical prints occupied the first floor. In the evening gloom, Ganelon and the prince couldn't see much more of the fourth floor than the flutter of curtains at the two large windows.

Next to the print-shop window was a doorway marked with two plaques: *The San Sebastiano Society for the Deaf* and *Madame Rosalie Paquin. Piano Given.*

The sound of young, unwilling fingers misusing a grand piano tumbled down upon their heads as Ganelon led the way up the narrow staircase. Beyond the second-floor offices of the Society for the Deaf where the staircase took a particularly sharp turn, Ganelon looked back over his shoulder and said, "There's Captain Maurice's hold over his landlady. Tenants who'd take this kind of racket don't grow on trees." They passed the third-floor studio, where a metronome beat out its elusive time and the piano stumbled after it. They mounted to the fourth floor. Ganelon glanced up the final staircase to Madame Rosalie's apartment and then knocked on Captain Maurice's door.

It was several moments before there was any sound. Then Ganelon heard the action of a shotgun behind the door. A careful voice asked, "Who is it?"

"Ambrose Ganelon," answered the detective. "His Highness Prince Raoul and I are here to help you."

Ganelon's most recognizable feature was his voice, the result of *The Ganelon Hour*, the popular weekly radio show on which he read accounts of the adventures of his three predecessors to support the upkeep of the Ganeloniana Wing of the Biblioteque du Prince.

The Ganelon Hour did the trick. Locks clattered, bolts pulled back, and the door opened on a chain. The double muzzle of a shotgun and the eye of a seated man appeared on the crack of the door. Ganelon was ready with a hundred-franc coin to hand through so the man could compare it with the profile Prince Raoul dutifully displayed for him.

"Inside!" urged Captain Maurice, taking the door off its chain and locking it again right behind them.

Madame Rosalie's taste in furniture ran to the bowlegged, underslung, and faded. A chalk mark wavered across the floor three feet in front of the open windows, drawn by the man, Ganelon had no doubt, to warn himself not to get close enough to be seen from the street.

Captain Maurice was a balding man with white feathers of hair about his ears. His eyes wore a hunted expression and his fingers plucked nervously at the shotgun barrel. He offered them the sofa and shook his head with bewilderment. "I can't understand what Grotz is up to," he said. "He knows I'm not going to let any damned refrigerator through that door."

"Why not tell us about it?" suggested the Prince.

The man looked at them bleakly. Then he slapped his upper legs. "I lost the rest of these crewing an Imperial Airlines flying boat on the Brindisi-Alexandria run in 1936. I was the youngest co-pilot in the air at the time. Some say Mussolini's people tampered with the controls.

"So there I was with a small pension and a lump sum by way of compensation, a young man who considered flying his life. Well, I remembered this story about the bird of paradise. They used to think the damn thing hadn't any legs, either. They thought the bird of paradise had to fly from the time it hatched until it died, feeding on the colors of the sunrise and sunset and drinking nectar on the wing from the topmost tree blossoms. A short life but a happy one, that was good enough for me!"

He smiled, remembering himself as a young man. Then he told them how he bought a Prentiss-Jenkins Hedgehog bi-wing two-seater fitted out with manual controls and sailed with it to Borneo where adventures were to be had and fortunes to be made in opals. In this rough-and-tumble, a legless man needed a partner. Enter Grotz, a brooding little dandy of a man whose bad luck had hounded him around the world and run him to ground in one of the corrugated-metal mining towns in the jungle. The peacock and the bird of paradise, that was how Maurice described their partnership of close scraps and tight corners. After five years they'd parlayed a small bankroll, a lot of hard work, and a little larceny into a leather pouch containing a king's ransom in opals. When Loo Choy and his cutthroats came bucking out through the weeds to the torchlit runway in that tin-lizzie of theirs, guns ablaze, Maurice and Grotz were already airborne up into the darkness.

Maurice was staring ahead of him into the night, imagining a whole king's ransom for himself when the Hedgehog sputtered and stalled. Grotz, his bad luck written all over his face, slapped him on the shoulder and shouted, "What's wrong?" As the wind whistled around them, Maurice shouted back over his shoulder, "They hit the gas tank. We'll have to jump. You go first. I'll keep her nose up!" So Grotz parachuted down into a jungle the luckiest man in the world couldn't walk out of. And Maurice switched to the auxiliary tank and flew away.

Maurice used the opals to start Bird of Paradise Air Freight. But into its second year of operation, the Japanese occupied Borneo and he fled to Australia with the shirt on his back and his second best wheelchair on the last plane out. He was with Australian air intelligence during the war. Then he came back home and for twenty years shuffled papers behind a desk for Air San Sebastiano.

"But Grotz hadn't died in the jungle," said Ganelon.

Captain Maurice gave his head a grim shake. Grotz had stumbled onto a mission hospital in the jungle. He lay near death for months. The first day he was up and around, the Japanese marched in and interned everyone.

Now Grotz had heard the Hedgehog's motor start up as he floated down and knew he'd been betrayed. He burned to avenge himself, but it wasn't until 1944, just two weeks before the camp was liberated, that he escaped. After six months in the jungle he was captured by a tribe of headhunters. He cowed them with some sleight-of-hand from card-sharping days and they made him their chief and taught him their ways, including their custom of sacrificing their chief during eclipses of the sun.

Ten years later, Grotz fled in the daylight darkness, and though wounded by blowgun darts reached a plantation doorstep before he collapsed. When he came to weeks later, his memory was blank. The Dutch plantation-owner liked Grotz and offered him work. Five years later he married the man's only child, a beautiful woman who bore him several wonderful children. But on their fifth wedding anniversary, Grotz's wife presented him with opal cufflinks and his memory came rushing back. On the spot, the man's only object in life was to kill Maurice.

"And how do you know all this?" interrupted Ganelon.

"His first call came from Singapore," said Maurice. "He guessed that if I was still alive I'd be back in San Sebastiano. The operator found me in the book. Before he hung up, Grotz told me he was going to rob the bank next door to finance his revenge."

But Maurice wasn't to hear from him for another seven years, which was the sentence he was given for attempting to rob a bank while thirty armed police cadets from the academy around the corner were cashing their paychecks. The next call came from Burma, where Grotz had gone to prospect for rubies to bankroll Maurice's death. Maurice was apprehensive but not particularly worried for he was counting on Grotz's bad luck. And the man did leave Burma penniless. But while he was there, his father-in-law, his wife, and his children were killed when fire swept their plantation home. Grotz inherited everything.

"Well, a legless man can't run very far," said Maurice, "and I couldn't hide for long. So I decided to make a stand. What I needed was a place with a little sky for an old bird-of-paradise aviator to nibble on and only one way in."

He patted the shotgun. "Well, he found me fast enough. Yesterday he called. He asked me what I could see from my window, and when I told him I could tell he was nodding and that he was seeing the same sky. He's here. Cocksure and determined. I expected something better than this refrigerator business."

"No police?" asked Ganelon.

"It's between the two of us," said Maurice. "I'm the guilty party, after all. Such terrible, terrible luck. Why did he have to get his memory back?"

They were out on the street on their way to rescue the royal napkins from the wash when Ganelon remembered he hadn't gotten back the hundred-franc piece he'd given Maurice to compare with Prince Raoul's profile.

At nine forty-five the next morning, as they had arranged with the besieged man, Ganelon and Prince Raoul, both in simple sun-glass disguises, returned to the cool breezes of the Quai des Matelots. The street was busy and expectant as they strode along in the direction of the rue Nicholas.

"All right," the Prince was saying, "so the stairs are too narrow for the damned refrigerator. Doesn't that just mean Captain Maurice is safe and Madame Rosalie is out of luck? What does a grand piano have to do with anything?"

Madame Rosalie was already standing at the curb, looking nervously down the quai toward the rue Rivarol. As the last one on the block, she was more anxious than anyone to see the truck arrive. As they passed behind her, Ganelon stopped to look up under the roof where the roof tree beam extended out from under the eaves. Then he smiled and went inside. Raoul followed after him up the stairs muttering. "As your prince, I could order you to tell me what's going on," he threatened.

"They couldn't have gotten a grand piano up these stairs, either. But it's up there," said Ganelon. "They hoisted the piano up from the outside. You can be damned sure that's the way the refrigerator will come." Then he raised his hand for silence. On the second-floor landing outside the Society for the Deaf a well dressed old gentleman with gloves and cane stood leaning against the wall as though waiting for someone. As Ganelon and the prince passed, a woman with a hearing-aid emerged from the office leading a small fretting child by the hand. The old man winked at the child and then reached down and to her wide-eyed amazement, pulled a fifty-centime piece from her ear and handed it to her. The prince laughed but Ganelon did not. They continued on their way up the stairs.

The prearranged knock got them into Captain Maurice's apartment again. The clock read five to ten.

Maurice sat for a moment without speaking, rocking back and forth in his wheelchair. Ganelon decided it was the old man's equivalent of pacing.

"I've been hashing it over about Grotz and myself all night," Maurice said with a decisive shake of his head. "The guy should thank me. I mean really. I'm the only thing that pulled him through the jungle, the Japs, the headhunters, all of it. He wanted to kill me that bad." His voice turned cheery. "So maybe we're even, right?"

But they were not and Maurice knew it. He hid his face in his hands. "Damn," he said through his fingers, "it's hard to find a friend and lose him in the same second. Standing there on the wing of the Hedgehog ready to jump, he looked back over his shoulder. 'What about you?' he shouted. 'I'll be right behind you!' I shouted. 'Jump! I'm okay!' And he jumped."

"New refrigerators for old," came the bullhorn. Ganelon crossed to the window. The truck had returned at the promised hour. But it had approached the quai from the other direction, stopping first at the curb where the delighted Madame Rosalie stood.

"So it's started then," said Captain Maurice. "So be it. But I'd sure feel a lot better if I knew what 'it' was."

As Ganelon watched, two large men jumped from the back of the truck with a rope net and the components of a block and tackle and followed the music teacher into the building. Behind him, Ganelon could hear the prince explain to Maurice the various ideas they had rejected and the process of reasoning that had led Ganelon to the conclusion that Grotz would come up the outside of the building in the refrigerator. Then many footsteps passed outside the door and pounded upstairs to Madame Rosalie's apartment.

"I might add in conclusion," smiled the prince, "that we never even briefly considered the possibility that one of the old refrigerators might harbor a genii in mittens and a muffler who'd grant wishes provided they involved frozen food."

Ganelon turned from the window to give the prince a thoughtful look.

Maurice patted his shotgun. "Well, then I have him, right? Kill or be killed, right? And with the prince himself and Mr. Ganelon here to testify it was self-defense, right?" The man wheeled around and took up a defensive position behind a sofa rampart, setting his gun at the ready.

Ganelon leaned back against the wall between the two windows and watched with crossed arms. Overhead an old refrigerator was being moved across the ceiling to the window. Then a rope went uncoiling past the window on his left down to the man with the bullhorn.

"Blam! Blam!" rehearsed Maurice. "Gotcha!" Then he ordered the prince out of the line of fire. After a moment he wheeled out from behind the sofa and began pushing furniture close to the wall to give himself a clearer shot at the window.

"It's the waiting that gets you," he said. "You've got to keep busy." As he started back, the phone on the end-table rang. "There's Grotz," said Maurice with a decisive nod. "I know my man. A word or two before he slips in the knife. Well, this time he's in for a surprise."

As the bottom of Madame Rosalie's old refrigerator appeared at the top of the window, the man in the wheelchair started past the telephone to take up his position behind the sofa. Then he stopped and looked at the ringing telephone. "But it's not going to be that easy. I'm the one who did him wrong, remember?" He considered this for a moment. Then he said, "Suppose I tell him flat out that I know what he's up to. Suppose instead of killing him in self-defense, I warn him off, tell him I know he's going to come up in the new refrigerator. I'd be giving back the same life I took from him so long ago."

Captain Maurice liked the idea. He lay the shotgun across his knees and reached for the phone. "Hello?" he said. But there was no answer at the other end of the line. "Hello?" he said again.

Ganelon watched and waited. At this point, the old refrigerator was filling the window. It stopped in its downward progress, spinning around gently in its rope net. As Captain Maurice stared into the mouthpiece of the receiver with a perplexed look on his face, the refrigerator door opened as much as the rope net would allow and the end of a tube protruded from the crack. Yes, thought Ganelon, the Borneo headhunters had taught Grotz their blowgun ways. And like a true sleight-of-hand artist, Grotz would have arranged things to have his audience watching the wrong refrigerator. Reaching over, the detective slammed the refrigerator door shut on the tube.

When they arrived at the blue door in the palace wall, Prince Raoul turned and shook Ganelon's hand. "Thou hast done wisely, as always, O faithful Vizier," he said. "And you negotiated the reconciliation like a seasoned diplomat. A touching scene."

"Until our next adventure, O mighty Caliph," said Ganelon, struggling to ignore the aroma of Princess Dixie's Texas pot roast (the detective's favorite) wafting over the wall.

As the door closed behind the prince, Ganelon rattled the few coins remaining in his pocket and sighed. Then he started back toward the rue Blondin, where he would transform himself into Benoit, the failed middleweight pug whose broken nose had become a dinner-hour fixture in the soup line at the Abbey of the Holy Vernicle.

A Checklist of the Mystery Writings of James Powell

PUBLISHED SHORT STORIES

Collections

A Murder Coming: Stories by James Powell, ed. Peter Sellers (Toronto: Yonge and Bloor Publishing, 1990)
A Japanese collection with the title in translation: *A Dirge for Clowntown and Other Stories*, by James Powell (Tokyo: Kawade Shobo Shinsha, 2008)
A Pocketful of Noses: Stories of One Ganelon or Another (Norfolk: Crippen & Landru, 2009)

Individual Stories

"The Friends of Hector Jouvet," *Ellery Queen's Mystery Magazine* [hereafter, EQMM], April 1966; reprinted in *Ellery Queen's All-Star Lineup*, ed. Ellery Queen (New York: New American Library, 1967); *Ellery Queen's Anthology, Fall-Winter, 1982*, ed. by Ellery Queen (New York: Davis, 1982); *Ellery Queen's Book of First Appearances*, ed. Ellery Queen (New York: Dial, 1982; *Murder Takes a Holiday*, ed. Cynthia Manson (New York Marlboro Books, 1992); collected in *A Murder Coming* (1990)
"The Stollmeyer Sonnets," EQMM, October 1966); reprinted in *Best Detective Stories of the Year #22*, ed. Anthony Boucher (New York: Dutton, 1967); *Boucher's Choicest: A Collection of Anthony Boucher's Favorites from the Best Detective Stories of the Year*, selected by Jeanne F. Bernkopf (New York: Dutton, 1969); *The Menace Masters*, edited by Jeanne F. Bernkopf (New York: Dell 1972); *Masterpieces of Mystery: Amateurs and*

213

Professionals, ed. Ellery Queen (New York: Davis, 1978); *Maddened by Mystery: A Casebook of Canadian Detective Fiction*, ed. Michael Richardson (Toronto: Lester & Orpen Dennys, 1982)

"Have You Heard the Latest?" *Caper Magazine*, April 1967; Collected in *A Murder Coming* (1990)

"The Beddoes Scheme," EQMM, October 1967 and subsequent large; print edition; reprinted in *Best Detective Stories of the Year, #23*, ed. Anthony Boucher (New York: Dutton, 1968); *Ellery Queen's Eyes of Mystery*, ed. Ellery Queen (New York: Dial, 1981); *Ellery Queen's Anthology, Fall-Winter 1981*, ed. Ellery Queen (New York: Davis, 1981, and subsequent large type edition; collected in *A Murder Coming* (1990)

"The Eye of Shafti," EQMM, February 1968; reprinted in *Every Crime in the Book: An Anthology of Mystery Stories by the Mystery Writers of America*, ed. Robert L. Fish (New York: Putnam, 1975); collected in *A Murder Coming* (1990)

"The Maze in the Elevator," EQMM, July 1968; reprinted in *Ellery Queen's Murder Menu*, ed. Ellery Queen (New York: World, 1969), and in a Norwegian anthology (Mortensen); collected in *A Murder Coming* (1990)

"The Daring Daylight Melon Robbery," EQMM, October 1968

"The Great Paleontologist Murder Mystery," EQMM, November 1968

"The Altdorf Syndrome," EQMM, May 1969; reprinted in *Ellery Queen's Grand Slam*, ed. Ellery Queen (New York: World, 1970) and subsequent paperback edition (New York: Popular Library, 1972); *Over the Edge*, ed. Peter Sellers and Robert J. Sawyer (East Lawrenceton, NS: Pottersfield Press, 2000); collected in *A Murder* Coming (1990) and in the Japanese collection *A Dirge for Clowntown* (2008)

"Kleber on Murder in Thirty Volumes," EQMM, (October 1969; reprinted in *Best Detective Stories of the Year, 24th Annual Collection*, ed. Allen J. Hubin (New York: Dutton, 1970); *Argosy* (UK), January/February 1971; collected in *A Murder Coming* (1990)

"Coins in the Frascati Fountain," EQMM, May 1970; reprinted in *Best Detective Stories of the Year, 25th Annual Collection*, ed. Allen J. Hubin (New York: Dutton, 1971): collected in *A Pocketful of Noses* (2008)

"The Plot Against Santa Claus," EQMM, January 1971; reprinted in *Lancaster Independent Press*, December 22, December 29, 1972; January 5, 1973; *Crime at Christmas*, ed. Jack Adrian (Wellingborough: Equation, 1987); *Mystery for Christmas*, ed. Cynthia Manson (New York: New American Library, 1990); *Merry Murder*, ed. Cynthia Manson (New York: Seafarer, 1994); *Christmas Stars*, ed. David G. Hartwell (New York: Tor, 1992);

A Yuletide Universe: Sixteen Fantastical Tales, ed. Brian M. Thomsen (New York: Warner Books, 2003)

"The Gobineau Necklace," EQMM, March 1971; reprinted in *Ellery Queen's Mystery Bag*, ed. Ellery Queen (New York: World, 1972) and subsequent paperback (New York: Manor, 1973); *Masterpieces of Mystery: the Seventies*, ed. Ellery Queen (New York: Davis, 1979); collected in *A Murder Coming* (1990)

"Three Men in a Tub," EQMM, September 1971; collected in *A Murder Coming* (1990)

"Trophy Day at the Chateau Gai," EQMM, February 1972; reprinted in *Ellery Queen's More Lost Ladies and Men*, ed. Eleanor Sullivan (New York: Davis, Summer 1985)

"The Mandalasian Garotte," EQMM, July 1972; reprinted in *Fingerprints: A Collection of Stories by the Crime Writers of Canada*, edited by Beverly Beetham-Endersby (Irwin Publishing, 1984)

"Ganelon and the Master Thief," EQMM, October 1972

"The Pomeranian's Whereabouts," EQMM, January 1973

"The Ascent of the Grimselhorn," EQMM, April 1973; collected in *A Murder Coming* (1990)

"A Murder Coming," EQMM, September 1973; reprinted in *Best Detective Stories of the Year, 1974*, ed. by Allen J. Hubin (Dutton, 1974); *Cold Blood: Murder in Canada*, ed. Peter Sellers (Oakville, ON: Mosaic Press, 1987; on cassette, *A Murder Coming*, Vol. II, Audio version of *Cold Blood*, Burlington, Ontario Durkin Hayes Publishing, 1993); *The Mammoth Book of Legal Thrillers*, ed. Michael Hemmingson (Robinson, 2001); *Revenge: A Noir Anthology About Getting Even*, ed. Kerry J. Schooley and Peter Sellers (Toronto: Insomniac Press, 2004); collected in *A Murder Coming* (1990)

"The Bee on the Finger," *Playboy Magazine*, September 1973; reprinted in *Playboy*, German edition, December, 1973; *Playboy*, Italian edition, September 1973; *Just My Luck* (Playboy Press paperback, 1976 and subsequent foreign editions); collected in *A Murder Coming* (1990). There was also as short film version, as "The Sting of the Bee," Momentum Films, c/o Mr. Lawry Trevor-Deutsch, 468 Pleasant Park Road, Ottawa, Ontario K1H 5N1 Canada.

"The Spratt from the Stars," *Worlds of If* (sold, March 1974; publication date, if published, unknown

"The Theft of the Fabulous Hen," EQMM, November 1973; collected in the Japanese *A Dirge for Clowntown* (2008)

"The Oubliette Cipher," EQMM, November 1974; collected in *A Murder Coming* (1990)

"Bianca and the Seven Sleuths," EQMM, June 1975 and subsequent large print edition; reprinted in *Ellery Queen's Searches and Seizures*, ed. Ellery Queen (New York: Dial Press, 1977)

"The Trolls of God," *Playboy*, February 1977

"Blindman's Cuff," EQMM, July 1981

"The Notorious Snowman," EQMM, October 1981; reprinted in *Once Upon a Crime*, ed. Janet Hutchings (New York: St. Martin's, 1994)

"The Priest Without a Shadow," EQMM, January 1982; collected in *A Pocketful of Noses* (2009)

"A Pocketful of Noses," EQMM, March 1982; reprinted in *The Year's Best Mystery and Suspense Stories, 1983*, edited by Edward D. Hoch (New York: Walker, 1983); collected in *A Pocketful of Noses* (2009)

"The Vigil of Death," EQMM, July 1982; collected in the Japanese *A Dirge for Clowntown* (2008)

"The Haunted Bookcase," EQMM, August 1982; collected in *A Pocketful of Noses* (2009)

"A Bagdad Reckoning," EQMM, November 1982; on cassette in *Ellery Queen Presents "Custer's Ghost" and other Stories* (Listen For Pleasure, Books on Cassette, 1986)

"Death in the Christmas Hour," EQMM, January 1983; reprinted in *Sherlock Holmes Through Time and Space*, ed. Isaac Asimov, Martin Harry Greenberg and Charles Waugh (New York: Blue Jay Books, 1984, and subsequent paperback editions); *Sherlock Holmes nel tempo nello spazio* (Arnoldo Mondadori Editiore, 1990 as "Morte nell'ora del Natale"); *Murder at Christmas*, ed. Cynthia Manson (New York: New American Library, 1991); *Christmas Magic*, edited by David G. Hartwell (New York: Tor Books, 1994); and in a German anthology published by R. Piper GMBH & Company, 1995.

"The Scarlet Totem," EQMM, April 1983

"The Bird-of-Paradise Man," EQMM, July 1983; collected in *A Pocketful of Noses* (2008)

"The Phantom Haircut," EQMM, October 1983; on cassette in *Ellery Queen Presents "Midnight Strangler" and other stories* (Listen For Pleasure, Books on Cassette, 1986)

"The Meandering Pearl," EQMM, November 1983

"The Dark Elf Master of Crack of Doom, EQMM, December 1983; reprinted in *Secret Tales of the Arctic Trails: Stories of Crime and*

Adventure in Canada's Far North, ed. Skene-Melvin (Toronto: Simon & Pierre, 1997)

"The Labyrinth of Life," EQMM, February 1984; on cassette in *Ellery Queen Presents "Custer's Ghost" and other Stories* (Listen For Pleasure, Books on Cassette, 1986)

"The Stranger at the Crossroads," EQMM, May 1984

"The Polygon from Alpha Centauri," EQMM July 1984

"Under the Spangled Roger," EQMM, November 1984; reprinted in *Dead in the Water*, ed. Violette Malan and Therese Greenwood (Toronto: RendezVous Press, 2006)

"The Verbatim Reply," EQMM, March 1985; collected in *A Pocketful of Noses* (2009)

"The Dawn of Captain Sunset," EQMM, April 1985

"The Brass Man," EQMM, June 1985

"The Dunderhead Bus," EQMM, August 1985; collected in the Japanese *A Dirge for Clowntown* (2008)

"The Hiccup Flask," EQMM, October 1985; reprinted in *Once Upon a Crime II*, ed. Janet Hutchings (New York: St. Martin's Press, 1996)

"The Bridge of Traded Dreams," EQMM, December, 1985

"The Coffee-table Book," EQMM, Mid-December 1985

"The Singular Bird," EQMM, April 1986

"A Baksheesh from the North," *Ellery Queen's Prime Crimes, #4*, ed. Eleanor Sullivan (New York: Davis, 1986); collected in *A Murder Coming* (1990)

"The Origami Moose," EQMM, June 1986; collected in the Japanese *A Dirge for Clowntown* (2008)

"Death's Sandwich-man," EQMM, August 1986

"The Cannibal Gourmet," EQMM, December 1986; reprinted in *Mystère, Mystère* (Paris: Éditions Denoel, 1996)

"The Brim Whistle," EQMM, February 1987

"The Mad Scientist, J/G," EQMM, April 1987

"Wingtips," EQMM, June 1987

"The Tulip Juggernaut," EQMM, September 1987

"The Talking Donkey," EQMM, Mid-December 1987; collected in the Japanese *A Dirge for Clowntown* (2008)

"The Quick and the Dead," EQMM, February 1988

"The Kidnap of Bounding Mane," EQMM, June 1988; reprinted in *Roger Caras' Treasury of Great Horse Stories*, ed. Roger Caras (New York: Dutton, 1989) and subsequent (Galahad Books, 1993) edition.

"Midnight Pumpkins," EQMM, September 1988

"The Cerebus Emerald," EQMM, October 1988

"Still Life with Orioles," EQMM, December 1988; nominated for the Crime Writers of Canada 1989 Arthur Ellis Award for Short Fiction; reprinted in *Murder on Main Street*, ed. Cynthia Manson (New York: Marboro Books, 1992)

"A New Leaf," EQMM, January 1989

"Burning Bridges," EQMM, February 198; nominated for the Crime Writers of Canada 1990 Parker Prize for Short Fiction; reprinted in *Fifty Years of the Best from Ellery Queen's Mystery Magazine*, ed, Eleanor Sullivan (New York: Carroll and Graf, 1991); *Ellery Queen's Mystery Magazine: The First Fifty Years, The Best Fifty Stories*, ed. Eleanor Sullivan (New York: Galahad, 1993); *Fifty Best Mysteries*, ed. Eleanor Sullivan (New York: Carroll and Graf, 1992)

"The Snood of Night," EQMM, March 1989

"The Greenhouse Dogs," EQMM, June 1989; reprinted in *Criminal Shorts: Mysteries by Canadian Crime Writers*, ed. Eric Wright and Howard Engle (Rexdale, ON:Macmillan Canada, 1992); *Bloody York; Tales of Mayhem, Murder and Mystery in Toronto Past, Present and Future*, edited by David Skene-Melvin (Simon & Pierre, 1996)

"The Sting of the Hoop Snake," EQMM, July 1989

"The Doors of Spring," EQMM, September 1989

"A Dirge for Clowntown," EQMM, November 1989; winner of the 1989 EQMM Readers Award; reprinted in *The Year's Best Mystery and Suspense Stories, 1990*, ed. Edward D. Hoch (New York: Walker, 1990); *Ellery Queen Presents Readers' Choice*, ed. Eleanor Sullivan (New York: Davis Publications, 1990); *The Year's Best Fantasy and Horror (Third Annual Collection)*, ed. Ellen Datlow and Terri Windling (New York: St. Martin's Press, 1990); *Mystères 91* (Librairie des Champs-Elysees, 1991); *Detectives: Stories for Thinking, Solving and Writing*, ed, Robert Eidelberg (Amsco School Publications, 2000); the story will also be in an upcoming original Japanese anthology published by Kadokawa Shoten Publishing Co. Ltd.; on cassette in *Best Fantasy Fiction*, edited by Martin H. Greenberg (Dercum Audio, 1990); collected in the Japanese *A Dirge for Clowntown* (2008)

"The Hot-Stove League," EQMM, January 1990

"Mrs. Brodie's Cow," EQMM, April 1990

"The Code of the Poodles," EQMM, October 1990; reprinted in *Northern Frights II*, ed. Don Hutchison (Oakville, ON: Mosaic Press, 1994); collected in the Japanese *A Dirge for Clowntown* (2008)

"The Valley of Dead Millionaires," EQMM, November 1990

"The Tamerlane Crutch," *Cold Blood III*, ed. Peter Sellers (Oakville: Mosaic Press, 1990); nominated for the Crime Writers of Canada 1991 Arthur Ellis Award for Short Fiction; reprinted in *Christmas Forever*, ed. David G. Hartwell (New York: Tor Books, 1993); EQMM, January 1995; *The Best of Cold Blood*, ed, Peter Sellers and John North (Oakville: Mosaic Press, 1998)

"The Van Winkle Loaf," EQMM, March 1991

"The Baltman Bird's-Eye View," EQMM, April 1991

"Yesterday's Dark Tomorrow," EQMM, August 1991

"Winter Hiatus," EQMM, October 1991; nominated for the Crime Writers of Canada 1992 Arthur Ellis Award for Short Fiction; reprinted in *Iced: The New Noire Anthology of Cold, Hard Fiction*, ed. Peter Sellers & Kerry J. Schooley (Toronto: Insomniac Press, 2001)

"Funeral Pie," EQMM, December 1991

"Santa's Way," EQMM, Mid-December 1991; nominated for the Crime Writers of Canada 1992 Arthur Ellis Award for Short Fiction; reprinted in *Murder Under the Mistletoe and Other Stories*, ed. Cynthia Manson (New York: New American Library, 1992); *The Year's Best Fantasy and Horror, (Fifth Annual Collection)*, ed. Ellen Datlow and Terri Windling (New York: St. Martin's Press, 1992); *Murder Most Merry: 32 Christmas Crime Stories from the World's Best Mystery Writers*, ed. Abigail Browning (New York: Random House Value Publishing, 2002)

"Dark Possessions," EQMM, February 1992; reprinted in *Il Giallo Mondatori* (March, 1992) as "uno spettro in poltrona"; *Crossing the Line: Canadian Mysteries with a Fantastic Twist*, ed. David Skene-Melvin and Robert J. Sawyer (East Lawrenceton: Pottersfield Press, 1998)

"Unquiet Graves," EQMM, June 1992; collected in *A Pocketful of Noses* (2009)

"The King of the Orangutans," EQMM, September 1992; collected in the Japanese *A Dirge for Clowntown* (2008)

"Ruby Laughter, Tears of Pearl," EQMM, Mid-December 1992; reprinted in *The Year's Best Fantasy and Horror, (Sixth Annual Collection)*, ed. Ellen Datlow and Terri Windling (New York: St. Martin's Press, 1993)

"The Tale of the Blind Man's Lantern," EQMM, January 1993

"The Blue Bread of Happiness," EQMM, March 1993

"The Fixer-Upper," EQMM, May 1993; nominated for the Crime Writers of Canada 1994 Arthur Ellis Award for Short Fiction

"A Keyhole in Time," EQMM, September 1993; collected in the Japanese *A Dirge for Clowntown* (2008)

"Household Hints," EQMM, December 1993

"Harps of Gold," EQMM, Mid-December 1993; collected in *A Pocketful of Noses* (2009)

"A Bequest for Mr. Nugent," EQMM, February 1994; collected in the Japanese *A Dirge for Clowntown* (2008)

"The Black Daffodil," EQMM, August 1994

"Midnight at Manger's Bird and Beast," EQMM, December 1994; nominated for the Crime Writers of Canada 1995 Arthur Ellis Award for Short Fiction; reprinted in *The Matilda Ziegler Magazine for the Blind*, braille and cassette editions, December 1995

"Grist for the Mills of Christmas," EQMM, Mid-December 1994; reprinted in *Northern Frights III*, ed. Don Hutchison (Oakville: Mosaic Press, 1995); *Christmas Crimes*, ed. Cynthia Manson (New York: Signet, 1996); *Murder Most Merry: 32 Christmas Crime Stories from the World's Best Mystery Writers*, ed. Abigail Browning (New York: Random House Value Publishing, 2002)

"The Rasputin Faberge," EQMM, October 1995; Nominated for the Crime Writers of Canada 1996 Arthur Ellis Award for Short Fiction

"Break Out from Mistletoe Five," EQMM, Mid-December 1995; nominated for the Crime Writers of Canada 1996 Arthur Ellis Award for Short Fiction

"The Dibble and Noah Webster," EQMM, September 1996

"Strangers on a Sleigh," EQMM, January 1998; nominated for the Crime Writers of Canada 1999 Arthur Ellis Award for Short Fiction

"The Colossus of Lilliput," EQMM, September-October 1998

"A Gallows Song," EQMM, January 1999

"Jerrold's Meat," EQMM, April 1999; nominated for the Crime Writers of Canada 2000 Arthur Ellis Award for Short Fiction

"A Quilt of Crazies," EQMM, May 1999

"Jane's Head," *Northern Frights 5*, ed. Don Hutchison (Oakville: Mosaic Press, 1999)

"The Flower Diet," EQMM, April 2000; collected in *A Pocketful of Noses* (2009)

"The Gooseberry Fool," EQMM, September-October 2000; collected in *A Pocketful of Noses* (2009)

"Honeydew Wine," EQMM, April 2001; reprinted in *Mystery: The Best of 2001*, edited by Jon L. Breen (ibooks, 2002)

"The Zoroaster Grin," EQMM, January 2002; collected in *A Pocketful of Noses* (2008)

"Bottom Walker," EQMM, May 2002; winner of the Crime Writers of Canada 2002 Arthur Ellis Award for Short Fiction; reprinted in *Hard Boiled Love*, ed. Peter Sellers and Kerry J. Schooley (Lawrenceton: Insomniac Press, 2003); *Revue Alibis No. 9* (Hiver, 2004); *Alfred Hitchcock Presenterar: Mord äinte särskilt trevligt* (Pagina Förlags AB/Optimal Förlag, 2007)

"The Jewels of Atlantis," EQMM, November 2002; nominated for the Private Eye Writers of America 2002 Shamus Award for Best P. I. Short Story
"The Firebird's Feather," EQMM, April 2003
"The Amontillado Club," EQMM, May 2003
"MacNaughton or MacNeice," EQMM, January 2004
"The Blunderbus Trick," EQMM, May 2004
"The Secret of Wolfe Island," published on James Powell's web site (www.james-powell.com) in 2004
"A Bigfoot Christmas," EQMM, January 2005; reprinted in *Blood on the Holly*, edited by Caro Soles (Toronto: Baskerville Books, 2007)
"The Caravan of Wonders Lady," EQMM, March-April 2005; printed as a separate booklet to accompany the limited edition of *A Pocketful of Noses* (2009)
"The Algonquin Rose," in *The* (Kingston, ON) *Whig Standard* and other newspapers of the Osprey Media group chain, weekend of July 4, 2005; reprinted in *Mystery Ink*, ed. Jake Doherty and Therese Greenwood (Owen Sound: The Ginger Press, 2007)
"The Headless Horseman and the Horseless Carriage," EQMM, September-October 2005; nominated for the Crime Writers of Canada 2005 Arthur Ellis Award for Short Fiction
"A Tale of Too Much Dickens," *Alfred Hitchcock Mystery Magazine*, January-February 2006
"The Ripper Prince," EQMM, May 2006
"Aardvark by Gaslight," EQMM, June 2006)
"At Willow-Walk-Behind," EQMM, December 2006; collected in *A Pocketful of Noses* (2008)
"Candy Cane Wars," EQMM, January 2007
"Ivory Crossroads," EQMM, March-April 2007
"A Cozy for the Jack-o'-Lanterns," EQMM, September-October 2007
"The Quest for Creeping Charlie," *Magazine of Fantasy & Science Fiction*, January 2008
"Red-Herring House," *Alfred Hitchcock Mystery Magazine*, May 2008
"Clay Pillows," EQMM, June 2008
"Clowntown Pajamas," EQMM, February 2009
"The Black Whatever," EQMM, forthcoming

PUBLISHED MYSTERY ARTICLE

"Chekov's Snowshovel," *Mystery Readers' Journal* ("Cool Canadian Crime" issue), Winter 2003-2004

A Pocketful of Noses

A Pocketful of Noses: Stories of One Ganelon or Another by James Powell, is set in Times New Roman and printed on sixty-pound Natures acid-free recycled paper. The cover is by Gail Cross. The first edition was printed in two forms: trade softcover, notchbound; and one hundred sixty numbered copies sewn in cloth, signed by the author. Each of the clothbound copies includes a separate pamphlet, *The Caravan of Wonders Lady* by James Powell.

A Pocketful of Noses was printed and bound by Thomson-Shore, Inc., Dexter, Michigan and published in June 2009 by Crippen & Landru Publishers, Inc., Norfolk, Virginia.

CRIPPEN & LANDRU, PUBLISHERS
P. O. Box 9315
Norfolk, VA 23505
www.crippenlandru.com
E-mail: info@ crippenlandru.com

Crippen & Landru publishes first editions of short-story collections by important detective and mystery writers.

☞ This is the best edited, most attractively packaged line of mystery books introduced in this decade. The books are equally valuable to collectors and readers. [*Mystery Scene Magazine*]

☞ The specialty publisher with the most star-studded list is Crippen & Landru, which has produced short story collections by some of the biggest names in contemporary crime fiction. [*Ellery Queen's Mystery Magazine*]

☞ God Bless Crippen & Landru. [*The Strand Magazine*]

☞ A monument in the making is appearing year by year from Crippen & Landru, a small press devoted exclusively to publishing the criminous short story. [*Alfred Hitchcock's Mystery Magazine*]

SUBSCRIPTIONS

Crippen & Landru offers discounts to individuals and institutions who place Standing Order Subscriptions for its forthcoming publications, either all the Regular Series or all the Lost Classics or (preferably) both. Collectors can thereby guarantee receiving limited editions, and readers won't miss any favorite stories. Standing Order Subscribers receive a specially commissioned story in a deluxe edition as a gift at the end of the year. Please write or e-mail for more details.